The
Forbidden
FRESHMAN

BOOK ONE
NOLAN

Katy ♡ xoxo
Archer

KATY ARCHER

―――――

ISBN: 978-1-991138-07-1 (Paperback)
ISBN: 978-1-991138-04-0 (Kindle)

Archer Street Romance
www.katyarcher.com

CHAPTER 1
MIKAYLA

"Yeah, I'm not doing that." I cross my arms, wishing for height. Even just a couple inches would be nice so I don't actually have to look *up* at Miss Sigma Beta Mu President with her icy blue gaze and relentless smirk.

Seriously, how does she not get muscle cramps in her face?

I bet she was born with this contemptuous look. Just popped right out of her mother's V-jay screaming indignantly, then throwing a haughty glare at the medical staff. *"Feed and clothe me immediately!"*

"You have to." Aimee smooths a long lock of shiny blonde hair over her shoulder and crosses her arms right back at me. "If you want a permanent place in this house, then you must finish the final initiation task."

"But it's stupid." I flick my arms up while Fiona gasps like I've just hexed the house.

"It's okay, Fee." Aimee raises her hands, her icy gaze darkening around the edges as that irritating smirk grows a little higher on her cheek. "Are you saying you want out?"

I clench my jaw, wishing it were that easy. Wishing I could flip all these preppy, superior girls the bird and flounce out of this sorority house like it means nothing to me. But I don't have that luxury, now do I?

Thanks to stupid fire damage in Buckley Hall, and Nolan U's sudden housing crisis, Greek Row was forced to step up and house the homeless, which means I'm in this uppity sorority house way earlier than I expected. And if I don't play my cards right and find a permanent place here, I'm kinda screwed.

Throwing a glance across the room, I cast my eye at the two other twitchy freshmen who I endured rush week with. "Louisa and Trinity don't have to do it."

"Well, you're special." Aimee's saccharine voice is sweet enough to put me in a coma.

I force air through my nose and remind myself not to lose it.

Remember what's at stake here. Suck. It. Up!

Gritting my teeth, I attempt a smile. "I thought being a legacy meant I get automatic entry."

The senior girls share this comical look before laughter bubbles out of them. I can practically here them thinking, *"Poor, naive Mikayla. She's so clueless."*

I guess I kind of am. Sorority life is so not my jam.

My little sister, Megan, would be in her element, swanning in and out of this house like it was made for her. She would have breezed through this entire process and no doubt been welcomed into the fold, the pretty poppet that she is.

But not me.

I don't fit.

But I have to fit—dammit!

Aimee reaches out her manicured hand, lightly tugging on the end of my messy ponytail. "Being a legacy means you have the right to rush. You only just scraped through, and now we want to see some real commitment. If you want to be invited to the initiation ceremony at the beginning of next month, then you need to complete this task. You need to show us that you really want to be a Sig Be sister."

I resist the urge to roll my eyes and tell them that I actually don't give two shits about being a Sig Be sister, but I can't say that. I need to be one whether I'm interested or not.

Fiona tips her head, her bottom lip popping out in a mock pout. "If you can't complete this final task, then I think it's clear you're really not Sigma Beta Mu material."

"Not a good fit." Claudia wrinkles her nose and hisses while Aimee's blue gaze drills into mine.

"And we really want you to be a good fit."

Hey, sarcasm, how you doin'?

I keep the thought to myself and try to force a smile, but I just can't do it! This is insane, stupid, dumb.

Everything about sorority life is!

Shut up, Mick. You know why you have to do this. Seriously, get over yourself and do this for the good of your future. Do it for Mom.

My expression bunches as my mouth revolts and gives it one more shot. "Seriously, though. You can't think of any other initiation to give me? How 'bout scrubbing frat house toilets with a toothbrush? Or walking through campus in a string bikini?"

"Oh please, freshman, that's child's play." Aimee rolls her eyes like I'm the world's biggest waste of space. "You know what? You shouldn't even be here. This is a favor to your mother, because I really respect her."

Yeah, right.

"I don't want to let her down, so we've been very lenient with you. Most pledges wouldn't have been given so many chances. Do you have any idea how prestigious this sorority is? How many people would do anything to be in your shoes right now?"

"Yeah." Claudia nods. "We have to protect our family, which is why this selection process is so intense."

"You know, if you don't want to be here, you can just —" Fiona tinkles her fingers, indicating the door, and I actually turn around and look at it. The white wood somehow calls to me, begging me to see sense and run like the frickin' wind.

But then I hear my mother's conditions for attending Nolan U. I see the weepy look in her eyes as she begs me to make her proud, and I'm forced to turn back around and sigh. "Okay, I get it. You're important." Three blistering glares are fired at me, so I try to soften my tone. "Can you go over the details again for me, please?"

Aimee threads her fingers together, her eyes taking on a glint of malicious elation as she repeats my heinous initiation task. "You must make Ethan Galloway fall in love with you, then publicly break his heart. Easy."

I scoff. "Yeah, sure. Who is this guy?"

The two freshmen gasp and bulge their eyes at me. "You don't know who Ethan Galloway is?"

"Have you been living in a cave?"

"I've been busy studying and getting an education," I retort.

Aimee tsks. "We've all been doing that, but we still know who Nolan U's biggest player is."

I frown. "So, why would he fall for me?"

There's a gleam in Aimee's eye. "It's not hard to get his attention. Even *you* should be able to pull that off."

"You have to at least try to make him like you." Teah gives me a sweet smile, then checks with the other girls. "Right? I mean, she'll be showing her commitment. You can't *make* someone fall in love with you."

Fiona's right eyebrow arches, and then she douses me with a haughty look that could rival President Aimee's. "If she fails, she fails."

"Come on, sisters. Be fair." Teah turns to her leader.

After a tut and an exaggerated eye roll, Aimee relents with a bored sigh. "If she can woo him enough to then publicly humiliate him, she's in."

Teah grins while my face bunches into a frown. "That's so horrible. Why would I do that to someone?"

"Because he's an asshole manwhore who's left a trail of broken hearts all over campus. Believe me, he deserves it."

Now my eyebrows are rising. Aimee's sharp, snappy tone makes me wonder if this diva got rejected by the big man on campus and she's out for major payback. I can practically see the claws popping out of her fingers.

So, why the hell did she choose me for this task?

I'm not some strutting princess who catches the eye and makes men drool.

Ugh, the thought of wooing some player just to stay in this stupid sorority is a new form of torture.

I seriously don't think I can do it, and my head is shaking before I can stop myself. "This is really dumb."

"Fine." Aimee points over my shoulder. "There's the door."

I close my eyes with a tired sigh. "But—"

"There's! The door!" Aimee's voice pitches, her gaze flashing. That smirk of hers has been replaced with an implacable scowl.

Grrr! I can't believe I have to associate with this uptight bitch.

You don't. Just walk out the door.

Fine! I will!

Balling my hands into two fists, I push my way through the line of Barbie dolls and storm into the room I've been sleeping in. It's more of a closet than anything. Think Harry Potter's stair cupboard but with the added torment of potpourri and pink wallpaper.

Snatching my duffel bag from under the bed, I start shoving my clothes into it. My brain is frantically trying to get my attention—*be logical about this, Mikayla!*—but I'm too pissed to do anything but snatch and shove.

This whole situation is ridiculous. They can't make me do this!

Surely Mom can understand how senseless this all is. Surely she'll cut me some slack and give me an out.

Hauling the bag onto my shoulder, I storm past the horrified-looking freshmen, their glossy lips popping open with surprise.

"See you later, loser," Fiona mutters as I brush past her.

Claudia titters behind her hand, and Aimee's smirk has just been upgraded to punchable.

But I resist the urge. I don't even give her the finger as I swing the door open and stomp down the stairs.

Screw this stupid sorority.

Screw Aimee fucking Walters.

And screw that insane initiation. I don't need this shit.

As I walk into the darkness, that voice of reason tries to reach me again, and all I can think as I march away from the house is *Yes you do. Yes, you do.*

CHAPTER 2
ETHAN

I grip the edge of the vanity, a low grunt reverberating in my throat. The party sounds distant. The thick beat vibrating the walls of the house seems far away as I run my fingers into shiny brunette locks and fist them.

Ruby moans, her red tongue licking my cock like a popsicle stick before that luscious mouth takes me fully and a groan builds in my chest.

Someone bangs on the bathroom door, and I manage a strangled "Occupied!" before I become incapable of speech. Ruby works me like the magician she is, and rockets are soon firing through me, my body convulsing with the release. She swallows it down like she always does, and I can't help a satisfied smile.

Glancing down at her sultry gaze, I blow her a kiss as she rises to her feet. She wipes the edge of her lips before planting them against mine. My tongue glides over hers as we drink deeply from each other before she pulls away to smirk at me.

I rest my hands lightly on her hips, giving them a gentle squeeze. "Thanks for that."

"After what you just did for me..." She pulls her dress back down over her tight little ass before snatching her G-string off the floor and shoving it into her purse. "Not a problem."

Looking in the mirror, she touches up her lipstick, then rearranges her tits.

This seems to be our usual party routine. We don't hook up that often, but the second our eyes met across the room tonight, I knew we'd be getting each other off in the bathroom. It never turns into more than that. I'm not even sure why.

"Later, Galloway." She wiggles her eyebrows at me, then saunters out the door.

I watch her curvy body disappear before straightening myself out and returning to the real world again.

A girl pushes past me to get into the bathroom, her dirty frown enough to tell me she's not impressed that we took so long in there. I snicker and murmur to her back, "All good things take time, sweetness."

Searching for my friends, I saunter through the party, raising my chin at various people, winking at the ladies, and checking out the talent for later. It's the usual drill. At least until hockey season starts. We're still in light training mode, which means we can get away with midweek parties like this.

As soon as the season starts, we won't have this luxury anymore, so we're all trying to take advantage.

Grabbing a can of beer, I crack it open, figuring I'll just have the one tonight. I have a workout scheduled for the morning, plus training in the afternoon. Coach gets super pissed if we're not on form, and I take my hockey seriously.

Which is why it grates so fucking badly that Jason got made captain instead of me.

When Coach announced it, everyone was expecting to hear my name, but then the word "Jason" came out of his mouth, and the Earth stopped spinning for a second.

Liam and Casey shot me confused frowns that quickly turned dark on my behalf. Shit, even Asher was pissed for me. Jason sauntered up to the front with a cocky grin and gave some long-winded speech about all he was going to do this season, like it only takes one man to win a fucking game.

I clenched my jaw and didn't say a word. Coach couldn't even look me in the eye for a week, which makes me wonder if his hands were tied on the decision. Jason's family has a lot of sway at Nolan U. He's like a fifth-generation legacy or some shit. Apparently his great-great-grandfather founded the first hockey team. I don't know. I don't care. I just have to lump Coach's shitty decision.

"You're backup captain for now."

But that's only if he puts Jason and me on separate lines. And who knows what dumb shit is gonna come out of Jason's mouth whenever he does interviews for the team. Seriously. It's such an epic fuckup.

I'm not trying to be an arrogant douche or anything, but Jason's an idiot. All I can hope is that he doesn't embarrass the team this year.

"It's all yours after Jason graduates." Liam keeps trying to reassure me with that thought, and I guess it's kind of working.

I just have to play my best and not think about the rest.

"Ethan!"

I turn at the sound of my name, spotting Liam and Casey near the kitchen.

"'Sup, brothers?" I find a place between them and tap my beer can against Casey's.

"Where you been?" Liam asks like he always does. I don't know when it happened, maybe it was from day one, but Liam's the guy who looks out for everyone. That's why we call him Padre. He's always the designated driver, always the guy with the listening ear, and if you had to bury a body, he'd be the one to call.

"Just getting a little taste of Ruby." I grin.

Casey crows and slaps me on the back. "Lemme guess: serviced in the bathroom."

"You know it."

"Hope you thanked her like a true gentleman."

"In more ways than one, bro."

He laughs and starts searching the crowd for a honey of his own. Casey and I have the same philosophy when it comes to college romances, and that is... college isn't meant for romance. College is meant for hookups and fun. I've seen too many couples get bogged down by relationship drama, and I don't want that. It's four years of my life before I go pro and things get super serious. I've loved my first two years here, and I plan to enjoy my last two just as much... if not more.

We need to live it up while we can, and I won't be tied down by some girl who expects me to toe the line and play boyfriend.

I want to play hard, study hard, party hard, and experience all I can, while I can. Once I've got a degree in my pocket and an Avalanche jersey, I can get serious.

"You guys bored yet?" Asher appears, slapping his hands on my shoulders and giving them a hard squeeze.

I roll my eyes and share a quick look with Liam. He laughs and shakes his head.

If anyone knows how to rub me the wrong way, it's Asher Bensen. I'd avoid the guy altogether if he wasn't on the team... and I didn't live in his uncle's house. When he scored the six-bedroom house and invited us to move in, we jumped at the chance. I just didn't realize how annoying he'd be to live with.

I mean, he's not all bad. I guess I'm still there, right?

"Come on, assholes. Let's ditch this place and head back to Hockey House."

Yep, he named it. He named our house.

It's kind of an appropriate title. Only hockey guys live there, and the team treats it like a base. We always have guys coming and going. The occasional girl sleeps over, but that's usually because she's too drunk to make it home safely. I've never had someone stay. Hooking up and then spending the night? That's romance territory and definitely not for me.

"Let's go, let's go." Asher throws the keys to Liam, and we trail him out the door.

It's not the worst idea. This party is nothing new, and we do have to work out in the morning. A few whines of complaint follow us as we're touched and pawed by different girls while we weave our way outside.

Casey hands out a few kisses, and for a second, I think he's gonna stay, but then he pulls away from some blonde with a "Later, honey" and catches up to us.

Piling into Asher's truck, I rest my head back and try to figure out this irritation in my chest.

Am I still pissed over the captaincy thing?

When Kirby came down with mono, we were all gutted for him. He would have been an amazing captain this year. But it did open up a chance for me, and Kirby even called to congratulate me personally.

"This fucking sucks, but I'll be back once I'm healthy again. I'm not letting this take me out. So, just keep the team running for me, will ya? I know you'll kick ass as captain."

I was so honored by that and promised him I'd try to live up to the type of captain he'd be.

But then Coach chose Jason.

Damn, that idiot better not be at the house when we get there. Thankfully, he doesn't live at Hockey House, but he often walks in the door like he owns the place and is oblivious to the *fuck off* vibes radiating his way. The guy is such a clueless douche. Shit, I can't believe he's captain.

"Stop looking so dark." Casey nudges me with his elbow. "It sucks. We get it. But you can't change it, so just focus on the fact that you got a Ruby Red BJ and that life is fucking awesome."

I grin and force a nod. "Yeah, man."

"We're kings of campus. Woo!" Asher raises his hands with a whoop, and I can't help a soft snicker.

Casey's right. I can't let this shit drag me down.

Liam pulls into our driveway. The lights are already on in the house, which means Riley and Connor must be in. They don't live here, but they may as well. With the number of times they crash on the couch, I'm surprised Asher hasn't converted one of his two bedrooms so he can earn himself more rent.

But the guy is stuck in his ways. The rich prick can't live without his own room, plus a spare for all his shit. He calls it his office, but I don't know how he gets any studying done in there when he's set it up like his personal mancave with a monster TV, mini fridge, pinball machine, and graphic novels dominating every spare shelf there is.

"Riley!" Asher walks into the house. "'Sup, man?"

"Hey, dudes." Our youngest D-man gives us all high fives as we trail past him, making a beeline for the den, which we turned into a pool room.

"Stack 'em and rack 'em," Casey calls to Connor as he shrugs out of his jacket. "You playin', Padre?"

Liam chucks the keys back to Asher. "Sure."

And soon we've got a game of pool going. Asher's handing out more beers while pouring himself a tumbler of whiskey like he's lord of the manor. Grabbing a pool cue, he walks around the table, eyeing the triangle of balls like he's about to play the game of his life.

"Just fucking break, man," I mumble.

"Someone's got his panties in a twist." He gives me a dry glare before doing as he's told.

I clench my jaw as the balls scatter, one going immediately into the pocket. If Asher beats me at this game tonight, I might have to snap my pool cue in half.

Casey gets some tunes going, and I don't know how it happens, but soon this friendly game of pool has turned into a serious showdown between me and Ash.

I want to take this irritating prick down, but damn if he isn't making me work for it.

I swear, burying that eight ball in the corner pocket is

more satisfying than even Ruby's luscious lips on my dick. He gives me a tight scowl, handing me a fifty.

Slipping it into my pocket with a cocky smirk, I raise my eyebrows at him. "Anything else you want to try and beat me at?"

"Yes, you asshole. Let's play again."

I take him down two more times and am three hundred bucks up by the time we change to darts.

I drink another beer, even though I told myself I wouldn't. It's good to relax and blow off some steam. I'm feeling better as I gather up the darts and start throwing them at the board.

I've convinced myself I can make the most of this year. In spite of the fact that I'm not captain, the guys still look to me for leadership, and I can't go letting them down.

"Yes!" Asher roars as his dart hits a twenty, bringing his score down below mine.

Liam's keeping track and tells me I need to score thirty points in this round and I'll win.

"No sweat." I shrug, lining up to throw while Asher groans.

"You are such a cocky asshole."

I laugh. "Jealous?"

"No, you know what? You can't just get thirty points *no sweat*. You're not that good."

"Wanna bet?" I smirk.

His eyebrows pucker. "Yeah, I do."

"You haven't lost enough money already tonight?"

With a dark glare he shakes his head. But then he starts to grin. "Who says the bet has to be financial?"

"Okay." I fist the darts and turn to face him. "What've you got?"

"You win this game, in this round—three throws, thirty points *exactly*—or you go without sex for a month." Laughter explodes around us, the guys whooping and slapping their knees while Asher raises his hands to shut them all up. "That includes Ruby BJs at parties. No hand jobs. Nothing."

I snicker. "You saying I can't even service myself?"

Pointing at me, he laughs. "You can't come for a month."

The guys all balk.

"What?"

"Damn, that's brutal."

"Is that even medically safe?"

The guys crack up, falling against each other after Riley's comment. I raise my hand to settle this pack of hyenas.

Crossing my arms, I meet Asher's challenging gaze head-on. "Anything else?"

"You can't tell anyone about it."

Casey crows. "Girls are gonna think you don't want some anymore."

"No they won't," I bite back, my smile growing. "Because I'm not gonna lose."

"Whooo!" Catcalls fire around the room as the guys quickly pick sides.

I share a glance with Liam, who just shakes his head with a grin.

"And... and!" Asher calls above the noise. "If he breaks the rules, he has to spend the day walking around campus butt naked."

That stops me for a second. I could get suspended for that shit. Coach would kill my ass, not to mention the college president.

"He can't do that." Liam shakes his head, pointing at Asher with a frown. "It'll affect the whole team."

"He's not the only player on the team," Asher bites back.

"He's one of the strongest players on the team, and we don't want to lose him."

Asher gives me a pointed look. "Then I guess it's the best way to make sure he follows the rules."

All the guys know I'd never do anything to jeopardize our season, so it's a pretty fucking good incentive.

But it's not necessary. Because I'm nailing these thirty points.

I shoot a glance at the dartboard, quickly calculating where I need to hit. No sweat.

Crossing my arms, I meet Asher's glittering stare with a smirk. "And if I win?"

He shrugs. "What do you want?"

"Your signed Gretzky jersey."

His lips part for a second. Oh yeah, I went after that one. Asher and his precious collection of hockey memorabilia. It could be enough to make him bow out.

But then he sticks out his hand and says, "Done."

I grab it, giving it a firm squeeze before turning for the dartboard.

No sex for a month. As if that could ever happen to me.

I fire the first dart with confidence, and it hits the ten, just. No problem. Only two more of those or a straight twenty.

I aim for the twenty and miss, the dart digging into the edge of the five-point space.

The guys are cheering me on like I'm competing for the world title. I grin at Liam, enjoying the way Asher's squirming beside me, his jaw clenching so hard I can practically hear his teeth grinding together.

With a little sniff, I focus back on the board.

Okay, fifteen, where are you?

Stretching my neck, I zero my gaze onto the space I'm aiming for and let that dart fly.

And what does that fucking dart do?

It betrays me, landing off my mark by a hair and digging into the two-point section of the board.

"Holy shit, he missed." Asher breathes the words at first, like he can't believe this is happening, and then he lets out this thunderous roar and starts whooping in my face. "You missed, bro! You missed!"

Tipping back his head with a laugh, he starts jumping around the room while the rest of my buddies crack up laughing.

"No sex for a month. No, wait, no *cum* for a month! Dude. Punishing." Casey slaps me on the shoulder, his sympathy pretty half assed. He's laughing so hard he has to bend over and rest his hands on his knees.

I fire a look at Liam, and even my best friend is fighting a grin.

Shit!

How the fuck did this happen?

I want to punch that grin off Asher's face right now. Maybe throw darts into his laughing mouth and watch him choke.

But I can't be a douche about this.

I shook, I lost, and now I'm gonna have to pay the price.

Raising my hands with a smile that's so fake it makes my face hurt, I bob my head at Asher, who's now wiping tears from his eyes. *Cheesedick.*

"Nicely played, man." Slapping his shoulder, I turn out of the room and head for the front door.

I just need a minute. A walk in the darkness to stop my head from spinning.

I lost.

I never lose.

But there it is. I'm not team captain, and now I can't have sex for a whole fucking month!

CHAPTER 3
MIKAYLA

I'm homeless.

It's that simple, really.

I just walked out of the sorority house, and now I have nowhere to go. Sure, I had a dorm room in my first week at this school, but then some genius decided that painting her nails by candlelight sounded romantic and didn't take into consideration the uneven surface of the pillow she had it perched on. She then thought dousing it with her nail polish remover would put the damn thing out.

Needless to say, she's not a science major, and she's lucky to be alive. Thankfully, everyone made it out safely, but not before most of us lost a bunch of stuff and were left without a place to stay. Which is why Greek Row had to open their doors, along with several houses surrounding the Nolan U campus.

I cross my arms, looking up at the night sky and finding little solace in the few stars I can see scattered among the clouds. The streetlamps emanate a lackluster glow that casts a pale light over the path I'm now walking.

This is just... fucking perfect, isn't it? I'm wandering the campus streets, alone, in the dark, and I have no idea what I'm supposed to do with myself.

I guess I could go to a motel, but the thought of wasting what precious money I do have for the "luxury" of a lumpy bed in a half-star room is too painful to consider.

You could just go back and say you're sorry.

"I could... or I could eat thumbtacks soaked in arsenic!" I answer myself out loud, because it's not like anyone's around to point fingers at the weird girl with the duffel bag who's talking to herself, right?

I just need to find somewhere to shelter for the night.

"Stupid sorority with its stupid rules and stupid freaking President Aimee." My anger is black and viscous, running through my veins as I storm down the street.

I'm pissed at my mother, and Jarrod, for putting me in this position. Ever since those two got engaged, they've been impossible.

Nolan U wasn't even my first-choice school!

My stomach knots as I think about all those delicious plans I'd come up with last year. My best friend, Rachel, and I sat there dreaming about what we'd do after graduation, and so far... none of it has come true.

Now I'm stuck in Colorado in this piddly university town with these piddly people and... Okay, fine, the education here is pretty good. Nolan U is considered an elite college. It certainly charges like an elite college, and I get why.

The facilities are top-of-the-line. I'm loving my classes, and all of my teachers and professors are great.

But I'm still pissed that Mom and her fiancé forced me here.

Dad never would have let this happen.

The thought is a cold lump in my chest. I growl, irritated with myself for even going there.

"Pull it together, Mikayla!" I bark, picking up my pace and storming down the street so fast, I don't even see the wall of muscle appear until I'm literally crashing into it.

"Whoa." Large hands catch me around the waist, steadying my feet before letting go.

I take a step back, my eyes traveling up his solid body before reaching his face, which seems just as chiseled as the rest of him. I mean, I can't see his chest or anything, but his T-shirt is fitted enough to give me a good idea of what lies beneath that white cotton, and my mouth is already pooling with water.

I frown, not liking the effect this stranger is having on me. I'm trying to be in a bad mood right now, not attracted to some college jock! He's got to be a jock, right? Tall, broad, with dark hair sneaking out beneath his backward baseball cap and a small scar on his square-cut chin.

I wonder what sport he plays.

No you don't!

I frown, so not needing these flutters in my belly or this rush of something hot and primal flooding my body.

With an irritated tut, I go to move around him, but he shifts and scowls down at me like I've done something wrong. "What are you doing walking around alone at night?"

I give him a pointed glare, wishing he was shorter so I could look him in the eye properly. The guy is a walking Empire State Building, and I feel like a country cottage next to him.

It irritates me, so I bite back with the only weapon I have—a snappy tone. "That would be none of your business."

He scoffs and looks around him. "Do you have any idea how many creepers lurk around campus at this time of night?"

"What, you mean like you?"

He gives me a dry glare. "Some drunk idiot could pick you up like that, Shorty." He snaps his fingers. "Any chick with half a brain knows not to take stupid risks like this. Aren't you girls always supposed to travel in packs? I thought that was Common Sense 101."

I raise my eyebrows at him.

Packs? What does he think I am, a wolf?

More like a meerkat.

I huff. "Great, so now I'm stupid *and* short. Well, aren't you just pleasant." I slap his arm, which feels like a perfectly shaped piece of marble, and I suddenly wish I hadn't touched him.

The tips of my fingers tingle as I skirt around him, trying to pick up my pace.

"Hey. Where are you going?"

"Like I'd tell you," I shoot over my shoulder.

"I can walk you. Make sure you get there safely."

I tip my head up to the sky with a scoffing laugh. "Seriously? Dude. I can see you have a blatant hero complex going on, and that's great for you. But I am very capable of looking after myself." I turn to give him my best pointed look. Hopefully the streetlamp above me can highlight how much I mean this. "I don't need you walking me anywhere. I'm a big girl."

"Well..." He tips his head, pulling a face that would have made me laugh if I wasn't having such a shitty night.

I've been hassled about my height most of my life, and early on, my dad taught me to run with it. *"You're always gonna be short, kiddo. Just own it."*

I try to give this hot jock a droll look, because I'm really not in the mood to be charmed. I even flip him the bird for good measure, but that just makes him laugh.

Holy Moses, his smile is beautiful—broad and wide with straight, white Colgate teeth and the kind of impact that probably makes most girls weak at the knees.

Dammit. I don't want to be most girls.

I spin and start walking away, hoping to escape this tingling sensation which is quickly spreading and making my lady parts sing like freaking sirens. I refuse to be bested by some guy. I'm not the type to swoon or bat my eyelashes. It's not my mission to score a boyfriend so that my life will be complete. I am perfectly fine on my own, thank you very much!

Glancing over my shoulder, I jerk to a stop and spin yet again. "Are you kidding me?"

He slows his pace, shoving his hands in his pockets but not changing his trajectory.

"Stop following me, you creeper!"

"I'm not." His lips twitch. "I happen to be going this way too."

"I call bullshit."

He sighs. "Fine. I just want to make sure you get to wherever you're going safely."

I roll my eyes with a groan, hating how much I like that sweet sentiment. But like hell I'm giving in to it. I am a strong, independent woman, and I don't need some nighttime protection detail.

"I don't need a bodyguard," I tell him. "Now stay." I point at him, narrowing my eyes in an attempt to combat the fluttering in my stomach.

Why does he have to be so freaking hot?

Why does the thought of some random stranger caring enough to walk me safely to... *anywhere*... feel so damn good?

I don't want to feel that way.

I can't afford to.

With a sharp frown, I point at him one more time, then spin on my heel, determined not to look back or interact with this guy for another second.

I'm on a mission to find someplace to sleep tonight, and I don't need him hounding me. Or judging me for storming out of a sorority house like a hissy-fitting toddler.

Okay, so maybe I haven't put much thought into my choices tonight.

But come on. How can I do what Aimee is asking of me? How can I possibly get some stupid playboy to fall in love with me? This Ethan Galloway dude who I'm then supposed to publicly humiliate.

I'm so not about that.

Bullies suck. I don't want to become one, even if Aimee does think this Ethan guy deserves it.

I will not—

"Hey, sweetness."

I jerk to the right when a van slows to a stop beside

me. It's mustard yellow with covered-up windows in the back, and from the leering looks these guys are throwing me, there should seriously be a *predator alert* label plastered to the side of that thing.

"Where you goin', honey?"

The voices calling out the window make my skin prickle... and not in a good way. This is no lust-fueled tingle—it's a *run like hell* warning.

And I accused the jock of being a creeper.

This can't be happening. Of all the nights to make a stand and tell Mr. Empire State Building I didn't need him. Of course I have to be approached by a van full of perverts.

My stomach hitches as I realize my little legs will never be able to carry me fast enough. Even if I break into a run, these two guys—no, wait, there are three of them— could jump out and grab me, haul me into their van, and do who knows what to me. I may fight like an alley cat, but three against one?

Shit. I can't believe I'm failing Common Sense 101.

I can't believe I'm gonna have to turn around, yet again, and hope to God Mr. Empire State Building didn't take me at my word.

CHAPTER 4
ETHAN

I stayed like she told me to, but I didn't take my eyes off her, and thank fuck for that.

As soon as that van slowed beside her, my muscles coiled. And yeah, there's a certain sense of satisfaction in knowing I'm right—I've heard too many rumors to not believe that some of them are true—but the thought of even one of those assholes touching her has me breaking into a run.

"Baby, wait up," I call, jogging up beside her and throwing my arm around her shoulders. The duffel bag bumps me in the stomach, but I ignore the buckle digging into me and pull her a little tighter to my side. Then I throw an icy glare in the direction of the van. My tone is anything but friendly as I seethe, "Hey, guys. What the fuck are you doing trying to pick up my girl?"

They all recognize me. I can tell by the way they jolt, the way their eyes round just a little.

They're not calculating if they can overpower me, because they know if they touch me, every guy on my hockey team will make it their personal mission to rain down a fucking hailstorm on them. You don't mess with the Nolan U Cougars. Anyone with half a brain knows that.

"We didn't know she was your girl, man." One of them laughs uneasily, and it looks like these douche nuggets might have a full brain between them, because moments later, the tires are squealing as they take off down the road.

"I hate you," she mutters.

"Well, you're fucking welcome," I snap. I can't help it. I'm still pissed at those assholes for approaching her. I'm raging that guys like that even exist.

With a soft sigh, she flicks my arm off her shoulders, her lips pursing to the side before she murmurs, "I mean, thank you… and I hate that I'm not bigger."

Her soft voice seems to smother my anger, not to mention the vulnerable look in her eyes. I force myself to relax, to take a breath and find my center the way Coach always tells us to. He likes us fired up on the ice, but we have to be able to control it—switch it on and off like a light bulb.

"*The best fighter is never angry.*" That's his favorite quote by some guy called Lao Tzu. I repeat it in my head a couple times, trying to shake off how fucked-up my night has turned out to be.

The girl blinks and clears her throat, lifting her pointed little chin like she's shaking off her vulnerability the way I'm trying to shake off my dark mood. The light above us casts a pale glow over her, and I take a second to study her petite features. Her straight nose has a smattering of freckles across it, her blue eyes piercing as she meets my stare with a challenging look that's all bravado. How I see right through it, I'm not sure, but it helps me soften my voice.

"You're welcome," I try again, this time grinning down at her and throwing in a wink that has her lips twitching. "Lucky I didn't listen to your bossy ass, right? That could have gone really badly for you. But never fear... I was here."

She rolls her eyes, tipping her head back with a groan. "Can we not talk about this anymore? I said thank you already. What do you want, a parade?"

A barking laugh pops out of me, which seems to surprise us both. I snicker, shaking my head. This chick is something else. The whole grumpy-ass persona on such a shorty is... well, it's adorable.

She tucks a clump of hair behind her ear, and I'm struck by what a wreck she looks. Not in a bad way, just in a *who gives a shit* kinda way. Most of the girls I associate with wouldn't leave the house without serious preening. This one looks like she doesn't believe in mirrors. Not that she needs to. Even with her messy hair, there's something about her that has my gaze glued.

She wrinkles her nose at me, then huffs. "All right, fine. You can walk me to my dorm."

"Thank you." I nod, grateful for the distraction after such a shitty night.

Her blue gaze brushes over my face, resting on my lips for a moment before darting to the ground.

I'm used to this kind of perusal. I can tell she thinks I'm hot. Most girls do. The thing that's refreshing is the fact that she's not trying to paw me or flirt with me. If anything, she's spent our entire interaction trying to repel me.

But it's not working.

I don't have a hero complex. I just can't walk away from a woman wandering around by herself in the dark. Shoving my hands in my pockets, I amble along beside her, slowing my pace to match her shorter steps.

The idea of what those guys could have done to her if I hadn't been here makes me want to punch a hole through the wall, or maybe straight through their bodies. Damn those fucking assholes. I hate that the world isn't safe enough for people to just live in however they want to. Anyone should be able to walk anywhere at any time.

But it doesn't work that way.

Shorty hitches the bag on her shoulder, and I figure we should at least introduce ourselves. She probably already knows who I am, but I've never seen her before, and I'd kind of like to know her name.

"So, my name's—"

"Nope." She raises her hand. "I don't want to know your name."

I snicker. *Is she for real?* "Why not?"

"Because then if I see you around campus, you'll expect me to be polite and say hi. I'm not interested in some faux friendship with a creeper who stalks innocent women at night."

Is she serious right now?

A surprised laugh punches out of me, cutting through the still night air and covering up the flash of irritation that just spiked through my chest. "Oh, you mean the guy who saved you from a carload of sleazebags and is generously walking you to your dorm?"

"I never asked you to do that, big guy."

"You know what, Shorty? I should just leave you right here."

She pauses to give me a challenging smirk. "But you're not going to do that, are you? Your conscience won't allow it."

I narrow my eyes at her pretty little face. Yeah, she's pretty, but... "Jeez, you're annoying."

"Thank you." She raises her chin, and another laugh pops out of me.

What the fuck is wrong with me? I only had two beers tonight. Why am I laughing so much?

This chick is a piece of work.

For one, she doesn't seem to know who I am, which is kind of refreshing. And two, she's not tripping over herself to make a good impression. If anything, she's working overtime to make sure I never want to speak to her again.

"So, what's your story, then?" She keeps walking. "Do you just prowl the campus at night, looking for lonely girls to rescue? Let me guess, you're a vigilante, right? What's your code name? The Jock? Tall Man? Captain Hero?"

I snort. "Those are the worst hero names ever. Have you even read a comic book before?"

"Hey, I happen to love Marvel and DC movies, okay?"

"And Captain Hero was the best you could come up with?"

"Gimme a break. I'm working on the fly here." Her lips stretch into a grin, which she can't quite catch in time.

The streetlamp gives me a taste of it, and I'm struck

again by the fact that she's pretty. Not knock-you-on-your-ass gorgeous, not cover model stunning, but a cute kind of pretty. What do they call it? The girl next door?

With her hair pulled back in a messy bun and those leggings paired with the Nolan U T-shirt, you can tell she's not the type to spend hours getting ready before walking out the door.

I'm kinda digging this unpreened, sporty vibe she's going with.

Damn, I wish she'd tell me her name.

"Do you live around here?" she asks. "What dorm are you in?"

I raise my eyebrows at her. "I thought you didn't want to know anything about me."

"Touché," she mutters and hitches her bag up again.

"Here." I take it off her.

"Hey." She tries to snatch it back, but I hold it out of reach. "I can carry my own bag."

"What the hell have you got in here?" I lift it up and down, trying to calculate the weight.

"That would be none of your business."

"Let me guess, you're one of those old-school chicks who feels like she needs to take half the library home, forgetting about this handy little thing called the Internet."

"I'm not eighty! And give me back my bag." She lunges for it, but I swing it out of the way again. "I don't need you to carry it for me like some knight in shining armor. Talk about old-school!"

I sigh, refusing to give the bag back. "You really don't want me to be a good guy, do you?"

She rolls her eyes. "I don't want you to make me feel

weak and like I can't handle myself," she retorts, then points to her right. "That's my dorm. Now hand it over."

I glance at the orange bricks of Hilton Hall before eyeing her up.

My tone drops to a quiet hum. "You're more than capable. I can instantly tell that about you. And accepting help doesn't make you weak." I hand back the bag while she blinks up at me, her bow-shaped lips parting.

For a second, I imagine kissing them, but that only makes my dick twitch, and I'm suddenly reminded of the stupid bet and how I'm out of action for the next month.

It's probably a good thing this chick has been so prickly tonight. I can't go pursuing anything with anyone right now.

Shoving my hands into my pockets, I take a step away from her and figure I'll bring us back to where we were when we started. "Well, I would say it's been nice meeting you, Shorty, but you're rude and you wouldn't throw me a parade for being your personal hero, so... as entertaining as this has been, I look forward to never seeing you again." I wink, unable to hide my grin.

She fights a laugh, clamping her lips together and nodding. "The feeling's mutual."

Her playful blue gaze captures me, and I'm locked in place by it for one, two, three seconds before my brain reminds me that I cannot engage with this girl.

She's off-limits. Every girl on campus is off-limits if I have any hope of surviving the next month.

With a nod, I take another step back. "Take care, Shorty."

Spinning away from her, I head back to Hockey House.

No point lingering out here. She's safely at her dorm, and I can't avoid the inevitable. It's time to go home and face the heat and hassles from my buddies before tackling this month-long torture.

Thank God hockey is starting up soon. I can throw all my energy into it. If I work my ass off, I might just get through the next four weeks without exploding.

CHAPTER 5
MIKAYLA

I watch the big guy walk away and have to bite my lip to stop myself from calling him back.

"I lied! This isn't my dorm! I have no place to go, Captain Hero!"

But I can't let myself say it.

He's too hot and... he laughed at my trash talk. He grinned at me as if I was likable. He stayed with me despite my every attempt to shoo him away, and then he went and lowered his voice to this husky timbre that sent my insides into chaos while telling me that accepting help doesn't make me weak.

He could make me weak, though.

If the throbbing between my legs and the mass of butterflies in my belly are any indication, he could turn my body, mind, and soul into putty.

It's good that he's walking away.

I don't want to be attracted to some tall hunk of a man.

I'm at Nolan U to study and earn my degree and

pursue my dreams. No one else is going to do that for me, and I won't let myself get distracted by Empire State Buildings. Even if they do smell good and laugh at my lame superhero code names.

"The Jock? Tall Man? Ugh!" I tip my head back in disgust. I could have done so much better than that. My dad introduced me to comic books when I was six, and I was hooked from day one. Sure, I haven't read any in a while, but still...

My chest seems to cave in, this unwanted pain pinching me as I picture sitting on Dad's knee while he introduced me to all his favorite characters. He used to read to me every night.

Until he didn't.

Until the only sound in the house was Mom's fussing and Megan's whining... and the clock that ticked above my bookshelf.

I haven't touched a comic book in years. How am I supposed to read them without him? Who the hell would I talk to about Captain Marvel and Black Widow? Who would I dissect storylines with?

With a short sniff, I turn on my heel, staring up at the five-story dorm and having no idea what it's even called.

I just needed to get the guy to hand me my bag back.

The way his muscles flexed when he held it away from me...holy hotcakes. I wanted to nibble every inch of his rounded biceps, run my fingers over his hard chest... maybe even my tongue.

He was way too damn sexy, and it's good that he walked away. It's good that I don't know his name.

I nod, trying to convince myself of this, yet I still turn

and look over my shoulder, searching the dimly lit street for him.

He's gone. And now I have to find a place to sleep.

My old dorm is another few blocks away, but it's unusable right now and probably won't be fixed for months. Besides, Mom really wants me to join the sorority and... Shit, she's going to be so let down when I tell her. She was desperate for me to become a Sig Be sister, just like she was. And I thought I could do it—be the good daughter and finally do something right for a change—but they're asking too much. I can't go hurting some guy just to score a permanent place in the house. That's so wrong.

Squeezing my eyes shut, I fight off the burn of irritation and break into a run. Tall Man would not be impressed that I'm careening through campus on my own at this time of night, but what choice do I have?

I need to find a place to crash. At least I'm running, right?

The bag whacks against my leg, growing heavier by the second, but I push on until I'm a puffing mess and slowing to a walk outside the hockey arena.

I won't be able to get into the building, but maybe I can find a shadowy patch against its looming edge. Someplace I can curl up, unseen, and try to get some sleep.

Exhaustion is tugging at me as I reach the end of the path and skirt the side of the building. I end up near the parking lot. It's well-lit, so I can see and hear people coming, but if I press my back against the wall, I'll be hidden in a strip of shadow. Dumping my duffel bag on the ground, I kick it up against the concrete and flop down beside it.

I'm drenched in darkness and feel safe enough. Even

if a vanload of sleazoids pulls up, they won't be able to see me.

Resting my head back against the cold surface of the building, I stare up at the night sky and shake my head.

What the fuck am I going to do?

Sleep here every night from now on?

Shit.

Mom will find out about my performance tonight. She always does, because her soon-to-be stepdaughter, Aimee fucking Walters, tells her everything.

Yep, that's right. My sorority president is going to be my stepsister, and if that's not a punch to the face, the fact that my mother is stupidly in love with her smarmy father is like a kick to the balls—if I had them, although I'm sure a kick to the V-jay hurts pretty bad too.

That's what the engagement announcement felt like, anyway.

Or maybe it's the fact that since hooking up with Jarrod, my mom has turned herself into someone I don't even recognize. Who knew that the Walters were the only family on the planet who knew absolutely everything and whatever they say isn't just opinion, it's irrefutable law.

"But Jarrod says Nolan U is the only college you should be considering. It's elite, Mikayla. The best of the bunch. He's happy to pay for your tuition if you go there."

"Jarrod believes this is the best choice for you, and so do I."

"Jarrod knows his stuff, Mikayla. Don't try to argue with him. You only embarrass yourself... and me."

"Grrr." I let out a disgusted huff and dig into my bag for my phone.

. . .

Me: Hey, you up?

I only have to wait a minute before I get a response.

Ray: Yep. You okay?

Me: Need to talk.

And my phone starts ringing.

"Hey, bestie," I murmur.

"Hey, you. What's up?" Rachel's sweet voice brings instant comfort, and I pull my knees to my chest, hugging myself and avoiding the question by asking one of my own.

"How's Cali?"

"It's good." I can hear the smile in her voice, and I know she's either with, or thinking about, her new boyfriend. "Not the same without you, though. Who knew Fontana could be so bland without the presence of Mikayla Hyde?" Her soft laughter hits my ears and I ache for home, especially when her voice quakes. "I did. I knew."

I sniff. "I miss you."

"Ditto times infinity."

The ache blooms and spreads across my entire chest. It's an effort to keep my voice upbeat. "How's the new job going?"

I should really ask about Theo. That's her favorite

topic of conversation these days, but I don't really want to talk about guys or to hear how happy she is with hers.

"Yeah, it's pretty good. I mean, waitressing isn't exactly my dream job."

"It's a foot into the food industry. You'll own your little bake shop one day."

"Yeah," she sighs. "That's what Theo keeps telling me. I wish I'd gotten that job at Sweet-a-licious. Can't believe I lost out to Amber Buchanan."

"I know, right? You are so much better at cake decorating than her, plus your customer service is far superior. Remember last time we went in and she basically snubbed us until we started incessantly ringing the bell?"

"*You* started incessantly ringing the bell, and I don't think I've ever seen her face go so red." Rachel starts giggling, and I can't help laughing along with her.

Tears burn my eyes, but I squeeze them shut and order them to dry out immediately. I will not start crying over the phone. It'll only make her worry, and I don't want to do that to her. She already has a propensity to stress about the smallest stuff, and I won't do anything to trigger her.

"Hey, so did I tell you my mom got that job in Jamaica?"

"Really?" I perk up. "Wow. She must be stoked."

"Yeah, she's pumped. She's wanted to get into international teaching for so long but knew it'd be too much for me. She's waited all this time for me to graduate, and it's her turn, you know?"

"When does she leave?"

"About three weeks. They're fast-tracking her visa to get her down there quicker."

"Oh, dude. That is so fast."

"I know. It's gonna be really weird without her around."

"Are you staying in the house?"

"She says I can, but I don't know. I don't really want to live on my own."

"You could get a roommate."

"Yeah, but the only one I'd want to live with is you, and you're stuck in Colorado for the next four years."

I wince, remembering how horrible our goodbye was. It's not like I can afford to fly back... unless my mother or Jarrod pays for it, and I'm already dependent enough on them.

"How's your mom doing?" She asks it softly, knowing it's a sensitive topic right now.

"Well, she's loving Aspen. Living it up in her new mansion with her two little Pekingese and my perfect little sister."

"I bet Megan's adjusting well to the move."

"Ugh." I stick out my tongue. "Megan adjusts well to everything."

"I'm just glad you guys didn't move until the summer. I would have hated graduating without you."

"I never would have let that happen." My voice dies off, strangled by the thought that I did let moving miles away from my best friend happen.

I originally wanted to go to UCLA, which would have been about a ninety-minute drive from the place I grew up in. But then Nolan University popped onto my radar when Mom told us we were moving to Aspen. Well, it had always kind of been there, since it's Mom's alma mater and she's often gone on about wishing I could go there but knowing she could never afford to send me. Until she met Jarrod. Turns out they bonded over their shared love of this college, regaling each other with stories of how they both went here.

After that, the inevitable was set in motion. They wouldn't have given me a dime toward college tuition if I hadn't agreed to come here. I mean, they never actually put it that bluntly, but I could read between the lines. The look on Mom's face when she was basically pleading with me to accept Nolan U was too much. She has these lofty dreams for me that will never happen because I'm not her. Yet I still felt compelled to do as she wanted. To not let her down. I hate that I feel this way sometimes. She caught me in a moment of weakness where all I could think about was how badly my dad had let her down over the years and how I couldn't be another person to do that to her.

So, I agreed and made her smile, and then... Jarrod asked me to sign a stupid contract, like paying for his future stepdaughter's college tuition was a business trans-action. Mom wasn't bothered by it.

"I've signed a prenup. What's the big deal? It'll keep you accountable. Jarrod likes things on paper. He's worked really hard for his money, and he deserves some guarantees. He's investing in your education. You should be happy about this."

"But look at these conditions." I tapped the second page, pointing out the clause about maintaining a minimum 3.5 GPA.

"Oh, sweetie. That's just a way to encourage you to keep your grades up and not slack off. I'm sure Aimee has the exact same contract."

I scoffed. "Does hers stipulate that she had to become a Sig Be sister too?"

Mom giggled while passing me a pen. "That's a privilege, Mikayla."

"But what if I can't do it?"

"Of course you can. Aimee's president this year. You're in. Don't you realize how happy I'll be seeing you two experiencing college together this way? It'll make your first year so much easier having her there to support you. Now, stop fussing and sign. You're getting yourself a world-class education for free. It's a no-brainer."

She made it sound so easy, yet it's been anything but.

Frustration builds like a firestorm inside me, and I'm sure Rachel can sense my angst through the phone.

"So... what horrible things are the sorority girls making you do this week?"

I work my jaw to the side and mutter, "Some stupid thing about embarrassing a guy they don't like."

"Ew, really? They're so immature."

"I know, right?"

"I can't believe your mom wants you to be one of them."

"Well, you know Melanie Hyde. I'm pretty sure her life's mission is to turn me into a mini Megan."

"A mini her."

"Megan *is* her." I sigh. "Talk about being a black sheep."

"I happen to love black sheep. They're my favorite because they stand out from the rest. They're like the badass sheep. Way cooler than those run-of-the-mill white ones."

I grin, adjusting my bag while I listen to the world's

nicest person try to make me feel better. Lying down, I rearrange my head until the bag is as close to a comfortable pillow as I can get it.

"I guess I better let you go. Is Theo there?"

"I'm at his place."

"You staying the night?"

I can picture the blush rising over her cheeks. She only lost her virginity to the guy a few weekends ago, and when she told me about it, she blushed so hard I thought she'd burst a blood vessel in her face.

It was kind of adorable and sounded way better than my first time. I'm happy for her, really I am. I've only met Theo over video chat once, but he seems like a nice enough guy, and I did love the way he kept looking at Ray —all loved-up, like she was the prettiest thing he'd ever seen.

Rachel deserves that in her life.

She's always been so quiet and shy. Never had a serious boyfriend in high school but always wanted one. She's the girl who read romance novels and pined for true love, always crushing on the hot jocks or the sexy bad boys but never scoring one. And then Theo walked into her life about a week after I moved to Aspen and swept her right off her feet.

He's a few years older than us and would have graduated from high school the year before we started, but I remember his dad cruising the streets in his cop car. He's a giant of a man, and I wouldn't say we feared him, but he wasn't the type you'd wave to as he drove by.

It's still early days for Rachel and Theo, but she wouldn't have slept with the guy if she wasn't feeling it. She told me she loves him and that he said it first, so she has no doubts about their relationship. I didn't even know it was possible to fall in love so fast, but she tumbled like she was kayaking over a waterfall.

It makes me wonder if I'll ever feel that strongly about someone.

If I even want it.

Love can be so... unpredictable.

It changes people. I think of how much my mother has changed since getting together with Jarrod, trying to become this perfect girlfriend and slide into this elegant rich world like she wasn't a single mother struggling to make ends meet.

And then I think about how much I changed when the guy I loved the most walked away from me. The one who was supposed to have my back and watch me grow. The one who was supposed to tell Simon Ekland to take good care of his daughter on prom night. The one who was supposed to attend my graduation ceremony and shout, "Yeah, Mickey Blue!" while raising his hands in the air.

But he wasn't there.

Because he left us for another woman, and I haven't seen him since.

CHAPTER 6
ETHAN

I slept pretty well considering it took me a good hour to get the conversation with Shorty out of my head. Thankfully, most of the guys had hit the sack by the time I finally walked in the door, except for Liam.

He looked pretty damn tired as he sat at the kitchen counter nursing a coffee, and I knew he was waiting up to check on me. That's just the kind of guy he is... and why we call him Padre.

"How you doin', man?"

"Yeah." I sighed, resting my shoulder against the pantry door. "Fuckin' darts."

"Can't believe you took that bet."

"I thought I could win."

He grinned at me. "You gonna last?"

"Have to." I shrugged. "Not about to walk around campus naked. Can you imagine the fallout? Coach would kill me."

"Well, yeah. And then resurrect you, just so he could sideline your ass for a couple weeks."

I snickered and clenched my jaw.

And that's how I woke up this morning. With a clenched jaw, because shit on a stick, last night was not a bad dream.

Today marks Day One of No Come.

Pulling up the calendar on my phone, I mark my freedom date—October 7. Yeah, it's gonna be a long four weeks, but I'm a man of my word, and everyone in this house knows it.

A cheer goes up when I step into the kitchen. I give them all the finger and have to force a smile when I look at Asher. Like I'm gonna give away how much losing riles me. He's not getting that satisfaction on top of everything else.

I'm gonna show all these fuckers what a man I am. Bet none of these douche nuggets could go dry for a month. It's like the ultimate challenge, and I'm going to make it my bitch.

Snatching the orange juice out of the fridge, I pour myself a tall glass and gulp it down before grabbing two bananas and the jar of peanut butter. I make quick work of my pre-workout snack, then grab my keys.

"Anyone coming with?"

"You know it." Casey gulps down the rest of his protein shake while Asher demolishes the last of his eggs and avocado.

Liam doesn't eat pre-workout and is measuring protein powder into his drink bottle while I shove my sneakers on.

Thursday mornings are always a workout day. We have practice in the afternoons, and I like to get my lifting done first thing. Hockey training is intense, and with the season just around the corner, we all have to up the ante. Practices are now four times a week, with two lifting sessions, one plyometrics workout, and two cardios expected in our own time. Between that and academic classes, we're pretty damn busy. And once the season starts, we'll have games twice a week too.

But bring it the fuck on.

If I'm gonna last this month, I need to work as hard as I can.

I start up my Ranger—a hand-me-down from my pop. It was my graduation present so I could easily make the two-hour trip to Denver without any hassle. I try to get down and see him once a month, and he'll drive up for home games whenever he can.

The trip to the arena only takes about five minutes, and I park in the sunshine-soaked lot and wait for the guys to peel out of the car before locking it. Nolan U is a pricey school, and when I turn to look up at the building I love so much, I'm grateful I got in. I'm grateful my dad saved his ass off so I could be part of one of the top NCAA programs in the country, playing and working in this world-class facility.

Nolan U is known for their sporting prowess, and every major team has the best. From the football stadium to the shiny new basketball courts, athletes at this school are treated like royalty... and expected to perform like Olympians.

Which is why we drag our asses out of bed so damn early to work out.

"Hey, look at that." Liam slaps my chest with the back of his hand, pointing to a lump near the arena door.

It's kind of cast in shadow, and it takes me a second to work out what it is.

"Some homeless guy sleeping it off."

My eyes narrow when I spot the duffel bag and immediately recognize it. A growl reverberates in my throat before I can stop myself.

"That's no guy," I mutter, jogging away from my friends and coming to stop by Shorty, huddled up in an uncomfortable-looking ball on the concrete.

What the fuck?

I walked her to her dorm. I made sure she was safe... and she spent the night out in the open?

She lied to me, the little shit.

Why'd she do that?

And what is she doing here?

Crouching down, I gently shake her shoulder. "Hey, wake up."

She groans, her face scrunching as she curls up like an armadillo.

"Hey." I shake her a little harder. "Come on, Shorty."

"What?" she whines, flicking my arm away. "Leave me alone. What are you doing?"

"What are *you* doing?" I bite back.

"Trying to sleep!" she snaps at me, her eyes still closed.

Casey starts snickering, and the sound jerks her awake. Her eyes pop open, her blue gaze hitting me hard before I'm distracted by the smattering of freckles across her nose. She's got a cute nose, refined and little, matching the rest of her.

She scrambles up into a sitting position, a clump of hair sticking out the side of her head as the messy ponytail from last night has gone askew after what must have been a restless sleep.

Shit. Does she have any idea what could have happened to her if some perv had found her here?

Another growl shoots out of me, and I stand up, bringing her with me. "I did not walk you safely back to your dorm last night so I could find you here. Do you have any idea the kind of assholes who might be lurking around?"

"Oh, you mean assholes who yell in your face at stupid o'clock in the morning?" She squints her eyes against the sun, her scowl downright adorable as she checks her watch, then gapes at me. "It's not even seven o'clock, you animal!"

"Who is this?" Casey asks.

She throws him a dark look and mutters, "That would be—"

"None of your business," I finish for her, pointing from Casey to her. "That's what she's gonna tell you, because Shorty here's allergic to sharing information. Like how she doesn't actually have a dorm room but is, in fact, homeless."

"I am not homeless."

"Then go home and rest someplace safe!" Snatching her bag off the ground, I grab her arm and start leading her to my truck. "I'll drive you."

"No you won't." She wrenches her arm out of my grasp. "I am perfectly capable of getting home by myself."

"Obviously." I point to the spot where she was just lying, then have a mini wrestling match as she tries to take her bag back.

After half a minute of watching her struggle, I let the

bag go and then catch her arm before she lands on her butt.

She grunts, shrugging me off and heaving the bag over her shoulder.

"Where do you live?" I bark. Yes, I'm being kind of forceful right now, but she just scared the shit out of me. Those guys in the van were lurking around for who knows how long, and she was just sleeping out in the open, like some invitation for them to snatch her into the back of their sicko van.

She lifts her chin, an obstinate set to her jaw.

Stubborn little—

I huff out my nose and force my tone to an even keel. "I'll drive you wherever you need to go, but you can't stay here sleeping outside. Now why aren't you home?"

Her blue gaze falters for a second, and she looks to the ground.

"I know you think this will be a creeper move, but I'm not letting you go until you tell me. I won't find you sleeping out on the street again, okay?"

Her jaw works to the side, and then she finally mutters, "Captain Hero," before letting out a heavy sigh. "I live on Greek Row, and I got into a big fight with my sorority sisters and needed a night off, okay?"

My head jerks back with surprise. "Which sorority?"

Her nostrils flare as she clenches her jaw. "Sigma Beta Mu."

It's hard not to laugh. "You're a Sig Be sis?"

No way. She *so* does not fit the bill. Those girls are intense.

"I'm a legacy," she grits out, looking like she hates that fact.

"I—"

Her phone cuts me off, ringing loudly in her pocket. She pulls it out and checks the screen, her shoulders slumping. "I gotta take this." She glances up, her gaze hitting mine as she lets out a resigned laugh. "I'm fine, big guy. Seriously."

I'm not sure I believe her but don't grab her arm when she walks around me. Instead, I turn to watch her leave, cringing as I hear her sigh the words "Hey, Mom."

I've got a feeling that call's not gonna go so well.

Part of me wants to follow her, but the sun is up now, and she should be safe enough to walk back to Greek Row without an escort.

"Ethan, come on, bro," Casey calls me from the doorway while Asher watches Shorty walk away.

But then she stops, dumping her bag in the middle of the parking lot and tipping her head up to the sky.

"In a minute." I wave Casey off. "You guys go ahead."

"You sure you don't need someone to keep an eye on *you*?"

I growl at Asher's question and turn back to put him in his place. "I just bumped into her last night and walked her back to her dorm. At least that's what I thought I was doing," I grumble, still annoyed that she lied to me.

And now I'm annoyed because I'm wondering why she even wants to be a Sig Be sister.

They're not your typical sorority girls. They're next level, like the kind who get mocked in college rom-coms. I've had some success with a few of them, but most are a little up themselves for my liking. Unless they get hella drunk at a party, and then all bets are off. Sorority girls can par-ty.

Turning back, I watch Shorty pace the parking lot, obviously agitated.

She seriously does not seem like the sisterhood type. Did I read her all wrong last night?

And why do I even care?

I don't need an irritating, pretty girl in my life right now.

Asher's still eyeing me up. I can feel his gaze on the back of my head. I whip around to glare at him. "Go. I'll meet you in there."

"Okay." He walks backward, pointing at me with a smirk. "Just be a man of your word. Remember what's at stake here."

"I'm not trying to bone her." I spread my arms wide. "I just want to make sure she's okay."

I don't know what my face is doing, but it must be believable, because he nods once and disappears inside the arena while I cross my arms and wait for Shorty to stop pacing circles around her duffel bag.

CHAPTER 7
MIKAYLA

"I told you, the task is ridiculous. You can't expect me to—"

"I expect you not to embarrass me," Mom cuts me off, and I dip my chin, unable to hold my sigh in check. "Don't go sighing in my ear. You are wasting this amazing chance by not being open-minded. Jarrod really went out on a limb for you over this. He got you into that school, he's paying for your education, and Aimee has been more than gracious helping you out during rush and ensuring you got a bid."

"Gracious?" I spit back. "This whole initiation thing is bullshit. I've done everything they've asked of me, but making some guy fall for me just so I can humiliate him? It's too much."

"Oh, stop being such a prude. It's just a little fun. You have to show your commitment to these girls. Once you've done that, they'll have your back for life. Believe me, it's worth it."

I grit my teeth, wishing for Rachel's mom. Why

couldn't I have been born into that family? Yes, Ray lost her dad when she was fourteen, and it sucked. It was heartbreaking. He was the nicest guy on the planet, and he died without warning. I don't know if Rachel will ever truly get over it. I don't know if I will. Ty Beauford was like a father to me, too, and Ray and I cried buckets together after that awful day. But her mom was solid. She was there for her, for me. She stayed strong... unlike my mother, who fell apart after Dad left, then didn't really pick herself back up again until Jarrod came into her life six years later. And then she became someone else all over again.

I've experienced three versions of my mother, and the only one I truly liked was the first one, but that's probably because I was too young to know any different.

"Mikayla, you go back to that house and you apologize. You grovel. I don't care what it takes, but you secure your place in Sigma Beta Mu."

"But Mom—"

"You know what's at stake here. I am marrying Aimee's father, and I expect you to do our family proud. Megan expects it too. She'll be joining you in less than three years, and I don't want you ruining her chances of getting in."

"I know, I just—"

"Jarrod and I made the conditions very clear when we agreed to pay for your education. It's all in the contract."

Fucking contract. Why the hell did I sign that thing?

"You want a degree. *I* want you to get this degree." She lets out a sigh—one of those disappointed ones that always make me feel bad. "Really, Mikayla, you don't need to make this so difficult. These conditions are in place to *help* you. I'm trying to secure your future here. Without Jarrod you'd be going to some little community college, but instead you have the opportunity of a lifetime at Nolan U. Don't waste it."

I huff and kick the bag at my feet, wishing I wasn't dependent on Jarrod, wishing my father was still around so he could go to bat for me. But he's not, so I signed that contract thinking it was for the best.

Shit. Double shit! Fuckity-fuck!

I clamp my teeth together, resisting the urge to scream.

"This is good for you, sweetie. Those sisters will teach you how to become a woman. I don't think it's asking too much to play along with a few silly games in order to secure a solid standing at Nolan U and have the support of these girls as you navigate college life. You don't want to screw this up. Now, go back there and do whatever you have to."

"I really—" Clamping my lips together, I swallow down my argument because I'm smart enough to know it will be a waste of air.

Jarrod has me in a headlock with that stupid contract, and as much as Mom is pissing me off right now, I really don't want to upset and embarrass her. She's put up with a lot of shit in her lifetime and... *Dammit!*

"Fine," I finally mutter.

"That's my girl." She ends the call with a bubbling laugh while I sneer at my phone, slapping it against my leg and muttering, "It's just so great that you get me, Mom."

Squeezing the phone in my hand, I'm about ready to

hurl the thing across the parking lot when a deep voice stops me.

"You okay?"

I spin around and notice Captain Hero still standing there. Seriously? The guy's frickin' relentless!

"I'm going! I'm going!" I flick my hands in the air.

"Need a ride?"

"No." Lifting my duffel bag with a grunt, I haul it over my shoulder.

"Need me to carry that heavy pack for you?"

I spin and flip him the bird.

"So fucking rude, Shorty." He grins, lifting his own finger to flip me off.

I can't help a laugh and quickly turn away before he realizes how funny I think he is. How adorable that look on his face was and how freaking hot his body is.

He probably knows it already. A jock like that?

He's probably got a girlfriend... or a harem of them. Or he's one of those meatheads who figures that sleeping his way through the female population is a healthy way to spend his time at Nolan U.

I'm so glad I never learned his name.

If I see him on campus again, I'll just walk the other way. Sure, he's a bit of nice eye candy, but so not worth my time.

Right now, I have to focus on swallowing the last of my pride and doing what I must to secure a college degree from a prestigious school. My dream is to become a sports agent. I only have to spend four years here studying sports management and business. And then I should probably go to law school. Agents need a solid understanding of contractual law. But maybe I can work for a few years or do some internships before hitting up law school. The sooner I can be independent from Jarrod and my mother the better.

But if I want any chance in hell of seeing my dreams come true, I need to toe the line on this one, which is why I walk my ass back to Greek Row and climb the front steps of the Sigma Beta Mu house.

I knock twice and am relieved when Teah opens the door.

"Oh, you came back. Yay. I was worried about you last night." She pulls me into the foyer just as Aimee and Fiona come trotting down the stairs.

"Well, well, well." Aimee tips her head, her eyes gleaming with triumph. "Hello, Mikayla."

"Thanks for calling my mom for me." I say the words with a smile, wondering if she can taste the sarcasm dripping off them.

She gives me a simpering laugh as she descends the last two steps and comes to a stop in front of me. I look up at her while my insides writhe. A quick rebellion is forming in my stomach, but I squash it down.

Think of your future. You can do this.

Swallowing the acid taste in my mouth, I try to sound as genuine as I can. "I'm sorry for leaving last night. I guess I was nervous about trying to pull off this initiation and didn't want to admit that I don't think I can do it." I spit out the speech I came up with on my walk.

How robotic does it sound?

I check Fiona's and Aimee's expressions. They're both looking a little bored, but they seem to believe me, so I force out the rest.

"I really do want to be a Sig Be sister. So... please, give

me a little more insight into this guy I'm supposed to destroy. Who is this *Ethan Galloway*?"

"I still can't believe you don't know him. You've been here for weeks. Have you been living under a rock this whole time?" Fiona pulls out her phone and starts searching for something.

"In fairness, hockey season hasn't started yet," Teah murmurs.

"Hockey?" My voice is barely more than a whisper as I think about the guys who arrived at the arena this morning.

Please don't let it be one of them.

Shit!

Hockey guys?

"Here he is." Fiona flips her phone around, and my heart sinks on the spot.

It's not just any hockey guy. Dammit. It's The Jock. Tall Man. Captain Hero.

I gaze at his picture. He's decked out in his Cougar hockey jersey, a proud, cheesy smile on his face.

His handsome, gorgeous, chiseled face.

His cocky, confident, bossy face.

I quickly try to think of all the annoying things about him—like the way he woke me up and told me off this morning. The way he's so damn persistent.

The way he laughed and gave me the finger.

My heart does a little hiccup, softening without warning.

No! Shit. Think about the bad stuff!

"I know it's a little overwhelming. He's hot property, and all the girls want him." Teah grins. "But that's your in. He's a total player and will pretty much bone anybody."

My mouth goes dry as an image of him naked on a bed suddenly pops into my mind. Tingles ripple through my downtown as I picture him thrusting into me, his body covering mine as he—

But I cut the thought off before I accidentally moan out loud.

"You don't have to sleep with him." Teah laughs, rubbing my arm. "The look on your face right now."

Aimee's eyebrow arches while I blink and order my expression to go bland, bland, bland!

"You just have to be a dick tease. Flirt with him enough that he'll want you." She smirks. "He likes a good challenge. Make him think you're a guarantee, and just when he's confident he's got you in the bag, we'll rip it away from him. I'm not exactly sure how I want to do that yet, but I'll keep you apprised of the plan. For now, pretty up and put on a smile. It's time to go meet your target." She lightly slaps my cheek, then looks sideways at Teah, her face bunching like she's just smelled a fart. "You might need to help her with this." She points at my face, then does this little circle, indicating my entire body, before turning away.

I narrow my eyes at Aimee's back as she struts off to the kitchen.

Teah takes my arm with a kind smile, and we wander back to my closet room.

Dumping my duffel on the bed, I stare down at the narrow mattress and wish I could flop back on it. That horrible night on the concrete was for nothing. I just want to crawl into bed, shut my eyes, and forget this whole thing.

But I have classes in an hour or two and...

Crapstick. I've got me some work to do with Ethan Galloway now.

"Here." Teah reaches for my hair, untangling the tie and combing her fingers through my fine locks.

She fluffs about, and I let her. Then she starts rifling through my duffel bag and pulls out an outfit for me.

"Yes." She puts a shirt aside. "No." She wrinkles her nose at my cargo pants, then pulls out a pair of ripped jeans that are a hand-me-down from Megan. "Love these."

Yeah, that's right. I get hand-me-downs from my little sister because she's a fashion diva and I apparently don't know the first thing about looking stylish.

So I let Teah clothe me and do my hair, then bypass the dining room and head for Java Jean's coffee shop.

I don't really want to start my day this way, but I've got a mission to complete. And the sooner I get this over with, the sooner I can get initiated into this stupid sorority and focus on the future I'm fighting so hard to obtain.

CHAPTER 8
ETHAN

I worked hard this morning. My muscles feel shredded, which is exactly the way they should be after an intense lifting session. I managed to channel some of my frustration into the workout, and I grunted and yelled my way through the heaviest lifting I've ever done.

Coach would be proud—maybe. It's hard to tell sometimes. Compliments are rare and usually grunted at you, but he's loyal to a fault and I'm pretty sure, when none of us are around, he won't shut up about how awesome we are. And that's why we give him our all.

Rubbing a towel over my head, I saunter out of the weight room, ready to shower up and get on with my day. But my step falters when I spot a short brunette loitering near the rink with a take-out coffee cup in each hand.

With a little snicker, I shoulder the glass door open and walk into the crisp air of the hockey rink.

"Hey, Shorty." I grab her attention. "How'd you get in here?"

She walks around the rink to meet me, and I watch

her face the whole time, trying to figure out what the hell she's doing here.

"Mr. Zamboni let me in."

"Did he now?"

She stops in front of me with an impish grin. "I can be persuasive when I need to be."

"Right." I drag my eyes down her body. She's changed clothes, and it's hard not to notice the way those jeans hug her little legs and that shirt tucks in at her waist, the V-neck accentuating her boobs. She really is petite, but I like her small curves on display this way.

Clearing her throat, she shoves a coffee cup at me.

I wrap my fingers around it. "What's this?"

"A thank you… for helping me out last night."

"Wow, how bad is this hurting you right now?"

"A lot." Her emphatic expression makes me laugh as I sniff the brew. Damn, that smells perfect.

"I don't know how you like your coffee, so you're having it the way I like mine. I always go for café au lait in the mornings because, you know, I'm classy that way."

With another laugh, I raise my cup and say, "Well, bonjour to you," before taking a sip. "Oh yeah, that's good."

"Excellent." She smiles, and I notice for the first time that her eyes are more of a gray-blue. It's hard not to stare at them.

Until she clears her throat and looks away from me.

"So, you went home, then?"

She snickers and shakes her head, muttering, "Home," before looking back at me with a sigh. "Yeah, Captain Hero. I went back to the Sig Be house and set things right with *El Presidente*."

"Ooooo, you pissed off the president?" I grin. "Nice."

Her nose wrinkles. "I think I pissed off everybody last night. Including you."

"I wasn't mad." I shake my head. "I was worried. I didn't want anything bad happening to you."

Her eyebrows pucker with confusion. I mirror her expression and state the obvious.

"I wouldn't want anything bad happening to any girl on campus. Walking around at night like that is just dumb. I wish it wasn't. I wish you could, but you have to face reality. What you did was kind of insane."

She works her jaw to the side, then shrugs. "Anger makes me stupid."

I laugh again. I don't know what it is about this chick. She's funny. It's not like she's trying to be, she just is.

But my smile gets cut in half when the door swings open and Asher walks in.

He eyes Shorty with suspicion before coming to stand beside me. Crossing his arms, he shows off his ripped biceps as he smirks down at her. "Where's my coffee?"

She raises her eyebrows at him, then puts on a sticky sweet smile. "Probably at Java Jean's waiting for you to walk your ass down there and buy one of your own."

A startled laugh punches out of him. "Sassy mouth. I like it." He tips his head at me. "Why'd you buy him one, then?"

"None of your business."

I snicker at her standard answer. It doesn't rile me so much when it's shot at Asher.

He narrows his eyes at her, and she points behind him.

"Disappear, tall person."

Asher shares a surprised look with me, like he can't quite believe this chick. I get it. We're used to girls stumbling over themselves to get our attention. We're used to shameless flirting. The girls who aren't interested seem to avoid us altogether, but most are keen, and most are of the eyelash-batting variety.

But not Shorty.

And damn if I don't think it's cool.

She's still giving Asher this pointed look, and all he can do is snicker, shake his head, and walk away.

"Stay put," I tell her. "I'm gonna shower up, then walk you to class...or wherever it is you're going next."

She rolls her eyes. "I just popped in to give you a thank-you coffee. I'm not waiting for you to *shower up*. I can look after myself. I don't need some bodyguard walking me to class."

"Sure." My lips fight a grin as I make a point of checking her out. "What are you? Five-nothing?"

Her lips part with an insulted scowl. "I am five-three... and a half, so just... you know!"

"Wow." I raise my eyebrows. "What a comeback. You're right, anger does make you stupid."

She gasps, her eyes flashing. "Give me that coffee back."

I hold it away from her, laughing some more as she makes a lunge for the cup. She grunts and tries again, jumping on me to reach the coffee and basically crawling up me like I'm the tree and she's the monkey. I cinch her around the waist, and the second her breath hits my cheek, we both go still.

I turn and am caught by those gray-blue eyes, held still by the way they study mine. Her breathing grows a little punchy, and natural instinct is making me want to lean forward and kiss those pink lips.

But I'm on Day fucking One of No Come. I'm on the *morning* of it, and if I kiss her now, it's just gonna make me ache in all the wrong places. I can already feel myself growing hard. Her little body nestled against mine, her boobs squished against my chest.

And now I'm getting even harder.

I lower her to the ground, and she swallows, taking a step back. "Seriously, I don't need you to walk me to... class..." Her voice trails off with a sigh as she obviously thinks of something. Squeezing her eyes shut, her face bunches and she quickly blurts, "But that would be really nice of you."

Wow. She actually agreed.

I raise my eyebrows in surprise, and she huffs. "Well, hurry up. It's freezing in here, and I don't want to be late."

I would offer to let her sit outside the locker room and wait for me, but I don't want Coach showing up and yelling at her.

She'll be less noticeable if she waits on the bleachers, so I direct her to a seat and tell her I'll be fast.

"Just stay, okay?"

She rolls her eyes again, plunking down with a little eye bulge before wrapping her hands around her coffee cup.

"Good girl." I wink at her, and she shoots me a very raw, dry glare.

It's hard not to laugh as I run off to the locker room.

She really is one entertaining chick.

One you should probably stay the hell away from.

Letting out a sigh, I down the last of the coffee before throwing the cup out and stripping off my gym gear.

So I wanted to kiss her for a second. Big deal. I can control this thing.

Once I walk her to class this morning, the chances of seeing her again are probably slim to none. I won't ask for her number or anything. I'll just deliver her to whichever building her first class is in and then be on my way.

Not a big deal at all.

CHAPTER 9
MIKAYLA

I sip my much-needed coffee, resisting the urge to guzzle it. After a horrible night where sleep only grabbed me in short bursts, I'm feeling somewhat jaded today, which is probably not a great state to be in when dealing with Ethan Galloway.

Why does he have to be so freaking hot?

And strong?

The way he held me against him, those hazel eyes of his. I swear he wanted to kiss me for a second, but then he just popped me onto the floor. Some player. He didn't even take advantage of the way I was clinging to him like a spider monkey.

Doubts knot my stomach as I think about this stupid initiation task and how I'm supposed to pull it off. I'm not like those other sorority girls. I don't flirt with guys. I've never really had a serious boyfriend. I dated in high school, but they were always short-lived mishaps that ended without too much fuss.

Most of the guys I hung with in high school were my

buddies... which is why I'm probably so useless at trying to attract any of them. They don't see me as a girl they can score with because I'm just *one of the guys*.

But I can't be that at Nolan U. I have to be girly like my sister. If I want an education, then I need to go against all of my natural instincts, which is why I'm sitting in this hockey rink waiting for Ethan to shower up and walk me to class.

Ugh. Getting walked to class. It's like I've been transported back to the 1950s?

My stomach turns over again, and I abandon the last of my coffee, resting it between my feet and hunching over on myself.

I study the rink, picturing players whizzing across the ice. I've only ever watched games on TV, and even then, it wasn't full games. I don't even know the rules of hockey. My dad was a basketball man, and I used to watch with him. He also taught me the ins and outs of football, but hockey was never on my radar. Although it probably should be. I bet there are plenty of female hockey players who need someone to represent them.

Maybe I should come check out a game sometime.

If I'm trying to woo Ethan, then I'll need to.

Closing my eyes with a sigh, I wonder how long this is going to take. What's the expected timeframe to make a guy fall for you?

And what the hell do I have to do in order to make him fall for me?

Digging out my phone, I wonder how lame it would be to google *how to woo a guy* when the door swings open and Ethan is sauntering back in to collect me.

As he draws near, I'm hit by a delicious scent that

makes my mouth pool with water. I don't know what the heck he's wearing, but it's spicy and manly. My nose twitches as I subtly inhale the air around me and feel that ache bloom between my legs again.

Damn this man and his sexy smell and gorgeous face and hot body.

Seriously. This assignment is going to be the freaking death of me.

"You good to go?"

I nod, snatching my coffee cup and walking to the stairwell. I trot down, and before I reach the bottom step, he grabs me around the waist and swings me down to my feet with a little grin.

It takes me a second to steady myself as his scent wraps around me, making my head spin.

This is insane!

I don't want to be affected this way.

Remember why you're here. Remember your future. Remember what you want.

I'm practically screaming the words to myself as we walk side by side out of the hockey arena.

The sun is warm and delicious the second it hits my face, and I soak it in, letting it burn off the chill from the arena.

"So, you gonna tell me your name, Shorty?"

I spin to glance up at him, shading my eyes from the sun while he slides on a pair of sunglasses. How is it possible to make such a simple gesture look so freaking cool?

Seriously, I hate this guy.

Everything about him is just—

He glances down at me, still waiting for my answer,

and I force a smile, reminding myself to play it cool. He can't know that I'm out to *get him*.

The thought sits ugly in my gut, and it's an effort to not let it show as I try to sound bright and breezy. "I guess after buying you coffee, I should probably learn yours too."

"It's Ethan." He sticks out his hand.

I stare at his long digits, his big palm, and finally slip my hand against his.

"I'm Mick. I mean Mikayla." I give him a firm shake, the way my daddy taught me, then let go before I can think about how strong his hand is.

"Anyone ever call you Mickey?" There's a playful twist to his smile, and if he wasn't wearing shades, I'm pretty sure I'd be able to catch the twinkle in his eyes.

"Only if they want to die." I throw a glare of warning in his direction.

He barks out a short laugh. "So, Mick."

"That's right. Not Shorty. It's Mick or Mikayla."

"Or mouse."

"What?"

"You know, because you're so little."

I try to make my glare even darker than the one before, and I'm ashamed to admit what an effort it is. Ethan's fighting a laugh as he keeps teasing me.

"And because your first name is Mickey. Like Mickey Mouse."

"Okay, I'm gonna have to kill you now."

"Good luck with that, lil' mouse." His lips stretch into an exquisite smile, but that's not enough to stop me forming a fist and throwing a punch his way.

I did say I'd have to kill him, right?

He grabs my fist, his large hand making it disappear within his grasp.

I grunt and try to pull it back. He gives it one little squeeze before dropping it and continuing to saunter along beside me.

He's still fighting a grin, his lips twitching up and down, and I'm irritated with myself for finding it charming.

Shit. I am in so much trouble.

I'm supposed to be making this guy fall for me so I can break his heart. But in only two small interactions, I can tell this whole fiasco is going to do me in. I'm not saying I'll be tumbling down Slope Swoon nursing a broken heart, but if Ethan keeps being so cool and likable, dumping on him this way is gonna sting.

Remember why you're here. Remember your future. Remember what you want.

I clench my jaw, repeating the little mantra and reminding myself that I am not one of those girls who needs a man to be happy.

I can simply make the choice not to fall for Ethan Galloway. I will not let myself be wrecked by his playful smile and charm. I'm on a mission to take this player down, and I will. I'm strong enough to do this.

Stealing a sideways glance at him, I grit my teeth and try to act bored and nonplussed when he strikes up a conversation about what my first class of the day is, then goes on to tell me how he's studying kinesiology.

Dammit. Even that's cool.

Yep. This guy is going to ruin me.

CHAPTER 10
ETHAN

My skates cut through the ice as I whip around the rink, building up speed when I round the back of the goal and hurl my puck at Baxter. He blocks, kicking it away to Asher, who slaps it back toward me.

We've been doing this drill for the last ten minutes, giving Baxter a decent goalie workout. Practice has been running for over an hour, and I'm damn tired. Sweat has been pouring down the back of my neck, and I'm itching for a scalding-hot shower. For reasons I don't even understand, I've been irritable ever since walking away from Mikayla. I don't get why she keeps plaguing me.

We had a fun flirt this morning, and that was it.

I can't pursue anything more.

And maybe that's it. I can usually get chicks out of my system pretty fast. Any attraction is acted on, and then I'm good to walk away.

But I can't hook up with Mikayla. I can't hook up with *anyone* until this damn month is over.

Shit.

Can't believe I lost at fucking darts. I was so damn cocky last night. Asher goaded me right into a corner, and now I'm lumped with this punishment that is a fresh type of torture.

But I refuse to complain to anyone on the team because I'm not some whiny baby. I'm a man who can complete a bet. A month doesn't have to be that long.

I slap another shot at goal and make it between Baxter's legs.

"Aw, shit!" He gathers it up, firing it back onto the ice, where Asher and I tussle for possession. It's a quick win for me, and I skate away from him, laughing, until I get blindsided by Jason, who checks me into the wall with a loud thud.

"What the fuck, man!" I push him off, and his hyena laugh scrapes down my spine as he skates backward with a whoop.

I want to down the guy so bad, but Coach blows his whistle and we're forced to skate to the side of the rink for our post-practice wrap-up.

We stand there puffing while he runs through what we did right, what we need to work on, and when our exhibition game is.

"I'm expecting a win, boys. Should be a guarantee against the Tigers as long as we can keep our defensive line strong." He points at Liam and Connor. "I'm expecting your best." Then he turns to Jason and me. "And no screwing around in the offense. I have you two on the same line, and I want to see efficient, coordinated play. No showboating."

I give Jason a quick side-eye. The coach is most definitely talking about him, but of course he has to lump us together, because apparently the sun shines out Jason's ass when it comes to Coach Bergeron... or whoever is pulling the hockey budget strings.

"All right, shower up. Get your butts out of here." He flicks a thumb over his shoulder, and we skate off the ice, trailing into the locker room.

Asher's right behind me, picking up where he left off before practice began.

"Seriously, where did you meet that little sassy mouth?"

"I told you already," I growl.

"Damn, bro. Must be killing you right now." I glance over my shoulder in time to see his eyebrows wiggle. "Knowing you can't tap that for a whole month. She'll have moved on by then, dude."

"Shut your mouth," I mutter. "I don't want to bang her."

"Shit, man, I sure as hell do. What I wouldn't give to shut up that sassy little mouth with my tongue. She was a firecracker. Bet she's a wildcat in the sack too." He makes a cat noise, scraping his "claws" through the air and causing a ripple of laughter to float through the locker room.

"Who are we talkin' about?" Jason calls from the corner.

"No one," I shout back, then throw a warning glare at Asher.

Thankfully, my roommate can't stand the new captain and seals his lips without a fight. I stalk to the showers, stripping off and soaking in that hot spray, trying to chase off my frustration with shampoo and soap.

It doesn't work.

I'm still riled as I grab my stuff and walk out of the rink.

Liam's leaning against my truck waiting for me. "We going home, or do you need to hit up Offside?"

Our local sports bar is a favorite—big-screen TVs dominate one end, along with pool tables, while the other side of the barn-sized establishment is a stage and dance floor. You can go there to hang with your bros or dance with some hos. That's not my saying, by the way, but it's damn catchy and hard not to think whenever Offside is mentioned.

I shrug and figure I could use a drink. But as I reach the driver's door, I change my mind.

"Screw it, let's just go back to Hockey House."

Liam slips into the passenger seat and gives me an assessing look. "No offense, man, but you look like you could use a drink."

"I could." I nod, the idea of a cold brewski feeling pretty damn sweet right now. "But I don't want to spend the night fending off women because I can't taste a one of 'em."

"I'm pretty sure you're allowed to taste. You're just not allowed to—"

I shut him up with a growl, but his words slipped apart with laughter anyway.

"I'm sorry, bro. Really." He sounds so fucking amused as I reverse out of the parking space and head for home. "I still can't believe you gave in to that bet so easily."

"Yeah." I sigh, running a hand through my wet hair. "I just couldn't let Asher get the better of me. If I didn't rise to the challenge, he was gonna hold it over me for weeks. You know how relentless the guy is."

"I do." Liam grins, then lightly slaps my arm with the back of his hand. "You can do this, though. You're strong enough to resist."

"Yeah," I murmur, thoughts of Mikayla dashing through my mind.

I can resist her.

I just wish I could stop thinking about her.

Every time I do, I can't help grinning over how rude she was. Girls don't act that way around me. They bat their eyelashes and giggle, or they give me their *fuck me* eyes and I deliver. But this lil' mouse gave me the finger and told me she was gonna kill me. It's classic. It's funny.

Which is why I should probably distance myself from her.

Or maybe not.

I can't imagine her doing any *I want to lick your face off* type moves on me, which means it's probably safe enough to talk to her when I see her. *If* I see her.

I just won't seek her out.

There, problem solved.

This doesn't have to be a big thing.

It's not like she's gonna track me down. To her, I'm just the jackass who called her lil' mouse... and I won't be able to help myself from doing it again, because the way her nose wrinkled and the way she fought her smile is too tempting to resist.

She's easy to tease because I know I'm not gonna offend her. She's a tough nugget and will just throw it straight back at me. I'm not dealing with a Little Miss Priss. Which is why my eyes are scanning the street as we drive past Greek Row, in spite of my decision to not go looking for her.

CHAPTER 11
MIKAYLA

I spent my weekend trying to be a good sorority sister. I didn't complain about the two-hour mani-pedi we had to sit through. I refused to go for pink nails and am now sporting navy blue, which I actually quite like. Painted nails are kind of fun, but I can never be bothered sitting around to let the paint dry.

While we were stuck with unusable hands, we were quizzed on the rules of the sorority house, and then Aimee did a presentation on what influential women wear.

"You can be both elegant and powerful." Her eyes darted my way several times throughout the presentation as if she was speaking specifically to me.

I tried not to let it rile me, but I was in a pretty foul mood by Sunday afternoon. I was so over "sisterhood" and missing Rachel with an ache that was physically painful.

She's the only girl I've ever truly connected with, and I was grateful for her texts and GIFs throughout the weekend. She keeps me going, although it doesn't help with the whole pining-for-California thing.

Rolling over in my bed with a soft groan, I can feel the day beginning to dawn. My brain slowly drags itself into thinking mode, and I'm just figuring out that it's Monday when an airhorn blasts outside my door.

I bolt upright, my heart taking off as I pant and try to regulate my fuzzy brain.

"Let's go! Let's go, ladies! Quiz time!"

Are you fucking kidding me?

Flopping back down with a thump, I muffle my scream under the bedsheets just as Fiona pops open my door.

"Get up, Mikayla! Breakfast!"

How anyone can eat at this ungodly hour, I have no idea. With a groan, I roll over and check the time. Six frickin' thirty. Do these people have no concept of how good sleep is for the body?

"Let's go!" someone shouts into my closet room, and I jerk my eyes open in time to see the megaphone. "Get your ass up!"

I'm so tempted to grab that thing and smash it on the floor, but then I'm reminded of my mother and tuition and what I want out of my life. So I sit up, feeling like a prisoner as I shove my hair into a ponytail and shuffle out to the kitchen.

The other two freshmen are already in there, happily making French toast. I sniff the coffee and try to imbibe some caffeine before being yanked toward a frying pan.

"Don't let anything burn!" Louisa fusses around me, all frenetic as she tries to prove just how much she deserves a permanent place in this sorority.

She obviously doesn't realize how perfect she already is. When they listed off the qualities of a Sig Be sister the other night, it was like reading from the Louisa Hartman study guide.

I flip the toast, not bothering to cover my yawn as I blink and try to shake some of the sludge from my brain. Mornings have never been my strong suit.

"Okay." Aimee swans into the kitchen, clapping her hands. "Why don't we sing the sorority song while you're preparing breakfast for everyone."

She starts us off, and the other girls join with enthusiasm while I sing about sisterhood glory through gritted teeth. You know Barney the Purple Dinosaur's song? Yeah, this one is worse than that. Some bubblegum tune that was probably composed by...

Actually, I should know this.

My slow brain struggles to hunt down the fact, but as I lay a new piece of toast into the pan, Clarita May Holbrook pops into my head. "1958," I murmur.

"Well done." Teah grins at me, collecting the plate of already-cooked toast and heading for the dining room.

I stay by that frying pan for what feels like ages before following Louisa and Trinity into the dining room and then having to endure a pop quiz on the history of Sigma Beta Mu.

I get three out of ten right, which makes me the loser of the morning comp and puts me on kitchen detail. I rush through the cleanup, worried I might be late for my first class. I have to sprint through campus, dodging clumps of students and hauling my ass in the door just as Professor Malcom starts talking.

The lecture is relatively interesting, although trying to

concentrate with zero caffeine is a major effort on my part. I try to take a myriad of notes that I'll have to dissect later, although whether I'll be able to decipher my drivel is another story. He also lumps us with our first major assignment, which I'll have to find some secret place to work on, because the sorority house is way too distracting.

Glancing at my watch, I figure I'll head to the library right now. I may as well get an early start. I want to ace this paper and—

"There you are." Teah grins, standing in my path while another sister, Bella, flanks my right side.

"Hey, guys." I look between them, alarm bells starting to clang. Bella's smile is freaking me out. "What's up?"

"Well, we didn't get a chance for a progress report this morning."

"Progress report?"

Teah leans in with a conspiratorial whisper. "On your special assignment."

"Special assign—oh. That."

She wiggles her eyebrows at me, and her smile would probably be cute if she was talking about anything else.

"Now, you've made first contact with Ethan, but we noticed no action throughout the weekend. Have you been in touch with him again? Sought him out? Do you have a plan for when you'll next interact with him?" Bella's thumbs are poised over her phone as if she's about to take detailed notes.

I tip my head, clamping my lips against telling them how stupidly ridiculous this entire thing is.

Don't be a smartass. If you don't play ball, you'll embarrass Mom and could ultimately lose your funding.

I clear my throat and try to look as though I've given Ethan more than a fleeting thought this weekend.

Actually, that's true. I gave him lots of thought this weekend, but every time he came to mind, I quickly shut the images down. And not once did I think about how I'm supposed to woo him.

"Well, I... should probably..." I leave the sentence hanging, hoping Teah will bail me out with a solution.

Which she does.

"Go on a date with him or something."

"Yeah, totally. That's what I was gonna say," I rush out the lie and force a smile.

Teah tucks a lock of strawberry blonde hair behind her ear and looks to Bella, who is typing up notes.

Seriously? Why?

"So, how are you going to do that?" Her expectant look makes my stomach writhe, and I'm about to shrug when Teah saves my ass again.

"She's going to casually approach him as though she hasn't been hunting the campus for him and ask him out for coffee. She'll charm him over a cup of joe and then ask for his number. Right?"

Coffee! My body starts humming for its caffeine kick.

"Yeah." I nod. "That's the plan."

"Great. So, you're doing that today, right? Because time is ticking by, and we don't want you to run out of it." Teah steps forward, pulling the tie out of my hair and obviously trying to give my fine brown locks more body. She fluffs them around my shoulders, then frowns and starts combing her fingers over the front to create this side part that I'm not used to before stepping back and nodding. "Wait. Take those studs out of your ears."

I frown at her, reluctantly doing what I'm told, while she hands me her hoop earrings and then extracts a tube of gloss from her bag. She fusses over my face, and I just have to stand there not complaining while Bella gathers up my loose T-shirt and ties it into a knot near my left hip.

"That's better," she mumbles.

They both stand back and peruse their handiwork with satisfied nods.

"Vast improvement."

I bob my head, forcing my tight lips to stretch into a smile, resisting the urge to tell them how freaking insulting this all is. They're basically telling me I'm not good enough the way I am. The way I'm most comfortable with.

Smacking my lips together, I choke out a thank-you and am about to head to the library when Bella grabs my arm with a gasp.

"Timing," she singsongs.

My stomach dips as I follow her line of sight and notice Ethan loping along the path. He's thirty seconds away from doing a walk-by. Thankfully, he's texting and hasn't even spotted me yet. I nearly tell the girls that I have this plan to catch him later, but I get no chance because they shove me onto the path, and once again I'm tripping near his feet.

His hand shoots out to steady my arm. "Whoa, careful," he murmurs, glancing up and then back to his phone.

He obviously hasn't recognized me yet, and this would be the perfect moment to slip away, but I can feel two laser beam stares between my shoulder blades, so I stand there until he looks up again and realizes it's me.

I flash him an alluring smile. At least that's what I try to do.

The move makes his head jerk back with a confused frown until I huff and roll my eyes.

As soon as I do that, his hazel gaze starts to twinkle with a grin... and here we go again.

CHAPTER 12
ETHAN

I didn't even see her until she was right beside me. I thought I was just steadying some random stranger, but then she stopped and waited for me to finish texting.

I figured it was just another chick trying to catch my attention, and I was getting ready to put on my polite smile because Get Some Ethan is on lockdown right now. But then she rolled her eyes, and I realized this girl with the lipstick and the hoop earrings is none other than...

"Hey, lil' mouse."

She huffs again, throwing in a noise of disgust. "You're really not going to drop that, are you?"

"Nope." I grin.

She tips her head back with a groan and looks seconds away from bailing when something stops her.

Her hands clench into two little fists and she takes a quick breath, like she's trying to win some internal battle before smiling up at me. "So, I bought you a coffee the other day. Think it's about time you return the favor."

Wow. Talk about blunt. I can't let that shit slide.

"Uh... that was an apology coffee. Shouldn't it be a plain freebie with no strings attached?"

She flicks her arms up like I'm impossible and ends up snapping, "Do you want to have a drink with me or not?"

"Oh, wait, is this you trying to be friendly? Because if you're asking me out, I don't tend to date mice."

Her right eyebrow arches as she crosses her arms and hits me with a challenging glare. "From what I've heard you don't tend to date women either."

"Excuse me?"

"Yeah, Mr. Hockey, I know all about you now. You think I'm allergic to sharing information, but I've heard that you're allergic to sharing anything more than your dick." She points at my pants, and I have to force out a scoff.

It's forced because okay, maybe she's right.

That kind of assumption has never bothered me before, but for some reason, hearing her sum it up in that derogatory tone kind of stings.

"So why would I waste my time asking you out on a date? All I'm trying to do is score myself a free coffee." Her eyes start to sparkle with a grin, and damn if I can't resist it.

"Okay, mouse, come on, then. I'll buy you a babyccino."

She struggles to contain her laughter, biting her lips together and shaking her head. "If you don't buy me something loaded with caffeine, you'll be in danger of bringing out my inner bitch, and I really wouldn't risk that if I were you."

I hiss. "Your inner bitch. Man, she must be a piece of work, because your outer bitch has got some bite."

She laughs like she can't believe I just said that but manages to compose herself enough to play along. "See? Why risk it? I'm doing this for your own health and safety."

And now I'm laughing too. Turning in the direction of Java Jean's, I set a slower pace than usual so she can keep up with me. Although, I get the feeling those short legs can probably run pretty fast when they need to. She seems like an athletic kind of chick.

The hoops in her ears bounce around while she's walking, and she keeps adjusting them, her eyebrows dipping like she's not used to wearing such big jewelry. Maybe she's trying something new with the whole T-shirt knot thing and the lip gloss. It's kinda cute, definitely shows off her figure a little more. Those frayed shorts she's wearing make her butt and legs—

Don't look!

My loyal brain starts reminding me why while my cock gives a little stir.

I clamp my lips together, forcing my gaze the other way... out across the green lawn to the smattering of sunbathers who will have to give up soon enough. Temperatures are already dropping, and within a couple months, this place will be covered in snow.

"You ski?" I ask. Yeah, it's random, but she doesn't seem to mind.

"I've done a little boarding, nothing too spectacular. I'm more of a water baby."

"Oh yeah? Where'd you grow up?"

"California."

"Nice. LA?"

"Fontana. It's about an hour east, but easy enough to get to the beaches."

"Wow. A Cali beach bunny. Nice." I grin and she snorts, shaking her head like I've said something ridiculous. "So, why are you in Colorado, then? Ain't no beaches around here."

She swallows, her lips pursing for a quick second before she murmurs, "I got into Nolan U."

"You didn't try for UCLA or USC?"

She looks up with a closed-mouth smile and shakes her head. "I got into Nolan U."

I frown, wondering what she's not saying. I'm about to ask, but she rushes ahead, opening the door for us and giving me a pointed look. "Let's go, big guy. Coffee awaits."

She ushers me up to the counter, and I don't even bother checking the board before placing the order. "One Americano and one café au lait in the biggest cup you've got. I'm talking bowl size, you feel me?"

The guy nods with a grin while Mikayla laughs, then taps the glass case.

"Throw in one of those apple cinnamon muffins, too, please."

I look down at her, pretending to be offended. "You didn't buy me a muffin. Since when was food part of this payback deal?"

She grins. "Think of it as an opportunity to show me what a gentleman you are." And with that, she spins to go look for a table.

Stopping near the window, I think she's about to slide up onto one of the high stools, and I'm already thinking of lines I can hassle her with, like "*How's the air up here?*" but then she frowns and turns toward the couch in the back corner.

I glance outside to try and figure out what she was looking at. There are a bunch of students milling around. Maybe one of them pissed her off at some point. Or maybe she just doesn't want to be stared at through the glass, because let's face it, if she's hanging with me, we're gonna get more looks than the average Joe.

I walk over to the couch with her mammoth muffin, then head back to the counter for our coffees.

Her mug is basically a bowl, and I'm feeling pretty triumphant as I place it down in front of her. The look on her face is priceless.

"Yes. Come to Mama, baby." She wraps her fingers around the mug and takes a big gulp. I'm pretty sure she just burned her tongue by the way her eyes are watering, and I jump up to grab her a glass of water from the cooler near the counter.

She chokes out a thank-you, guzzling the water down before attempting her coffee again. It's like it's her drug of choice the way she closes her eyes and sighs after a few more mouthfuls.

"I didn't get my fix this morning." She wipes a little foam off her top lip. "That first class was basically impossible to concentrate in. My notes are probably trash thanks to total brain fog."

"Ah, so that's why you approached me. It wasn't about hanging out, it was about getting your caffeine fix."

"Of course it was." She blinks like I'm stupid, but then her lips break into a grin.

I sip my Americano and lean back against the couch

cushions, studying her as she rips off a mouthful of muffin and pops it between her glossy lips. She licks the crumbs off her polished nails, and I seriously need to stop looking at her mouth.

I shift in my seat, clearing my throat and reminding myself of the damn bet. "So, what are you studying?"

Questions about study and schoolwork should take the edge off, right? There's nothing sexy about studying and assignments.

"Well, since it's my first year, I'm doing a bunch of general eds, but I'm planning to major in either business or sports management."

"Oh yeah?" I raise my eyebrows. "Where's that gonna take you?"

She hesitates for a minute, like she's not sure if she wants to tell me. There's this excited gleam in her eye as she fights a grin, then blurts, "I want to be a sports agent. But for female athletes. I want to get them the best deals I can. I want to give them the chance to shine just as brightly as the men. To get paid fairly. To get the best sponsorship deals. There are so many talented women out there, and they deserve all the same shots men get."

"Nice." I bob my head, impressed by her fervor. She probably has no idea how fast she's talking or how excited she sounds. "Well, you're in the perfect place. Nolan has an excellent business school, and we're not short on top-quality athletes."

"True fact." She nods, stuffing another mouthful of muffin between her lips. Her cheeks bulge out like a chipmunk as she chews. For a girl who's so petite, she knows how to devour food like an offensive lineman.

"UCLA would have been a good school too." I subtly

dangle the statement out there, hoping she'll elaborate a little more than she did earlier.

What? I'm curious.

She gives me a dry glare and delays by gulping down some more coffee. She's gonna finish that whole cup. It's kind of impressive.

After a thick beat of awkward silence, she finally gives in with a huff. "Fine. It was my first choice, but then my family was moving to Colorado, and Nolan U is my mom's alma mater, so..."

"So..." I raise my eyebrows. "You didn't want to be too far away from them?"

"It's not that," she clips. "I would have happily stayed in Cali, but my financial situation is..." Clenching her jaw, she looks away with a frown, then mumbles, "It's complicated. I don't want to talk about it."

"Right." I sit forward, resting my arms on my knees. "So you're just gonna make me guess, then?"

"Oh come on." She gives me a desperate little frown. "Don't you have things in your life you'd rather not talk about?"

"I'm pretty much an open book." I shrug. "Ask me anything."

"Fine." She huffs. "How much of a say did your parents have when it came to your college education?"

"None." I frown. "Why? Did yours?"

Her lips dip as she breaks off another piece of muffin, then mumbles, "They're the bank, so yeah... they had a pretty big say," before shoving it in her mouth.

CHAPTER 13
MIKAYLA

Shit! I can't believe I just said that.

Why did I open that crazy-ass can of worms around this guy?

He's going to want to know more, and I'd rather choke on this muffin than dissect my weird-ass family situation. I said *they,* which he's probably interpreting as my mother and father, when it's actually my mother and her dick fiancé. Having to explain that just might kill me.

Change the subject. Quick!

"So, where do your family live?" I swivel to face him, but all I see is a marked frown.

"Did your parents really say you had to go here because they're paying? You didn't get any choice in where you wanted to study? That's messed-up."

My nostrils flare, and I press on with my very unsubtle avoidance tactic. "Are you a Colorado boy, or...?"

He stares at me for a long beat that's thick with tension. But I don't budge, and eventually he sighs and slumps back in his chair. "I'm from Denver."

My shoulders drop with a relieved sigh, and I nestle back in my seat, bringing my coffee with me so I can nurse the cup in my hands. "That's cool. Easy for visiting, right?"

"Yeah." He nods, draining his cup. "My dad will drive up for games. It's pretty cool."

"What about your mom? Does she not like hockey?" The second the questions are out of my mouth, I regret them.

His expression tightens around the edges, his mouth dipping as he softly murmurs, "She loved it. She was the one who bought me my first pair of skates. Her dad used to play. He never went pro but had some fun playing college hockey until he busted his knee in a game and had to change course."

"Wow. They must be real proud that you're playing now."

"Uh-huh." He nods, and my mouth goes dry because something's off. I've said something to upset him, and crap! I hate it when things get emotional.

I'm scrambling for something funny to say, anything to lighten this moment, but then he sighs. "Truth is..." He glances at me, like he's weighing up whether or not I can handle what he's about to tell me.

I can't. I nearly say it out loud. *I don't like sad stuff or anything that will make me cry, so just tell me some cheesy joke. It can even be a crass one. Just don't—*

"My mother passed away a few years ago. She never got to see me play college hockey, and it kinda kills me. She would have loved it."

A fist of emotion jams up my throat, making it impossible to speak.

"Grandpa makes it to the games he can, but he's getting kind of frail now. He had a stroke after Mom passed." He shakes his head. "Shittiest year of my life. Nearly missed out on graduating from high school. I had to study like a demon over the summer, and they gave me special compensation, but I had to work my ass off senior year to get my grades up. I wanted Nolan U, because it's got one of the strongest hockey programs in the country and it's close to home, so I'm around if Dad needs me." Easing back into his chair with a sigh, he stares at his empty coffee mug for a second before looking back at me with a smile. "I like to think Mom watches me play. I don't know if she can, but... the thought makes me feel better anyway."

"She can." I bob my head, wanting to believe that. I don't actually know what happens to people after they pass, but I like the heaven theory. It sits well with me, the idea that there doesn't have to be an end, that those we love can still watch over us from afar.

Ethan's smile stretches across his face, and I'm caught by the beauty of it, softened by the knowledge that we both know what it's like to be raised by a single parent. My dad may not be dead, but I lost him. I understand this pain, and it makes me want to reach out and grab Ethan's hand.

My skin tingles with the idea of touching him, but I resist the urge and instead whisper, "I'm sorry you lost her."

"Thanks." Ethan's smile turns sad as he shuffles in his seat, and then Train Awkward pulls into the station.

I clear my throat, setting my coffee down and glancing across the shop to see Teah and Bella at the table by the window. Bella's looking over Teah's shoulder, obviously checking out how my coffee date is going.

Are they shitting me? They followed us in here?

Ugh!

When I saw them out the window, that was irritating enough, but I was too caught up listening to Ethan to notice them enter the coffee shop, and now my tingles have turned to prickles of irritation.

This is a nightmare. How am I supposed to be myself when they're monitoring me this way?

You're not supposed to be yourself. You're supposed to be the girl who can woo guys like Ethan Galloway.

Crappity-crap!

Fisting my hands, I force myself to take a breath, then angle my body so I'm even closer to him. With my breath on hold, I stare at his hand, lightly resting on his knee, then run my finger between his knuckles.

He stiffens and I nearly draw my hand away, but I've got a mission to accomplish here, so I force my finger to start tracing the bones of his long fingers.

"So... now that you've had a coffee date with a mouse... do you think you'd be up for a meal sometime?"

His eyebrows dip while his eyes dart from my finger to my face, to my mouth, then down to the floor.

"Uh..." He lets out an awkward chuckle and pulls his hand away. "You trying to score more free food off me?"

"Why else would I ask you out?" I wink at him.

His smile flashes with genuine amusement before he sits forward in his chair like he's ready to get up and go.

"Maybe." He nods. "Things are kind of busy for me right now, and hockey is gonna be heating up real soon, so I'll…" He winces, rubbing a hand over the back of his head. "I'll check my schedule and let you know."

And ouch.

I glance at the girls by the window, relieved they're too far away to hear what he just said or feel the icy burn of his rejection.

I told them I wasn't up for this. Didn't I make it blatantly clear that guys like Ethan don't fall for girls like me?

My insides flame as I stand, snatching my bag and hiking it up onto my shoulder. "Well, thanks for the freebie. We're all square now, so I won't bother you again."

His expression buckles. I turn my back on it, making a beeline for the door. I'm already outside when he catches up to me. He falls into stride beside me, and I turn to him with an irritated scowl. "What are you doing?"

"Walking you to your next class. I'm assuming you've got more than one class today."

I jerk to a stop. "I don't need you to walk me to class."

He turns to face me, smiling like he didn't just totally turn me down in the coffee shop.

Frustration courses through me, a nice healthy dose that will hopefully be strong enough to kill off the embarrassment I'm wrestling with.

"I've already told you, I don't need a bodyguard."

"Are you sure, lil' mouse?"

A hard laugh comes out of me, brittle and spiky. "You are such an ass."

"Perfect. An ass and a mouse. Isn't there some fable about that?"

"It's a mouse and an elephant, you idiot. And if you

don't want to hang out with me, why the fuck do you want to walk me to class?"

He sighs, his large shoulders slumping forward as he scuffs the concrete with his sneaker. "It's not that I don't want to hang out. It's just—"

"Forget it." I cut him off before this all becomes too feely and I give away how much his rejection is like a punch to the gut. "We're good. I got my coffee, and I don't need anything else from you."

His eyebrows dip into a sharp V.

"Chin up, big guy. This campus is crawling with girls who are probably more your style. Go ask one of them if you can be their personal protection detail." Forcing a bright smile, I start backing away from him. "Have a good day."

And then I flip him off, because I can't help myself.

He snickers and raises his middle finger right back at me.

It makes me laugh, dammit. Why does he have to be so fucking funny?

Spinning away, I storm off, trying to focus on the fact that he doesn't want to have dinner with me. He obviously doesn't mind my company as a friend or something.

What else is new?

A girl like me is always shoved into the friend zone because that's just who I am. No amount of lip gloss or hoop earrings is going to hide that.

With a growl, I untie the knot in my T-shirt and try to yank out the wrinkles. It doesn't work, and now I have to walk around campus with a mangled shirt. Perfect, it can match the scrunched-up feeling in my chest.

Dammit, I hate this so much.

Anger at Mom and Jarrod rears hot and fast. Damn them for putting me in this stupid position, and damn Aimee for giving me this impossible initiation task!

CHAPTER 14
ETHAN

Offside is going off tonight. Music is pumping, the dance floor is crowded with gyrating bodies, and all three pool tables are occupied. Thursdays are usually popular. Students are getting over an intense workweek, and they're already looking ahead to the weekend. May as well blow off a little pre-partying steam and get warmed up. Anyone can zombie their way through a Friday, right?

I wrap my fingers around the beer bottle Casey just set in front of me. I'm just having one tonight. Coach doesn't want us drinking at all, but come on... let's be realistic. After the practice we just endured, I'd say it's fair that we tip back one or two.

Man, he worked us hard.

I mean, he has to. The season starts in less than a month, and we need to be ready. I don't mind sweating it out for that reason. It's perfect prep for going pro, which I'm still set on doing. But I don't want to go pro until I have a degree in my back pocket. If my grandpa's experience taught me anything, it's to have a backup plan.

Casey perches on the stool beside me, resting his tattoo-covered arms on the table and scanning the dance floor for hotties. He's always on the lookout. Like me, the guy's after fun, not serious. We're too young to get tied down with that drama. There are plenty of women out there who just like to have a little fun, too, and Casey's radar is set to track 'em.

"Anything good out there?" Asher grins, resting his arms on the table.

Casey's left shoulder hitches. "Nothing poppin' yet."

"Come on, man. Don't be so damn picky." Asher snickers and glances over his shoulder. "I can see three I'd bang without hesitation. Red dress. Blonde curls. And... where'd she go? Yeah, that Latino goddess with the double-D rack."

Casey strains his neck to get a decent look and nods. "Not bad."

"So why the hell aren't you going for it?"

My friend takes another swig of his beer before giving me a sideways glance and shrugging.

I sigh, my shoulders slumping. "Dude, you don't have to serve this punishment with me. If you want to go get some, just go. I don't need sympathy celibacy."

"Just to be clear, there is no way in hell I'm going celibate. Need I remind you about a certain cowgirl I enjoyed last Friday?" His eyebrows rise and I shake my head, struggling to fight off my grin.

I'm still not sure if that night was a good idea. Casey swaggering into Hockey House after a quick fuck in the back seat of this chick's car lead to some weird ass conversations that will never be repeated outside of Hockey House. I now know how each of my bros lost their V-cards and I'm still not sure if I want to be privy to that shit.

Casey nudges me with his elbow. "It's the first night you've joined us since the big loss, and I was trying to be considerate. You've been in a shitty mood the last couple days, and I don't want to rub it in your face that no one's allowed to play with your wiener for the next month."

"It's down to three weeks now." Liam slaps me on the shoulder, obviously trying to encourage me.

I grunt, painting a line in the condensation of my beer bottle. I'm not grumpy because of losing the bet. Well, okay, I am... but I'm more pissed off with myself for the way it affected my conversation with Mikayla.

We were having a pretty decent time until she ran her finger down my hand and made my cock spring to attention. I don't think she noticed, because I was too busy telling her how I'm not available to feed her free food.

Shit!

The way she sprang out of her chair and practically ran out of the coffee shop. I tried to smooth things over, but it's not like I could tell her the truth, so I just had to act like I hadn't been the world's biggest asshole.

I haven't stopped feeling bad about it since. All week it's been bugging me, but I can't even seek her out to apologize because then I'm putting myself right back in the same position as before.

Hanging out with her was way more fun than I thought it'd be. She's so easy to tease. She takes it like a champ. I fight a grin, picturing her cheesy smile as she flipped me off and told me to have a good day.

But my smile disappears the second I relive that look on her face after I rejected her. Shit, we'd just been talking deep, and then I went and fucked it all up. I don't usually share about my mom with people, but it naturally progressed to that place, and when she agreed that my mom watches me play, I could have jumped right into those blue-gray eyes of hers. They held depth... understanding. And that's kind of rare.

It makes me want to get to know her more.

But then the little general got other ideas, and I had to cut her off.

I had to—

My breath catches, my arm freezing midair as I pause in taking another swig of beer and watch her walk through the door.

I blink, making sure I'm not hallucinating.

Nope. She's still there.

Damn, she looks good. She's gone and dolled herself up again, even more extreme than she did the other day. The ass-hugging jeans she's painted on show off her shape, and fuck it, there goes my dick again.

I scowl and check out the rest of her, my eyes skimming down to the heels she's sporting. Doesn't seem like her, and my suspicion is confirmed when she takes a step forward and her ankle turns.

She winces, then scowls down at her feet before looking at the girls around her.

Sorority babes.

"Here come the slut bags," Asher mutters, tipping his head toward the group I just happen to be ogling.

"That is so the wrong term for them." Liam laughs, shaking his head. "Sig Be girls are anything but slutty. Have you ever tried to flirt with any of them? They're like ice queens."

"Unless they get drunk." Casey laughs. "Remember that party last year? Shit, I don't even remember her name, but she was all over me. Damn, she was fine. What was her name again?" He goes all contemplative while he scours his memory banks, and my eyes are drawn back to the huddle.

They move to a table near the bar, Mikayla jumping up onto a stool. Her hoop earrings bang against her cheeks, and she adjusts them with a little wince before the girl opposite her says something.

I can't lip read, so I have no idea what was said, but Mikayla's shoulders slump as she tucks her hands under her thighs and swings her short legs back and forth.

My lips rise at the edges as I watch her. Yeah, she'd accuse me of being a creepy stalker, but it's kind of fun studying her from afar. I'm learning a lot.

Like the fact that she doesn't order alcohol, which means she either doesn't like it or doesn't have a fake ID... or maybe those Sig Be girls just won't let her. She sips on a root beer, her eyes tracking to the big-screen TVs on her left.

The girls around her are chatting and giggling, but Mikayla's not even paying attention. She's too busy watching the Broncos/Seahawks game. Her body jerks, a smile cresting over her face as she gives the air a little pump.

Glancing at the screen, I spot the Broncos' wide receiver doing a victory dance in the end zone.

Weird, I thought the little beach bunny would be a Rams fan, but maybe she's one of those people who just picks a team from any game she's watching and follows along. My mom was like that. Sure, she was loyal to

Colorado, particularly when it came to hockey, but she loved watching any game on the ice and would cheer for whichever teams were playing.

So, Mickey Mouse is a football girl. Interesting.

"What are you staring at?" Liam nudges me, looking over his shoulder.

"Oh, just... the game." I shrug.

His eyes dart to the screen, and he nods. "Sweet. We're up."

"Yeah, should be a guaranteed win, right?"

My comment sets off a quick discussion with Connor and Riley, who appeared a few minutes ago. Riley's brother plays Nolan U football. He's a senior this year and takes great delight in teasing lil' Ry-Ry about hockey. It's all in good fun, but man, I'd pay decent money to see those meatheads try playing on the ice. They'd get thrashed. You can't tell me it takes more skill to throw a leather ball down the field. And body checks in hockey can be just as brutal as football tackles.

"Hey, boys." Two girls sashay past the table, their hips swaying in a sultry rhythm that captures Riley's attention and diverts Connor. He's lured to the dance floor while I take another swig of beer and find my eyes tracking back to Mikayla.

She's still watching the game but flinches when the blonde beside her shakes her arm and says something with a sneer.

Mikayla angles her body back to the group, and even though I can't see her face anymore, I know she's bored.

Like really bored.

She has to be.

Because I know she'd rather sit in a bar watching a

football game than talk about whatever the hell Sig Be sisters obsess over.

It's time for a rescue.

It's probably a stupid decision. I'm supposed to be avoiding this girl. But that thought doesn't stop me from placing my beer on the table and muttering, "I'll be right back."

CHAPTER 15
MIKAYLA

I'm dying.

I've been transported into a new type of hell where football is playing on TV but I'm not allowed to watch it, and my toes are squished into pointy heels, and the jeans I'm wearing are so tight I'm getting an understanding of what those corset-wearing women had to suffer back in the day.

What I wouldn't give to be tucked up in my room studying economics or holed up in the library staying on top of my course reading. But no. I had to come out tonight because the Sig Be sisters were in the mood to party, and apparently, I'm not allowed to have my own opinions in that house... not until I've proven how committed I am.

Shitballs!

I go to rub my eye, and Teah quickly snatches my wrist before I can. "You'll smudge your makeup."

"Right." I force a smile and wrap my fingers around my root beer bottle instead. If I squeeze it hard enough, will the glass crack and shatter? Will the shards skirt across the table and bury themselves into Fiona's perfectly pale skin?

At least Aimee's not here, I suppose. She had to study for a test tomorrow, which feels monumentally unfair when I had to drag my ass out tonight. I wanted to study, too, dammit!

Gimme books to pore over. Gimme comfy pillows to lean against. Gimme boxer shorts, no bra, and a baggy T-shirt.

"Hello, ladies." The deep voice makes my nipples stand to attention, and I whip a look over my shoulder, my body completely betraying me when I catch Ethan's smile.

He smells good. He smells so frickin' good, and now that tingling sensation is flooding my body, pooling between my legs, and—

Stop it! He doesn't want you, remember?

"Hey, Ethan." I don't know how she's doing it, but Fiona's bright gaze seems to be a combination of *fuck off* and *do me.* There are hints of both icy coolness and lust in her smile, and it's weirding me out.

I grab my drink and guzzle it, keeping my gaze diverted from the solid chest that's lingering right by my head. His arm is on the back of my stool, his bicep grazing my shoulder blade before he leans down and murmurs, "Nice to see you, Mick."

"Yep." I nod and keep my eyes drilled on the bottles of liquor behind the bar.

"Was just wondering if you wanted to come and meet my friends. I'll buy you a drink and —"

"I'm good." I turn to him with a smile that is all

plastic.

He works his jaw to the side, seeing straight through it. I can tell by the challenge in his gaze. "Just thought you might like to hang with some real men rather than watching those pansies on the screen up there." He winks, and a laugh spurts out of me.

Dammit. How does he do that every freaking time?

It's an effort to wrestle my smile back into hiding, and even more of an effort to refuse him two more times before he finally gives up.

"Well, if you change your mind..." Sliding his hands into his pockets, he pulls off *sex god* with the ease of Apollo and has my lady parts wailing in agony as he walks away, and I stupidly turn to check out his ass.

Holy hot cakes. Of course his ass is perfect!

I spin back with a huff and am immediately facing down five angry glares. I can't decide if they're jealous that I got invited over but none of them did, or if they're pissed at me because I blew him off.

"What are you doing?" Bella's voice pitches with urgency. "Why'd you just reject him like that? Are you completely stupid?"

Teah hisses. "Bells, harsh."

"Well, I'm sorry, but I don't get why she's not taking this opportunity. He practically handed himself over on a platter, and she said no."

"Well, I..." My mouth opens and shuts a couple times while I try to think of a plausible excuse.

The truth won't fly. I've already tried to tell them this plan won't work, but they're hell-bent on making me see it through.

"She was just playing hard to get." Louisa tips her head. "Right, Mikayla?"

"Uh... yeah. Obvi." I force out a little laugh, trying to look as though I know what I'm doing.

"You don't really have the time to do that." Fiona's eyebrow arches. "The initiation ceremony is just around the corner, and if you haven't fulfilled this final task, then you're not coming. And if you're not part of the initiation, then you're really not—"

"Yeah, I get it," I cut her off before I have to hear one more time that I'm not really Sigma Beta Mu material.

I already freaking know I'm not!

But I do have the right to earn a degree and pursue my dream of becoming a sports agent, so I force my butt off that stool and hit the ground with a little smack.

"Now that I've moved the power to my side of the court, I will approach for a little dick teasing."

The girls whoop while I try to strut away from the table, but my damn ankle rolls again, and I end up shuffling away from them and clunking to a stop next to Ethan's friends.

"Hey, mouse." He seems genuinely stoked to see me, which I don't understand.

Didn't he imply at our coffee on Monday that he wasn't interested in dinner?

Why the hell is he inviting over to meet his friends?

But then my friend-zone theory rises in the back of my brain again, and I'm forced to accept that I will only ever be one of the guys. Dressing me up doesn't work. I'm still just me underneath all this garb, and Ethan knows it. Which is why he didn't mind me meeting his buddies.

"Guys, this is Mick."

I raise my hand in a little wave, casting my eyes around the table. The tank of a man on Ethan's left gives me a soft, closed-mouth smile while the piece of artwork on his right eyes me up like I'm a lickable ice cream cone. His arm tats are impressive, and I skim my eyes over them before getting distracted by the tall one next to me.

"Hey, you're the coffee girl from the rink the other day." He grins, sticking out his hand. "I'm Asher. Nice to meet you."

I give his hand a tentative shake and try to work out why his eyes are glinting with amusement.

"So, you into my boy here?" He tips his head at Ethan, and I don't even have a chance to respond before Ethan speaks.

"No, of course not. We're just buddies."

I whip a look at Ethan, who grins at me while my stomach starts sinking down to my knees. Forcing a smile, I nod and try to ham it up. "Like I'd date this asshole, right? I got a little more class than that."

The guys crack up laughing. Even Ethan's grinning, shaking his head with an *I'll get you back later* kind of smile.

I turn away from it, smashing my teeth together and trying not to bemoan the fact that one: my body wants him—like seriously, I've got a wet panties situation going on down here; I'm blaming his cologne—and two: my brain knows I must have him.

This buddy-like banter is not going to cut it for much longer.

I need the guy to fall for me, and I don't know how the hell I'm supposed to do that.

CHAPTER 16
ETHAN

"No way!" Mikayla shakes her head. "LeBron kicks ass. You cannot leave him out of your top five players. I refuse to let you do it."

Asher tips his head back with a laugh. "It's *my* top five. I can do whatever the fuck I want."

"Well, you're an idiot to exclude him." She shrugs, and I can't take my eyes off her.

She's been at the table for nearly an hour, and the conversation has been lively and energetic.

We've covered almost every sport, and now she's arguing with Asher—the only guy in our group who follows basketball.

Mikayla follows it all. Well, almost. She seems clued up on everything except hockey. I'm really gonna have to do something about that.

What? Making future plans? Careful, man.

I shift in my seat, aggravated by my restrictions, and practically growl, "You need to get to a hockey game. Watch a real sport for a change."

Her lips stretch into a teasing grin. "Aw, are we talking out of your comfort zone right now, buddy? Unless it's hockey, you don't understand?"

I narrow my eyes at her, shaking my head and trying not to laugh at the baby voice she's putting on.

"Why don't you like hockey?" Liam asks.

This trips her up. She looks at him, then shrugs, shaking her head. "It's not that I don't. I just never got into it. Football and basketball always dominated, and... I don't know. I'd probably enjoy it."

"You'd love it." Casey leans forward. "You should come to our exhibition game. I'll get you a ticket."

"Thanks." She grins at him, and my stomach pinches into a tight knot.

I know that look in Casey's eye. He's into her, thinks he can tap my little mouse—woo her to a game, then go to town after our win.

Screw that.

It's not happening.

Why? She's not your mouse.

Fuck!

I clench my jaw and suddenly wish I hadn't invited her over here. It was a peace offering of sorts. A chance to make up for what I did to her the other day... and a rescue. When I compare her face here to the one I was looking at before, when she was stuck at the sorority table, I've done her a huge favor.

But now Casey's getting captured by that smile the same way I was.

I need to end this, *now*. I'm about to offer her a ride home when the Sig Be sisters approach the table.

"Well, hello, ladies." Asher turns to smile at them, conducting a little eye sex with the blonde near the front.

She simpers while her friend casts a look around the table. Her lips twitch when she reaches Liam and he gives her his standard polite smile. Unlike the others, he's not a hungry lion when it comes to the opposite sex.

He doesn't sleep around. I don't even think he's hooked up with anyone since breaking up with Kylie over the summer.

"Time to go, Mikayla." The one with the ice-queen glare gives me a prim smile before lifting her nose in the air.

Oh shit. I remember her now. She used to hang out with a girl I dated my freshman year. Aimee Walters. She was something. I spent several weeks with her before I realized that serious was not what I was after. Aimee was way too uptight for my liking. She had a great bod and a tongue that could do all manner of dirty things to me. That part was awesome and the reason why I stuck around at first, but then she started checking up on me, treating me like her boyfriend, pissed off when I wouldn't ditch my friends to spend time with her. She wanted to go exclusive, and I bailed before I was sucked into the vortex.

Let's just say she didn't take it well.

"Hey, there's a party coming up at Kappa Phi. You guys going?" Casey keeps his eyes on Mikayla while he's asking, and a flash of irritation spikes through me.

"Aw, we can't make it this weekend." The blonde next to Mikayla pouts.

"It's next weekend." Casey winks at Mikayla, and my irritation is turning into a blood-boil situation.

"Oh, well, in that case…" Blondie simpers. "We'll definitely be there."

"Cool. Gimme your number and I'll send you the deets." He grabs his phone, but I quickly pass Mikayla mine.

"I can let you know." I don't think my voice is casual enough because I can feel Liam's curious gaze and a little heat from Casey's.

"O-kay." Mikayla types in her number, then hands it back. It's impossible to hide my laugh when I see she's used a mouse emoji instead of her name.

Her lips twitch, and she shakes her head at the inquisitive look she's scoring from Blondie.

"Inside joke," she murmurs, dipping her head and moving away from the table.

I watch her walk out of sight, my lips still twitching with a grin.

"What's so funny?" Casey grumbles.

"Nothin'." I shove the phone into my back pocket with a little smirk.

"You're an ass," he mutters.

"Oh really? And what was that?" I growl, then put on a voice. "Hey, gimme your number. Join me at the party."

He snorts and raises his eyebrows at me. "What, dude? It's not like you can go for it. You're just buddies, remember? She's a cool chick. I like her."

I grit my teeth and lightly thump the table with my fist. Casey's gaze remains on me, and he finally nods. "Oh, okay. I get it. You're hoping to string her along until this ban is lifted and then you can have your fun. No worries." He shrugs. "There's plenty more candy out there for me to enjoy. I just liked her spunk, you know? She's different to the other girls."

I appreciate the sentiment, except for the stringing along part. Mikayla's a cool chick. I hate the idea of playing her just to get in her pants. But if I'm not after anything serious, then what the hell am I doing interacting with her at all? Do I honestly just want her as my friend?

That'd be cool. As long as she didn't touch me or walk into bars looking smoking hot, I'd totally be able to handle that.

"She's fun," Liam murmurs. "I can see why you like her."

"Yeah, she's pretty easy to hang with," I mutter, snatching my bottle off the table and wishing it wasn't empty, but it's a good excuse to stalk away from the table and not have to put up with any more questions from my buddies, or respond to Asher's laughing taunt.

"Better keep it in your pants, man! You're playing with fi-re!"

CHAPTER 17
MIKAYLA

The squeak of sneakers on a shiny court accompanied by the rhythm of a basketball dribbling has always been music to my ears. One of my first Christmas presents ever was a basketball. My dad specially built a toddler-sized hoop for me, and we'd spend hours in the driveway, dribbling back and forth, practicing my shots. He took me to basketball games on a regular basis. The Lakers were our team, and I've been a loyal supporter my whole life.

And then Dad left, taking the shine off my budding basketball career but not completely killing my passion for the game. I may not have seen it all the way through, but I still love to watch... and in the last five years, I've come to adore women's basketball. Which is why I'm sitting in the bleachers on a Wednesday afternoon watching the Nolan U girls light up the court.

I pretend I'm a sports agent, sitting in the stands, scoping out potential clients. Number 26 is tenacious. She might be one of the shortest girls on the team, but she's fast and strategic with her play. Her passing is impeccable, and I can't stop watching her as she makes another point-scoring move, passing off the ball to number 12, who does a sweet double clutch layup.

"Yes!" I clap along with the crowd, enjoying the energy around me but wishing there were more people here.

This is why I want to be an exclusively female sports agent. We need to shine more light on these talented athletes. Sure, women's sports coverage has gotten way better in the last decade, but there's still room for improvement. I want to see people lining up to get into a women's game—no matter what sport it is.

My phone buzzes, and I pull it out of my cargo pants pocket, grinning when I see Ethan's name pop up. Underneath is a string of emojis, which I try to decipher. He's been doing this to me all week. Ever since he got my phone number, I've been inundated with hilarious messages. It all started with a Mickey Mouse GIF that led into a string of bantering texts that had me cracking up in the middle of the Luxon dining hall. Yes, I got stared at like I was a crazy person.

Then it happened again that night, when he sent me a line of emojis that I couldn't work out. This started a lengthy texting conversation that led into a deep-dive discussion about nutrition and how strict his coach is. I threw in my two cents, since I studied health and nutrition in high school, and he had me in stitches as the evening wore on. He turned our serious food discussion into a string of exercise-fail GIFs that had me snorting into my pillow.

So yeah, it's been a week of texts. I haven't seen Ethan. I haven't spoken to him. I've just watched his words pop up on my screen and been sucked into one conversation after another. He's actually pretty smart. Knows way too much about hockey, but I guess if he's wanting to go pro, that makes sense. He's also obsessed with that show *How to Get Away with Murder* and... wait for it... *Dawson's Creek*! Although he made me swear not to tell anyone about that.

I nearly typed back, *Fool!*

Until he followed it up with the fact that he used to watch it with his mom. They'd sit there for hours when she was too sick to do anything else.

My heart started bleeding over that one, and I could do nothing else but type back, *Your secret is safe with me.*

He said I owed him one back, obviously trying to lighten the mood, so I admitted that on my sister's eleventh birthday, I laced her cake with laxatives because she'd called me a loveless ho.

Captain Hero: Yeeeeouch! And also... hilarious!

Mouse: It was pretty funny, and no one ever found out. They blamed it on the hot wings! And to this day, no one has ever questioned why I didn't feel like a slice of birthday cake.

Captain Hero: Kinda harsh that she called you a loveless ho.

Mouse: People say mean things when they're stressed and angry. I don't even remember what I did to her, but that's

Megan for ya. She doesn't hold anything back. She really is the biggest brat.

Captain Hero: Remind me never to piss you off... or eat any of your baking... ever.

I replied with a bunch of green-faced emojis and "I'm gonna throw up" GIFs. It was pretty funny and led to more laughter on my part. Whenever I send him another message, I always wonder if I'm making him laugh too. Or maybe he smirks at the screen or snickers or... I don't know. But he keeps texting back, so I can't be all bad.

Pursing my lips, I figure out that his emoji train must be telling me that he's done with studying for the day, his last class made his head explode, and now he's gonna blow off steam with a workout, since today is the only day of the week he doesn't have hockey practice.

I'm about to type back with emojis telling him about my day when my phone actually starts ringing.

Crap on a cracker. It's Mom.

Ugh!

Standing up, I quickly shuffle down the row of seating and run up the aisle, trying to get away from the noise of the game before answering. She hates me wasting time with sports when I should be studying or learning how to be a better Sig Be sister. Yes, I've told her I want to be a sports agent, but I'm pretty sure she's hoping this is something I'll grow out of. She was desperate for me to get to college and expand my options, no doubt hoping that by the time I graduate, I will have discovered a passion for something far more feminine and ladylike. I swear, for a modern woman, some of her ideas are so fucking old-school.

"Hey, Mom," I answer just as I reach the corridor that leads outside. "What's up?"

"Where are you right now?"

"Just walking back to the house." Pushing the door open with my shoulder, I run out into the sunlight and hope she can't hear how out of breath I am.

"Well, good, you've got some time to get your apology ready."

I stutter to a stop. "My apology? What are you talking about?"

"Aimee has informed her father that you have been making life very difficult at the house, shirking your responsibilities, constantly rolling your eyes, and making sarcastic comments."

I roll my eyes, grinding my teeth together.

"And she said you haven't been trying very hard at all with learning the history of the sorority house and—"

"That's bullshit," I cut her off before I have to hear any more of these lies.

"Don't you use that tone with me. And watch your language. No wonder Aimee has such a problem with you. You don't talk like this in the house, do you?"

"No," I mutter.

"You better not, Mikayla Evelyn Hyde. I raised you better than that. How could you embarrass me this way?"

"I'm not swearing in the house," I snap, then huff and clamp my lips together when a group of students walk past me with frowny faces on. I force a smile and keep walking back to the Sig Be house. I kind of want to storm

in there, find Aimee, and tear her shiny blonde hair out.
How could she dump on me like this?

"Well, you must be doing something wrong."

"I am trying. I really am. I don't know why she's got it
in for me."

"Aimee? Has it in for you? Don't be ridiculous. She's
trying to *help* you. She called her dad out of concern."

I'm sure she did.

"You're making life really hard on her, Mikayla. She
promised Jarrod she'd do her best to get you in, but she
only has so much sway. Being president gives her some
influence, but these girls are close, and if enough of them
don't like you, she'll have no choice but to ask you to
leave. And not only will that break my heart, but I can't
guarantee that Jarrod will be happy to keep funding your
education if you're going to treat his daughter with so
little respect."

This is un-fucking-believable!

I tip my head up to the sky, clenching my hand into a
fist as waves of desperation rage through me. I hate that
I'm in this position. I hate that I'm bound by all these
stupid conditions. If Mom wasn't trying to impress
Aimee's father so much, I wouldn't have to put up with
this crap. Why can't she just stand up for me and tell
Jarrod that I deserve this opportunity without having to
follow in his precious daughter's footsteps?

Mom's changed since meeting Jarrod. Sure, she's been
happy, and it's great to see her loved-up this way, but
there's also this underlying fear that seems to drive her,
like she's petrified that any one little thing will push him
away and she'll be left again. She'll go back to being a

stressed-out single mother—the woman she hated back in Fontana.

"Mom." I let out a sigh. "I know you want me to succeed here, I really do. I know the conditions, and I'm trying. I swear, I'm trying."

This seems to appease her, but still... she can't help a little sniff before muttering, "Well, you need to try harder. Okay, sweetie? I want your best effort. Now go do something good for those sisters. Do whatever it takes to make up for your misconduct, because I do not want Jarrod getting another call like that from Aimee." She sighs and then mumbles, "I love you. Now go make me proud," before hanging up.

I pull the phone away from my ear, giving it the finger before shoving it back in my pocket.

I am so livid right now. I could strangle perfect Miss Aimee Walters. I break into a run and reach the house in record time. I was hoping the exercise would help me burn off some of this steam, but it's only made me sweat and arrive at the house a heaving, mussed-up mess.

Stomping up the front steps, I fling the door open and yell, "Aimee!"

Yes, it's unladylike, probably undignified, but do I give a shit?

Nope on a rope!

"Aimee!" I call again, storming up the stairs into forbidden territory. That's right, only junior and senior sorority girls get top-floor privileges. I'll no doubt get told off for walking my dirty little self through this plush part of the house, but I am so beyond caring.

I reach the door that has SORORITY PRESIDENT

embossed on the front and am about to pound the wood when it swings open.

"Mikayla. I thought I heard you call. If you'd been patient, you wouldn't have had to walk all the way up here."

I cross my arms, trying to clamp down this torrent of emotion. "What have you been saying to your dad?"

She looks confused for a second, tipping her head like she's trying to figure out what I'm talking about.

"Aimee," I snap. "How could you complain about me behind my back?"

"I wasn't complaining." She blinks. "I was concerned."

"Oh, whatever! Cut the bullshit."

Her opaque blue eyes flash, that innocent veneer dropping away as she sighs and grips the edge of the door. "Fine. He asked after you, and I told him... *the truth.*"

"You painted the worst picture possible. And lemme guess, you didn't mention at all the fact that you're making me do the most ridiculous initiative ever invented!"

"It's not ridiculous. Other girls have done it before—with far more ease, I might add." Her voice spikes, her anger rising to match mine. "And it's not like Ethan Galloway doesn't deserve it."

I narrow my eyes at her, picking up the way her cheeks flush and her delicate nostrils flare. "What did he do to you?"

"Nothing I couldn't get over."

"Obviously." Okay, that sarcasm was impossible to hide. But come on.

She huffs and crosses her arms. "We dated freshman

year. Things were going perfectly and then *poof.*" She snaps her fingers. "The guy decides I'm not the only girl on campus worth boning. So he dumps me and turns himself into a man slut. That arrogant prick. *'I don't think we should be exclusive. It's not really my style.'*" She puts on this voice which is the worst imitation of Ethan I will ever hear.

I raise my eyebrows at her.

"As if any girl on this campus could be better than me."

"O-kay," I murmur, wondering if she can actually hear herself when she speaks. "So, if he didn't want to be exclusive with *you*, then why the hell do you think he's gonna fall for me?"

Her expression returns to that arrogant smirk she loves to wear so much, and finally, the penny drops.

I click my tongue, looking away from her as I try to contain the vibrating anger in my chest. "You chose this task on purpose. You want me to fail so I can't be part of this sorority, even though you told Daddy Dearest that you'd do everything in your power to get me in. But you can't admit how much you hate me, right? So instead, you give me an impossible task and then tell him with those fake doe eyes of yours that *'I did everything I could, but Mikayla just wasn't a good fit. I tried, Daddy, I really tried.'*"

Her cheeks flush red at my mocking imitation of her before she sneers. "You don't even want to be here."

Oh, how I want to lace her morning health shakes with laxatives!

I've been working my ass off to stay here, but of course she sees through my paper-thin veneer.

I don't belong. I'll never belong, but I have to. Because

of Jarrod's stupid contract. Why the fuck did I sign that thing?

Because it's senseless to get saddled with a huge student loan when I have the chance of free education at a really good school.

You could just bail. Head back to Cali, move in with Rachel, get a student loan.

Break your mother's heart. Piss off Jarrod, which will probably cause tension in Mom's relationship, and that will break her heart in a whole different way.

Shit!

I clench my jaw, trying to hide my angst from Aimee. Like I'll give her the satisfaction of knowing how much this is killing me.

Crossing my arms, I meet her challenging gaze with one of my own. I am on fucking fire right now, and I will not let this prissy president beat me.

"I'm not gonna fail." I point at her. "I *will* win Ethan's heart, and then I'll break it. You just watch me!"

She lets out a derisive snort before stepping back and shutting the door in my face.

"Grrrr!" I spin on my heel and stomp out of the house, slamming the door shut behind me and storming back across campus to the hockey arena.

CHAPTER 18
ETHAN

I'm on my own in the workout room. Liam finished up a few minutes ago and hit the showers. Asher was right behind him. I'm not ready to call it quits, and I can't explain why.

Except that I can.

Mikayla hasn't texted me back yet.

Pathetic. I know.

I shouldn't care if some chick didn't find my emoji thread funny, but I was expecting a response and I got nothing.

So I'm pushing out some extra reps, giving myself a little alone time to be pissed at the fact that I'm liking lil' mouse more and more with each text exchange, and I really shouldn't.

She's fire.

Which is why I haven't tried to seek her out and see her in person. Keeping it all via the phone works great... except for the fact that my body is craving contact with her, and I can't let it do that.

I can't even jerk off when I think about how damn sexy she looked in the bar. My mind is a cruel tormentor, and I've imagined kissing her in a hundred different places, peeling off her clothes and running my tongue over the plains of her skin, and—

Dammit!

I adjust my pants, growling at my tenting gym shorts and forcing out another seven reps on the leg extension machine. My thighs are burning by the time I'm done. I should wrap this up. Coach gets pissed if we push too hard and don't listen to our bodies. Too many players get injured that way, and I—

The gym door pops open, and a huffing little mouse stalks into the room. She looks livid, her pretty face bunched into a dark scowl. My eyes quickly trail her body, loving the cargo pants and tight little tank she's wearing. No hoop earrings, no heels. Just a messy pony-tail and clothes that scream *Mikayla*.

She huffs, fisting her hands, then jerking still when she spots me staring at her. Her eyes bulge, her lips parting as her gaze travels down my body. She legit licks her lips before catching herself and trying to hide the move with a gruff frown.

I glance down at my bare chest glistening with a fine sheen of sweat and can't help smirking. "Hey."

She tuts and spins away from me, pacing to the mirrors and back. She's muttering something under her breath as she dumps her bag by the leg press and turns back to glare at me.

O-kay.

"What did I do?"

"Nothing," she snaps.

I reach for my phone to check that I didn't accidentally send her some offensive emoji, but... none that I can tell.

Glancing up, I watch her pace to the chest press and then over to the free weights before I can't take it anymore.

"Seriously, would you just spill?"

"It's not you. I'm fine!"

"Yeah, you seem fine." I give her a deadpan stare to match my tone. That only scores me another lethal glare. "Want to talk about it?"

"No." She kind of laughs out the word, looking at me like I'm stupid.

I nod, reminding myself why I don't do girlfriends and drama.

Although, Mikayla's not your typical girl. Whatever is riling her must be pretty big. And I want to help.

Standing up from the machine, I wander over to her, blocking her path when she tries to pace past me.

She growls, and I can't help a soft snicker. She's like a grumpy-ass chihuahua—all snarly and snappy, but if she tried to bite me, I wouldn't even feel it.

Hmmm. Bite me.

I think about her hungry gaze from moments before and feel a semi forming. No, wait, I'm going hard as rock.

Swiveling my body away from her, I rake my fingers through my hair, desperate for any kind of distraction.

Help her blow off steam.

Images of our naked bodies thrusting together flash through my mind.

Another way, jackass!

Closing my eyes, I force my brain to think of her like a guy. That's the only way I'm gonna get through this.

"You need to do something to blow off whatever's going on in there." I grind out the words while pointing at her chest.

She's a guy. She's a guy. She's a guy!

Forcing my gaze away from her tits, I clap my hands and bark, "Drop and gimme fifty."

"Fifty?" She jerks her head back.

Yeah, I get it. I'm asking too much, but she's not frowning anymore, is she?

Her eyes narrow at my challenging smirk, then she crosses arms and eyes me up with this fiery sharp look that's sexy as hell. "Okay, fine."

Lifting that obstinate chin of hers, she drops to the floor, getting into push-up position and pumping out a quick ten. Holy shit, she's strong. Most of the girls I know probably can't even do one. Her form is impeccable.

I stand back, mouth agape, even when her pace starts to slow. She gets to twenty-eight before her arms give out on her.

I hiss, and she scowls up at me from the floor.

"Oh, shut up. You give me fifty."

I drop with a soft laugh and start pumping them out. She lets out an irritated tut, no doubt annoyed that I'm gonna hit fifty, no sweat.

I've just reached twenty-one when she huffs, then jumps on my back.

"Unfair advantage," I murmur, reaching twenty-five.

"Aw, you can't handle a little mouse on your back?" She digs her chin into my shoulder, whispering in my ear, her breath tickling the side of my neck and setting my imagination on fire again. The wicked things I want to do to this spitfire.

I'm at thirty-two when she starts running her fingers lightly up the back of my neck, and when I hit thirty-nine, she starts trailing them down my side, the pads of her fingers whispering over my rib cage while she taunts me.

"Eighteen, twenty-nine, thirty-four." She laughs in my ear. "You losing count yet?"

I need to shut this girl up... with my tongue.

Tipping sideways, I flip her off my back. She lands on the padded floor with a thud, then laughs as she tries to roll away from me. But that's not happening.

Grabbing her arm, I pin her underneath me and reset my push-up position while she goes still and breathless. There's no fear or surprise in her gaze. If anything, it's gleaming hotter than I've ever seen it before.

I lower myself over her and murmur, "Forty," against her cheek.

As I rise back up, I notice how blue her eyes are in this light.

"Forty-one."

I smell the vanilla in her hair.

"Forty-two."

Her lips don't have gloss on them today, but they're still pink and plump and—

"Forty-three."

Her eyes trace my face as if she's trying to memorize it.

"Forty-four."

A soft breath whispers out of her, hitting my chin.

"Forty-five."

My heart rate accelerates, and as I drop to forty-six, I can't fight it anymore. Planting my lips on hers, I sink against her mouth, holding my push-up until my arms start to tremble. Her lips are hot and soft and eager, her greedy tongue swiping over my bottom lip like she's been wanting to do that since the day we met.

I can't help grinning as I part my lips, flicking my tongue against the tip of hers before pulling back and resetting my push-up position.

I wink down at her and whisper, "What am I up to?"

"Forty-seven. Now get your ass back here." She grabs my neck, pulling me on top of her with a strength that takes me off guard.

I only just manage to catch myself before squashing her. Resting my arms on either side of her head, I deepen the kiss because I can't help it. She moans, and that hot, sweet sound sends a jolt of electricity through my body. I'm so hard it hurts, my erection poking against her thigh as she glides her hands up my bare back. She's painting pictures through that fine sheen of sweat on my body, and it feels fan-fucking-tastic.

Her fingers dig into my shoulder blades while mine gently fist her hair, and then my hips start rocking, grinding my hard ridge against her core and dry-humping her as my body seeks that relief I've been denying myself.

She lifts her hips, wrapping her leg around me, her heel digging into my ass like she wants more.

So I give it to her, grinding a little harder while I plunge my tongue into her mouth.

It's instinct. It's primal.

I want to make her moan again. I want to bury my

cock in her wet heat. I want to watch her come beneath me.

I want—

SNAP!

A sharp, stinging pain hits my ass, making me jerk up and throw daggers at the guy laughing over me.

"What the fuck?" I growl at Asher, snatching the offending towel out of his fist and throwing it behind me.

His lips rise into a playful smirk, but I don't miss that gleam of warning in his eyes.

"Whatchya doin' there, lover boy?" He crosses his arms, wiggling his eyebrows at me before raking his gaze over Mikayla, who's still half pinned on the floor beneath me.

I warn him away with a growl and have no choice but to rise to my knees and block Asher's view with my body.

Her cheeks are flushed, her eyes glimmering with amusement. But now that Asher's here, I can't even hold her gaze.

Shit! What the fuck was I doing, letting myself get carried away like that?

"Wait-ing," Asher singsongs, obviously expecting me to answer his redundant question.

Asshole.

"Nothing," I mumble. "Just showing her how to... work out."

Asher cracks up laughing. "Didn't realize X-rated workouts were allowed in this gym. You know every inch of this arena has security cameras, right? Except the locker rooms." He shrugs. "Maybe you should take your workout in there next time." He winks and then starts laughing again.

I grunt, rising to my feet and reaching out a hand to help Mikayla up.

She doesn't take it, instead jumping to her feet and brushing her hands on the sides of her cargo pants.

"Hey, Asher." She gives him a small wave, her cheeks tinging this delicious pink.

My stupid cock remains at attention. He's a little late in getting the memo. I still think he's struggling to accept the fact that he's not allowed to shoot off for a month. He's in denial.

Mikayla's gaze darts over my tented shorts before she shuffles to her bag. "I should go. Don't want anyone getting in trouble. I know I'm not supposed to be here."

"Don't worry about it." Asher flicks his hand through the air. "Ethan here would cover for you. He's good that way. A real man of his word. If he makes a mistake, he follows through on the consequences, you know? He's just that kinda guy."

I face my teammate and pin him with a glare that could turn wood to charcoal.

He just snickers and does that irritating eyebrow wiggle again before spinning back to Mikayla with a cocky smirk.

"So, would Ethan's little gym buddy like to come back to Hockey House for dinner?"

"Hockey House?" She gives him a pitiful frown. "You *named* your house?"

Asher shrugs. "What idiot doesn't?"

"Okay." She tips her head. "But I would like a word with the idiot who chose Hockey House, because that's just lame."

"Puck off." He frowns at her.

144

She raises her eyebrows, biting her lips against a smile as she points at him and wrinkles her nose. "That's lame too. Just say 'fuck,' man."

Walking past him, she gives him a little pat on the arm while I fight my own grin and try not to relive every second of that searing kiss.

Asher bulges his eyes at me—*is this chick for real?*—while pointing after Mikayla.

I snicker and nod. Apparently so.

Which is maybe why I'm finding her so refreshing. We're used to puck bunnies falling all over themselves to bag us. They'll say whatever they think we want to hear. It's a nice change to meet a girl who'll tell it to us straight.

My cock twitches again, trying to finish what we so happily started earlier.

"Down, boy. It's not happening," I mumble, adjusting my shorts and heading for the shower—a cold-as-fuck shower—because I don't think junior here is gonna understand anything else.

CHAPTER 19
MIKAYLA

Asher chases me down the corridor. "So, you coming or what?"

I glance over my shoulder, wishing my strides were longer so he can't catch me so easily. I kind of want to outrun my flaming red cheeks and maybe go into hiding after being busted by him and then finding out there are cameras in that workout room.

Ethan's chest is a freaking work of art. The second I spotted his glistening skin and perfectly carved torso, my V-jay started throbbing. Like nightclub, party-mix aching for the guy. This gush of hot liquid shot straight between my legs, and it was an effort not to drop to my knees and beg him to take me right on that padded floor.

Thankfully, he got me doing push-ups, which helped a little... until I thoughtlessly jumped on his back and his muscles flexed and moved beneath me. My pussy was purring, and then it melted and turned into a puddle of white-hot goo. When his lips touched mine, any coherent thought became impossible. When his tongue dove into my mouth, breathing was added to the list of struggles, and then he started grinding against me, and every cell in my brain turned to mush.

And the cameras probably caught it all.

Shit! Do they have sound too? Did they hear me moaning? Kill me now.

Just bury me in a grave marked:

Mikayla Evelyn Hyde
Died of Humiliation

I can't let this happen. What if someone leaks it?

And now all I can picture is a bunch of security guards standing around a black-and-white screen while they laugh and point, then start sharing it on TikTok and Insta.

Shit!

Spinning with a jerk, I hold my hand up for Asher to stop. "Do you have access to the camera footage in the workout room?"

His left eyebrow arches. "I could."

He's got a handsome face. Long and lean with this chiseled chin and nose. His hair is dark, from the scruff on his cheeks to the shiny hair swooshed back from his forehead. The guy cares about his appearance, that much is obvious, but there's a bright gleam in his eyes that tells me he loves a good game and winning is really his only option.

So how can I make him feel like he's gonna win this round while still getting what I want?

Unlike my little sister, I'm no master of manipulation, but I try to channel a little Megs and give the guy my sweetest smile.

"Excellent. Could you please make the footage of me being in that area disappear?"

He considers it for a moment, then nods. "Fine. On one condition..."

"What?" I'm beginning to despise the word *condition*.

"Come hang at Hockey House tonight."

I cross my arms. "And why would I do that?"

"Because... we have cold beer, hot pizza, and you're desperate to get to know Ethan's friends better."

I snicker and shake my head.

"Come on." He nudges my shoulder. "I'll sweet-talk the security guards into eliminating certain footage, and you'll give us an evening of entertainment."

"Ew. What exactly are you expecting me to do at your place?"

"Hang out." He rolls his eyes. "Get your mind out of the gutter, mouse. It's not like we have a permanent stripper pole set up in the living room. I just want you to hang. That's all. Just... help me figure out why Ethan can't stop texting you and why my playboy is turning into a one-woman show."

I laugh and shake my head. "He's so not doing that."

Hope skitters through me, and although it should be because I can gleefully think, *My plan is working!* I know it's more a sense of *Really? The guy likes me? Has he seriously not hooked up with anyone else?*

Ugh, I can feel my excitement blooming.

Stop acting like some fan-crazed teenager!

I try to harden myself against the flutters exploding in

my chest, but when Ethan appears around the corner, giving Asher a glare of warning, I end up blurting, "Okay. Fine. I'll come over."

Ethan's head jolts back with surprise, but then his lips start tipping up into this beautiful smile that makes me want to shout, *"Better yet, I'll move in."*

But thankfully my brain is coming back online now, and common sense is starting to prevail.

Going to Hockey House is a great idea.

Why?

Because it means Asher will sort out the whole camera situation. Plus, it saves me from going back to the sorority house, where I will no doubt have to endure an evening of pissed-off Aimee.

Cold ice queen or rowdy hockey boys.

It's really a no-brainer.

Although Asher offers me a ride, I hang back, chatting with Liam while we wait for Ethan to shower up. Liam's a really sweet guy—big and broad, he looks like a military man with his buzz cut and serious face. If you didn't know him, you'd probably find him intimidating, but the second he opens his mouth and starts talking in his soft husky voice... or he flashes one of those sweet smiles your way... you know he's just a big ol' teddy bear.

"So, how long have you guys been friends, then?"

"Ethan and I met in high school."

"Nice." I grin. "How cool that you can go to college together."

"Yeah, we planned it that way. Couldn't not have the best years of our lives together, right?" He grins at me, and I suddenly miss Rachel with an ache so deep it makes my chest hurt.

"My best friend still lives in Cali. I miss her."

His smile turns sympathetic. "When will you get to see her again?"

"Not sure yet." I shrug. "But we text and talk most days, so at least we're still in touch. I just hope that doesn't fade with time."

"Don't let it." He shrugs, like it's the easiest solution in the world.

Running feet grab my attention, and those butterflies are back, swarming my entire body as Ethan comes to a stop beside me.

"So, you're braving Hockey House, huh?"

I laugh. "If I can handle a mani-pedi spa day which also included a painful round of hair removal, then I figure Hockey House will be a cinch."

The guys both nod. "Yeah, you're right."

Their expressions make me laugh a little louder, and any doubts I may have been harboring disappear the second I walk through the front door.

Music is pumping from the speakers but not in the deafening party-time way. Guys' voices float across the air —hassling, playful jabs that make me grin. The house smells like this heady mix of cologne, sweat, and fried chicken, and all I can think is *Home, comfort, a place to chill.*

Kicking off my shoes, I follow Ethan and Liam into the main living area, where I'm introduced to a few other guys who don't live in the house but are hockey Cougars like the rest of them.

They eye me up with curiosity but have obviously been forewarned by Asher that I was coming. I wave my hand in greeting, tipping back on my heels and trying to think of something funny to say. But all that pops out of me is a loud gasp.

"Is that *Devil's Doorway*?" I gape at the large TV screen on the wall, jumping over the back of the couch and landing next to Casey. "I don't know anyone else who plays this."

Casey grins, smashing his thumb onto the controller and taking out three bad guys before spinning his horse around and charging out of Windy City.

"Have you got the gold bars from the westbound train yet?"

"Yep." He keeps riding, dodging a band of Indians as he passes through their territory.

"They're gonna shoot you. You need to stop and offer them something from your bag."

"No, I'll be fast enough," he murmurs, dipping low to the horse and trying to pick up speed.

"No you won't," I singsong, then grin when he's shot through the back with an arrow and falls to the ground. "Told ya," I crow with a grin that I hope is obnoxious enough.

"Fine," Casey grits out, although it's all for show. His dirty-blond locks shake as he tries to glare at me. He probably has no idea that he's looking more scarecrow than man right now.

"How long have you been playing this?" I try to hide my laughter.

He runs a hand through his hair, which is why it's such a mess, and I can't hold it in anymore.

"Lemme guess, you're one of those stubborn-ass dudes who hates asking for help on a game like this. You just have to figure it all out on your own," I tease him.

He huffs and narrows his eyes at me, but I can see the glimmer of amusement in his gaze. "Fine, you little brat, tell me how to get past the Cheyenne tribe."

"With pleasure, sir." I put on a posh voice, snatching the controller out of his hand and going back to Windy City, where I quickly take out the bandits and start heading for new territory. Like I told him to, I stop and ask for permission to pass through Cheyenne territory, offering them tobacco and grain from my sack before making friends with the chief's son and picking up a companion for the rest of my journey west.

"Holy puck. I've been trying to outrun those guys for like five games now."

I can't help a smug smirk, but it doesn't last long because the whole *puck* thing just registered.

"Please tell me you don't do that too."

"Do what?" He keeps his eyes on the screen while I negotiate the river crossing.

"Use the word *puck* instead of *fuck*. It's lame."

"It's not lame, it's totally cool, and if you don't like it, there's the door."

"Oooo." I rise to his snippety tone with a laugh. "Someone's precious about their pucking."

He starts to laugh, snatching the controller back off me. "You're our guest, so just get pucking used to the way we talk, okay?"

I flick a look at Ethan, who's found a spot on the couch adjacent to me. He grins, winking at me while I shake my head, throwing in an eye roll for good measure.

Is it weird that I feel more relaxed here than I do anywhere else on campus so far?

Should I be worried about that?

Ethan's searing-hot kiss in the workout room tells me he's not immune to the fact that I'm a woman, but I fit in so easily with this group. Am I doing that thing I always do and just naturally falling into the friend zone with these guys?

I should pull back, find my feminine side, and strut out of this place like the dick tease I'm supposed to be. But I don't want to leave... and even though I start telling myself it's because of my initiation task, I know the truth.

I like these guys. I've got the major hots for Ethan, and if he keeps being as cool and awesome and sexy as he has been so far, I'm gonna go tumbling over the edge...

And unless I can somehow get out of this initiation—doubtful—then I have to go and break his heart, which will inevitably break mine, so...

Yeah, I'm royally pucked.

CHAPTER 20
ETHAN

"Yee-haw!" Mikayla shouts, tipping her head back with a laugh.

Her slender neck is mouthwatering, her smile enough to ignite my insides. Shit, she's gorgeous and funny and having a blast in this house.

She's managed to draw every guy in the room around the couch, and they're all getting into *Devil's Doorway*, yelling warnings at the screen and hooting in triumph when Mikayla takes out another bad guy.

About an hour ago, she and Casey started a two-man game, and they're killing it.

Me? I've been sitting on the couch, nursing my beer and trying to command my pig-headed, stubborn-ass dick to stay the hell down.

But then Mikayla goes and laughs again—the musical sound reaching my ears and doing weird shit to my chest. Or she'll raise her hands and whoop, her triumph so fucking sexy that my cock decides it's spring-loaded.

I shift in my seat, my eyebrows dipping when I spot

Casey nudging her with his shoulder. She tips sideways with a laugh, and he pulls her back up, his fingers lingering to the point of making me growl.

But no one hears me because they're too busy yelling at these two to get on the train.

"Speed up!"

"Jump!"

They both make it without getting squished by the Midwest Express and then start talking strategy.

And I continue to sit here like a jealous douche as Casey—one of my best friends—gets to touch Mikayla and laugh with her and flirt because he doesn't have a no-sex rule hanging over his head.

Curse my cocky, arrogant self.

Curse that fucking dart for betraying me.

Mikayla's hot tongue peeks between her lips as she negotiates the gold heist they're pulling off. I know what it tastes like now. I want to snatch that remote out of her hands and grab her face. I want to suck the tip of that pink tongue into my mouth and hear her groan again.

My dick springs into action, and I lurch off the couch, stalking into the kitchen. Asher snickers as I walk past him and turns to follow me, but I push him back with a growl.

Raising his hands as two white flags, he backs away. "Chill, man."

"Fuck off," I mutter, wrenching the cupboard door open to throw away my empty beer bottle.

"So, you're in a good mood tonight." Liam strolls in behind me, as unruffled as ever. How the hell does he do it? Stay so even keel all the time?

All I can manage is a grunt as I down a glass of

water, wishing it was straight spirits. That would make these torturous weeks easier to get through, just get my cock completely wasted so it can't even rise to the occasion.

"Mikayla's a cool chick." Liam leans his hip against the breakfast counter, crossing his arms and going for conversational.

I grunt again, and he laughs at me.

"It's only a few more weeks, and then you can go for it. You can do this, man."

"I don't date," I grit out. "I'm not stringing her along just so I can bang her."

"Okay." Liam shrugs. "So just be her friend, then."

"I'm trying," I practically whine. "But she makes it fucking impossible."

"Oh, so it's her fault?"

"No." I spin around and scowl at him. "Of course not. I just..." I shake my head. "Having her over here was a bad idea. Asher's just trying to rub my face in it. He knows Casey likes her, too, and he's goading me."

"Casey said he wouldn't go for it. They're just playing a video game together."

I throw him a dark glare, feeling like an immature putz when I grumble, "I don't like it."

"Because you like her."

I clench my jaw and look away from him.

He sighs and bobs his head, his standard MO for when he's about to dish out some sound advice. "Any other day of the week, you'd meet her, bang her, and never talk to her again. This bet is forcing you to get to know her, and for some reason, that scares the shit out of you."

I sniff, refusing to tell him why. Maybe 'cuz I don't know.

Maybe because my *college isn't for romance* argument is just a thin veil to hide what I don't want to acknowledge, what Liam probably knows but is nice enough not to say. You don't dive deep into this shit when the house is filled with hockey bros and they're yelling at a TV screen.

"You just have to make a choice. Either be her friend, ditch her, or let yourself fall." Liam shrugs, acting like it's the simplest thing in the world.

I shoot him an incredulous look, hating the last two options and not even sure if I'm capable of the first one.

He counters my look with a cheesy smile before spinning and walking out of the kitchen. Gripping the edge of the sink, I huff and shake my head, jerking still when a loud groan rises from the TV room.

"Shitballs!" Mikayla yells above them all.

An instant smile tugs at my lips. I love her potty mouth. She's hilarious.

"This is your fault, Casey. You're too pucking slow."

Casey lets out an indignant gasp, which makes Mikayla laugh, and I'm drawn to the sound like I have no control over my own body.

"Wait, wait, wait... did you just say *pucking*?" His face lights with glee while she rolls her eyes.

"As a *joke*."

"Nah-uh, you were legit *pucking*." He whoops, then goes suddenly serious. "But I'm afraid you're not qualified to use that term. It's for hockey players only."

"Oh, good God!" She groans, tipping back her head. "You guys are ridiculous."

"Uh... I think not." Casey gives her an emphatic look.

"Now get your cute little ass out of here before you start using words that don't belong to you."

He goes to shove her off the couch, but she jumps up with an unladylike guffaw and throws him the double finger with the biggest, cheesiest smile I've ever seen.

Holy shit, she's cool.

I step into her line of sight, grinning at her because I can't help myself. "Need a ride?"

"Yeah." She nods. The angry, stressed-out spark she stormed into the workout room with has completely vanished, and I can't deny my sense of triumph. I did that. *We* did that—my hockey boys and me.

Holding the door for her, I follow her cute little ass out to my Ford Ranger. I would offer to help her in, but as soon as the alarm beeps, she pulls open the door and jumps up like she's not a shorty.

She's clicking her seat belt as I slide behind the wheel.

"This is a really sweet ride." She runs her hand over the dash.

"Thanks. Dad gave it to me for a graduation present."

"Wow." Her eyebrows rise. "That's impressive. I'm guessing these things go for around thirty Gs or more."

I'm forced to admit, "It's a hand me down. He upgraded and I got this, but it was only a few years old when he gave it to me."

I start the engine and drive her back to Greek Row.

"When I get enough cash together, which will probably be never," she mutters dryly, "I want to get myself a Jeep Gladiator. I love those things."

It's hard not to laugh as I picture her little body behind the wheel of a huge ride like that.

"What?" She slaps my arm with the back of her hand. "You can't picture my big, tough self cruising through town in one of those things?"

"I can, actually, which is why I'm laughing." I throw in a wink to soften my teasing, and thankfully she laughs along with me.

"You're such a jackass." She shakes her head but is fighting her laughter still. "Just wait, Mr. Ford Ranger. I'm gonna get my Gladiator one day, and I'm gonna drive straight over this little truck of yours."

Her threat sets us both laughing again, and by the time I pull up to Greek Row, all my angst from Hockey House has dissipated... until I park the car, cut the engine, and spot the tip of her pink tongue again.

CHAPTER 21
MIKAYLA

I lick my lips as I study Ethan's profile. I don't even realize I'm doing it until his gaze darts to my mouth, and now I'm suddenly conscious of every nerve in my body.

Is he going to kiss me again?

Please, yes!

But he's not making a move. He's just sitting there, staring at me, tapping his finger on the steering wheel while my heart drums so loudly I'm surprised the entire Nolan U campus can't hear it.

"So..." I let the word hang, glancing out the window and reminding myself where I am.

Shit. The Sigma Beta Mu house is right behind me. The lights are on across both floors, and there's a very high chance that spies are looking out the window. Ethan's truck is parked in the shadow of a tree, but they can probably tell it's his. What's the bet that more than one girl has done it right there in the back seat or in the bed of his truck with a cool breeze kissing her ass cheeks while she spreads eagle for the hot hockey player beside me?

That image should immediately kill my mood, but this pulse comes back between my legs, because now I'm picturing *my* wind-kissed ass poking into the air while Ethan takes me from behind.

Holy sweetness. My blood turns to molten lava, oozing through my system and making me light-headed. I should probably get out of this truck before I do something stupid, but one thought stops me.

Well, one thought and one animalistic instinct.

I'm supposed to be wooing this guy so I can secure a place here at Nolan U, and holy mother of sex gods, I need to kiss Ethan before I physically combust.

Moving before thought can stop me, I unbuckle my seat belt and practically launch myself at him. He catches me easily, his fingers diving into my hair as his tongue sweeps against mine.

He lets out this panty-melting groan that has me climbing into his lap. The steering wheel wedges into my back, but he quickly solves the problem, scrambling for a lever and shoving the seat back as far as it will go. I straddle his thighs, nestling my wet core over his erection and moaning into his mouth.

His tongue is sweet fire, hot and commanding, silently asking for more. I happily give it to him, deepening the kiss until I can't figure out how I ever survived life without doing this on a daily basis.

My hips start to rock of their own accord, my body seeking relief from the pulsing ache between my legs. He lets go of my hair, dragging his fingers across my shoulders before his large hands cup my breasts. A hungry whimper builds in my throat when his thumbs flick my hardened nipples. That feels so fucking good. I want to tell him so, but my tongue's too busy doing a deep dive into Ethan Galloway's mouth. I want to live here forever.

I want—

"Holy shit," I gasp when he pinches my nipple, sending a sharp spike of pleasure shooting through my body. "Magic hands," I rasp. "You have magic hands."

His throaty chuckle vibrates against my neck as he nibbles and licks his way to my collarbone.

Deft fingers are pulling my shirt and bra straps down, exposing an expectant, pleading nipple to Ethan's wet tongue. The second he latches on, I can't help tipping my head back with a moan so loud I'm sure every sorority girl on this street can hear it.

I thrust my chest toward him, begging for more. With his tongue working my nipple and his hard ridge grinding against my sensitive core, I feel like an implosion is inevitable. My brain cells are the consistency of chocolate mousse while my muscles are as taut as piano strings.

If even the tip of his finger brushes my clit, I'm gonna come with an embarrassingly loud, orgasmic scream, and right now... I don't even give a shit.

I just want—

Ethan's mouth rips away from me, his ragged breaths hitting my face as he whispers, "Maybe we should cool it."

Okay, well, I don't want that.

My insides deflate faster than a popped balloon, and I lean away from him, scanning his face for any signs of why he might suddenly want to pull the plug on this thing.

He winces and glances out the window. "We're on a public street."

People would have to walk right up to the windows to see us.

I want to argue that point, but he's already pulling my bra straps back into place. I can feel my breasts wailing in despair while my pulsing V-jay starts screaming out a *Why? Why? Why?*

I'll have to take care of that myself when I head inside, but I really wanted him to do it for me.

The thought of those long fingers stroking my insides only strengthens the pulsing ache.

"We could go someplace else," I whisper, my tone kind of desperate.

He swallows, his face bunching as he shakes his head. "I'm really sorry. I've got an early practice in the morning."

I nearly yell, *"It won't take much to make me come. I'll be quick!"*

But how desperate would that sound?

And do I honestly want to be quick with Ethan Galloway?

Uh, no. I want to enjoy every inch of his body. I want to watch his eyes fill with pleasure, hear that guttural groan he makes. I want to feel every inch of him feeling me and sending me to the moon and back.

Those types of things really shouldn't be rushed, and they should most definitely not be begged for when the guy who can give them to you is lifting you off his lap and silently telling you that time is up.

Ouch.

Painful.

Humiliating.

Why am I expecting anything less?

I'm not the hot girl people drool over. Ethan won't be obsessing over me as he drives away. If anything, he's probably gonna be grateful he dodged a bullet.

Obviously, my nipples don't taste like ice cream, and my tongue isn't as magical as I hoped it was. He's kissed and boinked enough girls to know what he likes, and I haven't made the cut.

While my brain was turning to mush, his was only getting sharper, making him aware of our surroundings and the fact that I'm not the girl to blow his mind.

Shit, does he know what I'm up to with this initiation task? Like, even on a subconscious level, so he's holding himself back?

Cold fear slices through me, and I nearly blurt out the truth right there. *"I'm sorry. It wasn't my idea. They're making me. I actually really like you and genuinely want to bone you and keep texting you and hanging out with you and..."*

But wait... how would he know?

It's far more likely that he pulled away just now because I'm not enough woman for him. He's tasted a vast array, and I... don't make the cut.

I never make the cut.

Clearing my throat, I bob my head and somehow manage to croak, "Thanks for a good night," before jumping out of his truck and slamming the door on his feeble call back.

"Mikayla, wait."

I run for the house, desperate for him not to follow me.

Slamming the door shut, I lean against it, my chest heaving as I await the impending knock.

But it never comes.

In fact, when I ease the door open again, all I catch are his red taillights as he brakes for the stop sign at the end of the street.

"Shitballs," I murmur, disappointment searing me despite the fact that I didn't want to be followed.

"Well, well, well." The smarmy voice behind me makes my skin crawl, but I paste on a smile and spin to survey the line of sorority girls in front of me.

"Hello, ladies."

"Someone had a good night." Teah wiggles her eyebrows, giggling as my cheeks turn crimson. I can feel the heat flooding my skin.

"Oh yeah, we know what you were up to in that truck." Bella laughs. "Sizzling, sister."

While my insides rebel against the fact that they all sat at the windows picturing me getting hot and heavy with Ethan, I force a mischievous grin.

Aimee and Fiona don't seem as impressed by my antics, but I put on the show I'm supposed to, desperate to sell the idea that I really wasn't into it.

"Guys are so gullible, right? One little moan and they're all over you." I dip my hip.

"Your cheeks are pretty flushed right now. You sure *you* weren't into it?" Aimee's glare is sharp with accusation.

I shrug. "You told me to woo him, and that's what I'm trying to do." I blink, a serious edge coating my words as I remind myself of what the hell I'm doing here. "I need a place in this house. I'm committed to becoming a Sig Be sister, and if wooing and breaking Ethan Galloway is what it takes, then that's what I'm gonna do."

The words reverberate in my skull as I give Aimee an emphatic nod, then slip through the row of sisters. They make a space for me, and I can feel their eyes on my back until I turn the corner.

It's not until I reach my bed that I flop down with a heavy sigh, staring up at the slanted ceiling and trying to figure out what I did wrong to make Ethan change his mind, then reminding myself to not be surprised.

Guys don't want me.

They never have.

I should have learned my lesson the day Dad walked out on me, but my dumbass brain just won't catch on.

"Stupid girl," I whisper, my voice catching as I fight off the wave of pain tearing through my chest.

CHAPTER 22
ETHAN

.

I didn't sleep last night. How could I possibly get any decent shut-eye after the way I left things with Mikayla? Shit. The look on her face when I basically rejected her hot little body.

My lame excuse of being in public was derailed by her legit suggestion that we take things somewhere else, so I had to play the hockey card.

Yes, I had an early practice, but still.

I threw everything I had into it, which wasn't much because I'm exhausted after a restless *no cum, no release, no sex* night. Thank God I could work off some of this energy on the ice, but it's not enough, and it will never be enough to douse the guilt I feel.

I never should have kissed her again, but the second her lips hit mine, I lost it. Instinct took over, all self-control flying out the window as her tight ass found its home on my cock. When her tits, which fit into my palms like a fucking dream, squished up against my chest. How could I not suck on those sweet nipples? The second I curled my lips around that pink bulb, I was done for.

But not completely.

I don't know what made my brain kick in. Maybe it was the fact that I became aware that any sleaze could walk past the window and get a clear shot of Mikayla's tits. The idea of some leering guy checking her out gave me pause, and then my brain snapped into action. I wanted to cover her up, keep her all to myself... which then reminded me that I didn't have any right to do that because I fucking lost the worst bet in the history of the world.

I've got just over two weeks to go. I should be able to manage, but not when Mikayla is right under my nose, smelling divine and making me laugh, and punching right through my chest cavity with one of her smiles.

The second I see her, I—

Holy shit, she's right there.

I stop in my tracks, lifting my shades to drink her in as she ambles along the pathway. She seems in no particular hurry to get wherever she's going, so against my better judgment, I change course and block her way.

"Hi." I grin.

Her nose wrinkles, and she looks to the ground between us. The crack in the concrete is separating my large black sneakers from her tiny green Converses.

"Hey." Her voice isn't snappy but has a sharp edge to it.

I really pissed her off last night, and I feel legit bad about it. Shit, I wish I could tell her. I wish I could break all the damn rules and explain, but if I'm doing that, I may as well crush the big one and give in to my desire.

Clearing my throat, I try to fill the awkward silence, but I'm kind of lost for what to say.

"Well, thanks for that chat." She bobs her head and goes to scoot around me.

"What chat?"

Her left shoulder hitches. "Well, I don't know what to call whatever this awkward-as-shit moment is we're having."

I sigh and reach for her, but she flinches out of the way.

"I'm not even allowed to touch you now?"

"You don't want to, so..." There goes that shoulder again, hitching away like it's got a tick.

I narrow my eyes at her. "I want to."

"Mm-hm." She nods but obviously doesn't believe me, so I step right into her space, bending low to talk directly in her ear.

"I'm sorry about last night, okay? I handled it... badly."

"Mm-hm."

"I wanted to explain before you took off, but..." I sigh.

"I get it." She steps back. "We were in public. Hockey is king. It's all good, man. Don't sweat it."

I can see right through this casual veneer, and I want to tell her so, but a group of students walks right past us.

"Hey, Ethan." The leggy blonde gives me a simpering smile while her friend flashes me her *fuck me* eyes.

Oh shit, it's Ruby.

I bob my head at them, muttering, "Hey, Rubes."

She frowns at my casual, less-than-flirtatious greeting, then glances between Mikayla and me. Her red lips part, her eyes quietly asking if I've been hooked.

I don't know how to respond to that, so I don't say anything at all.

Her soft giggle makes me tense, and I silently beg her to shut up and keep walking.

Her lips twitch with a knowing grin before she saunters off with her friend. "Always nice to see you, Ethan."

I avert my gaze from her swaying hips, focusing back on Mikayla.

Lil' mouse snorts, working her jaw to the side and shaking her head. "I shouldn't keep you. Those pussies are calling. I can practically hear them meowing your name."

With a pointed look, she goes to spin away, but I catch her arm before she can. "Please don't walk away pissed off again. I really am sorry about last night."

"It's fine."

Still don't believe her.

"I mean, my vagina was pretty pissed, but I took care of it."

I internally groan, the image of her working herself to climax enough to make me blow on the spot. Does she writhe in quiet ecstasy? Does her body quiver? Or maybe she's a screamer.

Holy hell.

I glance away, begging my body to behave itself.

"Don't worry about me," she murmurs and shakes me off, darting out of reach and heading down the path.

I chase after her, chuckling at her exaggerated groan when I fall in step beside her.

"Seriously? You're like a head cold I just can't shake."

"A head cold? Jeez, thanks."

"You're welcome." She flashes me that adorable, cheesy grin, and my insides fold like a deck of cards.

"So, the party this weekend..."

You're playing with fire, dude. Don't ask. Don't you fucking ask.

"How about I pick you up at nine?"

She jerks to a stop and frowns up at me. "What?"

"You know, the party Casey invited you and the girls to. Thought I'd pick you up."

"Why?" Her eyes narrow like she's waiting for me to prank her.

"I want to take you to it."

"But I'll already be going. Doesn't it make more sense to just meet you there?"

I tip my head to study her, lightly tugging the end of her braid. It's a loose one that's draped over her shoulder, locks of hair falling out of it. She huffs when I tease her, "You don't have one romantic bone in your body, do you?"

"Romantic? Oh, so you want me to go as your date to the party?"

"Sure, why not?"

Her face bunches with confusion as she shakes her head and sputters, "Could you be any more confusing?"

I blink and shake my head. "I'm not following."

"Exactly!" she spits. "Because it's so fucking confusing! One minute you're telling me off like an overprotective guardian, then you're teasing me like I'm your kid sister, and yesterday you tried to suck my tongue right out of mouth before bailing with an excuse about early morning hockey practice. I don't know what you want from me."

"I...I want..." With a little growl, I rest my hand on her

hip and finally sputter out some semblance of truth. "I want to take you to the party. I want to pick you up and walk you in the door so everyone in that place knows you're with me!"

My outburst shuts her up. For all of five seconds.

"So, you don't want me, but you don't want anyone else having me either. How lovely."

I snatch her wrist before she goes to walk away from me again and gruffly whisper, "I do want you," before planting my lips on hers.

She responds instantly, like our tongues were specifically designed for each other. Her initial squeak of surprise is lost to a moan that twitches my dick. As I plunge my fingers into her hair, all the blood rushes down to the guy, snapping him to attention.

Is it now?

Is the wait over?

Are you finally putting me out of my misery?

It kills me that I can't grant his wishes, but I force myself to slowly pull out of the kiss. Cupping Mikayla's cheeks, I enjoy the dazed look in her eyes. She blinks, slowly coming to, and I get it. Hot damn, I get it.

Her kisses are fire.

She scrapes her teeth over her shiny bottom lip, and my insides flare with an inferno of need. But then I catch a movement out of the corner of my eye and stand straight, instinctively shifting to block Mikayla from whoever's approaching.

Aw, crap on a cracker.

"Hey, guys," Asher singsongs, his grin growing wide as he leans around my body to wiggle his eyebrows at Mikayla. "Lil' mouse. Nice to see you."

"And you." She steps up beside me. "Any luck with that footage?"

"Gone." He winks at her. "You held up your end of the bargain, so I dealt with mine this morning."

"Bargain?" I look between them, hating that they've got something going on that I don't know about.

Mikayla glances up at me. "I agreed to hang at Hockey House last night on the condition that he get rid of whatever was recorded in the workout room."

I throw Asher a dry glare, but I'm actually grateful. I don't want Mikayla embarrassed by that, plus she could get in trouble for sneaking into the arena, plus Coach would fry my ass over an open flame if he knew I'd been getting it on in the workout room.

"Thanks," I mutter, holding out my fist.

He taps his knuckles against mine before flashing me that warning look again. "It's a great day, isn't it?"

I narrow my eyes at him, wondering where the fuck he's going with this.

"Yeah, temperature's good." He looks up at the blue sky. "You know... I could almost walk around campus naked on a sunny day like this."

Mikayla bulges her eyes at him before letting out a shocked bark. "Whatever floats your boat, I guess."

She shoots me a *your friend is weird* kind of look before squeezing my arm. "Catch you on Saturday."

"Yeah." I force a bright smile, glancing over my shoulder to watch her walk away.

As soon as she's a safe distance, I whip back around to glare at Asher. "You are such a—"

"Just keeping you on track, man." He flashes me a cheesy grin.

I grunt and start walking, but he spins and falls into step beside me.

"So, what's happening on Saturday?"

After a little side-eye action, I mutter, "I'm taking her to the party."

"Like a date?"

"I guess." I shrug, trying to play it cool.

Asher whistles. "Has the mighty Galloway fallen? I have never seen you focus on more than one chick for longer than twenty-four hours, bar the Aimee fiasco of freshman year. Oh, and there was that Shanna thing too, I guess. "

Clenching my jaw, I resist the urge to shove him away from me and start running, finally gritting out, "Yeah, well, I can usually get them out of my system, can't I?"

He snickers, his shoulders trembling like he's fighting hysterical laughter. "Has my bet really turned you from a coldhearted sex machine to actually pursuing a girl?"

"I've never been coldhearted," I snap. "Fuck you, man. We all know college is about casual flings. No one in the house is serious about anyone."

"Liam was last year."

"Yeah, and look how that turned out," I spit, irritation coursing through me.

Coldhearted.

Screw that. Just because I enjoy sex doesn't make me an asshole. I'm always up-front with the girls I hook up with. They know the deal.

Mikayla doesn't.

I smash my teeth together, sliding my shades back on so I have a shield between me and Asher's keen gaze.

He's still grinning at me, and I want to serve him up a swift, sharp punch to the face.

Coldhearted.

I don't know why that term is eating me so damn much.

"Well." Asher pats me on the shoulder. I shake him off with a little growl, which only makes him laugh. "Luckily, I'll be there on Saturday night to keep an eye on you."

"I don't need you to do that."

"Sure you don't."

"It was just kissing," I grumble, pointing back to the spot where Mikayla turned my insides to Jell-O.

"Didn't you know, bro? Kissing leads to sex... and you ain't allowed none of that for another—" He checks his phone. "—sixteen more days."

When he starts hissing in mock sympathy, I flip him the bird.

"Watching you burn is gonna be so much fun." He cracks up laughing, flipping me off while veering left and sauntering away with a goofy grin.

I scowl after him, fisting my hands and continuing on to class.

The last thing I feel like doing is sitting through an anatomy lecture, but I force myself there, because hockey may be king, but I'm not leaving this place without a decent education, and I won't get jack if I don't put in the work.

Besides, it might help distract me from the Mikayla dilemma.

Shit, maybe there'll be something in my textbook about how to control a misbehaving meat stick.

CHAPTER 23
MIKAYLA

I slide my feet into the heels Teah is insisting I wear, then totter over to the full-length mirror in her bedroom. I feel like a newborn giraffe in these stupid things.

"I look ridiculous," I grumble.

Teah stops applying her mascara to check me out, then starts to giggle. "You look freaking hot, girl."

I frown at her, then turn to face the mirror again.

I barely recognize the person gaping back at me. No, wait, I do... it's my little sister, Megan. Resting my hand on my throat, I stare at myself fitted out in this skintight green dress that looks like it's had a glitter bomb explode inside the fabric.

Adjusting the dress at my hips, I pull it down a little, wishing it covered more of my ass. If I bend over, everyone will get a full display.

"Stop doing that." Bella slaps my hands away and smooths her palms over my hips to straighten out the fabric. "Don't you dare ruin my dress." She gazes over my shoulder and is soon pouting into the mirror. "Dammit, why does it look better on you than on me?"

I huff out a soft laugh. "You look way hotter than I do."

I run my eyes over her red-and-gold dress with the intricate pattern on the front. It's a second skin that pushes her boobs up and makes her butt look round and squeezable.

"The guys are going to be drooling." I wink at her.

She gives me a simpering smile, dipping her hip and running her hands down her sides while she admires herself in the mirror.

I run a hand through my curled hair and score myself a huff from Teah. "Stop doing that. You'll lose all the body if you keep touching it."

With an exasperated sigh, she gets up from her makeup station—yes, it's like a freaking actress's dressing room with lights around the mirror and everything—and approaches me with this bulldog expression.

"I didn't spend all that time dolling you up only to have you ruin the look." She fluffs the curls she created with this hot iron thingy and then adds a touch more gloss to my lips. "There. Now, try and not touch your face or hair, okay?"

I nod, nerves powering through me as I adjust to the fact that I'm going to have to go out in public looking this way.

And then it gets a million times worse when I step into the living area to wait for Ethan and find Aimee standing by the window. She turns and spots me, her eyebrows rising with surprise.

"Well, don't you clean up nicely."

"Um... thank you?" I wobble on my heels, and she tuts, rolling her eyes.

A few of the Sig Be sisters snicker behind their hands, and it's enough to make me want to rip this dress off my body and shout, "I'm done."

But then I remind myself why I'm suffering through all of this, clenching my jaw and ignoring them.

"So, we've all heard about the kiss."

"The kiss?" I flush, thinking about how hot and heavy I got with Ethan the other night and wondering if any of the girls saw him sucking my nipples. My insides tingle as the memory flashes through me. It's this weird mix of heady need and gut-plummeting embarrassment.

"Yes, the one he gave you in front of everyone at school the other day. Ethan basically claimed you after insisting he pick you up for the party, which means it's time."

"Time?" I swallow, dread pooling in my stomach.

"Yes. He obviously likes you enough to pick you up and make this seem like a date, which is rare for that manwhore, so tonight is the perfect opportunity to break his heart."

Oh crap.

"I thought you wanted him to fall in love with me first."

Aimee's steely gaze flicks to mine, narrowing at the edges while I shut my trap and silently reprimand myself for speaking at all.

"You want this to keep going?" Her voice is sharp with suspicion.

"No, of course not." I force a smile. "Initiation night, here I come. Woo." I pump my arm in the air, feeling like an idiot. I must look like one, too, because more snickering skitters around the room.

Aimee's unimpressed glare is stripping the skin from my body. I squirm beneath it but stand my ground as she approaches me. "Here's the plan. Ethan will pick you up. You'll play nice, pretending he's your personal sex dream, and once you're both comfortable at the party, you'll start making out with someone else."

"What?" I recoil, stumbling back on my heels.

"The girls will make sure Ethan sees it."

"But—"

"He'll be super pissed and humiliated."

My chest starts heaving, and it's an effort to pull myself into line. "I don't want to go making out with some random guy."

Aimee's cutting gaze slices right through me. "What's the problem? You've been making out with Ethan."

I clench my jaw and force myself to nod. That's right. I have. And they all think it's been this chore on my part. They think I've been playing this role to get into this house, and I have to make them keep thinking that.

Shit!

Swallowing down my repulsion at the idea of this super-awkward and horrible plan, I force a smile. "Okay. So, who is this guy?"

"It's a friend of Claudia's." She points at the girl who's wiggling her eyebrows at me.

"He's in my psych class. He likes to think he's a bad boy, but that's just to hide his nerdy side." She giggles.

Fiona rolls her eyes but is fighting a grin. "His name's Damien, and he's happy to help us out."

"Great." I clear my throat and look back at Aimee,

hoping she can't see through my paper-thin veneer. "Well, thank you for letting me wrap this up tonight and not drag it out for the full month. I appreciate it. I seriously had no idea how I was going to get him to fall in love with me."

She gives me a magnanimous nod, like she's the queen of England and I'm one of her sniveling subjects who she's kindly helping out.

Obviously, my jabs from the other day are getting to her and she's changed her tune. Like my mother, Aimee seems hell-bent on keeping Jarrod happy. Shit, I probably am too. I did sign that contract, after all.

My stomach churns. The urge to bolt from the room and get the hell out of here is overwhelming. I want to flee, call Rachel, pour out my heart to my best friend, and ask her what the hell I'm doing.

But then there's a knock at the door and it's too late.

I'm in this now, and tonight is going to suck on every level possible.

"Hey, Ethan." Claudia greets him with a sultry smile, leaning against the door and making my eyes burn with jealousy.

Yes, okay, a green devil is pecking at my shoulders right now.

Ethan's hot and funny and gorgeous and... and tonight I'm basically going to slap him in the face. I'm going to intentionally hurt and embarrass him, and then some confident, sure-as-shit chick like Claudia is going to swoop in and have her way with the guy. My guy.

Not your guy, your target.

Keep your head on straight, Mikayla.

"Just here to pick up Mikayla." Ethan's deep voice

makes my insides tremble, and I nearly roll my ankle trying to get to the door.

Stepping around Claudia, I stare up at him, my breath catching. Holy shit, he's sex on a stick. Tall and handsome in his dark jeans and a shirt that's tight enough to show off the contours of his muscles. His hair is intentionally mussed, and he smells like heaven.

I feel completely overdressed and out of my league.

"Wow." He breathes the word more than says it, his bright eyes drinking me in.

Squirming in these heels, I tug at the sides of my dress. "Hey."

"Hey." His smile is... something special. He likes what he sees right now, and I could bask in this glow, like seriously sunbathe under the rays he's firing at me.

But then I remember what I'm supposed to do tonight.

And I can't feel the warmth of Ethan's smile anymore. I can only feel the sizzling laser beams Aimee's trying to liquefy me with.

I turn to glance at her, and she gives me a demure smirk. "Have fun tonight."

Bella grins beside her. "See you there soon!"

With another thick swallow, I nod and shuffle out the door. Ethan takes my hand, leading me to his truck and laughing again when he spins to look at me.

"What?" I frown.

"You look seriously hot, lil' mouse. I almost didn't recognize you."

"Oh, thanks. So you're saying I don't look hot all the time?"

He stops me against the passenger side door, leaning down close and whispering against my lips, "You look hot all the time. Tonight, you are fucking fire, baby." His mouth is on mine before I can take my next breath, and I basically inhale his tongue. It's warm and soft and hungry, sweeping into my mouth and claiming me against the car.

I grip his neck, rising to my tiptoes to lengthen this heady moment.

But then, inevitably, he pulls back. His eyes drink me in again, making me feel like I'm somehow special. Which is dangerous, because I'm not. If anything, I'm a full-blown bitch who is going to be humiliating him tonight.

Shit. I don't want to do this.

So just tell him the truth, then.

I gaze up at his handsome face, my lips parting as I toy with the idea of spilling all. He smiles down at me. That beautiful smile which I've loved since the first time I saw it. And now all I can picture is how that smile will transform to a look of disgust.

What kind of asshole plays someone this way?

He won't think it's funny because it's not. And then when I try to explain how I went after him at first but changed my mind and genuinely started liking him, what will make him believe me?

As far as he'll be concerned, I've been lying this whole time.

I can't tell him.

But I can't humiliate him either.

How the hell do I get out of this?

Spinning around, I open the door with trembling

fingers and go to lift my leg to jump in, but this damn dress is too tight.

I let out a squeak and realize I'm going to have to hike the thing all the way over my butt in order to climb into the truck. Ethan softly laughs against the back of my hair before his two large hands grip my hips and boost me into the truck like I weigh less than a sack of feathers.

"Thanks," I murmur, wriggling in my seat and adjusting the dress.

His gaze skims my legs, running down to those heels before bouncing back to my face. "Hottie." He grins, and I can't help but grin right back at him.

I've got to admit, it feels kinda cool to be looked at this way, with such open desire. I'm not usually the girl who guys find hot, but look at me go. Ethan Galloway, one of the sexiest guys on campus, is eyeing me up like I'm some kind of cover model.

My heart trills in spite of the fact that it shouldn't.

As Ethan walks around to get behind the wheel, I press my knuckles between my breasts, ordering my heart to slow the hell down.

It's like my body doesn't understand that this is not a real date. Ethan will never be my boyfriend or anything. This is a onetime thing, because tonight, I have to make out with some other guy, and then Ethan will never smile at me again.

CHAPTER 24
ETHAN

Mikayla looks off-the-charts sexy tonight. When I walked in the door and saw her in that dress, my mouth went bone dry. All I could manage was a "Wow." It kind of surprised me, actually, because I've been appreciating girls for a long time now, and it takes a lot to make me speechless. But there she went.

It makes me wonder if it's specifically her or if my unsatisfied manhood is weighing in. But when I glance across at her in the passenger seat, my eyes skimming her curves, this tingling sensation in my chest warns me that it's not all about my twitching dick.

And then she squirms in her seat, tugging on the hem of the dress again, and the tingles only get stronger.

Tingles? What the fuck is wrong with me?

I give my head a confused shake and focus back on the road, refusing to look at her again until we reach the house.

"Stay put," I murmur when I park the truck.

"What?" She almost looks offended by my command

and stubbornly opens the door before I get there. She's swiveling around, ready to jump to the curb when I reach her.

"I told you to stay."

"I'm not your puppy," she grumbles.

"No, you're my stubborn little mouse." I grab her around the waist, lifting her out of my truck and setting her down. "I didn't want you ripping that dress. It's okay to let people help you."

She narrows her eyes at me, then lets out a little sigh before mumbling, "Thank you."

I grin. "You're welcome." Then I kiss her.

Which is weird, because right this second, we look like a cutesy couple, and I've avoided this sort of scenario for years. So why the hell does it feel so damn good right now?

"Let's go." I thread my fingers through hers, dragging her up to the house. Her steps are reluctant, and I can sense her trepidation growing. Before we reach the door, I spin around to check on her. "You nervous about something?"

She tugs on the side of her dress. "I don't really do parties. I mean, like this." She raises her chin at the house. "I'm way better suited to, you know... parties where you play charades or watch a game or play poker or something."

She's too adorable.

I kiss the tip of her scrunched-up nose. I can't help it.

Grabbing her other hand, I hold her arms out wide and look down at her. "You're a smokin'-hot college girl entering a party with one of the coolest guys on campus."

She snorts.

"What? It's true. You know it. I know it."

She tips her head. "You just have confidence to spare, don't you?"

"Yeah. Which is why I'm lending some to you." I raise my eyebrows at her. "Now, repeat after me: I am sexy."

She wrinkles her nose, shaking her head.

Leaning down, I level my eyes at her and gruffly command her to "Say it. We're not leaving this spot until you do, and I can already tell people are looking at us and wondering what the hell we're talking about, so just do it."

With a heavy sigh, she mutters, "I am sexy."

"Come on, Mick, with a little conviction, please. Look at yourself."

Her gaze catches mine, and I don't know exactly what I'm showing her right now, but it makes her blush. Then her lips twitch, and she says with a little more confidence, "I am sexy."

My lips curl up in response. "I belong here."

"I belong here."

"I'm about to have the best night of my life."

She hesitates. Something flashing across her expression—maybe a touch of fear or dread. I can't work out where that's coming from. But just as I start to frown, she rushes out the words. "I'm about to have the best night of my life. Now, let's go."

Tugging my hand, she drags me into the party, and yes, I'm feeling pretty damn cocky that I managed to swing this thing around.

As we walk through the door, every head in the room seems to turn toward us. I guess they're not used to me arriving with someone, and yeah, it feels weird. But screw it. I like this girl, and—

Oh shit, I really do like her.

How did this happen?

When?

And why am I not freaking out a little more about it?

I'm flirting with girlfriend territory here. I promised myself I'd never go down this path. Not that Mikayla's my girlfriend. She's just a girl I brought along to this party.

You called her your *little mouse before.*

I shut the thought off and rest my hand on her lower back, propelling her past the gawking partygoers and pretending like this is the most normal thing in the world.

"Hey." I raise my chin and eyebrows at various people, fist-bumping a few of the football players I know, then spotting Ruby. She glances down at Mikayla, then back up to me with a little pout.

That's right, luscious lady. There will be no visits to the bathroom tonight.

She grins and shakes her head, walking past us with a wink. Mikayla frowns, glancing at me, but I just shake my head and make a beeline for the hockey guys.

Mikayla seems to relax when she greets Casey and Liam. Asher gives her a smile that makes my skin crawl because I know he's loving the fact that she looks freaking edible tonight. He can feel my pain and suffering, and I know I'm gonna get it later.

Shit. Why did I do this to myself?

Riley slides up a few seconds later. "Mick!" He raises his arms like seeing her has just made his day.

"Hey, Riley." She high-fives him with a laugh.

"You guys want a drink?" He points around the table, an enthusiastic waiter who has obviously had a few already. Yep, the drink turns him into an animated kid. It's pretty fucking funny.

Liam tracks our young teammate as he makes his way to the keg and starts grabbing Solo cups to fill, before turning to Mikayla.

"You don't have to drink if you don't want to." Liam tips his cup at her. "I never do."

"Really?" Her face bunches with surprise. "Why not?"

He shrugs. "Don't like it."

I clench my jaw the way I always do when Liam is confronted with that question. Maybe he doesn't like it. But I know that's not the reason he doesn't drink. I've told him a million times that if he wants to, he should, but he's convinced that if he lets loose with a bottle, he's gonna turn into his old man, so he doesn't touch a drop.

I guess it kind of works out well that we always have a DD in our group. Just as long as Liam feels like he's not missing out.

"You're underage. No one's gonna judge you for following the rules and staying sharp at a party like this." Liam's lips curl into a closed-mouth grin.

I lean down to assure her, "But if you do want a drink, go for it. I'll keep an eye on you."

"Thanks." She looks over her shoulder to smile at me, but then her expression drops. She swallows and mutters, "Back in a sec," before brushing past me and going to chat with her Sig Be sisters.

"Still don't get why she wants to be in that sorority. She doesn't seem the type." Liam frowns after her.

I find a place next to him, watching her shoulders

tense as she reaches the girls and one of them starts talking like they're about to walk into an exam and haven't just entered a frat party.

I can't see Mikayla's face, and I wonder if she's rolling her eyes. The little frowns on two of their faces tells me she must be saying or doing something derogatory.

"She's lookin' pretty fuckin' hot tonight, bro. This must be killing you." Casey laughs, then takes a swig of his beer. "I don't get why you're doing this to yourself."

I groan and throw him a pained frown. "Neither do I. But she's... cool. I like hanging out with her."

"So, this is just a friendship thing?"

"Yeah." I nod, trying to sell it to myself. "Yeah, we're friends."

"You're looking at her like you want to tear that dress off and bone her right in the middle of the dance floor."

I groan again, then throw him a dirty look. "Stop picturing her naked."

"It's in there now. Can't help myself." Casey grins. "And since you guys are *just friends*, you don't mind if I—"

I cut him off with a growl that has him cracking up. Raising his hands as two white flags, he can barely get the words out. "Chill, bro. I'm messing with you. *Friends*, sure. Dude, I've never seen you like this over a chick before."

Clenching my jaw, I share a quick look with Liam before shooting my eyes back to Mikayla. She flicks her hand up like she's pissed, and I wonder if I should go over there and rescue her.

"Here you go." Riley shoves a cup in my hand. I take a gulp, keeping my eyes on Mikayla, who now has her hands clenched into little fists at her sides.

Yep. A rescue is in order.

I'm about to head over there when she spins, her expression mottled with annoyance as she storms back toward us.

"You okay?" I touch the small of her back as soon as she's within reach.

Darting a glance over her head, I glare at the group of girls, but they're already disbanding. Except the tall brunette who gives me a sultry smirk.

I frown and turn my attention back to Mick.

Her head's bobbing like one of those dolls you put on your dashboard. "Yeah, sure. I'm great. Is this yours?" She takes the cup out of my hand and downs the thing in one go, then wipes her mouth with the back of her hand and mutters, "I need a drink."

Casey snorts and then starts laughing while Mikayla makes a beeline for the keg.

"That chick is something else." He's shaking his head, and Asher starts grinning too.

"She really is. Good luck with that, man."

I growl at his teasing and swing my eyes back to Mick, who's working her way through a second cup of beer pretty damn fast.

"Help me keep an eye on her," I murmur to Liam.

"You bet." He nods and I turn to the rest of the table, silently asking for the same thing.

They all nod, raising their glasses at me and promising to do the same.

I relax a little, knowing they've got her back, before turning to see her fill her cup for a second time.

Three beers in under five minutes for a pint-size body like hers. Yeah, she's gonna be trashed before the hour's out.

I weave through the crowd toward her, taking the cup from her hand and slowing her down a notch.

"How about a glass of water in between, yeah?"

"Gimme that beer," she growls, snatching it back. "I'm not a kid you have to look after, Ethan. Just..." She shrugs me off her, this pained expression cresting over her face. "Just..." Shaking her head, she walks away from me, back to the hockey table before jerking still and veering away from the guys as well.

What the hell is up?

What did those sorority bitches say to her?

I nearly go and confront them but am too busy tailing Mikayla around as she downs another beer and then starts laughing with a couple of chicks on the dance floor. Resting my shoulder against the wall, I watch Mikayla's wild movements as she shakes her ass. I would join her, but I suck at dancing, and unless it's a slow shuffle with my hands resting on her hips and we're stepping side to side, I look like a complete idiot on any dance floor.

I may be a confident guy, but I've got a rep to uphold, and I will go down in burning flames if anyone here sees me trying to dance.

So I play bodyguard, standing back while Mikayla gets a little wild. It's kind of fun to watch. She's cute normally, but when she's got no inhibitions, she's even more hilarious. Her spaghetti arms fling through the air as she jumps to the thick beat pulsing through the house.

Guys check her out but seem a little put off by her wild dance moves to approach, and I relax, sipping my beer and enjoying the show. Liam comes over to chat with me, and we watch together before he has to hit the head.

Then Wily Wilson appears.

"Bro!" My face splits with a grin as the big guy holds out his hand. I grab it and come in for a hug, slapping his shoulder. "Good to see you, man."

I haven't caught him on campus since school started.

Wily and I went to high school together. He's a giant of a man. The kind of Mac truck you don't want to mess with. That's what makes him such a damn good offensive lineman.

He scored himself a football scholarship for Nolan U and is well on his way to the NFL if he keeps playing like he has been.

"Haven't seen you around much."

"Yeah." He shakes his head. "Been working my ass off, man. Coach is riding us about keeping our grades up and not partying too hard."

"Is this the new guy?"

"Yeah, and he don't take shit. Coach Watkins was only about the game. He couldn't care less what we did off the field. But Coach Jones..." He shakes his head. "He won't shut up about getting an education and being men of honor. If we screw up, we get benched, and he's hella serious." He snickers. "I just want to play ball, you know? That's why I'm here."

"Yeah but graduating with a degree isn't the worst thing either."

Wily nods but doesn't verbally agree with me.

I get it, I suppose. For guys like us, sports will always take priority, but I've learned so much since I've been here, and the classes I'm taking are really interesting. Dad always told me to study what appeals to me, and I took that on board. So far, I've only fallen into a couple of classes that were a drag. The rest, I've lapped up, and maybe that's why my grades are pretty good.

"Might try to find myself a tutor. Not sure." He shrugs, looking out over the dance floor and grinning. "Oh man, there are some hotties here tonight."

I follow his gaze with a grin, then jerk.

Shit. Where's Mikayla gone?

I scan the crowd again, hunting for her flailing arms, but she's... *Fuck!* She's gone.

"Gotta go, man." I slap Wily on the shoulder and head into the sweaty pit, weaving through the gyrating bodies as I try to find the girl I promised I'd keep an eye on.

Dammit. I turned my head for two seconds.

Pushing through the throng of people, I work my way outside, hoping her drunk little self just went to grab some fresh air.

CHAPTER 25
MIKAYLA

I don't know who grabbed my arm and pulled me off the dance floor, but they're kind of pissed with me.

"You're making a total fool of yourself," she snips. "Ugh! You're not even supposed to be drinking. What the hell is wrong with you?"

Miss Snippy is loud and annoying, and I don't like her.

I grunt when she yanks me to a stop and pushes me against the wall. "Pull it together!" She snaps her fingers in my face.

With a slow blink, I start to realize that Fiona has her talons in me. "You have a job to do. Now, this is Damien." She points to a guy behind her.

He's tall, but not super tall. Broad, but not super broad.

He's no Ethan Galloway, that's for sure.

Shit. Ethan.

I don't want to do this!

I figured if I got drunk enough and stayed away from

him tonight, I could somehow get through this. But even downing three beers hasn't murdered my brain. My head is spinning, but I still know what I have to do, and the thought repulses me.

How do I hurt Ethan when he's only been nice to me? When he's sweet and funny and he told me he'd keep an eye on me tonight? His hand on my lower back felt so damn good, and I wish it was still there. I wish he could get me out of this.

"Hey." Damien sidles up beside Fiona. She steps aside and says something I don't quite catch before disappearing. Now it's just me and this total stranger I'm supposed to kiss.

Ugh! Kill me now.

I lean my head back against the wall to counter the wave of dizziness.

"Okay, so Fee told me the plan is to head out to the dance floor, make sure we're in sight of Ethan, and start going for it."

"Don't want to," I mutter.

"Come on. It'll be fun." He snickers, stepping so close his body basically smothers mine. "We'll go out there and get a little busy." Hands slide down my body, rounding the curve of my butt and giving my cheeks a little squeeze.

"Hands off the goods." I push him away.

He grunts, frowning at me, before trying again. Resting his hands against the wall, he boxes me in and leans down close enough that I can smell the liquor on his breath. He's been drinking straight spirits. I can't tell what, but my eyeballs feel like they're burning.

My stomach roils.

"We need to put on a show. I'm doing you a favor. Stop being difficult and play along. I don't have all night."

"I don't want to do this," I slur, holding on to the *s* and dragging it out to try and make my point.

"Whatever. I know the drill. Claudia and Fee told me everything. You want a place in the house, you need to prove it." He grabs my hips and pulls me against him. "And oh, baby, I want to help you prove it."

I growl and shove him back. The move catches him a little off guard, and he stumbles a step before regaining his balance. "It's supposed to be a little making out, not a shit ton of groping. Control yourself."

He glances around, obviously checking this part of the hallway is still empty before he steps back into my space again. My insides pinch with fear for a second.

"We have to sell this," he snaps.

"Don't want to." I grit out the words, trying to sound tougher than I feel.

He huffs, letting out a string of expletives and a little accidental spittle on my cheek before barking, "I don't have to be doing this, you know. It's not like I need the money."

What the fuck?

"They're paying you?"

He gives me a smarmy smile. "Guess they really want you in the house with them, huh?"

Yeah right. Even my drunk-ass brain is smart enough to know that's bullshit.

They want Ethan to burn, and they're using me as their little toy to do it. If I succeed, they win. If I lose, they still win because they can kick me out of their house. Aimee's gonna get her triumph one way or another.

Clenching my jaw, I look away from Damien, and he must take my silence as consent because he grabs my wrist and pulls me away from the wall. "That's better. Now let's go do this."

Every cell in my body rebels against his touch, and I try to pull my arm free.

"Lemme go!" I sound like some whiny kid, but the idea of that guy's tongue in my mouth is enough to make me puke.

I hate being manhandled. I hate being bossed around.

I hate this whole damn thing!

"I don't want this." I try to wrench my wrist out of his grasp, but his fingers only dig in that much harder. My voice is too quiet against the thumping music and chaotic party noise, so I try to shout, "Let! Go!" And this time my pathetic voice is backed up by a full-blown roar.

"What the fuck are you doing?"

My head whips around in time to see Ethan charging down the hallway. He looks like a feral beast, his face mottled with anger as he grabs Damien and shoves him away from me. I stumble back against the wall while Ethan blocks my body with his, getting right in Damien's face.

"She said *let go*. Are you deaf?"

"I... I...," Damien sputters. "She... she wanted to dance, man."

"Bullshit!" Ethan fists the guy's shirt and shoves him. Damien's shoulders hit the wall with a smack.

He winces and I cringe, sort of feeling like I should step in and stop this but also too drunk to do anything but lean against the wall and watch the show. Captain Hero is taking down a sleazoid. It's kind of satisfying.

"Fuck this." Damien shoves Ethan away. Sort of. It's more a case of Damien slapping his arms against Ethan's chest and Ethan letting him go. Pulling his shirt straight, he throws me a dark glare that makes me shrink against the wall before storming down the hallway.

Ethan spins around to check on me.

"You okay?" All the fire has left his voice. It's now a tender lilt that makes my eyes water. "Come on, we're out of here." He gently takes my elbow, guiding me in the opposite direction of the pissed off Damien.

Shit. Shit. Shit!

The repercussions of what I've just let happen scuttle after me, climbing over my shoulders, down my throat, and raiding my belly.

My knees buckle, but Ethan moves like lightning, sweeping me into his arms.

Feels so good.

I rest my spinning head against his shoulder as he carries me past the kitchen. And then my stomach starts to churn a little more, clenching painfully when I spot the sisters glaring at me.

"I screwed up," I whisper.

"No you didn't, baby." Ethan brushes his lips against my forehead. "You didn't do anything wrong."

If only he were right.

CHAPTER 26
ETHAN

When I came down the hallway and saw that shithead yanking Mikayla's arm while she yelled at him that she *didn't want this* and to *let her go*, I lost it. What kind of fucker treats a woman that way?

And she's drunk off her ass.

Shit, if I hadn't found her...

My stomach clenches as I buckle her into the passenger seat and stalk around my truck. There are too many stories of rape and roofies. It's a nationwide problem, and Nolan U is not immune to it. I should have punched that asshole in the face. What if he goes after another girl?

I glance at Mikayla, pulling out my phone before starting the engine. "Who was that guy?"

She shrugs, closing her eyes and looking sick.

"Did you get his name?"

"Why?" she manages.

"Because I want the guys to keep an eye on him, make sure he doesn't go after any other girls."

"He only wanted me," she mumbles.

"How do you know?"

Her jaw clenches, and she shakes her head, then winces and covers her eyes with a trembling hand.

Shit, she's gonna cry.

I fire off a quick text to Liam, telling him what happened and what I'm doing. I won't need to ask anything else of him. Liam's a protector, and as soon as he reads my text, he'll take it upon himself to walk the party, keeping an eye on anyone who's looking vulnerable. He'll probably be feeling bad about losing sight of Mikayla anyway, which will make him extra vigilant. When I was frantically searching the house for her, I bumped into the guys, and they all went pale when I told them I'd lost her. I've never seen them move so fast, breaking away from the table and combing the house for her.

Shit, what if I hadn't walked into the hallway when I did? What if that asshole had dragged lil' mouse into a room before I'd found her? She may be feisty, but she's drunk right now. And I don't care what she says, she *is* little. A guy that size could do whatever the hell he wanted with her, and she wouldn't have been able to fight him off. I feel sick with rage as I drive straight for Hockey House. She's staying with me tonight. At least until she's sober. I have to know she'll be okay.

The thought that he was after Mikayla churns through me. I want to ask her about it, but I don't want to make things worse. She's probably just had the shit scared out of her, and she doesn't need me firing off questions. I'll follow up tomorrow after she's had some sleep and feels better.

Resting her head against the glass, she lets out a soft groan when I turn the corner.

"You gonna be sick?" I slow down a little.

She shakes her head, but I don't know if I believe her.

As soon as we get to the house, I jerk to a stop in the driveway and race around the truck. I'm expecting her to complain that I'm opening the door for her, but she doesn't say a word and lets me carry her into the house and all the way up to my bedroom.

Laying her down on the bed, I take off her heels and figure she can sleep in the dress. I've just taken her away from one creep; I'm not about to go undressing her, even if she would be more comfortable sleeping in her underwear.

"C'mere," she mumbles.

"Huh?"

"Come." Slow, uncoordinated fingers beckon me, and I snicker at her drunken smile, walking back up the bed while she rises to her knees. "Thank you." She rests her hands on my waist. "Thank you for saving me tonight."

My throat grows thick, and all I can do is brush my hands lightly through her hair and swallow whatever this feeling is.

Her glazed eyes are dreamy, glimmering with a smile as she tugs on my shirt and pulls me down. I go with it, sliding my tongue against hers as she wrecks me with a kiss that's uninhibited. It's scorching, sloppy, wet, and I can't resist it when she moans into my mouth and deepens it a little further. I drop to my knees on the edge of the bed, gliding my hands around her hips and up her back while this blaring alarm goes off in the back of my brain.

She's drunk!

Don't take advantage!

Step away!

"Do you really want to be doing this?" I murmur between kisses.

"Yes." She leans back, giving me this incredulous look. "Do you have any idea how hot you are?"

I grin, brushing my thumb across her glossy lips. "Yeah, but you're drunk. I don't want you kissing me if you don't know what you're doing."

"Oh, I know what I'm doing." Her smirk is comically smug. "I know exactly what I'm doing."

That sultry voice turns my semi into a ridge of granite, and when she unzips my jeans, then yanks down my boxer briefs, it springs free—hungry and eager to party.

"Well, hello, beautiful." Her giggle is relaxed and breathy.

I should stop this.

But then she wraps her fingers around my shaft and I'm blinded for a second. The moment the tip of her tongue licks that bead of moisture off my head, I let out an aching groan that makes all thought impossible.

Her sweet lips suck me while her fingers grip the base of my cock and scatter stars across my vision. It's impossible not to sink my fingers into her hair, not to let out a guttural moan. I'm gonna blow like a fucking fireworks display in her mouth.

Clenching my butt cheeks, I try to hold out, gain some control.

No cum for a month.

The thought hits me and is then followed by a succession of painful darts.

She's drunk.
You can't sleep with her.
You don't want to walk around campus naked.
Don't take this risk.
It's just a blow job.
No one has to know.
I'll *know!*
Be the better man.
Be a man of your word.
Fuck! I can't let this happen.

"Wait," I rasp. "Just... wait." I jerk back, gently pushing on her shoulders until her lips pop off the end of my cock. My body aches with the abrupt loss while she looks up with a confused frown. But then her eyes seem to light with understanding, and she flops back on the bed and starts pushing the dress straps off her shoulders.

"What are you doing?"

"I want you. Let's do it." Her words are slow and slurred, which helps me battle off the near overwhelming temptation.

She's not wearing a bra, and those nipples of hers are sexy as sin. Pink and puckered, begging me to suck them again.

I close my eyes and grit out, "I'm not sure that's a great idea. You're wasted."

"I can still turn you on, baby." She giggles, and she's not wrong. When I open my eyes and catch a glimpse of her exposed torso, I can barely breathe.

I want to touch, explore every inch of that smooth skin with my fingertips, then follow it up with my tongue. I want to yank that dress off her hips, spread those legs, and—

The bet. Remember the fucking bet!

I wince, snapping my eyes shut again.

"What's wrong?"

"Uh..." I scrape my fingers through my hair. My hands are shaking as I fight for control and scramble for an answer that doesn't give away the truth. I'm not supposed to tell anyone.

I've never hated Asher more.

I've never hated *myself* more!

She huffs. "I'm not a virgin, if that's the problem. I mean, technically."

My eyes pop back open. "Technically?"

"Yeah, I've done it." Her eyebrows bunch. "Sort of."

"Sort of?"

She flops back on the bed with a sigh, her breasts jiggling. I avert my gaze, trying to focus on the fact that she's practically a virgin. It's actually helping, because there's no way in hell I'm doing this with her if she's not 100 percent aware of it. She's not some puck bunny who gets off on tipsy sex romps. She's a freshman who has sort of, technically, done it once.

"I don't know if he finished." She groans, her eyes dipping shut. "It was kind of fast, and then he got off me and was fire-engine red and mumbled something, then left. And I was like... that's it? Why do people make such a big deal about this, you know?" She starts giggling, then rolls onto her side and looks at me. Her floppy hand drags down my arm. "But then I see you, and I'm pretty sure I'd feel it and it wouldn't be quick and you'd make me come. And I want to make you come. I want to make you feel good. And then you can make me feel good, and it'll be allllllllll good." Her words are getting sloppier by the second, and...

Holy shit, the guy didn't even make her come?

What kind of fucktard doesn't pleasure his woman?

What kind of asshole doesn't understand the art of foreplay?

We're not taking this one step further. If I ever get the chance to give this girl an orgasm, I want that memory tattooed on her brain for eternity.

Her eyes drift shut again, her words wispy and slurred. "Let's come together." And then she's gone, drifting away on a sleep she never even saw coming.

I gaze down at her relaxed face, skimming my finger over her ear and down her jawline.

"One day, baby. And you'll remember every second of it," I whisper, brushing my lips over her forehead. "I just need you to wait for me."

For some reason, my voice has gone thick with emotion. I don't know what's wrong with me or what this sensation in my chest means, but it's disconcerting.

Clearing my throat, I go into practical mode, hiking the dress back up her body and making her decent again. I'd prefer to strip it off and let her sleep in one of my T-shirts, but I don't want the guys making all the wrong assumptions. They will anyway, but at least if they walk in, trying to bust me, they'll see her tucked up in my bed, fully dressed, with me lying on the outside of the covers.

I wrestle the duvet out from under her body and get her tucked into my bed before lying down beside her. I rest my arm under my head and gaze up at the ceiling as Mikayla lets out these soft snores that are downright adorable.

What I wouldn't give to roll over right now and spoon with her.

What I wouldn't give to do exactly what she'd asked me to and make her come, then make her feel every inch of me as I took her over the edge of ecstasy.

My cock stirs, reminding me he's still there and still waiting... all the more impatiently.

But I won't break this bet.

Just like I shouldn't break any other rules, like bringing romance into my college experience.

Clenching my jaw, I grip my fist beneath my head and try to fall asleep, reminding myself of that very thing.

I'm not here to fall in love. I'm here to make the pros and get a degree. That's all. That's all it can be.

CHAPTER 27
MIKAYLA

I crack my eyes open, my slushy brain wrestling free of this black oblivion that—

Nope.

I snap my eyes shut again.

The searing light that's trying to burn a hole through my retinas is pure torture. As is the pounding in my head, and the fact that I'm pretty sure a skunk farted in my mouth last night.

I groan, my stomach roiling as I lick my lips and try to sit up.

Nope.

I flop back down again, my feeble moan disrupted by a soft snicker.

"Rough night?"

"What?" I croak.

"Here." The bed moves beside me, and I smell him— the sweet, fresh scent that is all heaven.

Ethan.

"Drink this." His fingers are feather soft as he brushes them over my ear.

Braving the light again, I force my eyes back open and eventually make out his thick, jean-clad thighs, his crumpled T-shirt, and then the glass of water he's holding.

"You need to rehydrate."

Wincing, I try to sit up, but my body seriously feels like it's been hit by a bulldozer.

What the hell did I do last night?

Ethan's arm comes around me, helping me to sit. I lean against him, my hand shaking as I hold the glass and try to drink. Water dribbles down my chin, but I force it down, knowing Ethan's probably right about the whole hydrating thing.

Hangovers suck.

This is why I don't drink.

The first time I got drunk off my ass was at Rachel's place. We were sixteen and curious, and it's lucky we both didn't die of alcohol poisoning. When her mom walked in the door, she read us the riot act. Apparently. I don't remember it, so she did a replay the next morning as we sat there nursing killer migraines. She made us clean her entire house, and then we had to go to my place and confess all... then clean Mom's house too.

Worst. Day. Of. My. Life.

Well, second worst.

A pain that seems more vibrant in my current condition scorches me, and I'm suddenly fighting the urge to sob uncontrollably.

"Hey, it's okay." Ethan takes the glass off me and lays me back down. "You'll feel better soon. Let me get you some Advil."

He walks out of the room, and my eyes rove the space. I'm on a big double bed, tucked under the covers. The space beside me is still neatly made, which makes me think we didn't do anything last night.

My scrambled brain tries to piece together what went down, fragments of unease filtering through me as the blurry images flash past my mind's eye. We kissed on this bed, but then... I can't remember.

My eyes bulge as I picture myself giving him a blow job, but... I don't remember how that ended, and then my stomach starts churning as I recall some guy's hands on my ass, me pushing him away. Ethan roared. He shoved a guy. I remember that. And then—

I bolt upright, my head spinning. I hold it with a groan as the faces of my Sig Be sisters appear crystal clear. They were pissed.

"I screwed up," I whisper.

The door pops open, and Ethan reappears with two red pills. I take them without question, trusting him because he's good and kind and carried me out of the party and doesn't deserve to be publicly humiliated.

I guzzle the pills, willing them to work at lightning speed. Setting the glass down, I nearly spill it, and Ethan grabs it before it hits the floor.

"I take it you don't drink much," he murmurs.

"No," I croak.

"So, why'd you get so wasted last night?"

"Because I'm an idiot?" I frown.

He laughs and tucks my hair behind my ears before his gaze turns serious. "It could have gone pretty bad, lil' mouse. You scared me. Who was that guy?"

I shake my head, trying to get out of this. I can't tell

him. How do I look at that beautiful face and confess the truth? He'll be so pissed, and then he'll stop tucking my hair behind my ear and giving me these gentle smiles.

So, I lie.

Like a coward, I mumble, "What guy?"

His expression turns dark, and for a moment, I think he's pissed at me for trying to pull a fast one on him, but then he growls, "The one who was dragging you down the hallway. Ignoring you when you told him you weren't interested. You yelled at him to let go, and he still wouldn't take his fucking hands off you."

I touch Ethan's arm, the move instantly calming him. Sort of. His breaths are kind of punchy and his muscles are vibrating beneath my fingers.

"Thank you for keeping an eye on me."

"I didn't do a very good job." He shakes his head, his expression pained. "I couldn't find you... and what if I'd been too late?"

My expression crumples, and there are those tears again, burning the back of my throat. I swallow them down and manage to whisper, "But you weren't."

Touching his face, I rub my thumb across his cheek and give him a grateful smile.

Crap, I can't hurt this man. I have to come clean and tell him about the initiation. My stomach clenches as my muddy brain tries to conjure the best words for this big confession.

"Ethan," I rasp.

"Yeah?" His eyes soften with a look I've never seen before.

It steals all my words, and I'm frozen still as his lips curl at the corners and he flashes me one of his smiles.

I don't want to lose that. I want him to keep staring at me this way for the rest of... forever.

With a soft snicker, he leans into me with a feather-light kiss that I want to deepen, but the door swings open before I can.

"Ah-huh! Busted!" Asher crows, then takes in the scene, his face bunching with confusion. "Wait. What did you guys do last night?"

Ethan stands with this dark look on his face, stalking toward the door. "Nothing happened, and fucking knock next time!" Shoving his friend out the door with one hard push, Ethan slams it shut and turns back to face me.

"What was that all about?" I try to laugh, but it comes out like a croaky snicker.

"Nothin'." Ethan shakes his head, and I can tell he's not being honest, but that's okay because I can't tell him the truth about the party, so let's just call it even.

I lean back against the headboard and take in the rest of his room. It's pretty simple with just a few hockey posters on the wall—action shots that no doubt inspire him. His dresser is in the corner, two of the drawers not closed properly as T-shirts and a pair of socks pop out over the side. There's a framed family photo on the top, which I must check out when I can find the strength to make my concrete body stand and move around the room.

And then there's his desk, covered with open books and obvious study notes along with his laptop.

"Studious," I mumble.

"Huh?" He looks over his shoulder.

"Your desk. You obviously study."

"Oh, yeah." He shrugs. "What's the point of being here if I don't?"

"I thought you'd be all about hockey."

I watch his face as he turns back to grin at me.

"Hockey is king, but study's queen. I need it as my backup. And I like what I'm learning, so it's not that bad. Sports science is interesting, you know?"

I nod, knowing it is. Anatomy, nutrition, all that stuff has always interested me too. But I've still got my heart set on being an agent.

"So... lil' mouse." Ethan shoves his hands in his pockets, walking around the bed and taking another seat beside me. His arm comes over my legs, and I can't help smiling as he boxes me in.

It feels good, safe, thrilling.

"What are we gonna do today?" His eyes seem to sparkle, and I can't take tear my gaze away from his.

My lips flirt with a giddy grin while my pounding head reminds me that I won't be up for much.

"I'm thinking—" He runs his fingers gently down my arm. "—some carbs, a ton more fluids, and even more rest."

"Wow," I croak. "Sounds exciting."

He laughs, then kisses the tip of my nose. "Stay here. Rest. I'll be back soon."

And once again, he's gone. I close my eyes with a relaxed sigh until images of sisterly glares fill my brain.

"Shit," I mutter, rubbing my forehead and wondering how the hell I'm gonna walk back into the house today. They'll slaughter me. Not literally, but they'll make me feel like crap for not following through last night.

I'm gonna get kicked out of that house, and then I'm screwed.

"Here we go." Ethan swans back in with a tray full of food and a smile so damn sweet that I'll be breaking my own heart into a thousand pieces when I hurt him.

I have to get out of this initiation somehow.

Placing the tray of toast beside me, he snatches a triangle and starts munching while I tentatively pick off a corner and nibble it between my lips.

A large T-shirt lands on my head. "Hey."

I pull the cotton away while Ethan stands there chuckling. "Feel free to put that on if it'll be more comfortable for you. The bathroom is down the hall, on your left."

Slipping off the bed, I pad out of the room to relieve myself, then change into Ethan's monstrous T-shirt. It must be big on him, surely, because it practically touches my knees. Sneaking back out into the hallway, I'm relieved there's no one else around as I dash back to his room.

He's on the bed, setting up his laptop when I close the door behind me. He glances up, his smile faltering when he drinks me in, and then he swallows.

For a second, I think I spot pure hunger, but it's gone so fast I must have just imagined it. A blurry memory of me trying to give him a blow job, then him gently pushing me away, makes my stomach pitch. I busy myself by laying the dress over his desk chair so I don't have to look at him.

"Can I borrow a pair of socks? My feet are cold."

"Of course."

I grab the pair sticking out of his drawer and take a

minute to look at the family photo. A young Ethan is standing in between his parents, beaming at the camera. His mother is laughing while his father grins at her. It's a happy, beautiful moment in time, and my throat swells, thinking about how Ethan will never have that again. His mother will never drape her arm around his shoulders again. He'll never hear her laughter. He'll try to remember it, but the sound will inevitably fade.

I know.

Because I can't hear my dad anymore.

Swallowing, I shuffle back to the bed and pull Ethan's socks on while lifting my chin at his laptop. "What are you doing?"

"When I'm hungover, I want comfort TV."

"Oh yeah?" I grab a triangle of toast. "And what's your comfort TV?"

"Sports movies."

"Of course." I laugh. "Let me guess: hockey, right?"

"Not necessarily."

Oh my gosh, his face is adorable.

"I've seen *The Blind Side* and *We Are Marshall* about ten times each, and *Point Break* is my jam, although I prefer the original version."

"Smart man," I agree.

He grins. "But when I'm feeling as shitty as you are right now, there's really only one series that will suffice."

"O-kay." The look on his face is making me suspicious.

Then he starts wiggling his eyebrows. "Mighty Ducks."

I burst out laughing. "Mighty Ducks?"

"Oh yeah, baby. We're gonna watch all three."

With a mock groan, I cover my eyes while he lets out this gleeful little laugh and lines it up. We nestle into the pillows, instinctively leaning toward each other. My cheek is soon resting against his shoulder as I nibble my toast and watch. I think I've seen the first one, maybe. I can't quite remember. It's kind of old, but in my state, it's perfect.

And yes, I'm the girl shouting at the screen during the final game, begging the team to win and prove what they're made of. Not great for the headache, but totally worth it.

Ethan's laughing at me while he loads up the second movie, and I end up snuggled against his chest for that one, his arm around my back.

Yep. It's heaven.

And as the second movie comes to an end, my headache has eased while the rest of my body has become hyperaware of his every movement. The way his muscles shift and twitch beneath me. The strength of his body is phenomenal, and my entire body is tingling, making the third movie harder and harder to watch.

I rest my hand across his stomach, desperately wanting to lift the soft cotton and explore the skin beneath. But he pushed me away last night. As my head clears, the memory comes back with more clarity. I wanted to make him come. You know, kind of a little thank-you for carrying me out of that party. Plus, I wanted to hear him moan. I loved the way his fingers dug into my hair, and I wanted to feel his body jerk and fall apart.

I've given a couple of blow jobs in my time, and

there's a certain triumph to it, but it wasn't about that last night. I just wanted Ethan to feel pleasure. Bliss. Ecstasy.

But he wouldn't let me.

The thought sits ugly and heavy in my stomach, ruining the last movie for me. Why wouldn't he let me do that for him?

Unless he's just a really good guy who didn't want to take advantage of a drunk girl.

I try to focus on that fact, spinning it around until I feel better. He was just protecting me. Being a gentleman.

So, do I...?

My hand inches down his body. He tenses. I grin when I notice the rising tent in his pants, but then he shifts, letting out this awkward laugh.

"Good movie, right? I think the third one's my favorite."

I force my eyes back to the screen and nod. "Yeah, it's great."

Hiding my disappointment will be impossible if I keep talking, so I grit my teeth and keep my hand on his stomach, begging myself to just focus on the movie and the comfort of being wrapped in Ethan's embrace.

But it's damn hard work, and by the time the movie's done, I'm ready to leave. Being this close to the guy and not being able to do anything about the fire burning through my muscles is a weird kind of torture.

"Well, I should—"

"Wanna play a game?" Ethan sets his laptop on the desk and pulls out a pack of cards, wiggling them in the air with a grin.

"Huh?"

"A game. Rummy, maybe?"

"You... want to play rummy?"

"Yeah." He shrugs and grins at me. "Got a problem with that?"

"I just..." Closing my eyes, I shake my head. "I thought I should probably go."

"Aw, come on. You don't have to go yet."

I let out an awkward laugh, wishing I could explain how difficult it is to be around him without sounding like some kind of sex fiend.

"Look." He sighs. "It's my day off, and I just want to spend it with you. Hang with me, lil' mouse. Play cards. Eat junk food with me."

I narrow my eyes at him. "What are you really playing at?"

"Nothing." His eyebrows pop up. "I genuinely like spending time with you."

My cheeks burst with heat, and I have to look to the floor, biting my lips together so a giddy giggle doesn't burst out of me. With a little sniff, I pull myself together and try to sound unaffected as I murmur, "I like hanging out with you too."

"Excellent. Then come over here and sit down." He slaps the bed. "Let me kick your ass at rummy."

I laugh and walk over to the bed, dropping to my knees and collecting the cards he's dealing to me.

And that's how my afternoon goes. Playing rummy and laughing my ass off. I love the way we can play off each other's jokes and banter. He hassles me for being obsessed with Justin Bieber when I was twelve, and I hassle him for owning a Kanye West album.

"I can't believe you were into rap."

"It was a phase!" He shakes his head, his cheeks brighter than the sun.

We eat toast, popcorn, and enough gummy bears to make me feel sick again. If it wasn't for the gallons of water I was drinking, I'd be on a total sugar high. Along with all that, I find out that he's a damn good rummy player, that we've both read every Goosebumps novel ever published, and that visiting Hobbiton in New Zealand is on both our bucket lists.

So yeah, *not* falling for this guy has become an impossible task.

The feeling grows with each passing minute, and by the time five o'clock rolls around, I seriously need to bail or he'll have my heart for good.

I change back into my dress, staring at my reflection in the bathroom mirror and trying to quell the giddy bugs dancing in my chest.

He's freaking amazing!

Calm down. You can't have him.

But you can't stop yourself either!

Gritting my teeth, I shuffle back to the room, bumping into a shirtless Casey along the way. *Holy hell. Is drop-dead gorgeous a requirement to live in this place?* I can't help glancing over my shoulder and checking out his back, which is covered by a massive dragon tattoo. An entire Chinese scene that I want to stop and study. But he must sense my gaze, because he turns back and catches my eye, giving me an all-knowing grin that sets my cheeks on fire.

If I react that way to Casey, I'm pretty sure my entire body will melt if I ever get to see Ethan shirtless again.

"Hey, you good?" Ethan's sharp eyes must read something on my face when I walk in the door, and I scramble to even out my expression.

"Yeah." I throw the shirt at him. "Thanks for the loan."

"Anytime." He grins, tossing it on the end of his bed before raking his eyes over me.

I tug at the dress, pulling it down my thighs, before snatching my heels off the floor. "Well, I better get back."

"I'll drive you."

"No, that's okay. I'll walk."

He gives me a skeptical frown. "In those heels?"

I hold them up with a laugh. "These things? No way. I'm walking home barefoot."

This answer seems to please him. The smile on his face makes my heart kick out of rhythm, and yeah, I really need to leave now.

"Okay, well... um, thanks for the day. You're awesome... and I'm gonna go."

"Let me at least walk you."

"No." I shake my head. "I don't need an escort."

"What if I want to escort you?" He grins.

I smile right back. "What if I need a minute to call my girl in Cali and tell her about this super-hot guy I've been hanging with today?"

He saunters across the room with this cocky grin and stops right in front of me. Cupping my cheeks, he gazes down at me like I'm special, and even that's enough to turn my weak insides to goo.

And then he kisses me.

It's hot and searing and over too fast.

It turns my legs to sticks of chewed gum, making my walk down the stairs hard work. Liam notices me in the entrance and gives me a worried frown before spotting Ethan behind me.

I wonder what that look means, but then he's grinning. "Hey, Mick."

"Hey, Padre," I murmur, glancing over my shoulder at Ethan.

His smile is extra bright, making me wonder what he must have signaled to his friend behind my back. I want to ask him about it, but then I don't because I really should get out of here. I've gotta call Rachel. I need to unpack this stuff with the only person in this world I 100 percent trust.

"See ya."

"Definitely." Ethan leans against the doorframe, watching me walk down the path. "You're still coming to the exhibition game, right?"

I spin and smile at him. "You know it!" This answer makes him happy, and that goo in my chest goes all warm and soft and... yeah, I really need to call Ray-Ray.

Pulling out my phone, I touch Rachel's name on my screen.

She answers after four rings, sounding kind of breathless.

"Hey, bestie."

"Hey." I squint against the sunshine, wishing I had my shades. "What's up? Why are you out of breath?"

She giggles, and I groan.

"Ugh. Do I even want to know?"

She laughs again. "I was just doing a workout."

"Really? Since when? You haven't turned into a gym bunny since I've been away, have you?"

"No, I'm just doing these Zumba classes online. In my room."

"Wow." I raise my eyebrows, kind of impressed. Rachel's always been allergic to exercise. That's basically the one thing we don't have in common. I'd run track and she'd watch from the bleachers. I'd jump in on a basketball game while she cheered me on from the sidelines. In middle school, I'd actually get involved during PE classes and she'd linger in the background, avoiding the ball at all costs. She even tried the *I'm allergic to sweat* line once with our PE teacher but was made to run two extra laps for lying.

She quickly learned that her best defense was the *I have my period* card, and she served that up once a month like clockwork.

And now she's doing Zumba in her room.

"That's awesome. I'm proud of you." I grin. "You've always been a great dancer. Zumba is the perfect exercise for you."

"I know it." She laughs. "It was actually Theo's idea. He's into the gym and wants me to be fit and healthy too."

"Nice." I nod, impressed by the guy. I like that he's encouraging my girl this way. For a second, it makes me want to tell her about Ethan. About the awesome day I've just had—how he took care of me, nursed me through a hangover, made me forget about all the angst from the Sig Be house and just let me be myself.

That is why I called her, right?

But for some reason, I can't get the words out, because then I'll have to admit that I'm falling for him, and it'll no doubt come to light that I'm supposed to hurt the guy and she'll be totally ashamed of me.

"So, actually, I was going to call you today because I have some news," Rachel says.

"Oh yeah?" I blink, relieved by the fact that we can focus solely on her.

"Yeah, um... you know how Mom's leaving, and I was feeling kind of edgy about living on my own?"

I gasp. "Did you find a roommate?"

"Sort of."

"What do you mean, sort of?"

"Well... Theo's asked me to move in with him. And I've said yes."

I stutter to a stop, my bare feet scraping on the pavement. "What?"

"He asked me to move in with him." Her voice gets brighter and perkier. I can't tell if it's forced or if she really means it.

Dammit, why didn't I video-call her? I need to see her face for this.

I nearly tell her I'm hanging up to call her back, but she's gushing on about how great it is that everything is working out. The timing is perfect. Her mom will leave, they'll rent out the house for extra income, and she'll move in with Theo.

I really don't want to kill her happy buzz, but surely I have to say something, right?

"Wow, that's... really fast." I say it softly, hoping I don't ruin her happy vibe.

She doesn't seem to notice my obvious trepidation over her big news, because she lets out this giddy laugh. "Well, when you know, you know, right?"

My stomach sinks as images of Ethan's beautiful face flash through my mind. Crap. My heart totally gets what

Rachel is saying, because today, when I let myself forget everything else, I swear I knew. I knew I was already falling for Ethan, and it was the easiest thing in the world.

And somehow, I'm supposed to shit all over it... sabotage this beautiful thing so I can get myself a free education.

I can't let that happen.

So how do I get both?

CHAPTER 28
ETHAN

It's been four days, and I can't stop thinking about Mikayla. She's in my head night and day. And yeah, it's driving me crazy.

Sunday was one of the best days I've ever had.

All we did was watch movies, play cards, and talk while time disappeared. No big deal. But I've never done that with a girl before, and it was epic.

It was epic because it was Mikayla.

She's not just hot, she's awesome.

Checking my phone, I grin at her latest string of emojis. Yeah, we're still playing that game, and I've worked out that she's telling me good luck for tonight. She said she was coming. I have no idea where she'll be sitting, but I'll be looking out for her.

"Okay, boys, let's go! Five minutes!" Coach is clapping his hands, and I shove my phone in my locker, slapping it closed and trying to shake Mikayla from my mind.

I need to focus.

First game of the season. It's only an exhibition one, but in my mind, it still counts. We've got to come out strong, show we're a contender this year. I want to win, and I want to win good.

Stamping my skates on the ground, I grab my stick and thump it against my chest, closing my eyes and going through my usual pregame ritual. I've been doing it since I was six, when I joined my first team and my dad coached us.

He's given so much to me and this game. It's his heart and passion that inspired me, his devotion that kept me skating when I got bored during my tweens. He kept pushing and dragged me into high school hockey, where his desire became my own. I owe him so much.

He's here tonight. He drives up from Denver whenever he can, and I know he'll be watching me with pride. And so will Mom. The idea makes me smile, as does the thought that no matter how I play, Dad always finds a way to make me feel like I did all right. Even when I puck up—as he likes to call it—he'll be there with words of advice or comfort.

I'm his star player, and I want to make him proud.

Which is why I can't go fucking up on this bet. I can't sleep with Mikayla yet.

I can't risk having to walk around campus naked. I can't risk getting arrested or kicked off the team for acting like a douche nugget.

Which means I should probably stop texting Mikayla, thinking about her, hanging out with her.

If she wasn't so fun to be around, this would be a hell of a lot easier. Why do I have to find her so attractive? I'd love to just slip into the friend zone with her. It'd be awesome. But one look into those eyes and I'm done for. Those lips of hers—I've tasted them now, felt them around my cock. There's no way I can be *just friends* with this girl. The scary thing is I'd like to be more.

She's not a quick fuck. She's girlfriend material.

"Shit," I mutter under my breath, thrown from the visualization technique Dad taught me. The one where I picture myself on the ice, skating perfectly, controlling the puck, passing it off, gathering it up, firing it into the goal.

Instead, my mind is filled with Mikayla and how much I want her and how that's such dangerous ground.

With a soft growl, I try to shove her into the back of my brain and focus up.

"We have to win tonight, guys. No excuses. No fuck-ups!" Jason yells across the locker room.

Great pep talk, man. Thanks.

"Okay, men, let's do this!" Coach rounds us up for a quick pregame pep talk, which is actually a good one. He goes over a few of the key pointers we've been working on leading up to this game before sending us out to the ice.

The second my skates hit that smooth surface and I hear the roar of the crowd around me, I'm able to center myself again.

This is what it's about.

This team. This game.

I can't go messing it up over a girl.

Spotting my dad in the crowd, I raise my stick and earn myself a proud grin. Then I force myself not to hunt the crowd for Mikayla.

Even after the month is up and I can finally have her all the way... do I seriously want that?

College isn't for girlfriends and romance.

I need to get my head in the game and keep it there.

CHAPTER 29
MIKAYLA

The arena is packed when I get there, but I manage to find a seat next to a redhead with apple-green eyes who talks a mile a minute. She doesn't even know me, but the second I sit down, she introduces herself.

"Caroline." She grins, her smile a bright beam like she's in her personal happy place.

I give her a polite smile, then glance at her friend, who gives me an uninterested look before going back to her phone.

"That's Leilani. Ignore her. She's pissed at me because I made her come to the game. But who wants to come on their own, right?" Her cheery voice falters, her lips opening for a second as she stutters, "I-I mean, not that there's anything wrong with coming on your own, of course. Like, you're not a loser or anything."

"I know." I grin at her, trying not to laugh at how flustered she's getting or how pink her cheeks are turning right now.

"Maybe you should just stop talking, Caroline," her

friend mutters dryly. "You know, it's this thing you do where you close your mouth and don't let the words come out."

Caroline nudges her friend with an abashed grin before focusing on the players.

The Cougars have just skated onto the ice. The crowd was deafening, and I'm very aware that I am currently surrounded by passionate hockey fiends.

"That's Liam Carlisle." Caroline points, leaning into me like I'm her friend and I want to know all this stuff. "He's one of the strongest defensemen on this team. And that's Asher Bensen. He's on the wing along with... Casey Pierce!" Her voice hitches and she practically swoons against me, rattling off stats about the guy I saw shirtless on Sunday.

Oh man, what if I told her? She'd probably have a conniption.

I decide not to say anything, keeping my eyes on Ethan as soon as she points him out to me. He glides around the ice, looking in control and totally focused. It's kind of—100 percent—sexy and impressive how good he is. Damn, he's fast.

According to Caroline, who seems to be a walking Wikipedia page when it comes to this game, Ethan Galloway plays center and is one of the most dynamic players Nolan U has ever seen.

Pride punches through me, and I start watching the game with interest. Caroline must have some kind of sixth sense that I don't know much about hockey because she's firing out rules and teaching me as we go.

I nearly tell her she should be a hockey commentator, but I don't get a chance because the Cougars slap the puck into the goal, and the crowd is on their feet and jumping with wild shouts.

I join them, bolstered by the energy in this place. It's hard not to get into it.

We sit back down, and Caroline continues her jabbering while I get fully absorbed in the game. My eyes start to home in on that puck, and I follow it across the ice, my body jerking along with the players when they capture it or slap it toward the goal or pass it off with a little flick.

This is awesome!

It's a much-needed relief after the week I've had in the sorority house. The grief Aimee and Fiona gave me over the Damien debacle has been a nightmare. Apparently, he stopped by the house on Sunday and had this massive rant. Thank God I wasn't there.

But I still paid a price when I eventually got home. Talk about being chewed out. It was worse than a lecture from my mother. I then got put on cleaning detail. I mean, seriously, what is up with that? It's like everyone in my life knows the worst way to punish me is to make me clean shit. And not just clean; I had to make the house sparkle. One little screwup and I'm freaking Cinderella.

I have assured them that, yes, I may have gotten too drunk to follow through on Saturday, but I wasn't done yet. What I really wanted to say was "Everyone can just fuck off because I am *not* doing this anymore." But I chickened out when I thought about Aimee calling to complain to her dad about me and my funding getting instantly cut.

Instead, I managed to squeeze in the fact that Damien was way too handsy for his own good, which scored me sympathy and concern from a few sisters, but cold-hearted Fiona didn't seem to give a shit. I lost them money, and she's not gonna let me forget it.

Thankfully, I managed to argue my way out of it by pointing out that Ethan protected me and nursed me through my hangover, which means he obviously likes me. It was like pulling burning knives out of my throat to admit that, because the idea of hurting him is killing me.

I seriously can't go through with this, but I'm still not sure how to get out of it.

"You had your perfect moment, and you screwed it up," Aimee spat at me. "We're not giving you any more chances. You finish this, Mikayla... or you're out."

And so I dragged my butt to this game, telling myself it was under duress. But now that I'm here, I can stop lying to myself. Without the watchful gaze of the Sig Be sisters, I can pretend that I'm just some girl who wants to learn about hockey and watch the guy she's crushing on play a decent game.

I hiss when he's smashed against the dasher boards, then cheer when he gets his own back a few minutes later. I roar when he sets up a beautiful pass that results in a sweet goal, and I jump to my feet and start screaming when he ends the second period with a sweet flick into the net.

"Yes!"

Caroline and I jump beside each other like we're pals with years' worth of history.

"I love this game!" I shout at her.

She laughs, throwing her head back. "It's the best!"

CHAPTER 30
ETHAN

I raise my arms, skating in a circle and crashing into Casey, who's coming over to congratulate me. It's a pretty sweet moment and only made better when I spot Mikayla in the stands.

She's jumping and celebrating with some redhead.

The moment I catch her eye, her face lights with a grin so big, I swear my heart wants to beat across the ice and get to her as fast as it can.

I grin and skate away, my insides thumping as my resolve to distance myself from this girl flies out the window.

I swear, this is gonna do my head in, but damn if I don't play some of the best hockey I ever have, knowing she's in the stands cheering me on.

When the final buzzer sounds, the high-scoring game ends with a 7–4 victory for the Nolan U Cougars. The crowd is going ballistic. I raise my stick to my dad, who's clapping and grinning like I've just won a gold medal, and then I spin to find Mikayla. The smile on her face is something else again, and when I find her waiting for me after I've showered up, I can't help running over to her and plucking her off the ground. Her legs wrap around my waist as she hugs me tight and laughs in my ear.

"You were incredible!" Leaning back, she holds my face and stares at me in wonder. "I think I've found my new favorite sport."

"Seriously?" I grin.

She shrugs like it's no big deal, and I hold her for longer than I need to, carrying her all the way to my truck, because how the hell am I supposed to put her down after she's just admitted to loving hockey?

Liam and Casey pile into the back seat, and Mikayla spins around to gush about how well they played. They blush like schoolboys who have a crush on their teacher, and I swear I've never felt so high. What a game.

I glance to my right. What a girl.

We head back to Hockey House, and Dad shows up a few minutes after we walk in the door with a stack of pizzas. He gets a cheer from the guys as we crack open beers and swarm the table for a slice. Mikayla sits beside me, the only girl in the house right now. I'm surprised more aren't here already. We usually get puck bunnies clinging to us after a game like that, but as I do a quick head count, I figure half the team has probably gone to Offside and the girls have followed them there. The half who don't know Jack Galloway.

"So, you must be pretty proud of your boy, sir." Mikayla grins across the table, dropping her pizza crust on the lid. I snatch it up and finish it for her. She's leaving the best part. Crazy woman.

"I certainly am." Dad winks at her. "I'm proud of all

these boys. You played like champions tonight, Cougars. It's gonna be a good season."

"Puck yeah!" we all roar, punching our arms in the air while Mikayla cringes and then starts laughing and shaking her head.

I grab another slice of pizza, ravenous after playing so hard, and down the thing in about four bites.

"Holy crap." Mikayla laughs out the words. "You've heard of this thing called chewing, right?"

"I'm hungry," I argue, crumbs flying off my lips. My mouth is still full, muffling my words.

"You're just jealous you can't finish a slice in four," Asher hassles her, his eyebrows wiggling.

This spark lights her eyes as she spins to face him. Holy shit, I love that look on her face right now. "You don't think I can finish in four?"

"Uh... no." Asher turns to laugh with Riley, pointing at her like she's so cute.

Her eyes narrow as she leans her elbows on the table. "Oh, I can finish in four. I just choose not to because I'm not a pig."

"Sure, sweetheart." Asher winks at her, grabbing his beer and taking a long swig as he leans back in his chair. He doesn't take his eyes off her, and when he plops the beer back down, he's trying not to laugh at the riled look on her face.

"Twenty bucks says I can."

Casey starts to laugh, sharing a look with me before dipping his head with a snicker.

"You're on." Asher takes his time to choose the biggest slice before handing it to her.

She looks just a touch nervous as she grabs the

mammoth slice and folds it in half. She darts her gaze at me, and I raise my eyebrows and nearly say, *"You don't have to do this,"* but she's already jamming the slice in her mouth.

Her first bite is huge and makes her cheeks puff out like a chipmunk. Thankfully, this isn't being timed, because she makes sure the entire bite is swallowed down before tackling the second mouthful.

Riley starts laughing as she struggles not to choke on her second, and soon everyone in the room has been drawn into the bet. She stands from her chair for the third bite, having to take an even bigger one in order to win. I watch her carefully, ready to jump up and pound her back if she starts fighting for air. Her little mouth is stretched to the limit as she tries to keep all the food in.

She's got one massive bite left. There's no way she can fit all that crust in, but she pauses to take a swig of my beer, and then Casey starts to clap. "Come on, lil' mouse!"

The guys join him, cheering her on as she climbs onto the chair, standing above us all while she forces down the last bite. At one point, I don't think she's going to make it. Placing her fist against her lips, she leans forward, and I jump up to make sure she's okay, but she holds up her hand to stop me and I sink back into the chair, watching her with a beaming smile as she works her way through that last bite, then punches her arms into the air. Sticking out her tongue and opening her mouth wide, she shows us all that she's done.

And the guys go ballistic, hassling the shit out of Asher while he digs a twenty from his back pocket and throws it across the table.

Mikayla wiggles her hips in a happy dance before

flopping into my lap. I catch her easily, kissing her cheek, then catching Dad's eye across the table. He grins at me, his gaze telling me I've found a keeper, before he takes a swig of his beer and leans back with this satisfied look on his face.

My chest expands as I glance down at Mikayla, who is now making a big show of plucking Asher's twenty off the table and folding it in half. The guys are still whooping and laughing along with her, and my dad is probably right.

I have found a keeper.

And that scares the living shit out of me.

CHAPTER 31
MIKAYLA

Twenty bucks means nothing compared to the pure triumph I'm feeling right now. I swear, I thought I was gonna lose that pizza twice. For one, I hate the crust. It's usually tough and a little crunchy—gimme soft, cheese-covered dough any day. Second, I have never finished a slice that big in four bites before, but no way in hell was I gonna let Asher get the better of me.

Pocketing the bill with a victorious smirk, I wiggle my eyebrows at Asher, who tries to be all *giving me the evils,* but he can't do it. He ends up laughing and shaking his head before sharing a look with Ethan that I don't understand.

I glance over my shoulder when I feel Ethan tense beneath me, but he just puts on a smile and rubs my back before pulling me against him and kissing my cheek again.

Turning my face, I steal a quick taste of his lips, which in retrospect was probably a bad idea, because now my entire body wants him, and it's not like I can give in to my animal instincts when his dad is sitting right across the table from me.

He seems like a cool guy. Reminds me a little of my dad, actually, which burns in ways I don't want to analyze. I shove the thought aside and focus on the noises around me. The stories from the ice, the reliving of the game and how in sync everyone felt. I listen to Mr. Galloway's feedback, impressed by his observations and the way he's so encouraging of every player. They seem to really love and admire him.

Ethan's a lucky guy.

I want in on this thing.

This entire thing.

I want to hang out here all the time. I want to be friends with these lovable, funny, loud hockey players. I want to listen to Ethan's dad tell me stories about when Ethan was a kid.

And the thought that I still haven't figured a way out of this initiation yet kills me.

Don't think about it. Be in the now. Enjoy your night.

Glancing over my shoulder again, I drink in Ethan's gorgeous face. The way he throws his head back with laughter, his hand resting on my hip while he talks to Casey. It all feels so easy and natural, sitting on his knee this way, pretending like I'm his girl.

I want to stay.

The thought of going back to the sorority house is like a bucket of ice on my head, so when there's a lull and the guys break away to different parts of the living area, I lean back against Ethan and guide his ear down to my lips.

"I'm having so much fun."

I feel his cheek rise with a grin. "Me too."

"I want to stay. Can I spend the night here?"

"Uh..." He tenses beneath me again, and that instant reaction is enough to kill my happy buzz in a heartbeat. I jump off his knee before he can stop me, creating a little distance between us with a few quick steps around the table.

He reaches out to grab my wrist, but I pull my hand back, forcing a smile in case anyone's watching.

Thankfully, they all seem distracted by an NHL game on the TV, and I can work through this humiliation without an attentive audience.

I can't believe I read it wrong.

He doesn't want me. I can tell by that awkward look on his face, that tight, almost cringing smile... that deep regret in his hazel eyes. He's about to say something hideous like "I'm sorry if I led you on, but... we're not a thing."

You're not worth sticking around for. You're not worth fighting for.

The words ring in my head.

He doesn't mind kissing me a little, but spending the night... sleeping with me... taking whatever the hell is going on between us to the next level?

Yeah, that's not going to happen.

And why should it? I'm a little mouse who he hardly knows. I'm not a hottie—one of those big-boobed puck bunnies who flaunts her body with ease. I'm the girl who shoves a slice of pizza down her throat for a measly twenty bucks.

I don't know why I'm upset, really. This is all for the best. I'm supposed to be publicly dumping his ass, not wanting to sleep with him or become his girlfriend or something.

We've just had some flirty fun, and Ethan's made it clear that's all he wants. It kind of solves my problem in some ways. I can just carry through with this bet and guarantee myself a place in the Sig Be house.

My chest feels like it's crumpling in on itself—a piece of aluminum foil being crushed by an unforgiving fist.

I try to ignore the painful sensation as I shove my hand in my pocket and point my thumb over my shoulder. "Well, I'm gonna get going, then."

"I thought you wanted to stay," he croaks, rising from his chair.

I shuffle away from the table, walking backward as he slowly moves toward me. With a forced laugh that I was hoping would sound light and unaffected but actually sounds more like a dog bark, I shake my head. "I don't think you want that."

His expression buckles with this agonized frown, and I turn my back on it, gripping the doorframe and forcing myself to call into the room. "Thanks for a good night, guys. I'm out!"

I raise my hand and wave at them.

There's a collective groan, a few complaints, one guy calls for me to stay... but it's not Ethan.

He's just standing there, staring at me with a look I don't want to decipher.

"See ya." I don't know what my lips are doing right now. I'm ordering them to smile, but my facial muscles are so tight and rigid, I honestly can't say if I'm grinning or grimacing.

"Mick, wait."

I don't.

I bolt for the door, trying to flee my embarrassment.

Why the hell did I have to ask?

Running down the front steps, I bump into Ethan's dad, who's walking back inside.

"Whoa." He steadies my arm. "You okay?"

"Yeah, I'm great." My voice is so forced and fake anyone could see through it.

His thick eyebrows dip into a frown, and he glances past me, exchanging a concerned look with Ethan.

"See ya," I squeak for the second time tonight and make a beeline for the sidewalk.

I don't give a shit that it's dark. I'm walking back to Greek Row, and Ethan is not going to stop me.

"Mikayla!" he calls again.

I pick up my pace, but so does he, and his long strides decimate the distance between us.

"Wait." He gently grabs my arm, pulling me to a stop.

"It's okay. I get it." I shake him off me, spinning to get this over with. "You like me as a friend. I'm just one of the guys. It happens all the time. Don't feel bad."

He tips his head with a droll look. "I don't kiss my guy friends. You're *not* just one of the guys, believe me."

"But I'm not your girl either, am I?" The words pop out before I can stop them, and I bite my lips together, wincing and regretting every syllable.

Especially when he doesn't deny it.

He just stands there, his mouth opening and closing like he's not sure what to say.

Well, he doesn't have to say a damn thing.

Actions always speak louder than words anyway, and I can tell by the tension vibrating off him right now that

I've said exactly what he's too scared to. It's sweet that he doesn't want to hurt my feelings and all, but why the fuck did he kiss me in the first place?

Maybe he did like me at first but quickly realized I'm just friend material.

I should be used to this by now, but for some reason, Ethan's rejection is the most brutal, the most painful.

Shit, I'm gonna cry.

I spin away from him, fighting the thickening in my throat and that horrible burning in my eyes.

"Mikayla, please, let's just talk about—"

"I don't want to talk about it." I rush out the words, raising my arm when I spot a car cruising past the house.

"What are you doing?" His voice takes on an urgent quality.

"Catching a ride." I run toward the car when it slows to a stop, grateful when I recognize the girl behind the wheel. "Hey, Lisa, are you heading past Greek Row?"

"Sure. I can go that way." She smiles at me, then spots Ethan over my shoulder. Her eyes light with pleasure.

"Hi." She lets out this nervous laugh, tinkling her fingers at him.

My stomach clenches as I fight the urge to scratch her eyes out and run around the side of the car.

Ethan stands there, eyeing me with this disappointed look on his face. He wasn't done talking, but tough shit. I was. I can't hear another man tell me they don't want me. Sure, they never say it so bluntly, but a girl knows.

I've put up with it enough times to read all the signs, and I can't hear those awkward excuses come out of Ethan's mouth.

I just can't.

CHAPTER 32
ETHAN

"Shit."

The car drives away, and I'm left there on the sidewalk watching my epic night turn to dust.

Why couldn't I have said, "Sure, you can stay"?

A million reasons crowd out my brain, from the commitment to not have a serious girlfriend in college to the very real concern that I can't spend another night with her and not give in to my desire.

She's so hot. Even stuffing pizza in her mouth.

If anything, that turned me on. Sure, not the chipmunk cheeks—as adorable as those were—but the fact that she fucking did it. She stuck it to Asher, and it was a thing of beauty.

She's fire. I love her spirit, and I wanted to wrap my arms around her, carry her up to my room, and follow through on every fantasy I've been having about this girl.

Every fantasy that I can't follow through on yet.

Dammit!

I've got one week to go.

But even then... do I want to give in?

Running a hand through my hair, I stare down the empty street and have to admit that taking it all the way with Mikayla—as awesome as that would be—could be a fatal mistake. I said no romance in college, and I meant it. I won't get distracted from my goals here. I can't.

"Hey."

I turn at the sound of my dad's voice.

"You okay?"

I nod, letting out a heavy sigh as I walk back toward him. He's leaning against his car, flicking the keys around his finger, obviously ready to make the drive back to Denver.

"Thanks for coming," I murmur. "I always love having you at the games." Digging my hands into my pockets, I scuff the concrete driveway with the toe of my sneaker.

"You played good hockey tonight, kid."

"Yeah." I grin. "It felt good."

"You saw her in the stands... and you upped your game. You played for her."

I clench my jaw, not wanting to admit it.

"You're in love with her."

My eyes shoot up to his, and I shake my head. "I don't know. It's new. I don't really... know her."

"Yeah, you do... I mean, sure, you're gonna keep peeling back those layers, but I saw your face tonight. You love her."

I sigh, those words ringing true in spite of the fact that I don't want them to be. It feels so fucking fast. I'm blindsided.

"It scares the shit out of you, doesn't it?"

I nod, gripping the back of my neck as that sad look

on her face rides through me again. She felt rejected tonight. Shit. I did that to her.

"Why?" Dad's soft question captures my attention.

"Huh?" I look up at him.

"Why are you so scared? It's love, Ethan, not the plague."

I punch out a laugh that's hollow and wooden. The short sound disappears in the air, and we're quickly left with nothing but my breathing and the clink of Dad's keys.

The man can wait it out as long as it takes. He's stubborn in his patience, and I eventually give in with a sigh. "I said no romance in college."

"Why?"

"Because it's a distraction."

He lets out a surprised laugh. "Not necessarily. I mean, yeah, sure. It's a distraction, but not one you need to be afraid of. I met your mother in college. She was the love of my life."

Clenching my jaw, I look away from him, this ugly sensation making my stomach roil.

"What is it?" Dad's voice sharpens and he pushes away from the car. "Just say it."

I shake my head.

"Son."

That tone yanks the words right out of me. Years of conditioning and I'm blurting out the truth before I can stop myself. "I don't want that for me."

"What? Love?" Dad's expression is comically incredulous. "You don't ever want to fall in love?"

I nod. One sharp movement—concise and clear.

Dad lets out a breathy laugh, all shock and bewilderment. "Why?"

"Because I..." Running a hand through my hair, I cup the back of my head and worry that I'll hurt him. But he's gonna keep pushing for the truth, so I make sure to keep my voice soft. "Because I saw how Mom's death destroyed you, and I don't want to be like that."

A flash of pain crosses his face. He swallows, nodding a few times while staring down at his keys. "It didn't destroy me." His voice is gravelly, and I wonder how much of that lie he believes.

"You shut down... for months. And when you came back, you... It's never been the same. You've never even dated again."

He shrugs. "I'm a one-woman guy. I can't ever love someone like I loved her."

"So you're just gonna spend the rest of your life alone?" I stretch my arms wide, giving him a pointed look that surely settles this argument. Love opens you up to a world of pain. Dad's never been able to move on, and I don't want to spend my life celibate and lonely. I'd rather have a ton of casual flings than have my heart shattered into a million pieces.

Dad lets out a soft sigh. "I'm not opposed to dating again one day, but until I find someone as cool as your mom, I'm happy on my own."

I shake my head with a skeptical frown.

"I *am* happy, Ethan. I love my life."

"So do I. Which is why I like to keep things casual. It's easier. Way less complicated."

"Yeah, but..." Dad's expression crumples as he points down the road. "That girl. She's one of kind. And if you do casual with her, she's gonna walk out of your life and end up with someone else."

The words are a fist to the face. A green haze blurs my vision as I imagine some other guy holding her, kissing her, making her moan.

I snap my eyes shut with a soft growl.

"Don't do this to yourself." Dad's voice is a quiet lilt, a soft pleading for me to hear him. "You'll regret it. Knowing you could have had her and chose to walk away...that'll be on you for the rest of your life."

"What if I lose her?" My voice is raw and trembling.

Dad pauses, his sad smile enough to tear my heart in half. "Yeah." He nods, laying his hand on my shoulder. "What if you do?"

I stare down at him, shaking my head in confusion.

He sighs, patting me twice before dropping his arm back down to his side. "Do you want to know one of my biggest regrets that I will never get over?"

My eyes start burning. This is gonna be about Mom. I can tell.

"I never took your mom to Disneyland. She wanted to go, and at first it was a case of not having enough money, and then it was a case of not having enough time, and then she got sick and..." He swallows. "And we said we'd go when she got better."

I blink and rasp, "And she never got better."

Dad sniffs, his head bobbing in that way he does when the emotion is raw and painful. He squeezes the keys in his fist. "I couldn't do it after that. Couldn't go there without her."

So that's why he never took me. I had to go with my cousins instead. We did a family trip to Los Angeles, and Dad had to work. But maybe he didn't really have to.

"I'll never walk into that magical place... because she never got to. And that's on me." His eyes glimmer with unshed tears. "And I should have made it happen, because then I'd have this amazing memory of us being there together."

My memories are still pretty fresh. It was only two and a half years ago. It was a big graduation celebration for me and my cousin Lacey. It bothered me a little at the time that I had to be there without Dad, but I got it. Now it bothers me a whole lot because the truth fucking sucks.

"Life is meant to be lived in the here and now." Dad's voice is still thick with emotion, but it's clearing. His tears aren't slipping free as he gains control and looks at me with that confident wisdom he carries so easily. "You can plan for the future, but life will always throw surprises at you. Some of them good. Some of them bad." He swallows, clearing his throat before carrying on. "You only have this moment right here. We never know which one's gonna be our last." He shakes his head with a sad smile. "Money can always be found. You can always make the time, and I know you will hate yourself if you let fear stop you from having one-of-a-kind love. Even if you only get her for a short time, enjoy it. Turn it into a memory you can cherish, but don't push her away because you've convinced yourself romance is too complicated. It doesn't have to be. The right woman makes you a man. She brings out all the best things inside you, and it kills me that you want to deny yourself that. I'm sorry if I've made you think love will break you. It *made* me. And I will never regret giving my all to your mother. Never."

Tugging on my hoodie, he pulls me into a hug, his solid arms wrapping around me and reminding me how strong he is.

I grip him just as tight, fisting his jacket and fighting the swell of emotion in my throat.

"Now, you go call that girl, and you tell her how much she means to you." He pounds me twice on the back, then gives me one of his Galloway smiles. "I love you, son."

"Love you, too, Dad."

I close the driver's door for him and slap the roof of his car, standing in the driveway and waving him off. As soon as his taillights disappear down the road, I rip the phone from my back pocket and find Mikayla's number.

It rings eight times before going to voice mail.

I hang up with a growl and try again.

And then I try one more time before sufficing with a text.

Me: I'm sorry. Please let me talk to you about this.

I stand there like an idiot, staring at my phone and begging those reply dots to start flashing.

But they never do.

And eventually I have to give up, shoving my phone away and walking back into the house thinking about my mom and how she never got to go to Disneyland.

CHAPTER 33
MIKAYLA

I slipped into the house twenty minutes ago and thankfully got to my room without detection. I mean, a couple girls saw me flit from the front door and down the corridor, but I'm grateful it wasn't Aimee or Fiona... or Teah.

She's the nicest girl in this house, and if she gave me one of her sympathetic looks, I might just start crying. I hate crying.

I did so much of it when my dad first left. I couldn't seem to stop. It's like I used up a lifetime's worth in those weeks after he walked out, and now there's no more. Well, there's plenty more, but I just never like them appearing.

I'd rather take burning eyeballs and this torturous tingling in my nose than give in to the tears sliding down my cheeks.

I won't let some guy weaken me this way.

My phone buzzes with a text, and I don't bother

checking the screen. It's no doubt another attempt from Ethan. He's called three freaking times, and I don't want to hear what he has to say.

Can't he just leave me alone and let me wallow in my own private shame?

I'm not girlfriend material. I know this about myself, and I'm furious that I let him get under my skin.

The only reason I did was because of this stupid initiation.

I throw my anger back at Aimee and this whole stupid sorority. I funnel my black energy into hating my mother and Jarrod for a second.

Who forces their child to join a sorority? It's ridiculous! Insane! Stupid! Dumb!

Flopping back onto my pillow with a little scream, I thump the mattress and nearly grab my phone to call Rachel.

But she's probably busy with her boyfriend right now. The girl who got zero action in high school is moving in with a guy. And yeah, it's not like I got much action in high school either, but at least I was brave enough to go after some.

Rachel was too scared to even approach guys at school.

And now she's moving in with the love of her life because *she knows*.

My chin starts to tremble, needles poking my eyeballs as I fight another wave of tears.

I know too.

But I can't know, because Ethan doesn't want me, and I'm not supposed to want him. I'm supposed to be breaking his heart, and instead he's breaking mine.

And oh shit! How am I supposed to break his heart now?

He doesn't want me.

Which means he doesn't love me.

Which means I *can't* break his heart, and I'm gonna fail and Aimee will kick me out of the house. I'll be homeless, penniless, and have no way of getting the education I need to fulfill my dream of becoming a sports agent.

Yes, I'm spiraling, but what the fuck else am I supposed to do?

Thumping the mattress again, I fist the cover and give in to the tears, closing my eyes and letting them trickle down my cheeks.

Why did Dad leave us?

Why'd he turn his back on me?

The man I knew when I was a kid would never force me into this situation. He was the only one who understood me. He never tried to turn me into something I wasn't. I would have sworn black and blue that he loved me just the way I was.

But he didn't.

He walked out that door, and I never heard from him again. Mom told us he'd moved on with another family and we were part of his past now.

"He doesn't want us. He doesn't want to see you girls. It's over," Mom had said.

Because we're not worth fighting for. *I'm* not worth fighting for.

And I just really need to accept that and stop trying so fucking hard all the time.

There's nothing wrong with being a lone wolf.

Rolling onto my side, I curl into a ball and let the tears silently fall onto my pillow.

Nothing wrong with it at all.

CHAPTER 34
ETHAN

I couldn't stop thinking about Mikayla last night. She didn't return any of my calls or texts, and I have to find her this morning. I need to make this right. I've never been one to obsess over a girl. I'm not the guy who waits by the phone. But Mikayla's shutout is killing me, and I'm not gonna let her get away with it.

We need to talk about what happened last night. I don't give a shit if she doesn't want to. Last night cannot be the end of us. Not with Dad's words ringing in my brain. Picking up my pace, I jog toward Luxon Hall. I don't have Mikayla's schedule, but I managed to sweet-talk one of the Sig Be freshmen girls into telling me Mikayla had an Intro to Marketing class this morning. She giggled and blushed and quickly spilled the beans, and I took off, shouting, "Thank you!" over my shoulder as I ran.

I don't want to miss her, so I sprint up the stairs and spot her through the glass doors as she files out of the classroom with a bunch of other students.

"Mick!" I raise my hand to grab her attention.

She stops, looking like a deer in headlights for a second before rolling her eyes and turning her back to me.

I weave through the crowd and quickly catch up to her, grabbing her arm.

"Lemme go," she murmurs, and I do, but I don't slow my pace and am soon keeping up with her little steps without any trouble.

She glances up at me again, rolls her eyes, and finally huffs, "What? What do you want?"

"I need to talk to you."

Jerking to a stop, she crosses her arms and glares up at me. "I'm not sure if you're aware of this, but when a girl ignores your calls and doesn't reply to your texts, that's a pretty strong indicator that she doesn't want to talk to you."

I grin down at her. "Yeah, I get that. But this particular girl needs to talk to me, so I'm hounding her."

She growls. "I do not."

"Yeah you do." I lean down, getting in her space and hoping my eyes are reflecting whatever the hell is pounding in my chest right now, because it feels good and right and... shit, I've fallen for this girl. My dad's right. "Mick... I'm sorry about last night." The words come out as this husky croak, and she swallows, darting her eyes to the floor.

I spot someone to my left and glance her way, only to notice a dozen eyes on us. They're not even being subtle about it.

"Come on." Gently taking Mikayla's elbow, I lead her down the hallway until I find an empty classroom.

She's not fighting me, and I move fast, not wanting to lose this momentum. I guide her away from the door, and we shuffle past the tables and right into the back corner. I spot a door and try it, relieved when it opens into an office. I don't even know whose office it is, but it's empty and there's not much in here. Just a desk with a mug of pens, a box of tissues, and an empty coffee mug. The shelves are lined with textbooks that need dusting, and I can see why the professor doesn't spend much time in this windowless space.

But it's the perfect place to talk to Mikayla.

Closing the door, I flick on the light and finally let her go.

Her arms are crossed, and she's scanning the shelves of books. "Okay, so the creeper vibe is kinda strong in here. What the hell are you planning on doing with me in this solitary cell?"

I snort at her dry tone and shake my head. "I just needed a private space we could talk in." Perching my butt on the edge of the desk, I cross my ankles and look at her. "I really am sorry about how we left things last night. I wish I could explain. I just—"

"Don't worry about it. You don't have to explain." She shrugs. "I get it, okay? I like hanging out with you, too, and being friends is awesome. I'm used to guys feeling this way." Her resigned smile makes me frown. "Just because I think you're smoking hot doesn't mean you have to be attracted to me. No hard feelings, okay? Just give me a little minute to lament the fact that we're on different pages and I'll be fine. Don't go feeling guilty or whatever. You—"

"Wait. Stop." I raise my hand to cut her off. "You don't think I'm attracted to you?"

She grips her arms and looks back at the bookshelf, her jaw clenching.

"Are you kidding me?" I bolt off the desk and am against her in two quick strides. I don't even wait for permission to capture her mouth against mine.

I have to show her how damn attractive she is. How badly I want her. I wish I could tell her the truth. No one would hear me in here. Asher would never find out.

But I'd know. And I'm not the kind of guy to lie or break a bet. I'm no coward.

Mikayla lets out a soft moan, her tongue lashing against mine like she couldn't control it if she wanted to. I get that, since my hands are moving of their own accord, cresting her perfect boobs before whistling over her waist and hips.

Her bag drops off her shoulder, landing on the floor with a thud as she rises to her tiptoes, sucking my bottom lip into her mouth before changing angles and deepening the kiss all over again.

I curve my hands around her sweet ass and lift her off the floor, my rigid cock nestling between her legs and practically vibrating.

Oh man, I don't know if I can control it this time.

But right now, I don't give a shit.

She's gotta know how much I want her. How good I want to make her feel.

Carrying her over to the desk, I place her down, pulling back to revel in the hungry look in her eyes. They spark with a heat that makes me groan, and I capture her neck, pulling her back toward me for a searing kiss before trailing my lips along her jawline and down to her collar-bone. The tip of my tongue paints a line down the V-neck of her shirt. She whimpers as my fingers trail up her legs, nudging her denim skirt up past her butt, then drawing my feather-soft touch between her legs.

She jerks like it tickles, and I grin at her, crouching in front of the desk and kissing her knee before inching my way up to the wet heat I know is waiting for me.

She looks nervous for a second, her breath hitching, and I pause.

"Is this okay?"

"Yeah." The word shudders out of her. "Don't stop."

"Your wish is my command," I murmur against her inner thigh. Tugging her panties off, I slide them down her legs, letting them dangle off her right foot before hiking her knees over my shoulders and exploring the wonder of this woman.

She's ready and waiting, her folds glistening as I gently nibble and lick a path to her clit. When the tip of my tongue touches her sweet spot, she lets out a stran-gled moan, then starts panting my name.

It's the most beautiful fucking thing I've ever heard, and my cock is straining as I stroke my tongue across her heat before burying two fingers inside her.

"Holy shit," she rasps, bearing down on me before moving her hips and fisting my hair.

I smile against her sweet body, working her clit while she pants and moans. It doesn't take her long to fall apart, her cry of ecstasy enough to nearly make me come in my pants. But thankfully I hold it together.

She's trembling, her inner walls vibrating as she clutches my fingers and rides out the orgasm. Her breathless gasps are a song, and as I kiss my way back to her knee, it's taking everything in me not to stand and take her right here.

I want my cock inside her, wrapped within her hot pussy, pounding—

A door clicks and I whip my head around, jolting to my feet and scrambling to get Mikayla cleaned up before we get busted. Shoving a couple of tissues in her hand, I lunge for the light switch before blocking her with my body. The frenetic movements behind me indicate she's rushing to get dressed in the dark.

Leaning my ear against the wood, I think I hear students entering the classroom.

"Shit, shit, shit," Mikayla's muttering behind me.

"It's okay. I don't think they've started yet."

As soon as I hear her snatching our bags off the floor, I whip the door open, grabbing her hand and walking out of the office like I was meant to be in there.

We get a few glances as we rush out the door and nearly barrel into a man carrying a briefcase. He gives me an odd look before turning sideways to brush past me and enter his classroom.

As soon as he's behind us, I burst out laughing, pulling Mikayla down the hall and around the staircase.

I find a private alcove under the stairs and push her back against the wall, leaning down so I'm in line with her face.

"You okay?" I brush my thumb across her lips.

"Yeah." Her voice is trembling, and for a second, I'm clutched with doubt that I took it too far until she grins at me, her cheeks pink and beautiful. "I've never... That's the first time anyone's ever..." She tips her head back and lets out a breathy laugh. "Fuck, that was amazing."

I can't help kissing that smile of hers.

She sinks into it, moaning again, and I know I can't give a damn about this stupid bet anymore. I have to have this girl.

Gently gripping her hips, I lean my forehead against hers and speak before I can think better of it. "Come over after practice tonight? We can finish what we started."

"Okay," she whispers, her eyes flickering with a touch of uncertainty.

"Only if you want to," I whisper.

"I do. I just want to make sure you do too."

With a soft growl, I press my body against hers so she can feel how hard I am. "I want you. Believe me."

She laughs, her breath hitting my chin. "All right, big guy. I'll see you after practice, then."

Cupping her cheeks, I brush my thumb down her jawline, then gently kiss those sweet lips, because I have to have one more taste before walking away. It's like a teaser for what awaits me tonight, and I have no fucking idea how I'm gonna concentrate on anything else today.

CHAPTER 35
MIKAYLA

I stay against the wall when Ethan walks away. I need a minute to compose myself after... well, that.

Holy crap! I have never come like that before. I'm used to servicing myself in that department, but what Ethan just did freaking blew my mind.

"His tongue." I tip my head back against the wall with a soft laugh. "His magical tongue."

My insides are still buzzing. The wet tingling between my legs fires up all over again as I remember that seriously erotic moment. Ethan's warm, soft tongue licking circles against my clit while his fingers drove into me. I didn't even care where I was. I'm not sure I was even conscious of it. My body was blinded to everything but the sensations shooting through me. I can only imagine what it'll be like having his entire body pressed against mine. I want to feel him inside me, all around me.

Shit, I'm gonna start leaking down my legs.

I bolt for the bathroom and do a second cleanup, my

sensitive body still buzzing after that epically hot orgasm. The anticipation for tonight is going to kill me.

Checking my watch, I groan, calculating how many hours I'm gonna have to wait.

But as I wash my hands and glance at my reflection in the mirror, I'm smiling.

"He wants me," I tell myself. "He actually wants me."

It's kind of a mind trip after spending most of last night lamenting the fact that Ethan Galloway would never be into a girl like me. But after what just happened, I can't really deny it.

He's attracted to me—big-time.

Which means this initiation is over. I don't know how I'm going to tell Aimee that I'm done, but I'll find a way somehow. I just need to offer her up something else so she'll let me stay.

Pulling the bathroom door open, I head out of Luxon Hall, my brain trying to come up with something half decent, but it's failing because I can't get Ethan out of my head.

We like each other. It's kind of surreal. Ethan is cover-model hot. I've never had a guy I like this freaking much like me back.

I shake my head, nerves firing through me as I realize I more than like him. It feels insanely fast, but there's just something about him. Is it honestly possible for people to fall in love so quickly?

Snatching out my phone, I pull up Rachel's number as I head to my next class.

"Hey, sweets," she answers after two rings. "I'm at work, so I can't talk for long."

"Oh shit, sorry. I should have texted. I wasn't thinking. I can call you later."

"No, that's okay. What's up?" Sweet Ray. She's always so accommodating.

"Um... well, I was just wondering..." I wrinkle my nose, then rush out the words, trying to outrun the burning embarrassment I feel whenever I talk about this kind of thing. "How did you know when you were in love with Theo? It was fast, right? How did you know when to just go for it?"

"Oh." She giggles. "Where is this coming from?"

"I'm just curious. I mean, you guys are moving in together, and you said the other day that when you know, you know. So... how do you know?"

"I'm not sure. I guess he just makes me happy. When I'm around him, I can't stop smiling, and when I'm not with him, I'm thinking about him. You know, the usual stuff."

"And the speed with which you fell didn't scare you?"

"No. It... I mean, yeah, I guess logically it's kind of trippy to feel so strongly about someone so fast. And when he suggested we move in, my first thought was 'Whoa, this feels intense.' Mom was definitely surprised. But she's leaving me, and I don't want to live on my own. Screw logic, you know? Theo cares about me, and I want to focus on that. On the bubbly way he makes me feel." She giggles again, and I can just see the expression on her face right now. "He gives me love bubbles, Mick. Big ol' love bubbles."

I laugh. Oh man, she's nailed it. That's what is popping in my chest right now.

"Life's too short to second-guess ourselves," she goes

on. "Why can't we fall in love quickly? What's wrong with that? Theo makes me happy. The fact that I'm gonna get to wake up beside him each morning is so freaking cool. I love him, and I'm not going to hide that just because it's happening so fast, you know?"

She sounds like she's trying to sell me on this, justify her decisions, and I can't help laughing. "I get it, Ray. You don't have to convince me."

"Oh." She laughs. "Sorry. Some people don't get it."

"Like who?"

"Well, Mom at first, and there's also Jenna from work. And Ali. Remember? From school?"

"Yeah, totally. She's always been a skeptic over things like love, though. She's far too practical for her own good."

"Even you questioned me when I said I was moving in with Theo."

"Yeah." I wince. "I know. Sorry about that."

"It's okay. I'm confident in my decision." She pauses. "So... where is all this coming from?"

"Oh, I just... well..." I let out a soft laugh. "I've... met a guy."

"What!" she screeches. "One sec... Hey, Diana, I've got a bit of a family emergency. Nothing to panic about, but I need to take a quick break, is that cool? ... Thanks. I'll be right back." I hear muffled steps and then the click of a door before Rachel's back in my ear. "Tell me *everything*."

I tell her what I can, skipping over the sorority stuff and focusing on all the awesome things about Ethan, from how hot he is to how he can make me laugh. I relive some of our banter, and the more I tell her, the more I realize that I'm not just falling anymore.

I've fallen. Hard.

"And you're gonna have sex with him tonight?" Rachel's voice pitches with excitement.

"Uh... yeah."

"Omg, Mick! It's gonna be so epic. Do you have protection?"

"I was kinda hoping he would. The guy's got a rep, so he's probably got a permanent stash on him."

"Does that worry you? The rep thing?"

I bite my lip, pausing outside the student union. "I don't think so? I'm not sure. I don't think he's the kind to play with me just to get me into bed. From what I've heard, he's always been really open about the fact that he's a one-night kind of guy."

"So, will he be that way with you too?"

I swallow, doubts scouring me. "I don't know. I... don't think so. We've been hanging out a lot, and we get on great, you know? I think he really likes me. He said he likes hanging out with me."

"Has he told you he loves you?"

"No," I snicker. "He's not Theo."

She giggles. "He said it after only a week, but... you should have seen the look on his face." Her voice goes all swoony, and I wait out her gushing, having to relive the story. I'm not grimacing as much this time, though. Theo sounds like a romantic sap, and I can't imagine Ethan every saying shit like that to me.

I wouldn't even want him to.

I like our way. Our teasing banter, our heated kisses. I like that he feels like a friend with these huge benefits.

My insides start to dance again as I imagine the benefits I'm gonna get tonight.

"Shoot, I have to go. Diana needs me out front again."

"Okay. Thanks for being there for me."

"Always." I picture her smile and suddenly miss her with an ache that's painful. "Love you, bestie."

"Love you."

I hang up and nibble on my lip as I wander down the path, then through the sliding glass doors. I find a free couch against the wall and flop onto it. My class starts in about twenty minutes, so I pull out my latest reading, finishing off the last page before class begins. I'm really enjoying the variety of classes I have this semester, but trying to concentrate on the text is basically impossible. I have to reread most of it, and then when class begins, I can barely focus on what Professor Dutton is saying. Her voice becomes white noise as I once again think ahead to what awaits me in Ethan's bedroom.

CHAPTER 36
ETHAN

I skate off the ice, dropping my stick and helmet as soon as I reach the locker room.

"What is with you today, man?" Liam slaps me on the shoulder. "It was Mistake City out there."

"I know," I growl, frustrated with myself.

Today has been impossible. I've never been consumed by a person before. I appreciate women. I love the way they look, taste, feel. I get my fill, and then I move on. I don't tend to relive hot nights, but Mikayla's pussy is something else. I can't stop hearing her sweet moans in my head. I can't stop imagining what it will feel like to bury myself inside her.

My cock's twitching just thinking about it.

But practice today sucked, and it's because I'm torn.

I love hockey.

Seriously. It's all I've been living for these past few years, and if I follow through with Mikayla, I'm putting that in jeopardy. Not only could I get benched, but I'll be letting my team down as well.

I'm a man of my word. I've got this bet to see through, and if I break it, I'll have to walk through campus naked.

Getting busted is a guarantee, and there'll be consequences for that.

But not following through with Mikayla will suck as well.

I should just tell her the truth and wait it out.

You're not supposed to say anything either! If you're gonna break the rules, you might as well go all the way.

I close my eyes when I enter the shower, dipping my head beneath the spray. I want her. I want her so fucking bad, and the idea of waiting one more week is brutal. Plus, she needs to know how much I'm into her.

I can't believe she doubted me last night. That she went down that path of thinking she wasn't attractive to me. I've never been more turned on by a woman in my life. I have to show her that. I have to wipe away every doubt in her mind.

The thought makes me antsy, and I rush through my shower, changing faster than anyone.

"Where's the fire?" Casey snickers as I zip up my bag.

"Behind on an assignment," I mutter.

It's the lamest excuse in the world, but I don't want to stick around to try and justify it.

"Have fun at Offside." Making a beeline for the door, I race to my car and haul ass back to Hockey House.

Liam texts me to check in, and I message him back on my way to the front door.

Me: I'm all good. Just need some quiet time to catch up on everything.

. . .

Padre: Sweet. As long as you're good. I'm DD tonight, so I'll see you later.

I send him a thumbs-up and unlock the door, racing upstairs to clear off my messy bed and make sure the room is somewhat presentable. I stare at the duvet, picturing Mikayla on there, her legs wrapped around my hips, her heels digging into my ass as I thrust and—

The doorbell rings.

My insides dip and zing. Seriously. What the hell is up with me?

She's affecting me like no one else ever has.

Should I really be jumping down this rabbit hole?

Opening the door, I spot her nervous grin, my heart hitching at the cute line of freckles across her nose, then dipping at the hungry glow in her eyes.

I don't bother with words. Wrapping my arm around her waist, I drag her into the house, hauling her up my body and climbing the stairs. Her legs wrap around me, her hot tongue dragging against mine as I walk her up the stairs and into my room.

I flick the door shut with my heel, placing her down so she can tug my shirt off. I throw it over my shoulder before making quick work of her tank top and bra. She's still in that sexy denim skirt from this morning, and her standing there topless in that thing is making me horny as hell.

But I don't want to rush this, so I force my cock to stay within his denim prison and take my sweet time exploring her tits with my tongue and fingers. Lightly pinching one nipple, I suck the other between my lips and enjoy the sounds of her pleasure. Those panting little gasps as she threads her fingers into my hair is a melody I could get used to.

Walking her back toward the bed, I lightly push her onto it, enjoying the view as she scrambles back, then beckons me with her finger.

The way she drags her teeth over her bottom lip, the excited little puff of air that comes out of her as I crawl across the mattress, is making my granite dick want to fire off right now.

Holy fuck. This woman.

Planting my mouth over hers, I run my hands up her legs, loving the quiver of her muscles as I once again rid her of her panties. I want to keep the skirt on though. Shit, that thing is sexy.

Cupping her sweet ass, I rock against her, moaning into her mouth before kissing a line from her chin to her right nipple.

Her fingers race to unzip my jeans. She yanks them open, then scrambles to free my cock. Fisting my throbbing dick, she gives it a squeeze, and stars scatter my vision. I thrust into her hand with a groan, lightly scraping my teeth over her nipple while finding her clit with my thumb.

She whimpers, whispering something incoherent as she lifts her hips while cupping the back of my head, a silent plea for my mouth to keep working her tits.

"Feels so good," she moans, breaths punching out of her as she strokes my cock and writhes beneath my touch.

Her sweet nipples are pink and glistening as I pull away from her, taking a moment to drink in her ecstasy while my thumb continues teasing her clit. Her head is tipped back, her eyes closed, her perfect lips parted as another moan slips out of her, followed by a sweet gasp.

I lick the curve of her breast, feeling how close she is, then suck her nipple into my mouth. Her body starts to vibrate, and she arches her back, fisting my cock as the orgasm rips through her. Her mouth pops open, a strangled cry rising from her throat as she shudders and buries her face in my pillow.

It's a thing of beauty, watching her come apart like that.

My body wants to drop, cover her, find a home in that wet heat she's offering.

She flops back to the mattress, a limp mess as her fingers trail down my chest, her words muffled by my pillow.

"What?" I whisper, running my hand back under her ass.

"Condom," she rasps, her expression desperate with desire. Her vibrant eyes are lit with need and damn, do I want to be her fucking deliverance right now.

I yank open the drawer beside my bed and snatch one out.

Ripping the packet open with my teeth is so familiar. How many times have I done this? How many women have I taken right here?

I pause. It's different this time. Mikayla's not just any woman.

The expectations for her to leave after a quick fuck

are nowhere in sight. I'm gonna want her to stay. I'm gonna want to hold her against me and—

Shit. What the hell has happened to me?

"Are you okay?" Her head pops off the pillow.

"Yeah," I rasp, swallowing, but still not grabbing the condom out of the packet.

If she wakes up beside me in the morning, Asher's gonna know. I'm gonna break the terms of our bet, and I'll be screwed. I—

Mikayla sighs, shifting away from me.

I snatch her leg. "Where are you going?"

"You don't want to do this."

"No, that's not it. I—"

"Forget it." She pushes me away, jumping off the bed and grabbing her clothes off the floor. "You're obviously not into it."

"No, Mick. Please, that's not it. I..."

She pulls her shirt back on, not even bothering with her bra. I stare at those puckered nipples poking at the fabric and my mouth goes dry.

Every instinct in my body is telling me to grab her, throw her back on the bed, and show her that she's so fucking wrong right now.

But I've gone and killed the mood. My hesitation told her everything she didn't want to hear, and I have to somehow explain it to her.

"Just let me explain."

"I don't want to talk about it," she snips.

I can't help the scoff that punches out of me. "Of course you don't."

Her glare could boil the Atlantic. I swallow and wince

in apology, crawling to the edge of the bed, my semi swinging out of my open jeans.

She takes one glance at it, then tuts and spins out of the room.

"No, Mick. Wait!"

Her feet thunder down the steps as I scramble to do up my pants and chase after her.

But I don't get far. Asher's at the top of the stairs, slapping a hand against my bare chest. The look of glee on his face is punchable. "You didn't just have sex, did you?"

"Does it look like I did?" I growl.

"You're holding a condom packet." He points at my hand. "It's open."

"But the rubber's still in there." I shove it into his chest, smearing the lube on his shirt.

"Ew, dude." He jumps back in disgust, and I take the opportunity to brush past him. "Where are you going?"

"I've got to get Mikayla." Snatching a jacket off the hook by the door, I shove it on and wrench the door open.

"Don't forget the rules, man!" he shouts down the stairs.

I whip around and silence him with a glare that's lethal enough to make him shuffle back from the stairwell.

Slamming the door shut behind me, I scan the darkened street for Mikayla but don't see her anywhere.

"Shit," I mutter, running for my truck, determined to find her and explain.

Screw the fucking bet. I have to tell her the truth.

CHAPTER 37
MIKAYLA

I didn't have time to order an Uber. Instead, I sprinted like the wind through the darkness, arriving back at the sorority house out of breath and nearly keeling over. I'm a fit person, I keep up with my running and calisthenics, but I have never run that fast in my life.

Bending over, I brace my hands on my knees and suck air into my lungs. I need to pull myself together before walking in the front door.

Shit. Shit. Shit!

I thought Ethan wanted me. I was so fucking sure, and then he paused. That look on his face while he stared at the condom packet spoke volumes. It was almost like he was scared to go all the way with me, which is total bullshit because he's a freaking manwhore!

He must have just felt bad because he went and led me on like that, but then when it came to the crunch, I'm not enough for him.

I hate this feeling so much.

My chest hurts.

Pushing my fist against my rib cage, I squeeze my eyes shut and feel the burn fire down the entire length of my body. It makes me want to drop to my knees and cry, but the front door pops open and I jolt upright, staring at Aimee as she struts down the path toward me.

"What are you doing?" Her tone is so derogatory.

I puff, then force a deep breath through my nose. "Catching my breath," I finally tell her.

She gives me a weird, disgusted look before crossing her arms and glaring at me. "And where have you been?"

"Nowhere," I mutter.

But that's not good enough. Shit. She's gonna make me talk, and like hell I'm gonna tell her what just went down with Ethan.

And double shit.

I still need a place in this stupid sorority house. I'd spent my day trying and failing to come up with a good alternative to this stupid initiation and in the end gave up. My sole focus became all about my feelings for Ethan and how we were finally going to do the deed.

But he doesn't want me, which should make the whole initiation task a hell of a lot easier.

Yet I still don't want to go through with it.

My chest still hurts.

This burning, brutal ache is relentless as it pulses inside me.

"Were you with Ethan?"

"Yes," I grit out.

"And how are things progressing there? You're running out of time, you know."

"I know that."

"You had the perfect out. We arranged it all for you, but you had to go and get drunk, and make a total fool of yourself and us." She points at her chest, then flicks her hand at the house. The venom in her voice has me backing away from her. I'm so not in the mood for this shit.

I've got my own fucking crisis to deal with.

I want to tell her that. I want to yell it right in her pretty little face.

But she's still ranting.

"Now you're having to drag this thing out unnecessarily." Her eyes flash. "You are so not meant for this place, Mikayla. I don't understand why you're trying so hard to be one of us. I—" She cuts herself off, probably realizing how loud she's shouting, before crossing her arms. "All you had to do was"—her voice rises again—"make Ethan Galloway fall in love with you, then publicly break his heart!"

"I know that!" I thunder back, finally lowering myself to her level. "What do you think I've been trying to do? You can't just make someone fall in love with you!"

The words hurt coming out of me.

Here I was, pining after Ethan like some sap while he was probably figuring out ways to gently let me down.

"You sure about that?" Aimee arches her eyebrow, and my stomach pitches when I notice the wicked gleam in her eye.

Dread rises over my shoulder as I spin around and spot Ethan just behind me. The wounded look on his face crumples my insides.

Oh shit. He just heard every word of that... and he looks gutted.

"Ethan," I rasp.

He shakes his head. "So this is why you never want to talk about anything. Because none of it is fucking real."

I open my mouth, but all I can manage is a soft squeak.

His injured expression is brutal. I get one more look at it before he spins and starts walking down the road.

"No, wait..." My voice is a pathetic croak. I stumble after him but don't get very far.

Aimee snatches my arm and spins me to face her. "Well, not exactly the public heartbreak I wanted." She smirks.

"But it's close enough!" Teah grins. She's standing in the doorway next to Bella, who is watching her phone screen with glee, while I'm struggling not to throw up.

"I got a picture of it," Claudia sings from an upstairs window.

"I recorded the whole thing. As soon as I saw him walking toward the house." Bella's laughing. "You should see the look on his face."

A bunch of girls start crowding out the doorway, cackling as they watch the footage over Bella's shoulder.

Aimee grudgingly laughs, turning to eye me up with a look that might actually be appreciation. "I don't know how you got him to follow you here, but... nice work. I guess I have to say... *welcome to Sigma Beta Mu.*"

Teah and Bella both cheer, which sets off a round of applause.

I stare up at the house, at all the girls congratulating me, and feel like the ground beneath my feet is cracking open. I'm standing in my own personal earthquake, and

I'm begging it to swallow me right down to the Earth's core.

That look on Ethan's face.

I can't get it out of my head.

I hurt him.

And I broke my own heart too.

CHAPTER 38
ETHAN

I drive home in a rage, my heart pounding, my knuckles white as I grip the wheel.

I want to get shit-faced drunk. I want to punch a wall.

"Fuck!" I roar, slamming on the brakes and slapping the wheel a few times.

This is why I don't do fucking romance!

The first girl who has ever made me feel anything more than lust or mild interest, and it was all bullshit.

She was playing me.

And I fell for it like a fucking sap.

Damn those sorority girls. They think they're so fucking great. Well, screw them!

I thought she was different, but the only difference about her was that she was so good at playing the role. I fell for it like some clueless idiot.

Was any of it real?

Did she know that first night we met?

I slam the door shut behind me and storm into the house. It's busy with guys. They've all returned from the bar and are now surrounding the TV, watching Casey play *Devil's Doorway* while Liam cooks up grilled cheeses in the kitchen.

Storming in there, I grab a beer can off the bench and find it already empty. With a growl, I hurl it against the wall.

"Whoa." Liam whips around to gape at me. "What's up, man?"

The genuine concern on his face kills me. I can't admit it to him. I can't admit it to any of these guys.

Asher saunters into the room, snickering. "He's just pissed because he nearly lost the bet tonight. Good self-control, though, dude." He slaps my shoulder.

I shake him off with a growl, shoving him out of my way and stomping up the stairs.

"Ethan?" Liam chases after me.

"Back off," I shout, then wince, leaning against the railing and shaking my head at him. "Please, man, just... I'm okay."

He knows I'm not, but he lets me go.

I shuffle up the rest of the stairs, slipping into my room and staring at the bed. Less than an hour ago, Mikayla was lying on that thing, her legs spread open, begging me to come in. And I hesitated.

It's fucking good that I did.

She didn't mean it anyway.

But it had felt like it.

"Shit." I plunk down on the edge of the bed and drag my hands through my hair.

It had felt so real.

CHAPTER 39
MIKAYLA

I pound on the door with my fist, not letting up until it swings open.

Liam eyes me up. He looks confused and then a little suspicious. I have no idea what Ethan told him, and I can't help squirming as I stand there under the yellow glow of the porch light.

"I need to talk to Ethan." I step up to slip past him, but he blocks my way.

"He's not in a good space right now."

"I know that." I raise my eyebrows. "I'm the reason why. Please, I need to make this right."

He stays put, crossing his thick arms.

"Padre, please. I screwed up, and I have to apologize and tell him the truth."

He obviously doesn't know what went down between Ethan and me because he's fighting confusion.

"I'm not leaving," I warn him. "I will sleep on your doorstep if I have to."

That does the trick. He lets out a heavy sigh and

finally shifts so I can get past him. The house is busy but not chaotic. It's getting late, so some of the guys have probably turned in for the night or are in their rooms studying.

I bury my hands in my hoodie pockets and throw Liam a questioning look. "He in his room?"

Liam nods, still obviously uneasy about letting me in.

I give him an edgy smile, trying to reassure him, but I don't think it works. My legs are practically shaking as I climb the stairs and pause outside Ethan's door.

If I knock, he probably won't let me in. I hurt him. I can't get that look on his face out of my head. I have to make him understand that I didn't want to do the initiation. I'd already decided not to follow through with it and was trying to come up with ways around it. Surely he'll get that.

Sucking in a breath, I knock once and open the door before he can even ask who it is.

He's sitting at his desk in sweats and a T-shirt, his feet bare and beautiful. He's hunched over a textbook, his laptop buzzing. The second he spots me, he slams it shut and throws me a heated glare.

"What the fuck are you doing here?"

"We need to talk."

"You don't want to talk, remember? You hate that shit. And I'm fucking done." He shoots out of his chair, walking past me to the door I just closed.

Wrenching it open, he points into the hallway, silently telling me to get out.

I cross my arms and meet his heated glare. "I'm not leaving."

"Yes you are. I don't want you here. I don't want to

look at your face. I don't want to hear any more of your bullshit. I want you out!"

His thundering shout makes me flinch. I can't hide it, and for a second, I think I see him wince like he regrets what he's saying. But it's only a flash, and his face is soon back to that rigid anger I walked in on.

Shit. He has every right to be pissed at me. He has every right to kick me out of his room.

I played him. I lied to him.

And even though all of my feelings became real, I never said a word. I could have told him, risked that smile disappearing off his face, but I chickened out, and now I'm facing his rage.

And I deserve it.

Working my jaw to the side, I try to stop it trembling as tears build in my throat and start to burn my eyes. I won't let them fall. If I do that, Aimee wins.

Who am I kidding?

She's already won.

With a little sniff, I finally nod and inch toward his door. Pausing just before I leave, I murmur the only thing I can. "I didn't mean to hurt you."

His jaw clenches and he keeps his gaze on the floor, gently pushing me the rest of the way out his door before closing it behind me.

I'm frozen for a second, swaying on my feet and wondering what the hell I'm supposed to do now.

A door opens down the hallway, and it works like an electric shock to my system. Darting down the stairs, I rush past Liam and bolt out the front door, not even closing it behind me as I run back to Greek Row.

The closer I get to the sorority house, the sicker I feel.

I don't know if I've ever felt this awful in my entire life. Even after Dad left. That was brutal, but this is somehow worse.

I screwed up so fucking badly. I knew from the start that this initiation was a stupid idea, but I played along anyway. I let my mom convince me it was just a silly game. I let my strings be pulled by Aimee and those girls, all the while knowing I shouldn't go through with it.

And I wasn't going to.

But I didn't act fast enough, and now I've lost Ethan.

So what's the point of staying?

Pausing outside the sorority house, I stare up at the beautiful white building with its pillars out front and its rows of windows. It's a picture-perfect house that I should want a place in.

But I don't.

I'm not Sig Be material, and it's time to accept that and face the consequences.

Sucking in a breath, I walk through the front door and head for my room.

"Oh, you're back." Teah jumps up from the couch and follows me. "You just disappeared. I wondered where you'd gone. I tried texting you," she rabbits on, following me all the way to my room.

"I left my phone here." I pick it up off the bed and show it to her before dropping to my knees.

"What are you doing?"

Clenching my jaw, I pull my duffel bag out from beneath my bed and yank it open. I don't say anything. She's not stupid. She'll figure it out as soon as I start packing.

I yank open my drawers and scoop my clothes out.

"Mikayla?" Teah frowns, her lips parting. "Where are you going?"

"I don't belong here," I murmur, punching my clothes into the bag, then turning to grab my underwear and socks.

"But you just got in. You passed the initiation."

"No I didn't." I shake my head, that sick feeling rising up my throat.

"Yes, you totally did. Aimee will be inviting you to the initiation ceremony and—"

"I won't be going." My voice is flat, but my face must be bleeding whatever the hell I'm feeling, because Teah gasps.

Then she backs out of the room, running down the hallway with an urgent shout. "Aimee! We need you!"

I roll my eyes. Great, now I have to deal with her too. This is just perfect.

El Presidente appears in my doorway just as I'm securing my bag. I hitch it onto my shoulder and give her a pointed look.

She smirks. "Going somewhere?"

"You know it." I knock her shoulder as I brush past her.

She lets out an indignant huff and clips after me. "What do you think you're doing? You've got a place in the house. You made it."

I spin back, anger flashing through me. "I don't want a place in this house. I don't belong here." I let out a hard laugh. "It kills me to say it, but you were right all along."

Aimee's eyes flash, her bright gaze fierce. "You're not leaving. You passed the test. Dad expects you to stay. You can't just walk out now."

"You don't want me here!" I spit back. "How many times have I heard you say I'm not Sigma Beta Mu material? I get it. I'm not one of you, and that's fine. I'm sick of playing your stupid games anyway."

She rolls her shoulders, her eyes darting around the other girls before she puts on a smile. "I never said I didn't want you here." She lets out a plastic laugh. "We just wanted you to prove your commitment, which you did. Right, girls?"

They nod, but their usual enthusiasm is a little lackluster, no doubt squashed by the vibrating tension in the air.

"Mikayla, come on. Don't be ridiculous. You're a Sig Be sister now."

I shake my head, pausing in the entranceway. "I'm not. I never wanted to do that initiation, and I was gonna pull out of it. If Ethan hadn't come along without me knowing, he never would have heard you, and..." My voice trails off, my chest aching as I relive that look on his face again.

Her blue eyes sparkle with amusement. "But he did, so lucky you. You're in."

"I'm out."

Her face bunches with indignant confusion, and then she gasps. "Wait. Oh, do not tell me you actually fell for that asshole."

I clench my jaw, staring down at the shiny tiles. "I never wanted to hurt him. I never wanted to hurt anybody."

"Oh please. He deserves it. The guy is a shameless man slut. We did you a favor."

I shake my head, my chin bunching as I'm tortured by

his sad face, his biting words... the way he gently pushed me out his door.

I've lost him. I screwed up, and I lost him.

It hurts so fucking bad.

"Mikayla, seriously. Stop acting like a crazy person," Teah pleads. "You don't need some guy. You've got us now."

I glance up with a frown. How are they not getting this? Why would I want them over Ethan—or any of the guys in Hockey House, for that matter? They're my people.

The thought that I'll never step foot in Hockey House again clutches my throat, making it hard to breathe.

Shit. I've lost it all.

Aimee's nodding, oblivious to my internal meltdown. "She's right. Stop messing around and accept this honor."

Her words snap me back to attention. "Honor?"

"Yes, honor. Do you know how many girls would love to be in your position right now?"

"Probably hundreds." I shrug. "But the point is..." I let out a breath, and despite the fist that's squeezing my heart to dust, I feel a sense of liberation as I look Aimee in the face and tell her, "The point is... *I* don't want to be here."

I spin for the door, kind of surprised that the thought of being homeless right now is more appealing than staying in this place. The chains around me are dropping off as I reach for the door handle.

"Argh!" Aimee screeches. "You are impossible. Your mother's right about you. No wonder she had such a hard time raising you. All she wants to do is help you, and you just keep throwing it back in her face. And now you're doing the same thing to me. To us!"

I whip around, struggling to hide my shock. Has she been having secret powwows with Mom behind my back? Talking shit about me?

The betrayal is brutal and fires off sparks of rage that build to an inferno in my chest.

"You have *not* been trying to help me," I shout. "If anything, you've taken great pleasure in torturing me, and I'm done. I'm *done*!" I wrench the door open, ignoring the gasps from the line of pajama-clad girls watching me.

"Oh, you *are* done, Mikayla Hyde. We are through, do you understand me? Don't expect any more kind gestures on my part. If you walk out that door—if you choose him over us—you are burning all your bridges."

I pause, yet again wondering if this clueless bitch can hear herself.

Kind gestures? When has she ever given me one of those?

"You know what, Aimee?" I turn to face her. "Go fuck yourself."

A chorus of gasps echoes around me as I give my future stepsister a pointed look, then raise my middle finger and walk out the door.

CHAPTER 40
ETHAN

It's one thirty in the morning, and I can't sleep. Dragging my ass out of bed, I storm down the stairs, frustration coursing through me. Mikayla's soft words have been ringing in my head since I pushed her out the door.

"I never meant to hurt you."

Yeah, right. Is that why she strung me along? Played me like a fucking fiddle?

I could have lost the bet because of her.

I had every right to push her out of my room.

So why the fuck do I feel so bad about it?

Yanking the fridge open, I eye the beer cans. It's a day off tomorrow. I could get rip-roaring drunk right now and it wouldn't hurt anybody.

Sounds fucking good to me.

I snatch the six-pack out of the fridge and go to pop one open when Liam appears in the doorway. He's in boxer shorts, his chest bare, his big arms folded as he eyes me up for a second, then glances at the beer can.

"Really?"

I snap it open and guzzle half the can. "Really." I slump onto the stool, letting out a loud burp before wiping my mouth and dumping the rest of the six-pack on the counter.

"Classy." He takes a seat opposite me and snickers, but the amusement on his face quickly dies. "I'm sorry, man. It sucks."

He doesn't even know what went down and he's giving me sympathy. I should probably tell him, but it's fucking humiliating, and I'm not sure if I can get the words out. Even to Liam.

"I know how much you liked her."

I snort and shake my head, taking another swig of beer.

"You can deny it all you want, but she was different to the rest. The way you looked at her was..." His lips curl into a half smile. "She's a cool chick."

"Yep." I accentuate the *p* and finish off the can, crumpling it in my fist before chucking it over my shoulder. It clatters on the kitchen floor, and Liam rolls his eyes, standing up to throw it away.

"You don't have to do that, man. I'll get it later."

But he ignores me, placing it in the recycling box with the other empty cans before walking back to me.

I wrestle another can out of the plastic yoke and am poised to open it when Liam's fingers curl over mine. "You sure you want to do that?"

With a derisive snort, I yank my hand out of his grasp. "Yes. I'm sure."

He winces and I pause, closing my eyes and not wanting to think about how many times he saw his dad get wasted and then violent.

"I just want a little bit of numb," I mumble.

"Yeah, I get it." He sits down with a sigh but then gives me a closed-mouth smile.

"You don't have to keep me company."

"I know." He shrugs and stays put anyway.

I eye him up, popping the can and gulping back a few more mouthfuls.

"Any chance you can work out this thing with Mikayla? Whatever it is?"

My lips curl into a deep frown as I shake my head. "Nah. It's over. It..." I let out a cynical laugh. "It never even really began, so I don't know why I'm feeling so fucking sorry for myself."

He tips his head, his smile sad as he picks at a speck on the counter.

I sigh, figuring he deserves to know why I'm saying this shit. Opening my mouth, I'm about to bag a bunch of sorority bitches when a key in the door stops me. We both pause, listening to the front door creaking open and the shuffle of feet.

"Hello?" Liam calls into the entranceway.

The can of beer is poised halfway to my mouth as I wait for whoever just walked in to show his face. It better not be fucking Jason.

Shit, we need to stop handing out keys to this place.

I tense, my jaw clenching until Baxter appears, his face bunched with confusion as he scratches the back of his head.

"Where've you been?" Liam kind of laughs out the words.

Baxter's not a late-night party man. He's quiet,

studious... a bit of a mystery, if I'm honest, but a damn good goalie.

"I pulled a late one at the library."

"I didn't know it was open this late." Liam frowns.

"It's not." He shrugs. "After I was done, I decided to take a walk to clear my head before going back to my car."

I nod, sharing a quick grin with Liam. Baxter's hair is now standing on end, his face still puckered with this weird frown.

"You good, man?" I ask him.

"Yeah, I just, uh"—he points at me—"saw your girl."

I tense. "I don't have a girl."

"Oh..." His frown deepens. "Okay, well, the shorty who hangs out here sometimes... She not your girl?"

"Nope." I shake my head, draining the beer before slapping the empty can down. It topples over then rolls to the floor, pinging its way to the fridge.

Liam lets out a soft snicker, giving me a pained frown as I reach for another beer, then glance at Baxter. "Where'd you see her?"

"At the library."

I go still, a warning flashing through my brain. "The library? You mean, just now?"

"Yeah. As I was walking to my car, I spotted her. She was carrying this big duffel bag, and she dumped it on the ground, kicked it a couple times, then took a seat next to it." He scratches his head. "It was kind of weird."

I shoot off the stool. "Just now? As in, it's dark as fuck outside and she's huddled up on the ground by the library?"

Baxter bobs his head. "Weird, right?"

"And you just left her there?" I can't help shouting the question at him.

His head jerks back like I've just offended him. "She's not *my* girl."

"Bax, what the shit?" I'm running up the stairs and snatching the keys off my desk before I can think better of it.

Liam's blocking my way when I reach the front door, pulling on a jacket and boots. He looks ridiculous with only his boxers on, but I don't think he cares right now.

"You've been drinking." He holds out his hand, ready to drive me.

"But I'm not drunk," I argue. "I've had two beers."

"I don't give a shit." He snatches the keys out of my hand, and I follow him out the door, swearing under my breath the whole way.

Jumping into the passenger side, I slam the door shut as he starts the engine and reverses out of the driveway.

Thankfully, he doesn't drive like a grandma, and we're soon pulling into the library parking lot just as a mustard-yellow van is leaving.

"Fuck," I whisper, my insides running so cold I think my lungs have stopped working. "Please, no, no, no."

"What?" Liam frowns at me, punching the brakes as I shoulder the door open. "Ethan, what!"

"It's the pervert van," I call over my shoulder, sprinting up the steps and bolting over the grass. The cold seeps into the soles of my bare feet, but I don't stop running until I reach the edge of the library. Mikayla's not there, and my heartbeat ratchets up as I spin to shout at Liam. "You check that way." I point to my right before racing around the left of the building, searching for her.

If those guys took her, I'm gonna hunt them down and kill them. I don't give a shit what it'll do to my future. If they've touched her, they're dead.

The thought of her in the back of that van, scared and being forced to do—

Holy fuck, I can't go there. I squeeze my eyes shut for a second.

The maelstrom in my body is at breaking point, fear and rage firing through me in equal measure as I round the next corner of the building and spot a black huddle along the edge.

It's deep in shadow, and I would have missed it if I hadn't been looking so hard.

Relief pulses through me in a wave so thick and strong I nearly keel over.

Taking a second to steady myself, I swallow down the aching in my throat just as Liam runs around the corner. I hold up my hand and he stops, glancing down at the black mound I'm pointing to before nodding and quietly backing away.

She's safe now. He can go wait in the truck while I...

Shit, I have no idea what to say to her. I'm still pissed at what she did to me, but when I thought she was in trouble, I would have given my life to get to her, save her, make sure she was okay.

I close my eyes, letting the relief at finding her ride through me again before shuffling closer. She's using her duffel bag as a pillow and is curled into a tiny ball with her back to me.

Crouching down behind her, I gently rest my hand on her shoulder. The second I touch her, she spins with a growl, her face a mask of terror as she goes to punch me.

I grab her fist. "It's okay. It's me. I'm not gonna hurt you."

She blinks, pulling in a shaky breath before slumping back down against her bag. The dim light makes it hard to see her features clearly, but I can sense her relief. I can feel the tension passing between us.

Pain courses through me, overriding the heady relief when she murmurs, "I'm sure you want to, though."

I shake my head, my voice coming out in a husky whisper. "No matter how pissed I get, I would never do that to you. I would never hit you or hurt you or..." My voice dries up as I relive that kick of ugly black emotion that tore through me when I saw that pervert van drive past my window.

"I know." Her voice breaks and she sniffs, pressing the back of her hand under her nose before sitting up. "What are you doing here?"

"Baxter saw you. As soon as I heard where you were, I had to come."

She nods.

"I saw the pervert van, and I thought—" I shake my head, balling my fingers into a fist and clenching my jaw as depraved images run through my mind, torturing me.

She lets out a soft sigh, her little fingers brushing over my knuckles. "They pulled in just after I arrived. Thankfully, they didn't see me, and I managed to sneak around the building. For a second, I thought you were one of them."

That look of panic washes over her face again, and I have to touch her. Cupping her cheek, I graze my thumb across her lip, my voice husky and pained when I ask, "What are you doing out here, Mick?"

She tips her head and shrugs. "What do you think?"

She left the house again. Walked out the door because of a fight with the sorority sisters.

Was it a fight about me?

Something stirs in my chest, and I drop my hand from her face, not sure I'm ready to forgive her so quickly. But my mixed emotions are going into battle. The logic that she played me wars with the hope that maybe she hadn't meant to.

But do I really want to go down that path?

I never wanted romance at college anyway. This is my perfect out.

As I gaze at her face, my insides begin to crumple, and it's only made worse when she sniffs and lets out this shaky laugh that does nothing to hide her vulnerability.

"At least I'm not camped outside the hockey arena, right?"

I huff out a laugh and stand up, reaching for her hand. "Come on. Let's go."

"Where?"

Grabbing her fingers, I haul her to her feet. "You're not spending the night out here. You're coming back to my place."

"But you don't want me there." She pulls out of my grasp and backs up against the building.

I let out a heavy sigh and snatch her bag off the ground. "I don't want you out here, so let's go."

CHAPTER 41
MIKAYLA

Liam's waiting behind the wheel, spying me through the glass as Ethan pulls me over to his truck and opens the back door for me.

I give him a skeptical frown.

"Just get in," he murmurs.

He's still mad. He's trying to hide it, but he can't. And I'm not sure if I want to spend the night at his house.

"Mikayla. Get. In."

But I guess it's better than spending the night out here. If that creeper van came around the block again, I was pretty sure a pants-peeing situation would have been going down. Trying to sneak away from them the first time nearly made my heart stop. Or beat so hard I felt like fainting.

I curled into the darkest corner I could find, my fist tucked against my chest as I got ready to defend myself. I should have probably run somewhere else, but I didn't want to draw their attention and have them chase me. So

I stayed in the shadows and begged the universe to make me invisible.

But then Ethan found me.

I glance at his face, set like stone, his eyebrows dented into a sharp V.

He might still be pissed at me, but he's not a creeper. He's Captain Hero, and even though I hurt him, he still came looking for me.

Climbing into the back of the truck, I buckle up and am grateful that Liam gives me no more than a quiet greeting.

Silence reigns as we head back to Hockey House, and it's damn near suffocating. I open the door as soon as we arrive, hauling my bag out after me and walking for the front door ahead of them.

It's locked, so I can't bust in and make a bed on the couch. As soon as Ethan reaches me, he takes the bag out of my hand. I fight the urge to wrestle it back off him. It's instinctual. But he's still annoyed, and I was in the wrong, so I'll shut my mouth and cross my arms and try not say a damn thing.

Liam opens the door for us, and I trail the guys inside, heading for the couch.

"Nope." Ethan points up the stairs. "You're taking my bed."

"No I'm not." I shake my head.

"Yeah, you are."

"No. I'm not." Snatching the bag off him, I dump it on the tiles in the entryway.

"Mikayla, get your ass upstairs," he snaps.

"I'm not taking your bed! If anything, I deserve the floor, so just go upstairs and leave me alone!"

"Are you fucking kidding me right now?" he yells back, and I'm about to tell him to shove it when Liam steps between us.

"So, I'm thinking you guys should both go upstairs and have yourselves a little chat." Lightly patting our shoulders, he glances between us, smiling like the padre he is.

My shoulders slump as I point at Ethan. "He doesn't want to talk to me."

"You're the one who doesn't like talking," he grumbles.

I snap my gaze to his, meeting his glare with one of my own. "I wanted to talk before. Remember? When you kicked me out?"

"Oh really?" He starts climbing the stairs. "So, you showed up here to tell me how you *feel,* did you?"

"Yeah, I did, actually." I thump up after him, following him into his room.

"Or maybe you were here to explain why you and your little sorority bitches created some big hoax to burn me." He slams the door shut, and I flinch again.

Shit. My nerves are stretched to breaking point, and I honestly don't know if I can handle this right now.

As much as I want to yell and rant about this whole shitty night, I also just want it to be over.

Letting out a shaky sigh, I run my fingers through my hair and fist the back. "Okay. Fine. You're right. It did start out that way, but it changed pretty damn fast. And I wanted to tell you, but—"

"Oh, bullshit," he scoffs. "You've been playing me this whole time."

"That's not true."

"Don't!" he growls, his eyes flashing bright, his gaze almost dangerous. "Don't fucking string me along anymore. I never thought I'd ever be capable of feeling this way about anyone, and then you make me fall. You make me fall so damn hard, only to find out that none of it is real!"

His words blow me back a step, and I blink at him, scrambling to digest what he's telling me while trying to line it up with the fact that he keeps hesitating every time we get too close.

"R-Real?" I sputter. "Falling? What are you talking about? You're the one who doesn't want me!"

"I *do* want you." He leans forward, then pings back with an exasperated scoff. "I told you that. I *showed* you that."

"And then you pull away. Every time. If I get too close, you pull away, so there must be something wrong with me, because rumor has it you've slept with half the girls in this school. So why can't you sleep with me?"

"There is nothing wrong with you," he bites back. "You are perfect, okay? Everything about you is amazing. From the way you dress, to the way you talk, to the way you watch hockey and play video games and eat fucking pizza!" He flings his arms wide. "Everything about you is what I want, and then I find out it was all a joke!"

My heart is beating so hard I don't even know how I'm gonna form words right now, but somehow they punch out of me. "It wasn't a joke. And I am *not* perfect. You are. I love everything about *you*, from your messy hair to your giant feet." I point at them, and it suddenly occurs to me that he must have run out of the house barefoot to reach me tonight. "You're Captain Hero. And you came for me, even when I didn't deserve it."

His forehead wrinkles, like my words are taking him off guard somehow.

My voice drops to a husky whisper, the fire draining out of me as I keep going with my list. "I love the way you play hockey and look after your friends... and watched *Dawson's Creek* with your mom." I flash him a watery smile. "You're good and you're loyal and you work so hard, and I love all those things about you so much. I love..." I point at him, the air whooshing out of me as my shoulders slump and I finally admit the truth out loud. "I love you. All of you. I love you."

I've never said that to a guy before, and holy shit, do I feel vulnerable right now.

I suck in a shaky breath and look at him.

He's staring at me in stunned silence.

I cross my arms, shrinking in on myself and wondering if now is the time to bolt from the room. That couch is calling my name... or maybe I can run down the hall and lock myself in the bathroom. There's a tub in there, right? I could cozy up with some towels. It'll be great.

Ethan's still not saying anything, so I inch toward his door, nearly turning to grab the handle when he stops me with his gravelly voice.

"You love me? For real love me?"

My eyes shoot toward him, and I'm caught in his gaze, my throat burning as I nod, then struggle to ask, "Do you love me?"

He tips his head, his expression crumpling with a look so desperate that my heart can hardly take it. He closes the gap between us, cupping my face and murmuring against my lips, "Fuck yeah, I do," before kissing me.

It's a desperate kiss, humming with an emotion so strong my head is reeling.

He pulls back, gazing down at my face, his eyes lighting with tenderness before he closes the space between us again.

Wrapping my arms around him, I cling to his neck, letting out a ragged sob as he pulls me close, then sweeps his tongue into my mouth. His arms slide up my back, suctioning our bodies together.

Threading my fingers into his hair, I fist the back of his shirt, deepening our kiss like I can't get enough of him.

I can't.

I want him all. Every inch.

I want him to feel how much I meant what I just said.

Unzipping his hoodie, I'm pleased to find his bare chest ready and waiting for me. His body is rock-hard, sculpted muscle. Dragging my fingers over those perfect contours, I drink him in with a smile.

"So perfect," I whisper before kissing his pecs, then sucking his nipple.

He hisses, gripping my hair with a choked groan when I graze my teeth over the sensitive spot, then keep inching my way to his waistline.

He leans his hands against the wall, bracing himself when I drop to my knees and yank his sweats down. He's going commando, and his cock springs out to greet me. It's still beautiful, and I grin like a cat who's got the cream, biting my bottom lip with a playful grin.

Ethan's groan sends a shiver right through me as I grab his manhood, licking a path from base to tip. His guttural moaning spurs me on, and I suck him into my mouth, gripping the base and squeezing.

"Holy shit, that feels good." He can barely speak past his heavy breathing, and I feel a surge of triumph that I'm able to pleasure him this way.

One hand drops from the wall, resting on the top of my head as I draw him even farther into my mouth. I glide my hand up his muscular thigh, the hard muscle and the curve of his perfect ass making my panties wet.

My need for him is pulsing strong, and when he chokes out, "Stop, stop," and pulls away, I nearly whine, *"Why? No! Don't make me stop."*

But then I capture his smile as he takes my hand and pulls me to my feet. "I want to come inside you."

To date, those are the sexiest words I have ever heard in my life.

My insides trill as he kicks the sweats off his beautiful feet and strips me of my clothes. I raise my arms, my breath kissing his chest as my shirt and skirt hit the floor. My panties end up who knows where, and I press my body against his, the sensation of his hard length and bare skin making my entire body ignite.

I already thought I was running an inferno here, but this heat is next level.

I push him back so he flops onto the mattress, and now it's my turn to crawl toward him as he nestles himself against the pillows.

I straddle his thighs, gazing down at his straining penis but still having to ask, "You want this, right? Like... you really want it?"

He tips my chin until I'm forced to look him in the eye, and I swear I could drown in that gaze. "I want it," he whispers. "Now, suit me up."

I grin, yanking his drawer open and pulling out a condom. I roll it onto him, hoping I'm doing it right. He checks that it's secure, then lightly rests his hands on my hips when I rise over him.

I've only done this once before, and I can't help that flash of uncertainty riding through me. He's big and beautiful, and I want this so badly, but I don't want to screw it up either.

"It's okay." He cups my cheek, pulling me forward and kissing me. "We can take this slow. We can do it any way you want."

I let out a soft breath, smiling at him as I rise to my knees and line myself up over him. His deft fingers find my opening, slipping inside and making me groan.

"You're so wet." He grins.

"For you," I whisper, then start lowering myself onto him.

He lines us up, and the second his head starts to part my aching lips, I let out a soft gasp. It's pure delight, pure ecstasy, as he stretches and fills me. I take it slow, my body adjusting to this overwhelming mix of pleasure and maybe a touch of pain. But a good pain. He's big, but it's also a relief to finally satisfy this achy need for him.

I had no idea how badly I'd been craving this connection, how much my body had to have this man... and only this man.

Ethan's fingers dig into my hips, and I swear his eyes roll backward as I sink farther onto him. "So fucking tight," he rasps. "Shit, you feel amazing."

I let him in a little deeper, inch by inch, until he's all the way inside me. Tipping my head back with a soft moan, I rest my hands on his chest and revel in this sensation. His body is quivering beneath mine; I can feel his strain to not start thrusting, to let me take my time and adjust to him.

It doesn't take long. Pure instinct starts to drive me, and I'm soon rising and falling, riding Ethan to a rhythm that is for him alone.

CHAPTER 42
ETHAN

Mikayla's wet heat is so perfect, I nearly blew the second she sat on me. It's taking every ounce of control not to lose it after only a few quick thrusts. I can't let that happen. I need this to last. After three weeks of no action, my cock's not playing fair, and I clench my butt cheeks, willing Mikayla's tight pussy to let me play for a little longer.

Her beautiful tits bounce as she picks up her pace, her pants and sexy whimpers igniting my insides to a white-hot fire. I cup them, giving them a gentle squeeze and loving the way they fit so perfectly in my palms. Everything about her fits me perfectly, and I revel in this feeling. Her skin is smooth and soft. I trail my knuckle over her stomach, then find the sweet spot between her legs, giving her clit a flick with my thumb.

She gasps, her eyes popping open like she's just tasted chocolate for the first time. The delighted look on her face makes my heart sing.

I keep rubbing gentle circles, the distraction helping

me hang on while she rides me and skyrockets toward her own orgasm.

She tips her head back with a groan, and I feel her thighs quivering against mine. She's close. She's so fucking close. I watch in wonder as her body pings tight and she cries out my name.

It's the most beautiful fucking sound in the world, her strangled gasp calling me like a siren while her insides clutch my cock, her walls spasming.

Grabbing her ass, I hold her close and, in one swift move, flip her onto her back. Her legs wrap around me, drawing me into her with another cry of pleasure. I thrust deep, unable to take my eyes off her face. She's beautiful. She's so damn beautiful.

And then her eyes open, that blue gaze of hers drinking me in, and I swear I catch a glimpse of her soul. It's the most intimate thing I've ever experienced, and I can't help croaking, "I love you," as I thrust a little deeper —one, two, three times and then finally let myself go.

A guttural groan slips out of me, the orgasm feeling a thousand times stronger than anything I've had before. It drives through me, shutting down each muscle until I'm a floppy, weak mess, barely able to hold myself above her.

I sink onto my elbows, breathing hard and trying to get control of my wild heartbeat. It pounds against her chest as I brush my lips across her neck and whisper, "I love you so fucking much."

She giggles, her body vibrating beneath me. "I love you too."

Her lips caress my shoulder, her hands trailing down my back as she lets out a satisfied moan. "That was so awesome. You know I'm gonna need to do that again, right?"

I laugh, lifting my head with a smirk. "Just give me a minute and I'll be good to go."

Her throaty chuckle is followed by a whoop as she raises her hands in the air and tips her head back with a loud "Yes!"

I watch her celebrate, laughing with her and figuring it won't take long before I'm ready for round two.

This woman is something else, and I already can't wait to see her come in a thousand different ways. I can't wait to *make* her come in a thousand different ways. Just me. Because she's mine, and I can't see myself ever wanting to let her go.

CHAPTER 43
MIKAYLA

Ethan Galloway is an Olympic god. If sex was a sport at the games, he'd win the gold medal. I am sure of it.

As my languid, sweaty body flops against his chest, I can't help yet another triumphant laugh. "Round three was also great. The judges are, once again, very impressed by your performance."

His chest rumbles beneath me, his hand gliding over my naked back and nudging me closer to him. I curl my leg up over his thighs and snuggle closer.

It's like three o'clock in the morning, and we've yet to sleep. How am I supposed to drift away when the hottest human on the planet is lying naked beside me?

His lips brush my forehead as he nestles into the pillows and rests his cheek against mine. I close my eyes, floating on this languid, post-sex cloud. It's a pretty awesome feeling, and maybe I can fall asleep this way.

Until Ethan murmurs, "So, this whole publicly breaking my heart thing. What's happening with that now?"

I sigh, cringing as I rise on my elbow so I can look down at his face. I trace the line of his jaw and stop at the tip of his chin. "They recorded you outside the house, so... that kind of covers it."

"And..." He searches my face, his expression serious. "They kicked you out anyway? What happened?"

I shrug, then nestle back against his chest.

"Mick, come on. Why were you outside the library?"

I press my lips together before releasing a soft sigh. "I left. I told Aimee she can shove her sorority up her ass. Even though I knew I'd already lost you, I couldn't stay in that place."

He lets out a surprised laugh, then squeezes me against him, kissing the top of my head. "You haven't lost me."

I swallow, not wanting to think about how monumentally I may have screwed up my future. Wrapping my arm around Ethan's stomach, I cling to him, reminding myself what I've gotten out of this whole shit show.

Him. And I never want him doubting how I feel about him.

"You know I..." I hold my breath, having to resist the urge to avoid my feelings and actually let a few of them out. "That night we first met... I had just told the girls that I wasn't gonna do anything so cruel. I didn't know this Ethan Galloway person they were talking about, and I didn't care who he might have pissed off. I walked out... and then bumped into you."

"Should have asked for my name, huh?"

I laugh against his chest, loving the way he's playing with my hair. The sweet, soft movement of his fingers is both thrilling and comforting.

"So, why'd you go back, then?"

"I needed a place to stay. I..." Wincing, I have to fight to get out the truth. "My mom and her fiancé are paying for my education. One of the conditions was that they wanted me to join Sigma Beta Mu. I had to do whatever it took, and... I tried. But I shouldn't have done it. I'm sorry I hurt you."

"You didn't."

"Yes I did. That look on your face." I lift my chin so I can catch his eye.

He kisses the tip of my nose. "That's when I thought it wasn't real. But I know it is now." He smiles. "When did it become real for you?"

"I don't know, probably when you called me Mickey Mouse."

He laughs. "That was right at the start."

"I know!" I flick my hand up in mock exasperation. "And then I had to pretend like I wasn't into you when I was around the girls and then lie to myself when I was with you, saying how this was all for the sorority. It's been a serious nightmare." I climb on top of him, my breasts squishing against his chest as I gaze down at his gorgeous grin. I want to smile and be playful about it, but there's a somber note to my voice. "Tonight... when I saw your face, when you thought I didn't mean any of it, I just... I couldn't stay in that house."

The look in his eyes is enough to melt my heart, and then he goes and tucks my hair behind my ears. "I never thought you fit in there anyway."

I grin and snuggle against him, pretty sure using him for a mattress would be a damn comfortable sleep. "You know, you're way comfier than the concrete outside the library."

"I better fucking hope so," he growls and pokes me in the side. I jump, letting out this embarrassing squeak when he finds my ticklish spot.

"Oh really?" His eyes take on a playful glint as he goes for it again.

"Ethan," I warn him, grabbing his finger, but he's too strong.

I soon find myself in fits of laughter, pinned beneath him as he tickle-tortures me until the heat between us rises once more.

His hot tongue is soon painting my nipples while his deft fingers glide over my curves.

And let round four begin.

CHAPTER 44

ETHAN

Mikayla snores when she sleeps.

It's not a loud jet plane kind of roar. More like a soft buzz that I could fall asleep to. A rhythmic lilt that is lulling me toward dreamland... until my brain stops it just before I completely drift away.

Sleep's been kind of impossible tonight. For some reason, I can't black out. It's like I don't want to miss one second of this.

Mikayla's small body is spooned within mine, my hand tucked beneath her right boob, my head on the pillow behind her.

My cock has finally had his fill after four rounds, each one blowing my mind in a different way. Just the reminder makes him twitch, but I order him back into submission. I don't want to hurt her. She denied it, but I could tell that last time she was kind of sensitive, and I would have stopped if she hadn't begged me to keep going.

I'm glad she did. We came at the same time, our cries

mingling together while she milked me dry. I just lay on her, unable to move for a minute as I drank in her tired smile, then lightly pressed our lips together.

She loves me.

She left Sig Be house for me. Walked right out the door with all her stuff.

It's kind of epic, and I don't know if any other girl on campus would do that for me. Sure, they flirt and swoon and act like I'm a walking hockey god, but would they really give up so much to be with me?

I need to unpack the details a little more on her mother and that weird-ass condition she gave Mikayla. If she's quit the sorority, does that mean her mom will stop paying for her tuition? That's crazy.

Mikayla murmurs something incoherent in her sleep, and I can't help smiling, brushing my lips across her smooth shoulder and trying to wrap my head around the wonder of her.

I've never let a girl sleep over before. This is all so new. I thought I'd hate it—someone in my space, stealing my covers—but it's pretty fucking awesome.

Sure, I haven't slept much, but the feel of her curled up against me, completely relaxed in my arms is... I can't even describe how cool it is.

The level of trust that comes with that. She's naked right now, asleep in a house full of guys. Not that any of them would touch her, but still. I'm kind of honored. She knows I'll protect her... even if it's just on a subconscious level.

I'm her Captain Hero. I grin.

My eyes drift shut as I let my own body relax. My mind starts to float again, and this time I let it go, finally falling into darkness... until there's a pounding on my door.

"Time to pay up, big guy! Let's go!"

Shit! My head pops off the pillow, and I'm instantly alert while Mikayla lets out a soft moan of complaint.

"I know what you got up to last night, man! I'm not deaf," Asher calls through the wood. "Now, get your ass up and get dressed. Actually, scratch that. You don't need to get dressed." He starts laughing, and I clutch Mikayla a little tighter against me.

Shit, shit, shit!

The bet. The fucking bet.

Sure, it whistled through my brain a couple times last night, but I told it to fuck off, because there was no way I wasn't showing Mikayla how much I wanted her. We connected on a whole new level last night, and I wouldn't trade that for anything.

If it means I have to walk around campus naked today, then so be it.

I groan, squeezing my eyes shut and cursing my cocky ass for agreeing to such a stupid bet in the first place.

CHAPTER 45
MIKAYLA

The thumping on the door roused me, as did something about not bothering to get dressed this morning.

The words take a minute to register, my sleepy brain too slow to calculate them. With a little groan, I roll over and creep my eyes open.

Ethan is gazing at me, but the sweet smile on his face does absolutely nothing to hide his worry.

"What was all that about?" I mumble, my morning voice taking a minute to kick in.

"Uh... just this, um... I have this thing with Asher." His eyes dart past my shoulder, and I sit up with a jolt, my small boobs jiggling.

His gaze skims my body, and I resist the urge to cover up. He just spent the night exploring every inch of me; I can't go getting bashful now.

Lightly pinching his chin, I force him to look me in the eye and ask, "What thing? The look on your face tells me it's not good. So, spill."

He covers his eyes with a groan, then rattles off the

details so fast I struggle to keep up with them. "I made a bet with Asher and lost, so I'm not supposed to have sex for a month."

I blink. "No sex. For a month?"

"Yeah." He groans again.

I look down at our naked bodies. "You do realize that what we did last night is called sex, right?"

His dry glare is comical enough to make me laugh, but his lips aren't even twitching, so I quickly sober up.

"Okay." I swivel my body to face him, and his hand lands on my hip. I love the way his large fingers curve around my body. He's so big and broad and beautiful and—

Focus, Mick!

"So... what was the bet?"

He gives me a sheepish wince. "That I could beat him at darts. We'd been drinking," he adds, as if that explains everything.

"Okay, and you lost, so now you're not supposed to have sex for a month." A thought hits me—yes, my morning brain is slow—and I let out a gasp. "Wait. Is that why you kept hesitating over us?"

He gives me a *well, duh* look, and I can't help a huge grin. He did want me. He wanted me all along.

"Why didn't you just tell me? It could have saved a lot of angst, you know?"

"Yeah." He squeezes my hip, his eyes lingering over my body before he looks up at my face again. "But it was part of the deal. I wasn't allowed to tell anyone so that girls would think I wasn't into them."

"Well, it worked," I mutter, then narrow my eyes at

him. "So, you broke the rules last night. Obvi." I point between us. "What are the consequences for that?"

His expression buckles, and my insides jolt with alarm. Every guy, no matter how amazing they are, has at least one asshole gene. Some have many, and that look on Ethan's face is warning me that Asher has a whole bunch of them.

"What do you have to do?" I practically growl.

He throws back the covers with a sigh, exposing his long, glorious body to me as he rises out of bed. His ass cheeks clench when he mutters to the wall, "I have to spend the day naked."

"Naked?"

"Yeah." He spins around with a sigh. "I've got to walk around campus naked."

"What?" My eyes bulge. "No way! You are *not* doing that."

"I have to." He flings his arms wide and starts heading for the door.

I scramble off the bed and chase him, grabbing his arm and spinning him back around. He could get into so much trouble for that. Someone will call the campus police, and he'll get arrested. Sure, he might only get a slap on the wrist, but it'll still go on his record, and what is his coach going to say? He might get suspended and miss the start of the season, or worse! If he gets kicked off the team over this, I'll—

"No." I give him a pointed look. "You're not doing this."

"A bet's a bet, Mick. I'm a man of my word, and I have to follow through."

He goes to move again, but I squeeze his wrist and

keep him put, taking another step forward and wishing I was tall enough to eyeball him. I could spout off about all this hockey stuff, but I'm sure he's already thought that through.

Yet he still gave in to his desire for me. I made him break this bet. Sure, I didn't know it, but I was kind of demanding about the whole sex thing, needing to rid myself of these insecurities.

Dammit! I won't let him do this.

And besides all that, I'm not letting him walk out the door butt naked for the rest of the world to see.

"You're mine now," I tell him. "And you're not walking around campus so everyone can check out the goodies." I point at his glorious manhood. "That junk belongs to me, and it's for my eyes only."

He lets out a surprised laugh. "You can't own my junk."

My right eyebrow arches as I throw him the most challenging look I can muster.

He throws one right back at me, so I let him go, crossing my arms with a nod that makes my insides flail.

But it's the only thing I can think to do.

"Okay, fine." I go to move past him, reaching for the door handle.

"What are you doing?" His voice pitches with alarm.

I look over my shoulder at him. "If you're gonna walk around naked, then so am I."

"No fucking way." He wraps his arm around my waist, lifting me off my feet and pulling me back from the door.

"But you can't own my body. I can show it to whoever the hell I want to."

He growls, setting me down by the bed and pointing

at me. He's about to say something that will spark an argument between us, but bring it on.

I am *not* letting him do this!

He opens his mouth and snaps it shut when someone starts pounding on the door again. "Let's go, lover boy! Time to pay up!"

"In a minute!" Ethan thunders over his shoulder while I shout in a bright voice.

"Come in."

Ethan's head whips around, and he gapes at me with a horrified glare as the door pops open. Jumping in front of me, he covers my naked body with his own, reaching back to snatch my arms so I can't dart around him and show... oh, it's Asher... that I'm not wearing a stitch.

Ethan's broad frame blocks most of my view, but when I try to peek around his arm, he quickly jerks my body back behind his.

I can't see Asher's face right now, but I can tell he's grinning. "Looks like you're ready to go."

With a little grunt, I fight Ethan's hold and pop my head out around his arm. "Not yet. We're just discussing something."

Ethan growls and spins around, pulling me close so my breasts are squished against his hard torso. His protective arms keep me in place, and I stay still, figuring Asher even seeing one nipple might just kill Ethan on the spot.

"You've got three minutes, dude. Then it's on." Asher walks away with a laugh, and I wrestle myself free of Ethan's hold.

Looking up with an arched brow, I quietly warn him, "If I can't stop you doing this, then you can't stop me. You can try, but you will fail. I will strip my clothes off in the middle of the quad if I have to."

His nostrils flare as he points at the bed behind me. "I will tie you up in here and lock the door."

I can't help a short snicker. Ethan's angry face is kinda cute. I'm pretty sure he'll hate to know that, so I lick my lips and give him an unrelenting look. "No you won't, because I will get you back so hard for doing that to me." I point at him. "Now, you need to stop this, or I will."

"And how the hell are you gonna do that?" He crosses his arms, his frown annoyingly skeptical.

I wish I had some eloquent, genius thing to say, but I'm working on the fly here.

Truth is, Ethan's the wrong person to be arguing with.

"I need to talk to Asher," I mutter under my breath, grabbing Ethan's T-shirt off the floor and throwing it on before bolting from the room.

CHAPTER 46
ETHAN

I throw on some boxers and chase after Mikayla, my feet stumbling on the stairs as I try to grab her. She's too fucking fast, and I can't even nip the edge of my shirt as she flies into the living area where all the guys are sitting and standing around the kitchen counter.

Casey's nursing a coffee, looking a little blurry-eyed while Liam sits there in a sweaty T-shirt. He must have just gotten home from his morning run. Asher's standing there spinning a basketball on his finger, which he quickly catches when Mikayla marches toward him.

She's not wearing a thing under my T-shirt. Holy shit. Can they see her nipples through the cotton? She better not raise her arms. My shirt's pretty long on her, but it's not touching her knees, which means it's too fucking short when she's panty-less.

I jerk to a stop behind her, grabbing the edges of the T-shirt and making sure it stays in place. I'm tempted to throw her over my shoulder and carry her back upstairs, no doubt kicking and screaming, but that will probably expose her very fine ass to these guys and—

Shit. She's right. I can't tell her she doesn't own my junk and then act like I own every inch of her body.

"Asher, we need to talk about this bet." She crosses her arms, seemingly unperturbed by the fact that she's being studied by three big hockey players... and what the fuck are Riley and Connor doing here? Those guys have dorm rooms. Do they ever use them?

They jump off the couch and wander over, eyeing up Mikayla with surprise before breaking into broad grins.

Great. Now five big guys are gawking at her.

"Did she stay the night?" Riley asks with a look so gleeful I want to punch him. "Does this mean—"

"It sure does." Asher nods, then turns back to Mikayla with a smirk. "Sorry, sweetheart, but your boy broke the rules, and we shook on terms. He can't go backing out now."

"I don't give a shit what terms you agreed upon. I'm not letting him walk around campus naked."

"You should be grateful it's a Saturday. There'll be minimal foot traffic. Well played, man." Asher holds out his fist, and I glare at his knuckles until he lowers his arm with a short laugh.

Casey snorts and shakes his head. I can't see what Mikayla's face is doing, but whatever look she throws at Casey shuts him up quick. Liam hides a grin behind his water bottle while Asher continues to stand there looking smug.

"Rules are rules, babe." He shrugs. "Things were set in motion before you even came along, and there's nothing you can do to stop it. Thank you, by the way." He winks at her, and I growl like a bear.

Asher laughs at me, and I'm about to grab Mikayla's arm and drag her back upstairs when she goes and makes my stomach drop.

"What if we set up a new bet?"

Panic sizzles through me. *What bet? What's she going to agree to?*

I move into her line of sight, tempted to cover her mouth with my hand before she says something stupid and ends up losing to Asher. Shit, the guy's relentless.

"Intriguing." He smirks, his eyebrows wiggling. "What do you have in mind?"

"I don't know..." She shrugs and waves her hand at him. "I'll play some one-on-one ball with you. If I win, Ethan's out of this stupid bet and the slate is clean."

Asher chuckles, resting the basketball against his hip and leaning forward. "And if I win?"

She swallows and looks around. "I'll, uh..." Her eyes light on the kitchen and she winces. "I'll play Cinderella for a month."

"Cinderella?" Asher frowns.

"You know, do dishes, mow lawns, wash cars and shit."

"What? No." I shake my head, gaping at the large pile of dishes scattered over the counter.

So, we're not the cleanest.

"And our laundry," Asher adds.

"Oooo. I like the sound of that," Casey murmurs into his coffee mug.

"Fuck off, you guys," I bark at them. "She's not doing that!"

"Deal." She speaks over me, sticking out her hand for Asher to shake.

"You don't have to do this." I try to intercept, but I'm too late.

Mikayla ducks around me, shaking Asher's hand before glancing up at me with a worried smile. "It'll be fine."

"Heads up." Asher shoots the basketball at her, and she only just gets her hands up in time, fumbling the thing before gripping it to her stomach.

"Shit," I mumble under my breath. "Don't do this, Mick. He's going to demolish you on the court."

"Too late, she already shook."

I ignore Asher's taunting and throw her a desperate frown, scrambling for a way out of this. "I'll just follow through on my bet. You don't need to do this for me."

"You're not walking around campus naked," she snaps, hugging the ball like a teddy bear. "Look, I played a little basketball in high school." She darts her eyes to Asher, who's shooting her a gleeful grin. "It'll be okay."

She doesn't believe that.

Shit! What have I gotten her into?

Following her out to the entrance, I hover over her while she pulls fresh clothes out of her bag, and then I carry it up to my room. We quickly get dressed, Mikayla donning a pair of ass-hugging shorts that make my mouth water. They're gym shorts, but holy shit, that body of hers is tight. If I wasn't so distracted by her impending loss, I'd be tempted to take her all over again. But I don't make a move or say a word as she throws on a tank top and ties up her hair.

"Seriously, Mick, you don't have to—"

"Would you stop saying that?" she cuts me off with a sharp frown. "I'm the one who made you break the rules. The least I can do is get you out of it."

"You didn't *make* me break anything. I chose to be with you because I wanted to. We needed last night."

She throws me a grateful smile, her eyes glimmering with enough emotion to blow me right off my feet.

"I'll help you with everything—dishes, lawns, cleaning, laundry." I guess it's another way of telling her I love her. "You don't have to do this alone."

"Thanks," she murmurs, patting my stomach as she walks past me before plucking the ball off the floor and heading back downstairs.

The guys are all waiting for us. Even Baxter's hauled his ass out of bed for this one. I throw a concerned frown at Liam, but he doesn't seem too worried by all of this, trailing out the door after Mikayla and Asher.

Fuck. This is gonna be a train wreck, and then my poor girl is gonna be a freaking housemaid for the next four weeks.

Shit, shit, shit!

I miserably walk to the basketball court, trying to figure a way out of this, but I'm pretty sure my lil' mouse won't let me do it. I kind of love that she's fighting for me. I just wish the feeling wasn't being overshadowed by the guilt lashing me.

I'll help her. I won't make her do any of the chores on her own.

The thought gives me some comfort, and I lean against the fence of the outdoor court, cringing as Mikayla dribbles the ball, then shoots a weak pass to Asher.

He's fucking crowing over this whole thing.

"Ouch," Liam hisses. "This is gonna be tough to watch."

A growl reverberates in my throat. Casey elbows me with a laugh. "Gotta love this girl. She's awesome, man." He shakes his head, then grins at me. "Congrats, by the way. I know you broke the rules, but I'm glad you got her. It's obvious how much she means to you."

I nod, flicking him a closed-mouth smile before glancing at the court where this game of one-on-one is just beginning. Asher towers over Mikayla, easily stealing the ball on her first attempt at a basket.

Liam hisses again while I cross my arms and watch in agony.

Asher quickly makes eleven points with one slam dunk, three lay-ups, and an annoying three-pointer that makes us all cringe. It's the first to twenty-one, and I've got a feeling we won't be out here long, until...

I shoot up straight, blinking in surprise when Mikayla does a quick spin, dribbling the ball around Asher and darting to the right. She jumps and scores a sweet three-pointer.

"Where the hell did that come from?" Casey laughs, clapping his hands and whooping. "Go, lil' mouse! Go!"

Asher shakes his head, still smirking at Mikayla's piece of luck, until she does it again. This time on his left, her quick feet dancing away from him as she dribbles the ball like a pro and does another three-pointer. The net swishes, and Asher gathers the ball with this confused look on his face.

"What is happening right now?" He shoots us a frown, then looks back at my girl.

Mikayla swipes the back of her hand over her forehead. "We're playing ball, dickhead."

She fires the ball at him so fast and hard he catches it with a soft "Oof."

And the biggest smile spreads across my face.

"I played a little basketball in high school."

A little basketball, my ass. She was probably one of the top players in her school.

Damn, I love this woman.

Asher dribbles the ball somewhat cautiously as he eyes up Mikayla. The cocky edge has dropped from his expression, and he's concentrating hard, studying his opponent like this game means everything.

She wiggles her eyebrows at him. He frowns, trying to get around her with a quick shuffle, but she pounces forward, easily stealing the ball and dribbling it to the basket for a perfectly timed bank shot.

"Holy shit, are you hustling me, lil' mouse? Is that what this is?"

"What do you think?" She walks over with a cocky grin, and I swear I love her so much in this moment my heart hurts.

Asher's eyebrows dip into a sharp frown, and he slaps her butt as she walks past.

"Hey!" I give him a warning roar, jumping away from the fence, but Mikayla brushes it off with a laugh while Casey holds me back.

"Don't worry, baby." She dribbles the ball, grinning over her shoulder at me. "Watch me make Asher cry."

My friend growls, lunging for the ball, but she spins away, making quick work of scoring another three-pointer.

The score is now tied at eleven, but it doesn't stay that way for long.

Mikayla is relentless and makes quick work of running Asher ragged. He manages a couple of lay-ups, but she demolishes him on three-pointers. The second the ball swishes through the net to make the score twenty-three to eighteen, we all start jumping in victory.

Casey springs onto Liam's back like we've just scored a winning goal in hockey. Riley and Connor are both cheering while Mikayla gathers the ball and skips past Asher with a girly grin.

"Here you go." She hands the basketball over, batting her eyelashes at him.

He glares at her, muttering, "Well played," but as she skips over to me, I see his lips twitching. There's a glow of admiration in his eyes, and I can't believe she's mine.

I catch her in my arms the second she's within reach, loving the way her legs tuck around my waist. I hold her securely with one arm while cradling the back of her neck with my hand.

"I fucking love you."

She laughs. "I fucking love you too."

Pulling her down to my mouth, I show her with a searing kiss that owns us both. Her tongue swipes against mine, her legs tightening around me as she clings to my shoulders and deepens the kiss.

I moan against her mouth, already calculating how fast I can run from the court to my bedroom, when a loud screech from the fence pulls us apart.

"Mikayla Evelyn Hyde, you stop that right now!"

Mick rips her mouth away from mine with a gasp, her entire body tensing as she gazes over my shoulder. I turn with her still in my arms and spot an immaculately dressed woman clipping her way onto the court.

"Oh shit," Mick whispers under her breath.

"Who is that?"

"My mother." Mikayla wriggles out of my arms. I set her down but keep a protective hand on the back of her neck until she murmurs, "Wait here, okay?"

She moves away from me, and I'm about to ignore her request. The woman storming toward us right now looks mega pissed.

But then my lil' mouse turns and fires a pleading look at me. "Please. Just… stay here. All of you." Her eyes brush over my friends, and we nod, respecting her need for privacy.

Against the instincts firing through me, I watch her run toward what feels like obvious danger and hold my ground. But I'm not taking my eyes off her for one second.

CHAPTER 47
MIKAYLA

"Hey, Mom." I try to keep my voice light as I slow to a stop in front of her.

She narrows her glare on me, a laser-focused look that fries my insides. Her nostrils are flaring too—never a good sign.

"What are you doing here?" I run a hand down my ponytail, wondering what she's most annoyed about.

Was it the fact that I was playing tongue twister in public with Ethan? Or maybe it's because I'm hanging with a bunch of guys—something she's always hated me doing. Apparently, ladies don't hang out with a bunch of sweaty men. It's improper.

Yeah, we're in the 2020s and my mother is still using words like *improper*.

I'm pretty sure if she had her way, she'd be strapping me into a corset and making sure my ankles were covered.

"Who is that?"

"Um..." I glance over my shoulder and cringe at

Ethan before turning back to just say it. "That's my boyfriend."

"Hm." She lifts her chin. "You've never mentioned him."

"Yeah, it's kinda new."

"It doesn't look new." Her steely voice and unimpressed glare have my gaze dropping to the concrete. "Does he have anything to do with your abhorrent behavior last night?"

I flush, biting my lips together and giving her an ambiguous shoulder hitch. Of course Aimee called her daddy, no doubt ranting about my rudely worded exit from the sorority house, and of course my mother found out and jumped in his chauffeur-driven car to come and "talk some sense into me."

"You signed a contract." Her French-manicured nails click together when she holds her thumb and fingers up like she's pinching thin air. "Does that mean nothing to you? You told me you were trying. You said you were giving it your best."

I tip to the edges of my sneakers, not sure when to jump in with my myriad of justifications. She must be pretty damn pissed if she drove all the way out here. Obviously, this kind of tongue-lashing can't be done over the phone. Bummer for me.

I wrinkle my nose, trying to figure out where to start. "So, yeah, I, uh... I don't belong in that place, and they were asking too much."

"Not too much." She spits out the words. "Loyalty. Commitment. Getting your priorities straight! They welcomed you in, and you walked out the door. You didn't even try!"

"I did." I throw my hands wide. "I learned all the sorority history, I sang their stupid song, I cleaned toilets with a toothbrush, I made breakfast for everybody. There was only one thing I wasn't willing to do, and I—"

"Do you have any idea how *humiliated* I am right now?" Her blue eyes glisten, her voice breaking with emotion. "Jarrod is furious. I can't believe you told his daughter to go... *screw herself*."

"I actually told her to—doesn't matter." I shake my head. "In fairness to me, she was being a bit—"

"Don't you dare try and justify your shameful behavior." She wags her finger at me. Her painted lips dip into a disgusted frown before she starts blinking at tears. "No matter how hard I try, I just can't help you. You won't let me."

"Help me?"

"You're just like him, you know." Her disappointment and repulsion make my head jolt back. "Your father was always so stubborn and set in his ways. He didn't care what anyone else thought. He just did what he wanted." Her hand flicks in the air, light glinting off the mammoth rock adorning her fourth finger. "And I tried. I didn't want you turning out like him, but you just *refuse* to bend. No matter what I do. No matter what I give."

I cross my arms, anger coursing through me. "I'm an adult now. You don't have to *try* anymore."

"Oh really? So you have the money to attend this prestigious school, do you?"

Her mockery deflates me, and I curl in on myself, crossing my arms and pinching my sweaty biceps.

"I didn't think so." Her voice stops quaking, replaced

with a steely edge that makes me squirm. "You need me. You need Jarrod."

I grit my teeth.

"So, you will apologize to him, then to Aimee. You will grovel, and you will do whatever it takes to get back into that Sig Be house." She glances over my shoulder, her eyes narrowing with disgust at the Hockey House guys. "*Whatever* it takes."

I'm already shaking my head.

"Yes. Yes, you will. Because you have embarrassed me for the last time. Jarrod very generously offered to fund your education and all he asked—all *we* asked—in return, is that you followed a few small conditions that would be helpful to you."

Helpful, my ass!

My nostrils flare and I open my mouth to protest, but she keeps ranting before I can.

"And you signed that contract. That was your choice, Mikayla. And right now, you are in breach. You need to fix this. If you don't, you won't be getting one more dime from Jarrod. Is that clear?"

I work my jaw to the side.

"Is that clear, Mikayla?" Mom practically shouts the question.

I sniff and look away from her, my insides writhing. "It's clear. It's *fucking bullshit*, but it's clear!"

"Don't you use that language with me. You're lucky he's even willing to give you a second chance after the way you treated Aimee."

"It's not fair," I bite back. "Does no one care how she treated me?"

Mom rolls her eyes. "I'm sure she wasn't that bad."

"But I am?"

Her unimpressed scowl speaks volumes. Clenching my fists, I resist the urge to stamp my foot like a petulant child. But come on!

"You're supposed to stand up for me. I'm your daughter. But you side with him every time. Who the hell *makes* their child join a sorority? Who the hell *forces* their child to go to a particular school?"

"Oh, stop being so dramatic. It was your choice."

"It wasn't my choice! You forced my hand. There's no way Jarrod would have given me money toward any other college, and you made it abundantly clear that I would be the world's worst daughter if I didn't do what you wanted me to. I tried! For you." I point at her. "But this isn't who I am. I can't be a Sig Be girl. I'm not like Megan."

"You're definitely not like Megan," she mutters.

Her derogatory tone is poison ivy, and it's an effort to keep the hurt from showing. "So you're just giving up on me, then?"

Her nostrils flare as she looks away, her lips pinching into a thin line. "I've been trying to help you. Give you the best chances life can offer. But you're so damn stubborn. Jarrod has been nothing but good to you, and all you've done is—"

"I don't give a shit about Jarrod." My anger spikes hard and fast. "I don't care what he thinks. He's not my dad!"

She whips back around to look at me, her eyes flashing. "No, your dad left you. He walked out the door, and he didn't look back. You think he'd be willing to pay for your education?" She scoffs like that's the most ludicrous thought in the world. "Jarrod's not even blood, and he's bending over backward to accommodate you."

"Oh really? So why can't he just pay for me to go to school, then? Why do I have to join this stupid sorority?"

"The sorority was to help you," she snaps. "And I knew that if he didn't put it in the contract you'd back out and ruin this opportunity for yourself. You'd fall into your old habits of hanging out with a bunch of loser guys who are going to do nothing but mess up your future. I want you to become somebody, not waste your life!"

"I'm not wasting my life. I know exactly where I'm going and—"

"I don't want to hear it! All I know is that we can't be a part of whatever it is you're trying to achieve here. We won't support you in throwing your life away." She points to the shiny black car waiting on the curb. "Now, you will get in that car. We're going to clean you up, and I'll drive you to the Sig Be house myself."

I stare at her for a long, thick beat. She's standing there puffing after all that shouting and I'm reeling in disbelief. How can she not see me? Why is she so hell bent on turning me into something I'm not?

I can't do it.

I can't give into her demands this time.

"No." I step back from her.

"No?" Mom's mouth drops open. "Have you not heard anything I just said?"

"I heard every word." My voice shakes, and I fight to keep it strong and even. "Now, you listen to me. I am not apologizing, because I am not sorry for leaving that house. I don't belong there. And I don't give two shits if Jarrod's annoyed with me, or you think I'm throwing my life away. I don't even want to be part of this dumb, blended family if I'm not allowed to be myself. So, you can take that contract and shove it up each other's asses for all I care!"

Mom's eyes flash as she sucks in a breath.

And then she cracks me across the face with her ring-clad hand.

She's never slapped me before, and I'm tipped sideways by the unexpected blow.

"Hey!" Ethan roars from behind me. "Get away from her!"

I glance over my shoulder to see him charging. His face is mottled with this mix of horror and indignant rage.

Mom takes a quick step back from me, her eyes jumping to Ethan, before looking at me like she doesn't even know who I am.

"You don't want to be part of this family?" Her voice trembles, the tears on her lashes finally spilling over. "Fine. Then don't be." Shaking her head, she walks away from me just as Ethan jerks to a stop by my side.

"Are you okay?" His voice is kind of urgent, his eyes etched with worry as he studies my face.

I clench my jaw, watching my mother clip to the car, not even bothering to look back once.

The other guys shuffle around me, all glaring at the shiny SUV as it takes off down the road.

"Seriously, Mick. Are you okay?" Ethan asks again.

"No." My voice quakes, and I swear if I cry right now, in front of all these guys, I'm gonna end myself.

Snatching the basketball off Asher, I throw it down with a loud roar. It hits the concrete with a sharp slap, then bounces high, swooping over my head as I walk away from the guys.

"Mikayla," Ethan tries to call me back, but I shake my head, raising my hand to stop him when he walks after me.

"Give me a second." I spin to face him, walking backward and shaking my head. "Just... please." And then I take off before he can reach me. Sprinting off the court, I turn left, not even sure where this path leads.

I just need to find somewhere private.

The tears are building, ugly sobs making my stomach convulse as I try to keep them in.

Mom's words ring inside my head, a deafening gong that reverberates through my body.

She doesn't care if I'm not part of her family anymore.

She's putting her stupid fiancé before her own flesh and blood... which means my time at Nolan U is about to expire.

And once again life proves me right—good things never last for me. And it's all thanks to the people who are supposed to love me in spite of everything. Why are they the ones who are always the first to walk away?

CHAPTER 48
ETHAN

I give Mikayla five full minutes before going to find her.

It's agony. The guys stand there, silently supporting me as I try to reconcile that the horrible bitch who slapped Mikayla is also the woman who birthed her. It doesn't seem possible that my lil' mouse could come from something so hideous.

"How could she slap her own kid? I mean, what the actual fuck!" I shouted at the guys.

They all nodded their agreement, Asher looking pretty dark over the whole thing.

"That bitch," he muttered while Casey murmured his agreement.

Liam stood silent, crossing his arms with a worried frown. I shared a quick glance with him and felt that chill run through me.

As far as I'm aware, he's never told anyone but me about the house he grew up in. He knows what it's like to get knocked around by a person you should be able to trust. Someone who's supposed to love and protect you.

Shit, I've been so lucky. I may have lost my mother way too soon, but when she was alive, she loved me. And my dad... he's given me everything I could ever need.

My heart hurts for Mikayla as I walk the fence line, following the path she took and soon finding her standing by a tree and punching the trunk.

"Hey, stop." I rush over to her, quickly grabbing her wrist before she can plow her knuckles into the rough bark again. Lightly kissing her grazed skin, I murmur, "No more tree punching, okay? You're hurting my girl."

She sniffs, letting out a watery laugh as she obviously tries to rein in her tears. "I told you anger makes me stupid."

I give her a pained frown, then pull her into my arms. As soon as her cheek hits my chest, it's like a switch goes off. A sob punches out of her—a deep sound that feels like it's being yanked from the center of her body. She starts to tremble, her arms looping around me and clinging tight while she quakes and cries against me.

I stand there, holding her in a protective cocoon, trying to be stoic. Trying not to let those tears rip me in half. My shirt is soon smeared with her snot, but I don't move an inch, not until her tears start to ebb.

As her cries turn to soft whimpers, I loosen my grip enough to sit with my back against the tree. I pull her down between my legs and nestle her against me.

She wipes her face with the back of her hand, sniffing and hiccupping a few more times before managing to rasp, "Shit, I hate crying so much."

"You needed to." I press my lips to the back of her head. "It's okay."

Leaning around her, I check her cheek, relieved

there's no red mark. It must have been a stinging, hard slap, but the pain would have died down already, and now she's just left with these internal wounds which cut so much deeper.

"What was the fight about?"

She sucks in a breath, letting it out in a rush before mumbling, "I should have tried harder to get scholarships. I should have looked at more options. But I played right into their hands."

"Okay," I whisper, trying to catch up with what she's telling me.

"Jarrod and Mom offered to pay for my education."

"That's kind of standard, isn't it?"

She scoffs. "There is *nothing* standard about those two. If I wanted the money, I had to play by their rules. He wrote a fucking contract and everything. And I signed it, like some idiot. But it was free education. I thought I was doing the right thing."

"What did the contract stipulate?"

"That I went to Nolan U, that I maintained a minimum of a 3.5 GPA, that I never did anything to get in trouble, and that I..." She huffs, tipping her head back against my shoulder. "And that I become a Sig Be sister."

"What kind of crazy-ass clause is that?"

"Mom's engaged to Aimee's dad," she sneers. "You know, Aimee? The Sig Be president."

I let out a tired sigh. "Yeah, I know Aimee."

"Well, my mother was a legacy, and it was one of the many things she and Jarrod bonded over. They mapped it out so perfectly. Their daughters would become besties, and this idyllic life they pictured would just unfold seamlessly before them. We'd become this happy blended family." Mikayla's voice sharpens, taking on a bitter edge. "But they forget to take into account the Mikayla factor. The daughter who won't conform because she's just like her father." Her voice starts to tremble, and I can tell we're hitting some pretty sensitive topics right now. "You know what? They probably *did* take it into account, and that's why that fucking contract exists in the first place."

I let her take a breath, waiting for the air to still around us before asking, "Where is your dad?"

"I don't know, and I don't want to talk about it. He left, and I never saw him again. End of story."

"Okay." I soothe her with a kiss to her cheek, wrapping my arms around her.

She grabs my wrist, her small fingers clinging. "Aimee never wanted me in that house. That's why she gave me the impossible task of making you fall in love with me."

"Well, that wasn't so impossible." I grin.

She turns to look at me. "But breaking your heart would have been."

"Again, not impossible." I tip my head with a sad smile. "For a minute there, I thought you had."

She sniffs and curls into me, turning sideways and wrapping her arms around her knees. She's so small and vulnerable right now. Is it weird that it feels like a privilege to see her this way? She's letting me in. Miss *I Don't Want to Talk About It* is going deep for a minute, and I'm the one she's trusting with all of this.

"I failed, Ethan."

"No, you chose me. And that's fucking awesome." I kiss the top of her head. "I'm sorry your mom's so pissed about it. The way she behaved on that court, I swear, I—"

She touches my cheek, leaning back to look at my

face. I swallow down the anger rising through me, softened by her gentle caress.

"I'd choose you every time." Her thumb brushes my cheek, the look in her eyes trying to melt my heart all over again. The sadness tingeing her expression constricts my chest. "Even though it means she's cutting me off."

"What?"

Mikayla drops her gaze, nodding as she struggles to talk past a fresh wave of tears. "I told her I didn't want to be part of this dumb blended family if I couldn't be myself... and she... she said, 'Fine. Don't be.'" Her voice cracks, and I squeeze her closer to me. "I don't think she's going to change her mind, and Jarrod definitely won't. I was rude to his precious daughter, and I'm now in breach of that contract. Once this semester's up, I'm not gonna have any money to pay my tuition."

"We can get you a loan."

She winces. "I don't want a loan. I..." She shakes her head, fresh tears dropping down her cheeks. "I don't even have a place to live anymore. I can't borrow enough money for everything. It's too much. Nolan U is too expensive. I'll just..." She shrugs. "I'll just have to find somewhere else or maybe work for a few years. Save up, you know? I can delay my plans." Her words break apart, and she bites her trembling lips together as new tears cascade down her cheeks.

"I don't want you to leave me. I feel like I only just found you."

She sniffs, giving me a hopeless shrug. "We may not have a choice."

"We'll find a way." Determination courses through me

as I wipe her tears with my thumbs, then pull her in for a firm kiss that leaves no room for argument.

"Come on." Standing tall, I pull her to her feet and head for Hockey House, figuring I can at least solve one of her immediate problems... if I can get the guys to agree.

CHAPTER 49
MIKAYLA

Ethan threads his fingers between mine as we walk. His hand is so big it engulfs mine, and the sense of comfort is complete. I rest my head against his arm as we walk, letting him lead me, take charge so I don't have to think.

My exhausted brain is mushy.

The past twenty-four hours has been a trip.

From ecstasy to heartache to elation to triumph to crashing into a burning heap.

And now Ethan is walking beside me, holding my hand and promising to find a way.

As upset as I am, I'm also grateful. Someone's in my corner for a change, and it feels so damn good.

I squeeze his hand, trying to fight off that wave of insecurity rising over my shoulders.

What if he changes his mind?

What if he leaves me?

"You're frowning. It's cute and all, but I prefer your smile." Ethan's gentle teasing makes my lips twitch. I look up at him, and he pulls us to a stop. Hockey House is just across the street, but we stand there on the sidewalk, him holding my shoulders, me unable to take my eyes off that beautiful face of his.

"I know it hurts right now, but it won't hurt forever." He gives me a quick peck on the lips. "I'm gonna make sure you're okay. I'm here for you."

I blink and swallow, my chin automatically dipping as I try to hide my biggest fear.

"Hey." He tips my chin back up. "I'm not gonna let you down. This may sound intense, but I seriously love you, and I've never felt this way about anyone before. I kinda like it." His lips rise into a grin that makes my heart soar. "So I'm not gonna let your bitchy mama steal what we've got going here. I'm fighting to keep you by my side."

And now my eyeballs are burning again. My nose starts to tingle as I battle more tears. "I seriously love you too. It's fast and it's terrifying, and I'm gonna have moments where I'll doubt. I mean... people leave me, you know? I'm very... leave-able."

"Not me." He leans down, holding my face so he can look me right in the eye. "I'm not leaving you, and you're not leaving me. Deal?"

I nod, a smile starting to tug at my lips. It's hard not to give in to it, so I let it spread across my face, and then it grows even wider when he peppers my cheeks and lips with quick kisses.

"Come on, lover. Let's go find you a place to live." He drags me across the street and into Hockey House. I'm assuming we'll head to his room and start looking for listings, but I'll have to find a job first in order to pay rent. That's not a bad thing necessarily, but it's gonna encroach on my study time and—

"Hey, hockey bros!" Ethan grabs everyone's attention when we walk into the living area.

Every head in the room turns my way, every face etched with concern. Even Baxter wanders out of his room, leaning against the doorframe and watching me. The guy's like the recluse of the house. I give him a tentative smile. The edge of his mouth twitches, and I figure that's like a full-on grin for Mr. Serious. At least that's what I tell myself it is.

"So, my lil' mouse here has an accommodation issue."

Oh, not listings, then. He's gonna start by asking if anyone knows someone who needs a roommate.

"Thanks to breaking bitchy mama's rules, she's been cut off."

My cheeks flush. Does he seriously have to tell *everyone* that?

I squeeze his hand, throwing him a sharp frown.

"It's okay, baby. We can trust these guys. What's said in this house stays in this house. It's an unspoken thing we all abide by. Right, guys?"

"Puck yeah!" they all shout.

I wrinkle my nose. That term is seriously ridiculous.

"So, what are you proposing?" Casey crosses his tattooed arms and grins at me. "We getting a temporary roommate?"

"Yeah. Until she can figure this out. You guys cool if she stays a while?"

"What?" I balk. "No! I didn't ask him to say that, you guys." I point at Ethan, shaking my head. "I know I can't move in here."

Asher's face is bunched into a sharp frown, and Liam's looking dubious.

"I don't want to get in the way of guy time," I rush out. "I'll figure something else out."

"You're staying," Asher clips, still looking pissed.

"But... I don't understand. I thought you guys would hate this idea. I'm a chick. Hockey House doesn't host chicks."

"You beat Ash at basketball, you've kicked my ass in *Devil's Doorway*, and you can finish a slice of pizza in four bites. You practically are a guy," Casey argues.

Ethan starts laughing while I stand there sputtering.

"But... but—"

"And your mom's a full-blown bitch!" Asher frowns, then mutters, "No offense. And you're staying."

I choke out a laugh. "Are you serious right now? You're seriously gonna let me stay?"

"You need a home." Liam shrugs.

"It's only temporary. Just until I can figure things out. And I won't move in unless it's unanimous." I rush over to the coffee table and climb onto it so everyone can see me. "All in favor?" I raise my hand.

"Puck yeah!" they shout in unison, and I can't help cringing again.

"That's so lame, you guys. You really need to come up with—"

"Don't talk shit, roomie. It's puckin' awesome." Casey grins while everyone cheers.

"Welcome to the house, lil' mouse!" Asher shouts, and then they all start chanting, "Lit-tle mouse, lit-tle mouse," like I'm some kind of hero.

Tears quickly build on my lashes, and I raise my hands to stop them. "Shut up, you guys. If any of you make me cry, I'm gonna have to kick your asses!"

They break into raucous laughter while Ethan walks over to the table and grabs me, throwing me over his shoulder.

"Come on. We've got a month's worth of sex to make up for."

I laugh as he walks me out toward the stairwell. "Wait, wait, wait!" I stop him with a slap to the back. "Kitchen. Kitchen."

"What for?" He diverts that way.

"Snacks. We're gonna be burning a lot of calories. Hunger is inevitable. In fact, I'm hungry now... and I know the perfect dinner plate I can eat my food from."

He chuckles. "And this is why I love you."

He pops me down, and we load up from the fridge and pantry. Then he chases me upstairs, where I do eat quite the buffet off his rock-hard abs before letting him lick honey and yogurt off my boobs.

And just like that, my day circles back around to ecstasy.

CHAPTER 50
ETHAN

"So, question." I circle my fingers over Mikayla's back while she lies naked beside me. I love the feel of her tits squished against my chest, the weight of her arm across my stomach and her leg across my thighs.

Trailing my fingers down her back, I palm her ass and ask, "How did you not get a basketball scholarship?"

She groans and rubs the tip of her nose against my pec. "That was the original plan, but then Mom met Jarrod, and he brought out her inner hoity-toity."

Ethan's chest rumbles with laughter.

"Anyway, suddenly me being all tomboy didn't fly anymore. She talked me out of playing basketball my senior year. I don't even know how I let her do it, but somehow I ended up becoming something I wasn't... all to please this new man in our lives. He talked a big game, you know? Promised us all this stuff. Bought expensive gifts. Mom was so freaking happy for a change that we all just went along with it, and it wasn't until I got here and started rush week that it suddenly hit me—this isn't who

I am. I don't want this. And then you pulled me into Hockey House... into your friend group, and I felt like I'd found home."

"You are home." I kiss her forehead, squeezing her against my side.

She looks up and softly reminds me, "This is temporary. I can't live here forever... and unless I can score myself a financial miracle, I can't even stay at Nolan U."

My insides tense, rebelling against that idea. I don't want her moving back to California. I need her here. With me.

"We'll figure something out. We'll find you the money somehow. Tomorrow we can start looking into financial aid, and you can maybe start job hunting. We're gonna make this work. We have to."

She doesn't say anything, and I wish she would. I want her to agree with me. But she's filling up with doubts again. I can feel it in the way she's tensing, her soft sighs against my chest, that little sniff. I'm starting to read her, and I love the idea that she'll be here with me. Hockey season starts next week, and life is pretty damn full-on. The fact that I'll get to come home to her for a while is pretty fucking awesome. I can learn all her little tells, and she can learn mine. Yes, it's fast, but it feels so damn right.

The thought of her leaving cannot be entertained.

As she drifts off to sleep against me, her light snores making me smile, I stare at the ceiling, determined to find a way to keep her at Nolan U.

I'm not losing the best thing that's ever happened to me.

"Her mother did what?" Dad balks, his face mottled with angry confusion.

I stare at the screen and nod. "Yeah, I know. I couldn't believe it." Scrubbing a hand down my face, I pinch my chin and admit, "So, I said she could stay with me for now."

"Good idea." Dad nods. I'm relieved he's on board.

I was pretty sure he would be. I asked Mikayla's permission before sharing the latest with my father. I tell the guy almost everything, and this is one of the big ones. For a second, I thought he might say I was playing with fire, basically letting her move in when we've only just gotten together, but these are unique circumstances and... well, she's my lil' mouse. I can't even explain why it feels so right. It just does.

"So, what's she gonna do about next semester?"

I shrug. "I don't know how to find her that money. I mean, there's different paths we can take, but she's pretty adamant she doesn't want to get a loan. At least not for Nolan U. It's too expensive."

"Is there a grandparent or some rich uncle she could hit up?"

I purse my lips to the side, glancing over my shoulder. Mikayla's in the shower. She said a quick hi to my dad, then gave us some privacy. I don't want to take advantage of that privacy, but...

Leaning toward the screen, I softly say, "She has a dad. He left when she was younger, and she hates talking about it, but I was wondering if I should try to track him down."

Dad frowns. "He left his kids? Who does that?"

"I don't know, but maybe if we can find him... reach out and tell him what's going on, he might be willing to offer some financial aid?"

"Did he pay child support after he left?"

"I'm not sure, but I doubt Mikayla will want me asking. She's kind of closed-off about the topic."

"Probably because she felt completely rejected by the one guy who was supposed to love and protect her no matter what."

The thought rattles through me. Dad's right. What kind of asshole leaves his family and doesn't even bother to stay in touch?

But the idea of trying to find him just won't leave me alone. I spent most of my night obsessing over it. Instinct is telling me to pursue this. And to pursue it quietly.

"You could always ask Asher's family. Aren't they loaded? They're the ones who own the house you live in."

"Yeah." I force out a laugh. "I doubt they'd want me showing up on their door asking for money. I don't really know them."

"Asher could ask on your behalf."

"Yeah." I tip my head to the side, wincing slightly. "I just hate the idea of Mikayla being indebted to that family. I don't know them that well, but Asher can be a total prick sometimes. He can be awesome one minute and a D-bag the next. I'm not sure I trust the family enough to give the money to Mikayla without a bunch of conditions attached to it."

"Good point." Dad nods, then lets out a heavy sigh. "I wish I had the funds, but you know how it is. I only managed to save enough for you. Sorry, kid."

"You've given me so much." I smile at him. "Seeing the way Mikayla got treated yesterday makes me all the more grateful for you. Thanks for being so cool, Dad."

He blushes and gives me his *aw, shucks* smile. "You make it easy."

We grin at each other, and then Mikayla walks back into the room. She's wrapped in a towel and gives my dad a little wave.

"Sorry. I forgot to take my clothes into the bathroom with me. I'll just grab some stuff and leave you guys to it."

"No, that's okay. We're just wrapping up." I swivel back to bulge my eyes at Dad, who's quietly laughing at me. "Have fun, son." He wiggles his eyebrows and hangs up.

I jump out of my chair, darting across the room and catching Mikayla against me before she can take off to the bathroom.

"Hey!" She squeals with laughter as I swing her around and throw her onto the bed.

She lands against the pillows, her towel coming loose and giving me an exquisite view of her right nipple.

Her teeth brush over her bottom lip as she flicks the rest of the towel aside. Her naked glory is spectacular enough to take my breath away, and then she sizzles my insides with a suggestive lip lick. "Want some sugar?" Sucking the tip of her finger, she trails it down her body, between her breasts, over her belly button... and I'm yanking off my sweats as she grazes her inner thigh.

Holy hell.

I pounce on the bed, making her laugh as I lunge at her with hungry kisses.

"I can't believe I just did that," she groans when I give her a chance to catch her breath.

"It was so fucking hot, baby." I suck her neck, lightly scraping my teeth across her collarbone before drawing her left nipple into my mouth.

She moans, fisting the back of my hair.

"You like that?" I grin, pinching her other nipple.

"You know I do," she pants, her head tipped back, exposing her luscious neck to me.

Taking her hand, I guide it back between her legs. "Touch yourself, baby. Let me see you do it."

Her head pops up, and she gives me a doubtful frown. I wiggle my eyebrows with a grin. "It was so hot it nearly melted my insides."

Biting her lip, she grins at me, then tentatively touches her clit. I suck in a breath, my cock turning into a steel rod. Gliding my hand up her inner thigh, I nudge her legs apart and settle between them. Kneeling on the floor, I nibble my way from her knee to the wet oasis begging me to touch it. She's still circling her clit, moaning and starting to writhe as the orgasm builds within her. I watch for a moment, entranced by her sexy beauty, before I can't take it anymore.

Parting her glistening folds, I plunge my tongue inside her, and she loses it. An exquisite cry bursts out of her as she arches her back. I hold her ass, keeping her up and licking her until she's a puddle of limp limbs. She drops back to the bed, and I smile at her.

"That was beautiful."

She blushes, shaking her head. "Or totally embarrassing."

"Beautiful." I give her a pointed look, then go to rise from the floor.

"Wait. What are you doing?"

Her sharp tone makes me pause. "I was gonna... snuggle?"

"Uh, no... you're getting in here." She points between her legs. "Don't leave me hanging."

I wince.

"What's wrong?"

I see that flash of doubt on her face and rush out my explanation. "I don't want to hurt you. We've been doing it a lot the last couple days, and you must be kind of tender down there."

"I can handle it. Now get inside me right now," she says emphatically, then throws in a sweet smile and a "Please."

I fight my grin, resting my hands on her knees. "You promise you'll tell me if it gets too much?"

"Yes! Now suit up." She tips her head back. "Seriously, my pussy needs you!"

I laugh and quickly do as I'm told before dragging her to the edge of the bed and easing into her. I take it gently, slowly, forcing my eager cock to behave itself... until she starts moaning and begging, "Deeper. Please." She hooks her legs around me, digging her heels into my ass and driving me forward.

Being the good boy I am, I once again do as I'm told, lifting her leg so I can plunge to the hilt.

"Yes," she groans.

And I do it again, driving farther, pushing harder until we're both panting messes.

Her inner walls are trembling, clenching. Stars scatter across my vision as I grip her hips and pump a little faster.

Slap—slap—slap. Our bodies make a song, the rhythm fast and heady.

"I'm close," she rasps. "Come with me, baby. Please."

Oh man, this begging is a heart stealer. I'm pretty sure she could get me to do anything if she asked me with her voice all strained and wispy like this.

Pulling her hips up, I change the angle for the last few thrusts.

"Holy shit," she moans the words. "You feel so fucking good. Baby... ba—" Her high pitched words are lost as the orgasm steals her breath.

Her inner walls clench me, setting off Rocket Ethan. I match her moaning ecstasy as I thrust deep one last time and we tumble over the edge together.

It's fucking amazing.

She's amazing.

We're amazing.

CHAPTER 51
MIKAYLA

I've been living at Hockey House for over two weeks now, and yeah, it'd be so easy to call it home. Sleeping with Ethan every night is heaven. And now that his season has officially begun, it's sometimes the only way I get to see him. Between practices, studying, and classes, his life is full. I don't want to be another burden on him, although he never makes me feel that way.

I grip my pen, shuffling in my library chair and trying to focus.

I haven't found a job yet. I seriously don't know what I want to do right now, because my plan had been to simply study while I was here so I could throw all my energy into getting the best grades possible.

But I don't have that luxury anymore.

Mom hasn't contacted me once, and I haven't reached out to her either. I got a couple of texts from Megan that I chose to ignore.

.   .   .

Megan: Are you fucking insane? Stop acting crazy!

Megan: I can't believe you're throwing this all away for some guy. Have you no standards?

Megan: So that's it. You're just gonna ignore me? Probably because you can't justify your stupid behavior.

Megan: Mom was right to cut you off.

That last one stung like a bitch. I turned my phone off for two whole days after that. It was only the thought of Ray not being able to reach me that forced me to turn the thing back on. That, and Ethan getting frustrated with the fact that he couldn't contact me. He had a really funny joke to tell me the other day, but he'd forgotten it by the time he got home.

"If I could have texted you, I wouldn't have forgotten."

"You could have just texted it anyway, and I would have seen it when I eventually turn my phone back on."

He shot me a droll look. "It's not the same. Turn your phone back on, lil' mouse. Please."

I gave in with a sigh, although I haven't fully ruled out buying a cheap burner phone that's just for Ethan and me.

While it was off, I'd missed several calls from Ray and a bunch of texts. She forgave me after I explained what went down but then made me promise not to do that to her again. She was getting ready to drive to Colorado and hunt me down.

So, I'm now contactable once more, and apart from Ethan and Ray, my phone's been basically silent. I should be stoked about this, but somehow it's like a bruise that just keeps getting bigger and more tender.

My mother, just like my father, has dumped me. Walked away because I didn't do what I was told. I wasn't good enough, and it cuts like a freaking knife through my heart.

Shoving my device a little farther away from me, I lean over my textbook, then glance up when my computer dings. It's an email from my marketing professor with the link for our next assignment outline. I procrastinate on my current essay to read up about it and am actually looking forward to diving into this thing. My mind is already buzzing with ideas, and I'm trying not to get bogged down by the fact that I'm gonna have to put all this on hold soon.

I'm being stubborn about getting a student loan. I really don't want to be saddled with a bunch of debt, so I think my best plan is to just see the semester out, then get a job and save every penny I can. Maybe I can take some community college classes—night classes or something —and keep chipping away at my degree until I have enough money to attend and get the qualifications I need.

It's not preferable at all, but what other choices do I have?

"Oh wow, it's the deserter."

I glance up and spot Teah hovering near my table. She's looking a lot hurt and a little annoyed with me. Still. Bella hovers next to her, trying to throw me the evils as well, although she doesn't seem as invested.

And then Fiona swans up. Oh joy.

Between the three of them, I'm getting the stare-down of a lifetime. It's basically impossible to ignore, so I just lean back in my chair and face it.

"I'm surprised you guys aren't over this yet. Don't you

have better things to do with your time than obsess over the fact that I don't want to be part of your little club?"

"It's not a club!" Fiona gasps, her indignation almost comical. "It's a sorority, you clueless loser."

I roll my eyes.

"I can't believe you chose that manwhore over us." Teah's trying to be snarking, but again, it's coming out all wounded and raspy.

She's taking this really personally, and I wish she wouldn't. I don't even get why. It's not like we were best buddies. Unless she's harboring some kind of secret crush on Ethan and it's just jealousy. Since they posted those pictures of Ethan's stricken face all over social media with headlines like *Hockey star burned by freshman bitch* and *The mighty man goes down in burning flames*, we've had to counter the rippling rumors with some open PDA. We're together. We're in love. And I think almost everyone on campus knows it.

Which has led to a variety of reactions. Girls still swoon and flirt around Ethan as if I'm not even standing there. Some of them sidle up to me, checking just how serious our relationship is and can I see it lasting. And then there's the ones who are just plain pissed.

Like the Sig Be sisters, and any other campus girl who thinks I either don't deserve Ethan or I'm a fool to fall for him.

Aimee thinks I'm the worst, but that's because she didn't best me.

I mean, I guess she kind of did. At this stage, I'm gonna be out of here by the end of the semester, but like hell she's gonna see me cry over it.

"You're gonna be sorry." Fiona shakes her head.

I raise my eyebrows. "Is that some kind of threat?"

"No," Bella scoffs. "It's consequences. You chose a guy who's gonna cheat on you over sisters who would have had your back no matter what."

"He's not going to cheat on me."

"What makes you so sure?" Fiona's mocking laughter grates my insides. "He's slept with half the school. You've been dating for less than a month. You don't know this guy. He's gonna get bored, and his eyes will stray, and you'll be left with nothing."

Teah nods. "He's never lasted more than a few weeks with any girl. He's not a one-woman guy. Get ready for some serious heartbreak, Mikayla."

"And you brought it all on yourself." Fiona raises her manicured eyebrows. The look of smug glee on her face makes my stomach squirm.

"You're wrong." My voice is annoyingly weak and tiny as I try to counter them, but it's getting harder to look them in the eye as they move around the table, circling me with their little taunts.

"He's gonna hurt you."

"You're insane to think this will last."

"And watching you fall will be a pleasure, because we warned you and you didn't listen."

I shrink further into my seat, gripping my pen and staring at my computer screen. It's hard not to let their biting words sink in.

It's hard to counter that ugly doubt.

I trust Ethan. I really do. He seems totally into me and I'm into him, and being together is easy and fun and—

You trusted Dad, too, and he left without warning.

My stomach clenches and my vision starts to blur until I hear a bark behind me.

"Hey! Leave her alone."

I flinch, swiveling in my chair as the girls scamper away, leaving a pissed-off Liam standing behind me. He stares after the girls, narrowing his eyes when Teah turns back to take another look. She yelps and clutches the binder to her chest, running after Bella.

"Thanks," I murmur, dropping my pen with a heavy sigh.

"They're relentless." He sits down beside me and lets out an irritated huff.

"I guess they've got nothing better to do with their time." I sniff, clenching my jaw and wishing I could brush their words off. I want them to be cobwebs I can flick away, but today's verbal attack felt more like an onslaught of parasites. I can feel them crawling around inside me, eating away at my confidence.

I hate days like this. I should blame hormones. I've got the whole period thing happening this week, and I always hit a low day or two around this time, but it's only being exacerbated by everything else I'm dealing with right now.

"You okay?" Liam rubs my shoulder, his compassionate smile enough to make my eyes burn.

"Yeah, I'm fine. They're just words."

"You know they're not true, though, right?"

I sigh and nod.

"Look at me."

I close my eyes, refusing to turn until he nudges my shoulder again.

"Come on, Mick. Look at me."

With a huff, I spin in my chair and give him a pointed look.

He grins. "Ethan's into you. He loves you. I've never seen him like this with anyone else before, and I've known the guy for years. Trust me. Trust *him*. He's not going anywhere, and he's not gonna let you walk away either."

"Yeah," I croak.

"You guys are good together. Don't let some bitchy, mouthy girls screw this up for you."

My lips twitch as I nod again.

"Come on. Let's go." He stands up and grabs my bag off the floor.

I close my laptop and textbook, gathering them against my chest. "Where are we going?"

"You can hang out at practice this afternoon. That way you can see Ethan as soon as we're done." He winks at me, and I follow him without question.

Watching the guys practice actually sounds like a pretty good way to spend the afternoon. It has to be better than hanging out here and potentially bumping into someone else who's gonna taunt me or gush about the fact that I'm dating Ethan Galloway.

I don't want to hear that he's the hottest thing on two legs. I already know that, and I don't need the added pressure of knowing how many people in this place want to get with him... or want to slap me for being the one who turned him monogamous.

CHAPTER 52
ETHAN

I secure my pads and throw on a hockey jersey, yanking it down before brushing my hair off my forehead. I'm fired up and ready to put in a good practice today. I'm focused and—

The locker room door swings open, catching my eye. I glance over in time to see Liam storming in, looking kind of dark.

"You okay, man?"

He wrenches his locker open and shakes his head at me.

"What's up?"

His jaw clenches, which means he doesn't really want to share. I stare at him for a little longer, wondering if he'll change his mind, before shrugging.

"Okay. Well, maybe you can burn it off on the ice."

"I was in the library." He sighs, pulling off his shirt, his tense muscles flexing as he gets changed. "I heard these girls being real bitchy, you know? So I figured I'd swing past the table on my way out, make sure whoever they were harassing was okay."

"Was she or he or... they?"

His lips dip into a sharp frown. "It was Mikayla."

"What?" I swivel to face him, my voice coming out hard and snappy. "Who was it? What'd they say?"

"It was those Sig Be girls. They were going on about how she'd made a huge mistake by choosing you over them and that you were gonna cheat on her. Just talking general shit, circling her like vultures." He grunts while I let out a string of curse words that draws the eyes of almost every guy in the room.

"What's going on?" Asher calls from his locker.

"Nothing!" I bark.

"This about our girl?" He moves closer, and I can't help a quick growl.

"She's not your girl, she's mine!"

"She's ours," he argues back, and my fingers curl into a fist. Ever since moving in, Mikayla's become like our house mascot. It's cute and all, but not when Asher starts talking shit about her belonging to all of us.

I stalk toward him and fist his collar. His eyes spark with challenge, and I'm seconds away from brawling when Liam's hand lands on my shoulder.

He glares at Asher. "Would you shut your damn mouth? This isn't helping."

"I just want to make sure she's okay. I heard you say something about circling vultures. And Mikayla might be *your* girl"—Asher gives me a pointed look—"but that doesn't mean the rest of us want to see her getting harassed or hurt. We're allowed to care about her too.

She's an awesome chick, and if someone is making her life hell, we're gonna do something about it."

I relax, letting go of Asher's collar and shoving him away.

Liam quickly tells the guys what he told me, and they all mutter their disgust. Casey crosses his arms, looking just as dark as Liam.

"That wasn't what got to me the most." Liam shakes his head, resting his hands on his hips with a heavy sigh. "For a second there, she looked... so beaten, you know? That's not Mick. She's tough. That's one of the things we love about her. She doesn't take shit. But she just sat there today. Didn't say a word."

My insides crumble. I knew she was struggling. It's been impossible not to notice her quiet spells and the look on her face when yet another post or video pops up on social media. I've tried to shield her from it, show her how much she means to me, but I can't protect her from everything, and it kills me.

"Where is she now?" I ask.

Liam tips his head toward the door. "I brought her to practice with me. Figured she could study in the stands or something. They can't get to her here."

I flash him a grateful smile and head for the door. The guys make a clear pathway for me, all appreciating my need to get to her, but I'm blocked before I can even reach the doors.

Jason crosses his arms, barring my way. "We've got practice. You can deal with your love life later."

I'm about to shove him back with a few harsh words when Coach steps in behind him.

"Okay, guys, let's get on the ice." He claps his hands.

"I just need to see—"

"Ice, Galloway! We're already running late. Get your ass out there. Whatever it is can wait until after practice."

"It really can't," I try to argue, but the look on his face leaves me zero room for argument.

"Shit," I mutter under my breath, knowing I can't muscle my way past Coach just to give my girl a kiss, to touch her face, look in her eyes, reassure myself that she's okay, tell her I'd never cheat on her.

Coach is a hard-ass, and he'd never understand.

So I spin with a scowl, ignoring Jason's snicker, and head for the rink.

As soon as my skates hit the ice, I look into the stands for Mikayla.

She's halfway up the bleachers, huddled against the cold. Liam's jacket is around her shoulders, which pisses me off, because it should be my jacket.

Dammit, why didn't I go to the library today?

Gliding across the ice, I raise my stick at her. She gives me a small smile and waves back, so I blow her a kiss off my glove. That makes her smile a little wider, and that tightness in my chest starts to ease.

I should be grateful that I've got a team ready to protect my girl when she needs it.

And I am.

I'm grateful Liam was there today, but it's up to me to make sure she understands that those girls were lying. Choosing me over them wasn't a mistake. I'm not going anywhere, and my eyes aren't wandering either.

No one can hold a candle to my lil' mouse.

She's it.

She's everything.

CHAPTER 53
MIKAYLA

Ethan's skating like a demon this practice, which means Liam must have told him about the library incident. I knew he would, so there was no point asking him not to say anything. When he wrapped his jacket around me, then headed off to the locker room, it was inevitable.

Ethan will want to talk about it, and I'm trying to prep myself for that.

Part of me wants to forget it.

So those girls got a little mouthy. Big deal.

I can brush that off.

Right?

I hunch over against the cold, curling in on myself like a little porcupine.

My phone starts ringing, and I pull it out of the back pocket of my jeans. The jacket falls off my shoulders and I shiver, answering the phone with a "One sec" before taking the time to pull the giant thing on.

It looks ridiculous on me. The shoulders are so wide,

they practically come down to my elbows, and my hands have been lost to the length of these sleeves.

I wrestle my digits free and snatch up my phone, pressing it against my ear. "Sorry about that. How's it going, Ray-Ray?"

"Yeah. Okay."

I sit up a little straighter. *Okay* in Ray speak is basically *My life is total shit.*

"What's up?"

"I was just calling to check on you."

My lips twitch. Ray can never just spill. She always has to work her way into things. She'll hide her angst, cover it with care for me before finally telling me what's going on.

Curiosity and worry make me rush through my stuff.

"It's good and bad. Living with Ethan and the guys is pretty cool. I know it's temporary, so I'm trying to enjoy what I can. I beat Casey's high score on *Devil's Doorway* the other night, so yay." My cheer is stupidly weak.

I keep my eyes on the rink, watching Ethan speed down the edge before whipping around the back of the goal. Whatever drill he's doing is giving him a pretty decent workout. He's flying right now, controlling the puck with these little taps and swooshes. It's like he was born to do this.

"And the bad stuff?"

I huff. "The girls are still horrible. My mom and I are still... not speaking, and I have no idea how I'm going to pay for next semester, let alone the rest of my degree, which means I'm trying to come to terms with the fact that I'm on a ticking clock here." My voice starts to wobble, tears burning my eyes.

"Aw, Mick, I'm so sorry. I always was a little afraid of your mom, but... I didn't think she was capable of cutting you off."

"Yeah, I guess... that's just what people do. They leave me, Ray-Ray."

"Not all of them. Not me. I will *never* abandon you. You are stuck with me for life."

My smile is weak. "You're miles away."

"Physically, but I'm always here. I'm here right now. With you."

I swallow and nod, appreciating the soft lilt of her voice and forgetting for a moment that she's got her own struggle that needs to be talked about. Sucking in a breath, I'm about to ask her when she cuts me off with a few more sweet words of comfort.

"And Ethan. I mean, I know I've only spoken to him twice on video, but he seems really cool. And from what you've told me... the connection you guys have... it sounds like he's in this for the long haul, sweets. He loves you."

"Yeah, that's what he says." I sigh. "It's also what my dad used to say. And my mom... when I was little."

She goes quiet, because how do you argue with that?

But she tries anyway. "Just because your parents suck doesn't mean everybody does. Ethan is good, and the way he looked at you when I met him that day? How he touched your neck and showed genuine interest in me because I'm your best friend? I don't know... I just got a good vibe about him."

"Thanks, Ray," I whisper, sniffing against my unshed tears and trying to believe every word out of her mouth. I want to. I so desperately want to. Closing my eyes, I take a short breath, then figure it's her turn. "So... what's with the *okay*?"

She doesn't respond, and I have to probe again.

"Come on. You can't leave me hanging. You've made me feel better, and now it's my turn to help you. What's made your day shitty?"

After a soft sniff, her quaking voice comes down the line. "Theo and I had our first fight."

"Aw, sweetie. How bad was it?"

"Awful. You know how much I hate conflict."

"I do, but it's also part of life. Couples fight."

"He was so mad," she whispers. "I've never seen him like that before. He was yelling, and then he slammed his bottle down, shoved the chair back. It was horrible."

I bite my lip, wincing when I think about it. Ray did not grow up in a house of shouters. Her mother never raised her voice, and when her dad was alive, he was one of those sweet, quiet types, always had a smile at the ready and a kind word to say.

Theo's outburst probably scared the crap out of her.

"Have you guys made up yet?"

"Sort of. He drove off in a huff and came back about twenty minutes later. The second he saw me crying, he rushed over and hugged me. He told me he never wants to fight again, and then we... well, you know."

I grin. "Makeup sex is the only good thing about arguing with your lover."

"Yeah. I guess." She sighs. "I should be telling you I'm great. Why do I still feel bad? Am I just being overly sensitive? I'm not used to yelling."

"My parents used to yell at each other sometimes. Mostly Mom, but..." I shrug, dropping my assurances quickly because hello, my parents got divorced. "What was the fight about?"

"Oh, I got home from work and the kitchen was a mess. It'd been a tough day, and I got a little snippy with him. Asked him how long he'd been home and kind of hinted at the fact that he was sitting there drinking a beer and relaxing when he could have been cleaning up the mess. I'd had a longer day than him, so why should I have to do it, you know? I'm working two jobs now, and it's—"

"You're working two jobs?"

"Yeah, I took on two shifts at the grocery store to help with finances. Theo suggested it, and I thought it was a good idea. We want to save up for a trip to Hawaii."

"Nice," I murmur, then snort. "So you're working two jobs and he's not helping out around the house. Guys can be so frickin' clueless sometimes."

"I didn't think I was expecting too much. I mean, sure, my jobs are probably less demanding than his, but he got home before me. I felt like it was fair that he pitch in too." She sighs. "But when I said that, he got all annoyed, saying how his job is harder than mine. I don't even know what I said to make him start yelling, but he did, and then he stormed off before I could say anything back."

"Dick move, Theo." I frown, wondering if I should try meeting this guy again. I've only had one short conversation with him, back when they first got together. Theo never seems to be around when I'm talking to Rachel. I'm about to suggest we amend this, but she starts talking before I can.

"I suppose this is just teething problems. New situations always have them."

"Do you regret moving in with him?"

"No. It's better than living on my own. I guess we just have to figure out what this looks like for us."

"Maybe if you talk to him when things are all happy and good. Work an angle to make him think that helping you out around the house is his idea. Or go on about how much it would mean to you. You said he's sweet and caring and loves buying you stuff, right? He obviously cares about you and wants to make you happy. You just need to tell him what your happy looks like."

"Yeah, you're right. I'm not very good at telling people what I want."

I smile. "I'm pretty sure guys need you to spell it out for them. They're not always the best at reading a woman's mind."

"Is Ethan like that with you? Totally clueless?"

"Uh... actually, no. I feel like he's great at reading me."

"You haven't had any teething problems staying with him?"

I cringe, almost feeling bad for her when I admit, "None. It's been awesome. The only downer is everything outside of Hockey House, but inside... it's great. Ethan and I are made for each other. It still makes my head spin when I think about it." I raise my hand in a wave, smiling when Ethan glances up to check on me. He grins back and skates into another drill. He really is hot on that ice. Damn, it still seems surreal that he's mine.

"I'm happy for you, Mick. You deserve it."

I just hope it lasts.

Fear clutches me for a beat, and I have to fight not to say that to Ray. Instead, I clear my throat and direct the conversation back to her. "Let me know how it goes with Theo. I'm sure you can work this out. You love him and he loves you, and this is just a little blip along the road, right? And remember, you don't have to keep living with him if these blips keep happening. Not all experiments are a success."

"Oh, but I want this one to be. The idea of rambling around in Mom's house by myself sucks, plus we've already rented it out. I can't go kicking out brand-new tenants. And... and Theo's great. I love him. I really do. We just had a bad day."

"A day that included makeup sex, so it can't have been all bad."

She lets out a soft laugh. "True. Thanks, Mick. You always make me feel better."

"Ditto times infinity."

I'm not quite ready to end the call, so I launch into a completely inane topic that has nothing to do with guys. Well, real guys anyway. "Hey, have you watched *The Night Agent* yet?"

She gasps. "Yes! And how hot is he? And so protective of Rose. I seriously would have binged the entire thing in one sitting if I hadn't had to go to work in the morning."

"I know. I was obsessed with the show. We ended up watching until like three the other morning. I could barely focus in class the next day, but worth it." I sing the last two words, then start laughing as she gushes over the twists she didn't see coming.

We unpack the show in detail, then move on to *Citadel*, which is another show peppered with hot men and heart-clutching action. I'm so absorbed in our breakdown that I nearly miss the fact that practice has ended and the guys are trailing past me, giving me little waves and smiles as they leave the arena.

Ethan is taking his sweet time showering, so I linger on the phone with Rachel until I see him coming.

"Hey, I better get going. Ethan's practice is done." I smile at him as he walks toward me, but then my stomach pinches. Why does he look so nervous?

"Okay." Rachel's voice is back to the sweet, cheerful one I'm used to. "Thanks again for making me feel so much better. I seriously love you, bestie."

"I love you too. Now go have more makeup sex with your man."

She giggles. "You have a good night too."

I mumble goodbye, not wanting to tell her that I'm suddenly worried about my night. What is up with that tight look on Ethan's face?

I slip my phone away as Ethan stops at the bottom of the stands, obviously waiting for me. His jaw clenches, and he looks out over the ice as I gather my stuff and trot down the stairs.

I'm three steps away when he turns to grin up at me. His smile is too tight.

"What's the matter?" Gripping my bag strap, I stop where I am, afraid to get too close. Not because I think he'll hurt me, just because I can feel a serious conversation coming, and I freaking hate those.

Shit, Rachel helped me de-stress after the library incident, and now Ethan's gonna want to unpack it.

"Listen, I'm good. We don't have to talk about my afternoon. Let's just—"

"I have to tell you something." His voice is deep and husky.

And now that pinching fear is taking chunks out of my stomach.

I tense, just waiting for those words to pop out of his mouth. *"This isn't working. I'll find you another place to live. We can't be together. I don't love you anymore."*

I'm so blinded by my panic that I nearly miss what he actually says.

"Wait. What?" I blink and try to hear him past the buzzing in my ears.

He winces and runs a hand over the back of his wet hair. His gaze glimmers with a hint of apology. "Please don't be mad with me, okay? I just want to help you."

"What did you do?" I need him to repeat it, to say it again so I can make sure I heard him correctly.

His face wrinkles with confusion, and he finally says it, says the one thing I never thought he would. "I found your dad, and... he wants to see you."

CHAPTER 54
ETHAN

Watching the blood drain from Mikayla's face kills me. I knew she was gonna be mad about this. Even though the news is fucking great, it's gonna take her a minute to get there. But I couldn't sit on this.

I only just got off the phone with her father. It took me a little time to find him. Ten days, to be exact. I've been scouring the Internet, working my way through a bunch of Michael Hydes with no success. But not today. This morning, I left a message for the owner of the Luna Luxury Resort in Northern California. The guy is loaded, the son-in-law of some business mogul who builds resorts all over the world. Michael Hyde designed this boutique getaway hotel in Northern California and has grown it into a world-class escape that's frequented by the rich and famous. There's no way he doesn't have the money to pay for Mikayla's education.

And he called me back just as I was hopping out of the shower, his voice shaking.

"You know my daughter?"

He'd sounded breathless with excitement, and I'd rushed out a few key questions that would reassure me he's the man I'm looking for.

And he was.

He fucking was!

And he wants to see Mikayla.

But will she be willing to see him?

That's the battle I'm facing right now, and as I watch her pale face start to mottle with anger, I know I'm in for a fight.

"Mick, please."

"You called my dad? What the fuck, Ethan!"

I close my eyes.

"How could you go behind my back like that? I trusted you, and you shit all over me?"

"I didn't shit on you. I..." I sigh. "Okay, yes, I went behind your back on this, but I didn't want to say anything unless it worked out, and he—"

"He doesn't want me. I told you that, yet you looked for him anyway!" She stomps down the stairs toward me. I go to reach for her, but she slaps my hands away with an angry growl, using Liam's sleeves as weapons to keep me back. It would be comical if she wasn't so angry with me.

"Mick, come on. He wants you. He called me back. He's excited to see you. He's flying all the way out here this weekend so he can—"

"No!" She shoves me aside, storming past me. "I can't do this. I'm not gonna talk about this with you, and I'm not going to meet up with some guy who abandoned me when I was eleven."

"Mick."

She throws me a dark glare that warns me off, but

dammit, I can't listen to it. So I follow her down the tunnel toward the exit and snatch her arm before she can run away from me. "Just stop and talk to me."

"I don't want to talk about it!" She tries to wrench her arm free, but I don't let go this time.

Instead, I pull her toward me. "I don't give a shit if you want to or not. You need to."

She growls again, sounding like a pissed-off little puppy, but I meet her raging gaze, refusing to be put off by it.

"I know he hurt you. I get that, okay? But you should have heard him on the phone. He was nearly crying. And he's flying out here. He didn't even hesitate. He wants to see you."

"Well, I don't want to see him."

"But you're going to, because this could solve all your problems."

"Or it could ruin me!" Her blue eyes glass with tears. "Don't you get that?"

My chest constricts, the look on her face like a punch to the balls.

I sigh, my voice dropping to a soft, husky rumble. "Why would he fly out to see you only to reject you again? If he didn't want you, he wouldn't have called me back, and he wouldn't have offered to meet up this weekend."

She tries to wrench her arm free again, and this time I let go, sensing that she's not about to bolt. But she's not about to respond to me either, so I take advantage of the silent space and keep talking.

"I know this is scary and emotional. And I know you hate *emotional*, but you need to do this."

She starts shaking her head.

"Mick, you've gotta go see him."

"No I don't."

"Yes you do." I bend down to look her right in the eye. "And I love you enough to make you."

Her eyes round, and then she darts her gaze away from me. I can tell by the trembling of her bottom lip that she's fighting tears, refusing to let them spill out of her eyes. I hate it when she cries, but this isn't about my comfort. It's about helping her. If she needs to, then she can just go ahead and rip my heart to pieces with her tears.

"It's gonna be okay," I whisper. "I'll be right beside you, and I would never let anyone hurt you."

She sniffs and swallows, hunching her shoulders and swiveling away from me.

She's not running out the door, so I take that as a positive sign.

Inching closer, I stand right behind her, gently weaving my arms around her and kissing the back of her head. "That's why I didn't tell you what I was up to. If I'd found him and he hadn't wanted to see you, I wouldn't have said anything. You never would have known."

"I hate that you hid this from me." Her voice is barely audible. "It feels like you were lying or something."

"I'm sorry. I didn't want to hurt you."

"But you did."

I close my eyes, resting my forehead on the top of her head. "I'm sorry." I swallow, my voice sounding thick and gummy. "I just want what's best for you. I was just trying to fight for you. For your future. For us."

With another little sniff, she spins and wraps her

arms around me, fisting the back of my hoodie and burying her face against my chest.

I kiss the top of her head, then cup the back of it, relief pulsing through me. She has every right to call me an asshole and dump me right here. But she's holding me.

Tightening my grip on her, I stand there in the dimming light of the arena entrance and hold her until she's ready to let go. It takes a really long time, but finally, she eases away from me. I smile down at her, tucking her hair behind her ears. Her lips twitch and she sniffs again, pushing up the massive sleeves of Liam's jacket.

My forehead wrinkles with a frown. "Here." I push it off her shoulders.

"What are you doing?"

Liam's jacket hits the floor as I unzip my hoodie and drape it around her shoulders. "That's better."

She gives me a droll look, her right eyebrow arching. "Are you gonna pee on me next?"

I snicker, grabbing Liam's jacket before tucking my arm around her shoulders and pulling her close as we walk to my truck. "My girl. My hoodie."

She doesn't say anything, but her lips are curling into a smile, and I take that as forgiveness. I can't shake the feeling that I'm still gonna have to fight to get her to see her dad this weekend, but hopefully she'll let me.

"I love you," I murmur when we reach my truck.

She stops and looks up at me, rising to her tiptoes and pressing her lips to mine. It's enough of a reassurance to settle my gut as I open the door for her, then drive us home to Hockey House.

CHAPTER 55
MIKAYLA

I've changed three times already, and for a girl who's not opposed to dragging clothes out of a laundry basket to re-wear them, that is a huge deal.

I stand in the mirror, adjusting my shirt and then rethinking these pants.

"No," Ethan growls from the bed. "You are not allowed to get changed again."

And just because he said that, I unzip my pants and kick them off my feet. He groans and flops back on the bed while I rummage through my bag and find a pair of cargo pants that are old but comfy.

You know what? Screw it. I know we're going to some fancy restaurant in town—like the only one there is—but I can wear cargo pants if I damn well want to. Apparently, my dad booked the restaurant yesterday. He called to let Ethan know we're doing brunch.

Brunch, for fuck's sake. Who the hell does brunch?

Assholes like Jarrod do, which does not bode well for this meetup.

My boyfriend was beaming. "He must be rolling in it if he's taking us there."

I didn't say anything. I couldn't.

Talking has been basically impossible since I found out I'm seeing my dad. If I manage to switch my brain off, then I can laugh with the guys and hang like everything's normal, but the second it hits me again, my mouth snaps shut, and all I can do is stare at the wall and obsess over the fact that I'm about to come face-to-face with my father.

I vacillate from anger to fear to excitement. It's such a weird roller-coaster ride, and I'm less than twenty minutes away from finally looking that man in the eye. What do I even want to say to him?

Part of me wants to scream in his face for abandoning me, maybe punch him in the balls and watch him fall.

But then another part of me just wants to ask him why. Ask him how he could have walked away from his daughters so easily.

The thought makes my throat swell, and my nose starts tingling as I shove my feet into my comfiest pair of Converses.

Ethan eyes me from the bed, and when I spin with a challenging glare, he closes his mouth against whatever he was about to say. Probably something along the lines of "*You know this place is pretty high class, right?*"

Instead, he smiles, his gaze softening with this look that always makes me feel like I'm the only girl in his world. "You look great."

And I nearly change again.

He's standing there like a freaking supermodel in his black jeans and button-down shirt. The leather jacket he's pulling on is enough to make my lady parts water, and I momentarily hate myself for being so damn attracted to him.

It makes it impossible to stay mad. Especially when he says sweet shit like wanting what's best for me.

Dammit! Why does he have to be so perfect?

Fisting my trembling fingers, I snatch my phone and shove it into my pocket.

Ethan swings open his bedroom door, and I eye the space I need to walk through. It suddenly seems like the entrance to some dark, haunted cave that's going to swallow me whole and spit out my bones.

"Bummer." I let out a shaky laugh. "My legs have stopped working. I guess I can't go after all."

Ethan huffs, looks up to the ceiling as if he's calling on a higher power to give him patience, then reaches me in two strides. Without a word, he lifts me into his arms and carries me down the stairs like I'm a princess.

I frown at him the whole way, but he ignores me, not setting me down until we've reached his Ranger.

"I'll carry you into that restaurant if I have to," he warns me, plucking me off the ground and even pulling the seat belt over me.

"I can do it." I snatch the belt off him and buckle myself in, fuming as he walks around the truck. I can't believe he's making me do this.

Crossing my arms and slumping down in my seat, I don't say a word to him as we drive into town. He finds a parking spot right outside the restaurant, and my insides start clenching all over again.

I seriously don't think I can do this. But then Ethan opens my door, takes my hand, and pulls me into the restaurant. By some miracle my legs carry me through those doors, and I spot my dad immediately. He's already waiting for us, fidgeting with his watch, checking the time, then straightening the cutlery in front of him. He adjusts the wineglass, then looks toward the entrance... and goes still.

His eyes light with recognition as we weave around the tables, and by the time we reach his spot, he's standing and staring at me with tear-filled eyes.

"Mickey Blue." He chokes out the nickname he used to call me, and my insides crumple as an earthquake of emotion rips me in half. "Look at you. So grown-up. So beautiful."

He's struggling to talk as tears spill out of his eyes.

I don't know what to do with myself, and if it wasn't for Ethan's reassuring hand on my lower back, I think I would have just stood there like a statue for the rest of the day.

"Please, sit." Dad motions to the chairs opposite him, and we take a seat.

Grabbing my menu, I flip it open, needing something to do. My eyes scan the selection, all fancy words written in a fancy font that's barely legible. I'm not taking any of it in.

Ethan shakes Dad's hand, introducing himself in person and then smiling as my dad thanks him repeatedly for reaching out.

"I've been waiting for so long," Dad rasps, his glimmering eyes drinking me in. "Hoping. Wishing. Praying for that moment when you'd finally forgive me and track me down."

I frown, slapping my menu onto the table and making the cutlery rattle. "What do you mean?"

He goes still, blinks at me like he doesn't understand my anger.

"Why should *I* be tracking *you* down? You're my father. Shouldn't you have been trying to find me? Make sure I was okay? Keep in touch!"

"I..." He blinks at me again. "Mikayla, I... I did."

Yeah, right? Does he honestly believe that bullshit?

I glare at him, ready to unleash a little hell—list out every time he let me down—until I realize that he's not lying. His face is so sincere, his eyes filled with sad bewilderment.

Holy shit.

But that can't be right.

I never heard from him. Not once.

Air whooshes out of me—a husky gasp that's more of a shudder. "When? When did you call me?"

His face bunches with confusion, and there he goes again, straightening his already straight cutlery and realigning his already aligned wineglass. "I... When your mother first kicked me out, I tried to keep in touch. I called you and Megan every day. But you didn't want to talk to me. I sent gifts for birthdays and Christmas, but they were sent right back because you didn't even want to open them."

"That's bullshit," I snap. "I cried myself to sleep for months. Of course I wanted to talk to you. I was desperate to know you still loved me. And there were zero gifts, by the way, so stop talking out your ass!"

Ethan's hand rests on my leg beneath the table. His gentle squeeze alerts me to the fact that I'm drawing every eye in the room. I clamp my lips together and look down at the menu. The words blur into black, unreadable blobs.

"Mikayla." Dad's voice breaks over my name. He clears his throat, but his voice remains gravelly. "Your mother told me you didn't want to see me. She told me you hated me and that I needed to give you space."

"That's a lie." Now my voice is breaking. "I never said that to her."

His blue eyes, so similar to mine, darken with realization while I wrestle with the same reality. I'm pretty sure someone's just punched me in the chest. I struggle for air while my dad clenches his jaw and shakes his head, looking sick.

I know how he feels. That... that bitch!

"How could you believe her so easily?" My voice quakes as I struggle with a fresh wave of rage at my mother. But the anger comes spitting out at my dad, because..." Why didn't you fight for custody or something? How could you just walk away?"

"Because, I..." He sighs, closing his eyes and pinching the bridge of his nose. "When my parents split up, I hated the fact that I had to go see my dad every other weekend. The guy was an asshole, and I didn't want to be near him. Those weekends sucked. I felt helpless. No matter how hard I begged, Mom would always make me go because the court said she had to send me." His face crumples with a look of pure agony. "I didn't want to put you through that."

"But you weren't an asshole," I rasp.

"Sweetie." He tips his head, his expression filled with

remorse. "I cheated on your mother. She had every right to kick me out."

I sniff and look away from him, pinching my lips against the sob brewing in my stomach. I won't cry in this place. I won't lose it in this fancy restaurant. The black rage against my lying mother builds like an inferno, rising up my chest until I want to scream.

But Ethan's rubbing my leg, his soft touch keeping me grounded.

"Mick, I am so sorry." Dad's voice hitches. "I let you down. I thought you hated me for cheating, for being kicked out. I thought you never wanted to see me again. It broke my heart to give up physical custody, but I didn't want to cause you any more pain. I was trying to do the right thing."

"And Melanie was trying to punish you." Ethan finally speaks. There's a hard edge to his voice. "She hated you for hurting her, so she took away the one thing that meant the most to you. Your daughters."

I glance at him, then dart my eyes to Dad, who's nodding and looking ready to smash his fist through something. Our gazes meet across the table and his anger disintegrates, his eyes flooding with pain. "I should have fought harder for you, baby girl. I'm so sorry."

Tears burn my eyes, and it's impossible to fight them. I dip my head as the first few fall, quietly whimpering into my hand. Ethan's fingers graze my shoulders, then come to rest on the back of my neck. He gives it a light squeeze, kissing the side of my head and murmuring in my ear, "It's okay. We can leave if you need to."

"No," I manage, shaking my head and wiping the tears off my cheeks. "I can do this."

"I know you can." He smiles at me, then turns to my father. "Truth is, Mr. Hyde—"

"Please, call me Michael."

Ethan nods. "Truth is, Michael, she's done it again. Your ex-wife is punishing Mikayla this time."

Dad jerks in his chair, his face bunching with annoyance. "What do you mean?"

"Well..." Ethan looks to me and I nod, giving him permission to speak on my behalf. My stomach is still jumping with silent sobs, and I'm afraid if I speak that I'll turn into a blubbering mess. "Her fiancé agreed to pay for Mikayla's education, and because she won't follow the letter of his law, he's reneged on that. And Melanie is backing him."

Dad's eyebrows dip a little deeper. "What? She told me you were sorted. For college. She said you didn't need any money for that."

I blink. "When did you speak to her?"

"I..." His face buckles with confusion. "She's my only avenue to you and Megan. We communicate through email."

"But... I... What? I thought you walked away and never looked back."

"Mickey Blue." He tips his head like the very idea of that is absurd. "I may not have forced you to see me, but I was still a part of your life. I kept in touch with your teachers and read every report card. I haven't missed one child support payment, and I'd already started a college fund for both you and Megan, but your mom told me she had already arranged all of that. I should have pushed harder for more information. What is this about her fiancé reneging on his promises?"

Dad looks pissed while I'm sitting here try to deal with this mindfuck.

She made me believe Dad didn't give two shits about us, but he's been watching from the sidelines this whole time?

"Mick?" he prompts me, and I blink, trying to pull my scrambled brain back together. "What happened?"

"I, uh... I failed to become a Sig Be sister." I sigh. "I embarrassed her and pissed off Aimee—her fiancé's daughter. He's kind of precious about her, and now he's hating on me and saying I breached the contract, so he won't pay another dime toward my education."

Dad's nostrils flare, and it's obvious he's struggling to remain calm.

"Okay, go back a bit," he grits out. "So, you're at Nolan U."

"Yes." I nod. "Mom and Jarrod wanted me to go there, because..."

"It was her college." Dad's lips twitch. "She really loved it there."

"Yeah, well..." I shrug. "She really wanted me to go, and it was the only school he'd agree to pay for, so I went along with it. But then they also wanted me to join her and Aimee's sorority... and it just wasn't my thing." I glance at Ethan, who makes my heart trill with a little wink. "So I pulled out and everyone got pissed, and now they're refusing to pay for anything."

"That's where you come in." Ethan points at my father.

I bulge my eyes at Ethan, trying to shut him up.

He ignores me and throws a dazzling smile at my dad. "Not only was I hoping that you'd be able to reconnect with your daughter, but I was also hoping that you might be able to help her get this degree she so desperately wants. A degree she deserves."

Dad pins Ethan with an appreciative look before turning his full attention to me. "What are you studying?"

"Oh, uh... business and sports management."

His eyes light like I've just given him his Christmas wish. "Are you playing any college ball? I notice you gave it up for your senior year. Kind of broke my heart there, kid."

"I..." I shake my head, letting out a watery laugh. "It was never the same after you left. I kept playing, but I never loved it as much without you."

His expression crumples with regret, but Ethan makes him grin by quickly retelling the story of how I hustled Asher. Dad's soon laughing, his smile filled with pride as he stares at me across the table.

It gives me the courage to tell him that "I want to be a sports agent. Representing female athletes."

His smile grows even wider. "That's perfect for you, Mickey."

Oh man, he looks so freaking proud of me right now. It makes me want to cry in a whole different way.

"Of course I'll help you achieve that goal. It'd be my pleasure. Like I said, I have the money already set aside." His shoulder hitches. "I'm still going to keep paying child support until Megan graduates, and I'll definitely offer her college funding if she wants it."

"So you've been paying child support all this time?" I shake my head, still reeling from his earlier revelation.

His head jolts back. "Of course I have. You're my daughters. I..." His voice trails off as another dark look storms across his face. "Did your mom tell you I haven't been?"

I swallow. "She never said either way. She just told us that you'd moved on, found a new family, and... didn't want us anymore."

"That's not true." He gives me an emphatic look, and then his shoulders slump with a sigh. "I mean, yes, I have a new family. And I'd really like for you to meet them when you're ready. But... I always wanted to be a part of your life. And I've missed you every single day." His eyes fill with tears again. "I love you, Mickey Blue. That's never gonna change."

Before I know what I'm doing, my chair is scraping back over this shiny restaurant floor and I'm bolting out of my seat. I round the table with quick steps while Dad stands and spreads his arms wide. Barreling into his chest, I wrap my arms around him and close my eyes, breathing in his scent, which is so familiar even after all these years.

Dad sniffs, holding me against him while I'm transported back in time to those days when he'd hug me tight after a basketball game or carry me on his shoulders as we walked out to the parking lot after watching the Dodgers play. All those moments he made me laugh, read to me, watched movies with me. He understood me better than my mother ever could, and he *did* want me.

He wanted me, and he's missed me.

And now he's here, and it's a chance to start again.

CHAPTER 56
ETHAN

"So, no offense, but I officially hate your mother." I tap my thumb on the steering wheel, agitation coursing through me as we drive back to Hockey House.

Mikayla snorts and shakes her head. "Asher's right. She's a full-blown bitch. I can't believe she lied to everyone that way."

"She robbed you of years with your father," I huff. "In an effort to punish him, she ended up majorly hurting you too. Stupid woman."

"I know." Mikayla rests her head back against the seat, looking surprisingly calm. "It kind of sucks that she's just getting away with it."

"She's not." I shake my head, reaching for Mikayla's hands and threading our fingers together. "She lost you, and that's a heavy price to pay."

Her smile is sweet, her eyes flickering with gratitude. "And he's back in my life again." I glance across to watch her smile grow even bigger. She squeezes my hand.

"Thank you for making me go today. Thank you for... finding him."

"Anything for you, Mickey Blue."

She laughs. "That nickname is reserved for my dad and him alone."

"Aw," I whine, then wink at her. "Doesn't matter, I prefer *lil' mouse* anyway."

Her soft chuckle is music to my ears. After all those tears in the restaurant, those brutal revelations, I thought the day might be a bust. But after their lengthy hug, Mikayla and Michael sat back down, and a waiter tentatively approached the table.

"Order whatever you want, guys. It's on me," Michael said.

I took him up on his offer and had the best steak of my life while Mikayla devoured a plate of eggs Benedict. Having eaten like a pigeon leading up to this, it was great to see her getting her appetite back. We talked about everything from Michael's family and the resort in Cali to what Mikayla's been doing. He was stoked to hear that his daughter was still best friends with Rachel and wanted updates on her too. Then he showed us pictures of his wife and their three children—Maddy, Marcus, and Kyle.

"They're six, nearly five, and three. And they will be so excited to meet you." His eyes danced, then washed with sadness when he asked, "Do you think... do you think Megan would like to meet them too? Will she be willing to see me?"

All Mikayla could do was shrug. "I can ask. I mean, we're not that close, but I can definitely text her. Pass on your number."

He nodded, obviously grateful that she was willing to try.

I was worried things would get depressing again after that, but Mikayla started talking about me, and her dad was super interested in my hockey and the fact that I want to go pro. It seemed to brighten up the conversation again, and by the time our second round of coffees rolled around, we were all laughing as he told me stories about what a terror Mikayla could be when she was little.

"She defined the terrible twos." Michael laughed. "The number of times I had to carry her kicking and screaming out of public places. She was one determined young lady." His eyes softened with affection as he smiled across the table. "I've always loved your spirit. I knew it would serve you well as an adult. But oh boy, it was a pain in the ass when you were little."

I cracked up laughing while Mikayla slapped a hand over her face and turned bright red.

All in all, a great brunch.

And we've already arranged to see Michael again in December. He's going to pay for Mikayla and me to fly out and meet his family over Christmas. Michael nearly started crying when Mikayla accepted on the spot. My dad will be disappointed, but we can do Thanksgiving with him, so it's all good.

"I'll put you up in the nicest suite at the resort."

It's gonna be freaking awesome.

"You ready to go home yet?" Mikayla suddenly asks.

I glance at her and shrug. "I thought that's where we were heading."

"I know you have a game tonight, but do you think

we've got time for a little walk in the woods before you're due at the arena?"

I check my phone screen. "I've got about an hour."

"Perfect." Her grin is adorable, and I turn off toward Berkeley Grove, parking in the gravel lot by the south side entrance. Mikayla jumps out of the truck, her smile playful as she grabs my hand and leads me down the first trail.

This park is a popular hangout for the whole town and often busy with people walking their dogs or exercising.

I thread my fingers through Mikayla's, ambling beside her as we both decompress after such an emotional meal.

And then she jerks me sideways.

"What are you doing?" I laugh as she pulls me off trail and we plunge into the thickening trees.

Glancing over my shoulder, I check the coast is clear before ducking beneath the branches and following her into the shadows of the wood. She's giggling, and that playful smile of hers quickly makes sense when she fists my jacket and pulls me down to meet her lips.

I happily take her up on the offer, swiping my tongue into her mouth while her deft fingers unzip my pants.

"You serious?" I murmur against her mouth. "Right here?"

"Yeah, baby. Doesn't it turn you on?"

"You turn me on." I nibble my lips along her jawline while she wraps her fingers around my pulsing cock.

"I just want to say thank you." She breathes the words in my ear, then sucks my lobe while my fingers start scrambling for her waistband.

The cool breeze kisses my ass when she yanks my

pants down, and there's something so fucking sexy about the high-risk stakes of doing it outside. We're far enough off the trail that the chances of getting caught are slim... but there's still a chance. And damn if that doesn't turn me on even more.

I shove her pants past her hips and wrestle one foot free so she can wrap her legs around me. Swiping my finger between her folds, I check that she's wet enough, and hot damn, she is.

My dick twitches, anticipation nearly making me blow on the spot as I check my wallet and am relieved to find a condom in there. She snatches it off me, ripping the packet open with her teeth while I finger her.

She moans, tipping her head back with soft little gasps that prevent her from finishing the suiting up job.

"Baby, please," I beg before sucking her neck.

She pulls it together, rolling the condom the rest of the way while I take her a little closer to the edge.

"Now, now, now." She grips my shoulders and I hike her up, pressing her against the tree and plunging inside her.

We groan in unison, her sweet gasp ringing inside me as I thrust into her. Her legs clamp around me, and I grip her ass cheeks, finding a quick, heady rhythm.

"Yes." She lets out a whimpering cry, and I take it even deeper, hammering into her while she pants in my ear.

The explosion comes so fast and strong, I feel like I'm floating as her inner walls clench me, milking me for all I'm worth. I push her back against the tree, puffing against her neck, my entire body trembling as I slowly nudge myself as deep as I can go and ride out the last strains of this mind-blowing orgasm.

"Fuck me, Mick. That was…" I lean back, shaking my head in wonder.

"I know." She grins. "We should totally do this more often. There's something about the breeze tickling my butt cheeks that just does it for me, you know?" Her eyebrows wiggle as she bites her bottom lip, then whispers, "Imagine what it'd be like if we were both fully naked."

I groan, nestling my forehead into the crook of her neck, still not willing to put her down, to slip out of her and resume life as normal. How will it ever be normal again? It can't. Because I've got Mikayla, and she is the best thing that has ever happened to me.

"I love you," she whispers against my cheek, brushing her fingers through my hair. "I love you so fucking much."

I smile against her skin, then kiss her neck before pulling away so I can look into her eyes. So she can see how much I mean it when I whisper back, "You and me. Forever."

"Forever." She smiles, and the look of trust in her eyes makes my insides bloom.

Then we seal the deal with a kiss.

CHAPTER 57
LIAM

Mikayla's been living at Hockey House for nearly a month. She keeps saying it's a temporary fix but seems pretty settled here. Plus, just quietly, I think she doesn't want to live alone but doesn't know how to find a room-mate either. It's not like she's got a bunch of girlfriends to hang out with. She's a tomboy at her core, and I can't imagine Ethan wanting her to move in with some other guy, even if it is just a platonic thing.

I wonder how long she'll stay.

Not that it bothers me. She's cool, and I don't mind having her around. Ethan's been the happiest I've ever seen him, but I'm not sure everyone is as cool with the arrangement as he is.

Baxter would never say anything, but he's a pretty private, reserved guy, and I don't think he appreciated walking into the bathroom to find Mikayla shaving her legs the other day. He was red for the rest of the afternoon.

Asher would have sprinted right up there to check it

out for himself if Ethan hadn't blocked his way with a feral snarl. Asher was only riling him up, but I'm worried that it might turn into a brawl if Asher doesn't figure out where the frickin' line is. The guy can be so damn clueless.

Running up to the front door, I wipe the sweat off my face with the bottom of my shirt. Despite the fact that it's mid-November, it's still pretty warm. I love the cold. Give me snow and ice and all things chilly.

We've had a bunch of frosts and two decent snowfalls, but I'm hanging out for those weeks where the entire campus turns into a winter wonderland. It may sound cheesy, but I love that North Pole promise. That crystal-white snow coating everything, your skin tingling with that icy chill while you sip a hot coffee.

I love standing in the middle of a snowfall, the flakes dancing through the sky and landing on my jacket and boots and beanie.

There's a silent beauty to snow. And waking up to a clear morning after a heavy dump is pure magic. There's no other way to describe it.

I open the front door and strip off my shirt, using it to wipe the sweat off my body. The house is toasty warm. Mikayla's gonna love that. She's a tiny speck with a very thin layer of fat to ward off the chill. She's used to Southern Californian winters, and she's already complaining about how freaking cold everything is.

Wait until January and February, Mick. You're gonna turn into a popsicle.

I don't feel the cold. I was born and raised in Colorado, got my first pair of skates when I was three. I spent my youth hanging by the rink—any excuse not to go home, right?

The dark thought makes me frown, and I whip out my phone, sending a quick text to my younger sister, Sofia.

Me: Checking in. How's your week going?

Sofia: All good, big bro. Nothing that interesting. School is boring. Math is the devil's spawn, and Mom's not letting me go out with Elena this weekend even though her older brother is coming with us to play bodyguard.

Me: Where were you gonna go?

Sofia: Just dancing.

In other words, clubbing with fake IDs. I shake my head, hearing my sister's voice as if she were in the room with me. She's a junior in high school, and I'm siding with Mama on this one.

Sofia: Maybe if you came too...

·   ·   ·

Me: Sorry, chica. I've got hockey. I'm sure you'll find something fun to do instead.

Sofia: Argh! You suck too.

I grin.

Me: I love you.

She makes me wait it out before finally replying with a "love you" GIF that cracks me up. The fact that she's complaining about math and Mama is a good sign. No mention of Dad, which is what I always like to see.

Clenching my jaw, I stalk into the kitchen, trying to shake off memories—screams and the dull sound of knuckles hitting flesh followed by those stomach-convulsing whimpers and the soft begging to stop.

I'd hide in the closet with my two sisters, trying to be brave and strong while Mama took those beatings. I wanted to go help her, rescue her, but she made me promise not to. Seeing her son black and blue was more than she could handle. After the first few times I got in the way, she made me swear to hide my sisters and keep them safe. Even though I was the middle child, she looked to me. Treated me like I was the oldest and strong-est. It was my job to protect the girls.

And that's exactly what I did, until I was big enough to make a difference.

Until the night he nearly killed her, and I broke my promise.

I chug down a glass of water and lean against the counter, staring out the window. My lips start to twitch as I notice some flakes dancing past the glass. Snow. It's only a few flakes, and it won't turn into a proper snowfall, but just the promise is enough to make me feel better.

Glancing at my watch, I check the time and figure the guys will all be piling in soon enough. The due date for my big assignment is looming, so I bailed on Offside and figured I'd jog home for my cardio today. Yes, I've already done practice, but it wasn't an intense one, and I still had energy to burn.

Ethan was happy to be designated driver, so I'm off duty and like being a free man for the night. Zero responsibility. It's a nice change.

I've got the house pretty much to myself—I can hear Baxter in the shower—so I'll take the chance to get some reading done and try to nail down my assignment plan before the house is bustling with bodies and noise.

Wandering through to the stairwell, I'm about to climb up to my room when the doorbell rings.

Not thinking twice about answering the door shirtless, I swing it open and am surprised by the audible gasp that greets me.

Big green eyes hooded by a long set of bangs bulge at me before the nervy woman looks at the ground. "Um... uh... Hi."

"Hey." I grin, gripping the door and relaxing my pose, hoping to put her at ease.

Her gaze flutters over mine again before running down the length of my body. I figure since she's perusing,

I can do the same thing, so I study her from head to toe. She looks around my age with a long, lean body. Like, really lean. Her leggings leave nothing to the imagination. I can already tell that if she turns away from me, I'll get a perfect view of a very tight little butt. I swallow and track my eyes back up her body, lingering on her oval face and struck still by those big green eyes. They really are beautiful.

My chest constricts, and I grip the door a little tighter when I think I spot a flash of fear coursing through them. But then she blinks, and it's gone.

She gives me a polite, closed-mouth smile, then looks to the ground, the porch light above her highlighting the chestnut brown of her long, straight hair.

"Can I help you with something?" I keep my tone light and friendly.

"Maybe." She rubs her forehead, messing up her bangs with those shaky fingers.

This one's twitchy.

Oh man, I hope she's not standing at the door with some surprise pregnancy news. The rate the guys in this house sleep around, it really wouldn't be that surprising.

I wince, just waiting for her to ask for Asher or Casey —yep, it's got to be Casey—but instead she murmurs, "I'm looking for Mikayla Hyde. I think she lives here?"

"Oh yeah." My voice brightens. "She does."

Her shoulders sink with relief, and that's when I notice the suitcase at her feet.

"She's not home right now."

The girl's eyes jump back up to mine. And there's that flash of fear again.

"But you're welcome to come in and wait for her," I

continue, adding a smile for good measure. "I don't think she'll be too much longer. She's out with—"

"Ethan," she finishes for me, then let's out a soft laugh that almost sounds sad. "Of course she is."

I frown, wondering who this woman is and why she has a problem with Ethan. Her jacket rustles as she crosses her arms and looks over her shoulder. The snow is picking up just a little. A few light flakes float around her, some landing on the ends of her hair before melting away.

"So... do you want to come in and wait for her?" I step aside, gesturing for her to get her cute little butt inside.

She gives me a cautious look, her dark eyebrows crinkling.

"It's perfectly safe." I grin. "I'm a gentleman, I swear. I'll set you up in the living room with a coffee or hot chocolate, and I'll leave you alone if you want me to... or I can sit and keep you company. Whatever you need."

She stares at me for a long beat, and then out of nowhere her eyes fill with tears. Covering her mouth with her hand, she dips her head as a sob shudders her body.

I move without thinking, darting out the door and wrapping my arm around her. She stiffens at my touch, and something horrible snakes through me. A warning. A sinking dread that's all too familiar.

"I'm not gonna hurt you," I whisper. "I promise."

She sniffs and lets me gently nudge her into the house. As the door swings shut behind us and her suitcase, I let her go, keeping my hand lightly on her elbow as I check on her.

"It's gonna be okay," I murmur, then throw in a comforting smile. "I'm Liam, by the way."

Her lips tremble as she attempts a smile of her own, then rasps, "I'm Rachel."

———

Thank you so much for reading THE FORBIDDEN FRESHMAN. I hope you loved Ethan and Mikayla's romance... and are now up for a different kind of love.

Liam's a quiet, protective giant and that's exactly what Rachel needs right now. When her world is turned upside down by a shocking revelation from Theo, she runs to her safe place—her bestie, Mikayla—but she'll find more than she bargained for at Hockey House. She'll find a family of men who will do anything to protect her. And a guy who will show her the true meaning of love.

THE HEART STEALER is now available from your favorite online book retailer.

If you want to read a sneak peek first, sign up for Katy's newsletter. You'll also get the *Nolan U. Sports Digest* filled with images and character interviews, plus a chat with the author!

SIGN UP HERE:
subscribepage.com/katyarcher-bookreader

And if you're not quite done with Ethan and Mikayla, keep reading for a special bonus epilogue. It's time for Mikayla to meet her dad's family, and Ethan might just have some special plans for how to celebrate Christmas with his girl at the luxurious resort in Northern California.

Santa doesn't need snow or a big red coat to deliver Christmas gifts now, does he?

Maybe just a Santa hat will do (*insert eyebrow wiggle*).

For a sizzling Christmas-themed treat, read the Bonus Epilogue...

A NOTE FROM KATY

Dear reader,

Thank you so much for taking a chance on my debut novel. It's so humbling to know that you made time in your busy life to read my work. I really hope you enjoyed it.

Writing this series has lit a fire within me and I can't begin to express how much I pucking love Nolan U and Hockey House. I can't wait for you to spend more time there!

Rachel and Liam's book is just around the corner and although it has a different vibe to Ethan and Mikayla's flirty teasing, it's been a rush writing their romance. Nothing gives me the tingles like a protective hockey player growling, "Who did this to you?"

If you enjoyed *The Forbidden Freshman*, I would so appreciate you leaving an honest review on Amazon and/or Goodreads. Even just a star rating is helpful. You don't have to write anything if you don't want to. But star ratings and even short reviews really help validate the book, letting readers know it's worth a shot. It also tells Amazon and Goodreads that this book is worth shining a spotlight on. I know there are a bunch of readers out there who love college sports romance just as much as we do. If you can help me reach them, then that would be freaking fantastic.

Thanks for the assist!

I'd also like to thank a few key people who have been instrumental in helping me get this book off the ground —Megan, Kristin, Beth, Rachael, Meredith, Melissa. Working with you guys is so freaking amazing. I'm honored and privileged to have your support. You seriously are the best team.

Maggie—one of my favorite people in the world. Thank you for getting me and putting up with my ranting, my dreaming, my stressing and the odd freak out. You're the G.O.A.T.!

Trudi and Nicky—thanks for the regular catch ups. There's nothing like sitting down with fellow writers and speaking in a language that is all our own. Thanks for introducing me to so many awesome cafés as well! May our monthly lunches continue for a long time to come.

Elle Kennedy and Cambria Hebert—thank you for inspiring me to write this series. Thank you for writing such brilliant books that suck me in. Thank you for introducing me to characters I have fallen in love with. Keep writing forever, pretty please.

My fellas—thanks for always making me laugh, not telling me to shut up when I've been talking for way too long about plot lines and character development, supporting me when I'm chasing after a deadline and giving me cuddles when I'm frazzled after a long day. I'll love you guys for the rest of my life.

My first love—thank you for every story. Thank you for the unconditional love you have brought into my life and for giving me the courage to do something you created me to do. I love you.

And last, but absolutely not least—my readers. Thank you for reading this book. Thank you for all the emails, the reviews, the words of encouragement. Thank you for making this experience so incredibly awesome. I couldn't do this without you!

xoxo
Katy

BONUS EPILOGUE

There's nothing like a little extra when you fall in love with book characters. It helps ease that book hangover when you're not quite ready to say goodbye.

Because you were awesome enough to buy this book direct, pre-order your copy or grab it on release day, you get this extra treat as a thank you from me to you 🩶

Enjoy!

xoxo Katy

MIKAYLA

So, it turns out my dad's father-in-law owns a private jet. WTF!

And you want to know the best part?

He didn't need it over the Christmas break, so he let his newly acquired "granddaughter" catch a ride from Denver to Sacramento with three of her buddies.

I know, right!

Talk about the best way ever to start Christmas. I was kind of nervous about meeting my dad's new wife and my half siblings, but I seriously didn't have anything to worry about.

Being distracted by luxury rides in small planes and big cars helped a lot, and by the time we pulled into the Luna Luxury Resort and wound our way through the lush golf course and palm trees, I was pumped. Dad ran out to greet me like I was his prodigal daughter, he hugged Rachel, shook Ethan's and Liam's hands, and then I was meeting three of the most adorable children ever created.

They instantly loved me, which means Dad must have talked me up big-time. And now Maddy is sitting on my knee while I read her *The Night Before Christmas*. Marcus and Kyle are only half listening because they're too busy sneaking glances at the mammoth hockey players who have taken over the couch next to me. I think they're in love with my boyfriend and his bestie. The guys played with them in the indoor pool this afternoon, putting them on their shoulders and throwing them around. The boys have been cling-ons ever since.

Dad's wife, Emilia, looks on with quiet amusement. She's pretty cool. So different from my mom. Like polar opposite, which is a little weird, right? How could Dad love two completely different women? Or is it just that he never really loved Mom?

I guess I get it.

Mom's hard work, high maintenance.

My gut twists as I think about the wedding invite she sent me last week. After months of radio silence—being cut from her life like I meant nothing to her—she's invited me to her freaking wedding, and I have no idea how I'm supposed to respond.

"Merry Christmas to all, and to all a good night." I put on my best Santa voice, ending the book with a flourish.

"Again! Again!" Kyle pumps his little arms in the air.

"I don't think so, mister." Emilia rises from her chair with a laugh. "You've got to go to bed or Santa won't come."

Maddy gasps. "But I've been good!"

I try not to snicker as I bend down and whisper in her ear, "Oh, he'll definitely come for you, kiddo. You're way too cool to miss out."

She beams me an adoring smile before kissing my cheek, then jumping off my knee.

"Come on, you guys." She waves at her brothers. "The sooner we go to sleep, the sooner it'll be Christmas!"

We watch them barrel out of the room, and I share a *they're too cute!* grin with Rachel. She bobs her head while Dad walks for the door.

"We'll be back soon, guys. Feel free to wait for us in the restaurant if you want. I've reserved the private room, and Emilia's put together a special Christmas Eve feast. We'll get started as soon as the kids are settled."

"Sounds great." I jump up, still in awe of the fact that my dad is living this uber-luxurious life now.

I mean, sure, he probably works his ass off to keep this classy place running, but how cool that he owns it? I mean, this is his baby. Apparently, he was a huge part of the whole design and everything. I'm proud of the guy... and he seems so incredibly happy.

He was never like this with Mom. Even as a kid, I can remember there being this underlying strain and tension all the time. I've been around the guy for two days and I don't think I've seen one frown yet. He's happy. Content. In love.

I glance up at my boyfriend as he throws his arm around my shoulders and winks down at me.

I get it.

Being in love changes everything.

With a grin, I wrap my arm around his waist, and we wander through to one of the five-star restaurants. The resort is kitted out with every luxury you can imagine. The suite we're staying in has three bedrooms and this huge living area in the middle. The TV is so massive, it takes over most of the wall. It's insane.

There are multiple restaurants, including an '80s-style bar with pool tables and a jukebox that plays a stream of Michael Jackson and Madonna hits—I felt like I should have been wearing a neon bubble skirt and leg warmers when we hung out in there. Along with that coolness, there are also tennis courts, pools, a golf course, a spa, a library that made Rachel swoon, and a mini movie theater.

And the staff treat us like we're royalty.

Seriously. This is like the best Christmas ever!

"This way, please, Miss Hyde." The maître d' guides us through the elegant restaurant to the private room, offering us drinks and canapés while we wait for Dad and Emilia.

By the time they finally get there, I'm nearly full on

predinner snacks, but I make room for more food, because holy crap, I can't say no to any of the deliciousness that's placed in front of me.

As Christmas Eve draws that much closer to Christmas Day, I sit back in my seat with a groan.

Dad snickers, shaking his head at me. "You never could resist a good feed."

"I know." I put on a strained voice, but I'm smiling because that was freaking epic. The white chocolate mousse dessert was melt-in-my-mouth divine. Rachel sure loved it. She's been talking off Emilia's ear most of the night, raving about how much she loves cooking and the quality of the food.

She's in heaven.

And I'm here with all my favorite people... so I'm in heaven too.

Dad's awesome. He loved me all along, and I never had anything to doubt or fear. It sucks in huge ways that he didn't put in more effort to get in touch with me, but I understand where he was coming from. I've been able to forgive him with relative ease.

It's my mom that I'm struggling with.

That manipulative bitch stole years from me and Dad. She punished us both, and then she freaking cut me off. I want to hate her for the rest of my life.

But... she invited me to her wedding.

Shit!

Why'd she have to go and do that?

It would have been so much easier if she'd just pretended like I didn't exist. We could move on with our lives and—

Ugh! Why does she even want me there?

I'm her wayward, impossible daughter! I'm—

"Hey." Dad nudges me, leaning closer and lowering his voice. "You okay, kid?"

I blow out a sigh, sitting forward and resting my elbows on the table.

Do I tell him?

Working my jaw to the side, I sneak a glance at Ethan, who is fully immersed in some hockey discussion with Liam. He knows about the invite. He walked into his bedroom just as I was opening it and stood through quite the rant on my part. I have no idea what I said now, but his eyebrows were kind of high by the time I'd finished. And then he hugged me. One of those I'm-gonna-swallow-you-whole kinda hugs that I didn't even realize I needed until his arms were around me.

"Mickey Blue." Dad nudges me with his elbow again. "I know you've grown and changed in so many ways since the last time I lived with you, but I can tell something's up. You get this look on your face when you're trying to hide the fact that something is bugging you." A little smile tugs at his lips. "You can't fool your old man."

I give in to his playful wink with a soft snicker and finally blurt, "Mom's invited me to her wedding."

"Oh." Dad's head tips to the side like he's trying to formulate the perfect response but can't think of a good one.

With a huff, I answer for him. "I want to send her back a big F-you, with a side of *Are you fucking kidding me?* And maybe a dash of *You're a psycho bitch* would really round out my RSVP." I give him a pointed look. "What do you think?"

He smothers his laughter with his hand, his gold

wedding band glinting at me while he rubs his face. "Aw, kid, I..." With a sad sigh, he shakes his head. "As satisfying as that would be, I'm not sure it's the best reply. This is obviously your mom's way of trying to reconnect with you."

I snort and look away from him, clenching my jaw. I don't even know if I want to reconnect with her. What she did was so shitty.

Dad's soft hand on my wrist makes me turn back to face him. He's looking at me like he's about to say something all mature and sensible. I seriously don't know if I'm in the mood.

It's Christmas Eve, for fuck's sake! This is supposed to be a time of joy and merriment!

"Look, I know it's tough." His thumb rubs the back of my hand. "I've had my fair share of rants about your mother. Poor Emilia's heard it all, but you know what she said to me?"

I really *don't* want to know, because it's probably going to be something wise that will crush my resentment and make me feel small and petty.

Gritting my teeth, I throw a sideways glance at the woman who's brought my father to life before turning back to Dad.

"She told me to let go and forgive her. Because if I hold on to all this angst and burning rage over what she let happen, then I'm only hurting myself."

My nose twitches as I sniff and hitch my shoulder.

"Mick, I get it. I do. Part of you wants to punish her for hurting you. And that's justified. But it's not going to make you feel better."

"Are you sure?"

"Pretty darn." He gives me a dry look, although is fighting a grin the whole time.

Tipping my head back with a heavy sigh, I blink up at the wood panel ceiling. The funky design is kind of mesmerizing, and I focus on that so I don't have to look at my dad who is probably right. Dammit.

"You know what? I think you should go to that wedding. Take your hunky boyfriend, walk in there with your chin held high, and you show Jarrod and your mom that you're doing better than ever." He lets out a soft laugh. "Hell, if you really want to have some fun, you could *thank* them, because if she hadn't cut you off, Ethan never would have found me, and we never would have reconnected."

I sit forward, staring at the candles in the middle of the table as the thought sinks in. Finally, a smile twitches my lips. "Holy shit, you're right." Laughter pops out of me, loud enough to draw every eye at the table. I point my thumb at Dad and shrug. "He's right."

I grin at the confused frowns being thrown at me and turn to Dad. He's smiling like he loves me, and I wrap him in a hug.

Resting my chin on his shoulder, I give him a tight squeeze. "I've really missed you."

"You never have to again, kiddo. I'll always be here for you."

Pulling out of his embrace, I give him a watery smile. "I love you."

"Ditto." He grins.

My head starts to bob as the weight of what I agreed to starts to sink in. The thought of seeing my mom again is brutal. But the thought of walking into her wedding with the sexiest guy on the planet is kind of awesome. And the idea of thanking her and Jarrod is freaking epic.

I've got a lot I can thank them for, actually... including the fact that I no longer have to be one of her bridesmaids.

The thought makes me giggle, and I reach for my champagne flute, raising it high in the air. "To being grateful."

I laugh, sharing one more secret smile with my dad before clinking my glass with Ethan's.

ETHAN

I have no idea what Mikayla and her dad were talking about after dessert. It looked kind of serious, and curiosity made me want to muscle in, but I behaved myself and stayed focused on Liam.

We talked hockey mostly. I don't know how we never get tired of that topic, but it was the foundation of our friendship initially, so I guess it makes sense.

As we wander back to the lush suite, I can feel the dopiness of my smile. So, I'm kinda buzzed. It's hard not to be with so much tasty alcohol flowing. Even Mick's got a giddy look on her face.

I'm glad she's put behind whatever was bothering her over dinner, because I've got some Christmas Eve plans that I want to enjoy.

Laughter bubbles in my stomach as I think about my pre-Christmas gift. Shit, I hope she likes it.

At the time I bought it, I thought it was the funniest

fucking thing in the world. I had visions of her reaction and walked out of the store laughing away to myself.

I hope I'm right, because if she doesn't find it funny, it's gonna be fucking humiliating.

Maybe that's why I drank just a little too much. I need this buzz to get me in the zone for this shit.

I'm no grinch, but Christmas isn't my favorite holiday, and Christmas shopping is a total bitch. Then there are all the decorations and endless traditions. Ever since Mom died, I just haven't been as into them. But this year, I've got myself a girl, and I want our first Christmas together to be all kinds of awesome.

And it starts tonight.

She jumps on my back when we're halfway down the path. Hitching her up, I enjoy the feel of her short legs wrapping around my waist.

I give her tight little ass a squeeze while Liam opens the hotel room door, then call out a quick goodnight. "Happy Christmas Eve, bitches."

Liam laughs. "You, too, man."

"I'm gonna go do dirty things to my woman." I wiggle my eyebrows at him while Rachel's cheeks turn neon.

She bites her lips together, staring at the blank TV while Liam raises his hand in farewell.

"You have fun with that."

Mikayla giggles, sucking my neck and shouting, "Oh, we will," just before I swing our door shut.

Dropping her onto the bed, I shed my jacket and throw it over the armchair in the corner.

"So, dirty things, huh? What do you have in mind, Mr. Galloway?"

I spin around, my stomach pooling with red-hot

desire when she bites the tip of her finger and gives me her *I want to fuck your brains out* look.

Oh, baby, it is so on.

Stumbling back toward the bathroom, I raise one finger, asking her to wait while I resist the urge to pounce. "I want to give you something first, okay?"

I didn't go shopping for no reason, now did I?

"Okay." She gives me a curious look.

"Just a little pre-Christmas present."

"Oh, really?" Her face lights with glee, and now I'm worried that I'm overselling this.

"Just... just wait right here." Diving into the bathroom, I strip off my clothes, whacking my knee on the counter and cursing up a storm when I stub my toe on the edge of the shower.

Slow is smooth and smooth is fast, you dumb fuck!

Taking a breath, I slide off my boxer briefs and hunt through my toiletry bag for the little Santa hat I bought.

Thankfully, my dick knows what's coming and is already standing to attention, making it easy to slip the Santa hat on. I glance at my reflection in the mirror and laugh at myself.

Oh man, she better find this funny!

Clearing my throat, I pull my shoulders back and march into our bedroom, my proud dick sporting the little red hat. Resting my hands on my hips, I strike a pose and loudly announce, "Merry Christmas! Ho, ho, ho!"

There's a thick beat of painful silence before the cutest snort pops out of Mikayla's nose and she tips sideways on the bed, her laughter filling the room as she beckons me over with her finger.

"You..." She sits up on her knees, her siren finger still

calling me. "Are..." Her hands rest on my hips as she stares down at my cock. "The sexiest Santa in the universe."

"Why, thank you." I'm still putting on this deep, ridiculous voice, but I'm blaming her smile, because she's so fucking gorgeous, and I always want to see her grinning at me like I'm the best thing that's ever happened to her.

"So, Santa..." She bites her bottom lip, her finger trailing down the edge of the V that leads to my straining cock. "You might not know this about me, but..."

Oh fuck, her eyes. That hungry look is gonna undo me on the spot.

"I'm not always such a good girl. In fact..." She licks her top lip. "I can be quite naughty."

Laughter rumbles in my chest as I lean over her, capturing her face in my hands. "That's okay. This Santa's all about his naughty lil' mouse."

"Oh yeah?" Her fingertips tickle the hairs on my upper thigh. "And what are you gonna do with me?"

With a little growl, I grab her shirt, ripping it off her body before pushing her back on the bed. She hits the mattress with a squeal that busts apart into musical laughter, which sends my heart soaring.

My nimble fingers make quick work of her belt and pants, and the second her very fine ass is exposed, I give it a light slap.

"Oh!" she squeaks, her mouth dropping open with delighted shock. "Santa baby!"

Her grin is delicious as I grab the edge of her flimsy panties and tear them off her body. I'll buy her a new pair. She doesn't seem to mind as I throw the trashed material over my shoulder and part her pretty legs.

"Slow or fast, lil' mouse?" I run my thumb across her shining folds, pleased that she's already so fucking wet. And because I can't resist, I lean over her, sucking her pink nipple into my mouth while she decides. She's taking her sweet time to answer me, but that could be because I'm now teasing her clit with my thumb.

"I... I want..." She whimpers, her breaths getting short and excited. "Oh fuck. Take me fast, Santa. Take me now!" The last few words come out in a sexy moan.

Rising back to my knees, I give her a playful smile, about to whip the Santa hat off my cock.

"Please, allow me." That addictive tongue of hers skims her lower lip as she ceremoniously pulls the Santa hat off my eager dick.

He's having a party now. Wiping the bead of moisture away with her thumb, Mick licks her lips again, pumping me while I scramble for a condom. What I wouldn't give to bury myself into her without a rubber. One day. And it's gonna be fucking epic.

She grabs the packet off me, ripping it open with urgent fingers and suiting me up while I continue to stroke her clit.

"Ahhhh," she lets out another sexy groan, her head tipping back while I take her to the edge. "I'm coming. Fuck, I'm coming." She gasps the words and I pick up my pace, bending down so I can run my tongue across her glistening opening just as her body starts to vibrate. The orgasm rockets through her like an earthquake and I grab her ass while she rides it out, capturing her sweet liquid with my tongue.

That seriously did not take much. I love that I can make her come so easily. Sitting back up, I gaze down at her heaving chest, then capture that hungry look in her eyes.

She wants me so fucking bad.

Yes! This Santa is falling hard for Christmas right about now.

Lifting her legs, I push her knees against her tits, giving her ass another light whack. She giggles, the sound wrapping around me as I check the condom is on properly and line myself up.

"Go," she begs me. "Please, baby. Hurry up."

I grin at her, teasing her opening with the tip of my cock.

"You better get inside me, Santa," she warns. "Now!"

So I do as I'm told, plunging deep and relishing the look of ecstasy on her face.

"Yes," she groans, fisting the duvet as I grab her ankles and take her fast and deep the way she wants me to.

It's blinding pleasure. My rigid cock pumping in and out of her is bliss. Our wet heat creates a suction symphony, enhanced by her sweet moans and breathy pants.

"Oh fuck." My body starts to burn, the build coming on faster than I expected. Gliding my hands down her calves, I tuck my fingers under her luscious ass and lift her hips, plunging even deeper for my last few thrusts.

I explode like a fucking volcano, my words incoherent as her inner walls clutch me and drain me dry. My fingers dig into her ass cheeks and I strain as deep as I can go until my heart rate starts to drop again.

Soon, all that remains is our heaving chests and these gooey smiles that we can't seem to stop giving each other.

"Thank you, Santa," she eventually manages.

"Anytime, naughty girl." Pulling her legs down, I lift her up against me, our bodies morphing into one as I run my hand up her back and hold her close. Her sexy scent envelopes me as I brush my lips across her cheek.

She's my present this year.

I don't care what she's bought me. She's the only present I will ever need.

"Fuck, I love you."

Her lips skims my shoulder as she nibbles her way up to my mouth. And just before I can claim those perfect lips, she leans back with a smile. "Thanks for being the best Christmas present ever. Like seriously. Ever." Her emphatic look fills my chest with that delicious feeling only she can give me.

"Merry Christmas, lil' mouse," I murmur against her smiling lips.

BOOKS BY KATY ARCHER

NOLAN U HOCKEY
Hockey House V-cards (prequel)
The Forbidden Freshman
The Heart Stealer

...Also coming out in 2024...
The Game Changer
The Love Penalty

NOLAN U FOOTBALL
In development

NOLAN U BASKETBALL
In development

CONTACT KATY

I love to hear from my readers, so feel free to email me anytime. You can also find out more on my website.

EMAIL: katy@katyarcher.com

WEBSITE: www.katyarcher.com

And if you want to connect with me on social and see pretty reels and teasers from the books, you can find me Addicted to College Sports Romance on...

INSTAGRAM
@addictedtocollegesportsromance

FACEBOOK
@collegesportsromancebooks

TIKTOK
@katyarcherauthor

Printed in Great Britain
by Amazon

43521385R00260